Praise for City of Windows

'A tough, wise, knowing narrative voice, a great plot, a
great setting, and even better characters - I loved this'
Lee Child, *Sunday Times* bestselling
author of the Jack Reacher series

'Told at a ferocious pace in staccato prose, this
thriller truly gets the blood racing'
Daily Mail

'CITY OF WINDOWS is that rarest of gems - a page-turner
painted with soaring prose that makes you want to read every
sentence twice. In Dr Lucas Page, Robert Pobi has created a
unique and modern protagonist. . . He'll be back and so will I'
Gregg Hurwitz, *Sunday Times* bestselling author of Orphan X

'Pulsating'
Sunday Times Culture

'CITY OF WINDOWS is a white knuckle ride hurtling
along at breakneck speed. A beautifully plotted thriller, but
the best thing of all is its lead character. With Dr Lucas Page
Robert Pobi has created one of the most fascinating and
unique protagonists since Jeffery Deaver's Lincoln Rhyme'
Martyn Waites, bestselling author of Angel of Death

'An absolute corker of a thriller'
Irish Independent

'A stunner. One of the most impressive, compelling
thrillers I've read in a long while. The plot moves at bullet
velocity. The writing has an electric surge. Robert Pobi
delivers a fresh, exciting new voice to thriller fiction'
David Morrell, author of Murder As a Fine Art

About the author

Robert Pobi is an internationally bestselling novelist whose work has been published in more than fifteen countries. He spends the summer months in a cabin in the mountains, and when he's not writing at a desk once owned by Robert Calvi, he fishes for everything that swims – from great white sharks off Montauk to the monstrous pike of northern Finland. He collects early twentieth century American art, listens to a little too much Motörhead, and doesn't do Twitter.

CITY OF
WINDOWS

ROBERT POBI

MULHOLLAND
BOOKS
HODDER

First published in Great Britain in 2019 by Mulholland Books
An imprint of Hodder & Stoughton
An Hachette UK company

This paperback edition published in 2020

3

A CIP catalogue record for this title is
available from the British Library

Paperback ISBN 978 1 529 35315 0

Printed and bound in Great Britain by Clays Ltd, Elcograf S.p.A.

Hodder & Stoughton policy is to use papers that are natural, renewable
and recyclable products and made from wood grown in sustainable
forests. The logging and manufacturing processes are expected to
conform to the environmental regulations of the country of origin.

Hodder & Stoughton Ltd
Carmelite House
50 Victoria Embankment
London EC4Y 0DZ

www.hodder.co.uk

For Reijo, who would have been proud

I can calculate the motion of heavenly bodies,
but not the madness of people.

—ISAAC NEWTON (ATTRIBUTED), CIRCA 1720–1721

CITY OF
WINDOWS

1

December 19
New York City—East Forty-second Street
and Park Avenue

Nimi Olsen made the mistake of trying to cross Forty-second half a block before the intersection and missed the light. She was now stranded on the spine of frozen slush that snaked down the middle of the street, freezing her ass off. Cars snapped by with homicidal vigor, and every few seconds a mirror brushed her hip.

Traffic was unusually aggressive—everyone was fed up, miserable, and ready to light shit on fire just to get a little heat going. It had been below zero for two weeks now, the biggest freeze in more than a century. Half the news stations were reporting this as climate change in real time and a warning that humankind was headed for an extinction event; the other half were claiming the deep freeze proof positive that global warming was a Chicken Little conspiracy dreamed up by Tesla-driving kale munchers who wanted to burn the Constitution. The only thing everyone actually agreed upon was that it was *cold*.

Balancing in the middle of the road, playing matador with angry cars, was a position every New Yorker experienced at one time or another. It was also a possible path to the obituary section. Nimi had grown up here, always thinking that *other people* got killed by cars;

each year, more than fifteen thousand pedestrians on the island got a taste of hood ornament followed by a ride in an ambulance. And even though only a couple of hundred succumbed to their wounds, it was not an exercise she wanted to take from the theoretical to the practical.

Nimi scouted both directions, looking for a break in the herd of cars stampeding by. She was five minutes into her balancing act and needed to put a little sidewalk under her boots.

Then, almost magically, the choreography of traffic changed and a black sedan coming down Forty-second slowed just as it cleared the Park viaduct. The driver waved her across. She lifted a foot and stepped into the void.

Nimi smiled as she stepped in front of his grille. Gave him a wave and mouthed, *Thank you.*

She made eye contact, and everything was fine. And then, somehow, it wasn't.

The car window disintegrated, and the driver's head disappeared— it was there, and then it was gone. And for a brief pinch of time, the clock stopped doing what it was supposed to, and everything ceased moving.

Then the sound of the shot thundered in.

Nimi began a scream.

The car—now driverless—surged forward.

In what could be written off as fast thinking but in clinical terms would be called instinct, Nimi began to run.

If it hadn't been so slippery, she might have had better traction.

If she'd had longer legs, she might have made it to the sidewalk.

If she had been a bigger girl, her bones and flesh might have protected her internal organs.

If it had been another day, she might have lived.

2

Columbia University

"So"—Dr. Lucas Page looked up a final time at the computer-generated cosmos blinking down from the ceiling—"if human reality is, in fact, nothing more than a highly specialized simulation, is it truly possible to decode our universe? And if it is, what would be the point?" With that, the time-lapse special effect generated by a million dollars' worth of optics faded and the recessed lighting of the auditorium cycled back up.

Page stepped away from the podium, gave a final nod to the class, and wished the students a prosperous Christmas break unfettered by contemplation or purpose. The hillside of undergrads rose in unison, clapping and cheering.

It was during the awkward post-lecture phase where the students were either still clapping or stuffing laptops into backpacks that Page slipped down the stairs and through the curtains. The adulation of his students was not a reciprocal relationship, and he avoided mingling with them, sometimes to comic lengths. He had absolutely no idea how to respond to *I really enjoyed your course, Dr. Page, and I hope you have a really nice Christmas vacation.* And it wasn't a skill he was interested in acquiring.

The incurious herds they fed through his auditorium were beginning to border on depressing. They all came preloaded with the belief that they were special, but very few had developed even basic critical-thinking skills. More and more, they asked questions that weren't really questions at all.

Out in the hall, he headed for the stairs. He wanted to get out early; there was a Christmas tree somewhere out there with his name on it.

Page climbed the stairs with the specialized mechanical gait it had taken years of rebuilds and adjustments to his prosthetic to get just right. He was now able to take the steps two at a time going up, no small feat for a man the surgeons said would need a walker for the rest of his life, and he completed the three flights almost as quickly as the old days.

With every step, the auditorium slipped further from his focus, a process he was consciously aware of. It wasn't that he didn't enjoy teaching this particular course—he detested it. Not that there weren't some bright kids on the roster—there were a few. But it was tedious weeding out the brains from the shitheads, and there were way too many of one and not nearly enough of the other.

His course, Simulation Theory and the Cosmos, had become the largest draw in the department, which was some kind of magic considering that Page had thought it up one night after too many drinks and not enough self-control in a sarcastic nod to the endless academic jack-offery that were the bearing walls of the other departments. It was a spoof—you had to be an idiot to miss it—but he left the single-paragraph outline on his desk, and the dean had picked it up during one of her rare visits. When she started yammering on about its merits, he didn't have the heart to tell her it had been a joke. So he now taught a course he thought was complete and absolute horseshit to a bunch of kids who wouldn't know the difference between a scientific theory and a conspiracy theory under an administration that couldn't differentiate sarcasm from earnestness. Things were swell.

The third floor was the academic equivalent of the 1914 Christmas truce: undergraduates, TAs, and faculty were doing their best to act like friends, if only for the night. Bottles of imported beer and cheap champagne were being consumed as they tried to look involved in their conversations while waiting for more interesting messages to light up their smartphones.

He slipped by a handful of hellos, three offers of beer, two of wine, one of champagne (Perrier-Jouët Grand Brut, no less), and one slap on the back. He opened the door, expecting to find Debbie grading papers to CNN.

She wiped out the question mark hanging in his thoughts by jabbing an arm at him, a stack of phone messages folded into her fingers. She didn't look up, but she acknowledged him with, "You had sixty-one calls." Then she nodded at her computer. "And a shitload of email."

The console beside her desk was stacked with wrapped Christmas gifts that experience taught him would be alcohol in various permutations—the university equivalent of apples for the teacher.

"Any drop-ins?" he asked.

Screening visitors—mostly of the whiny student variety—was the main reason Debbie was here. She was working on a Ph.D. in deep-space astronomy, a distinction she offset with very clear—and proudly worn—Asperger's. And it was her uncertainty with nonverbal cognitive cues that made her the ideal assistant; she was not susceptible to any of the weaponized histrionics the students liked to use. "Twenty-six. The only one you'll want to call back would be the Haagstrom kid. His father died."

Page stopped flipping through the pile of messages. "Email him and give him a two-week extension. Tell him to call me if he needs anything. Give him my cell number."

Debbie looked up, her face etched with surprise.

"It's his father, for Chrissake," he said. "And it's Christmas."

"I understand. I'm just surprised you do."

Lucas nodded over at the *Tetris*-stacked console of Christmas cheer. "Can you take care of thank-you cards for those?"

Debbie waved it away. "Already done except for two—your publisher and your literary agent. Your agent sent a decent scotch and your publisher went big with a magnum of champagne."

"Send the champagne to the dean with a note to have a merry Christmas."

"It's a thousand-dollar bottle of Bollinger."

"So add the word *very* to the note." He tried out a smile. "And take the rest home."

The video in the corner of Debbie's computer screen switched stories, and Page automatically shifted focus for an instant. As the chyron started its sales pitch, Page's chest lit up with a bolt of adrenaline. "Turn up the volume." He was pretty certain that he had sounded calm.

She hit the SPEAKER button on her keyboard.

The sallow face of the ersatz journalist looked into the camera as emergency lights flashed in the background. The text on the chyron ticking across the bottom of the screen was laced together with the clumsy, noncommittal vagaries of modern American journalism, but the yammering heads seemed to be certain of one fact: a sniper had shot someone.

Page might have let it go if a figure surrounded by FBI parkas hadn't caught his attention. There was no mistaking the walk. Or the tailored overcoat.

"Aren't those the people you used to work for?" Debbie asked without looking up from the monitor.

"No," he lied.

3

Forty-second Street and Park Avenue

Special Agent in Charge Brett Kehoe moved away from the crime-scene tent while Grover Graves followed on his flank, dictating computer model results—a term that at this particular junction in time was a euphemism for *guesses*. It was night now, but the lights of the city were amplified by the snow and gave the illusion of working under a full moon. Which made everyone on-site nervous—there was no reason to believe that the man with the rifle had closed up his toolbox and gone home.

Wind funneled down the street, blowing snow under Kehoe's scarf where it melted and soaked his collar. On any other night, the street would have been the perfect image of a New York Christmas. Now it was just a place where someone had been murdered. And the oversized ornaments hanging from the lampposts added a morbid humor to the situation that was not lost on him.

He looked up at the line of rooftops, the endless windows, and the snow coming down. Whoever planned this knew exactly what he was doing; these conditions would wear his people down.

As they walked, Kehoe automatically—and unconsciously—scanned the buildings. He had six FBI countersnipers on-site, keeping everyone—law enforcement, citizenry, and media ass-holes alike—safe. Or at least that was the intent. Two SWAT teams on standby combined with the NYPD's presence meant the shooter would have to be stupid—or suicidal—to still be in the area. Which translated to everyone being a little nervous.

The component that really made Kehoe uneasy on this one was the victimology. Federal agents got killed. It was one of those things. Not as often as people thought. And certainly not as often as the idiots on the news liked to proclaim. But everyone concerned knew that it was a statistical possibility. That someone had gone through this much trouble to kill one of his people hinted at a larger picture that he was as yet unable to see.

"How is it possible that you're standing there shrugging? This is pure physics: A-squared-plus-B-squared-equals-C-squared."

Graves held up a weatherproof tablet slaved to the modeling hardware back in the command vehicle. "Sure. Pythagoras knew his shit. But we can't manufacture either a horizontal *or* a vertical azimuth, and that doesn't give us a starting point."

Kehoe never gave in to displays of emotion at work; it was a personal point of pride, but he could only tolerate *I don't know* so many times. "We have a dead federal agent in that car and a civilian stapled to a lamppost. I won't accept *can't*."

Graves held up the tablet again as if it might illustrate his point. "To figure out where our shooter was, we need some values that simply aren't there. We don't know the angle of travel because there is no accurate way to string the shot. We can't reverse engineer a line of travel from the body because that slug tore his head up; there's nothing to work with. Different rounds act differently on impact, some even tumbling backward if you want to believe the Warren Commission."

"Don't editorialize with me," Kehoe said, allowing a little alpha dog to seep into his voice.

"Sorry, sir."

"Video?" Kehoe asked. One saving grace of omnipotent technology was that in any public arena, there were always eyes on the prize.

"We've checked every video feed, surveillance camera, traffic camera, and pedestrian cell phone, and we've come up with a big fat zero. We have one dashcam from a cab three cars ahead that demonstrates the downstream domino effect from the moment of impact, but there's no sound, so we can't be certain of the precise time the round came in. What we have come up with is a four-second window, which means the car could have been anywhere in the intersection when the shot came in. It just kept rolling until it hit the lamppost."

"You mean young woman."

Graves looked up from the tablet. "Yeah. Young woman."

How was it that in the second-most surveilled city in the world they couldn't find a guy carrying a rifle down one of its busiest streets? Kehoe realized that everything they needed seemed erased by evil spirits. Or someone who had a whole lot of know-how in the killing business. "What about our magic bullet?"

Graves gave him a shrug. "We're looking for it."

"*We're looking for it?*" He took a deep breath and let it oxygenate his lungs. He felt a very disturbing calm, the kind that comes on just before you drown. "We look like a troop of asshats."

Graves shrugged again.

Kehoe took another breath and let it power an even tone. "This snow is going to wipe out a lot more evidence if he took the shot from atop one of these buildings." They were looking at over 1,600 yards of rooftop and nearly 3,000 windows. His men were hoofing it across the skyline, but a thorough search would take all night. Which they didn't have.

"Unless you have a magic eyeball, this is the best we can do." Graves sounded defensive.

Kehoe turned back to Park Avenue. Back to the police cars and the emergency services vehicles and bureau men running around and the oversized Christmas ornaments and the snow and wind and the two victims. Then he lifted his focus to the windows stretching to the horizon before turning and walking away.

"Where are you going?" Graves asked.

Kehoe said, "To get you a magic eyeball."

4

The Upper East Side

Lucas Page loaded the dishwasher while Erin oversaw handwashing in preparation for their after-dinner story. Even with his early departure from school, he had managed to miss supper, which in this particular instance was not a bad thing because the kids didn't need him in a sour mood. He wanted to blame it on a general reticence toward grading term papers, but that would be a cop-out; the bogeyman on CNN had started it all. At least he had come home with a Christmas tree.

He generally made an effort to be there for supper. The kids thrived on routine; most of them hadn't eaten a vegetable or seen an alarm clock before they had become part of the family. But sometimes work at the lab kept him late. Tonight, dragging the big Scotch pine through the kitchen had bought him a lot of domestic air miles, and it was a welcome reprieve from all the bad juju the CNN broadcast had conjured up.

But this wasn't any night; they had a new child who needed to get comfortable with them. Erin had taken two months off so she wouldn't have to divide her attention between the hospital and home. And Lucas had promised her two full weeks during the Christmas break, yet he hadn't even been able to make it home for supper. What the hell did that say about his word? She wouldn't care that he had been rattled by the news and had spent a little too much time wandering the tree lot. This was a child, not an academic exercise—intentions didn't matter; results did.

He loaded cups into the rack while the storm came down beyond the window above the sink. The lights were on in Dingo's apartment over the garage, and smoke drifted from the chimney.

Winter had started in November, the first snow of the year hitting the city ten days before Thanksgiving. The backyard had been buried for weeks, and now only the superstructure of the swing set rose above the snow like a derelict oil rig designed by Dr. Seuss. And it wasn't giving up anytime soon—Lucas couldn't remember it ever looking like this; so far, the season's snowfall had surpassed all previous records. The scent of pine needles combined with the scenery outside was setting the mood, and to paraphrase Johnny Mathis, it was beginning to feel a lot like Christmas.

He tried to concentrate on the dishes, but his attention kept creeping back to the television.

The blinking screen usually lent an intangible warmth to the kitchen, but tonight it added a creepy, shimmery blue to the stainless steel and marble. He had the sound low as the news anchor in his peripheral vision did his best James Earl Jones. And with every little detail, his old machinery squeaked as it tried to start up.

He was wiping down the sink when that same figure from before caught his attention. Same silhouette. Same clothing. Only one man looked like that.

Lucas turned off the water, wiped his hands, and turned up the volume. He was leaning against the island when Erin came in. "What's with the news?" She froze as she saw his expression and turned to the television, then back to him, tractor-beaming him with one of her looks. "Luke?"

He watched her stare flick back and forth from his good eye to his bad one—it was something she only did when she was angry or disappointed, and right now he knew that she was both. There were a lot of things he could say, but the last thing he wanted was to sound defensive.

Anderson Cooper was now sharing the split screen with Wolf Blitzer back in the studio. Blitzer was doing his best to look grave as Cooper came back with vague answers about the unknown suspect, unknown motive, unknown victim, unknown type of weapon—the only certainty being that the weather would hamper the investigation.

Lucas nodded at the screen when they ran the loop, just as that figure crossed the street behind Cooper. "Remember him?" he asked.

Erin grudgingly shifted her focus to the screen. When she saw the figure he was referring to, her posture stiffened.

Maude called from the front hall. "We're ready!"

But Erin didn't move. She just watched the events unfolding on the screen. "That's Brett Kehoe," she said flatly.

"Yeah."

Maude called again.

"In a minute!" Erin snapped, quickly updating it with a softer, "Give me a minute, okay?" But she was still staring at the TV. "Does this involve you?" she asked Lucas.

Kehoe was now walking toward a group of men and women in FBI parkas. "I don't know."

Erin took the remote from the counter, snapped the television off, and tossed the controller back onto the marble. The battery cover flew off, rolling triple-As out onto the floor. "Well, stop watching that crap. It's story time."

Fifteen minutes later, images of the Ghost of Christmas Past had evaporated, and Lucas read from a Sesame Street book. The kids had lapsed into the usual almost-calm that followed playtime and pre-ceded bedtime. The book was a little dated, and he had trouble doing voices other than Mr. Snuffleupagus, but the children always got a kick out of his singing.

Maude was doing homework at the oak library table—no doubt

final prep for her algebra test tomorrow—and Erin was in the big Morris chair by the fire. Damien and Hector were on the floor by the tree, deeply immersed in a made-up game with the Ouija board (only they called it *the Luigi board*), and Alisha, who had been with them for three days now, was curled up with Laurie and the dog in the window seat. Alisha was making friends with Laurie, who enjoyed her role of being a big sister for the first time. Erin's body language had softened a little, no doubt in response to Lucas's Grover impression. And it was one of those moments where all seemed well in Page Land—almost.

He was in the midst of a very bad rendition of "The Alphabet Song" when Alisha's and Laurie's attention shifted out the window. At first, they just looked curious, but when Alisha's arms tightened around Lemmy, Lucas stopped singing, "*J* is for a jar of jam," closed the book, and went to the window. Behind him, Erin's reflection unfolded from the chair.

Two police cruisers bookended a pair of black SUVs at the curb. The cars were double-parked, and the lights pulsed. The doors on all four vehicles opened simultaneously, and more than enough manpower to field a football team stepped out into the snow. There were six police officers divided between the two cruisers and eight warm bodies between the SUVs. The only one that Lucas recognized was the well-tailored figure from the television—so make that seven warm bodies plus Brett Kehoe.

Kehoe broke off from the group and headed for the front door. The rest took up positions on the sidewalk that Lucas recognized as strategic; as always, Kehoe surrounded himself with good people.

Lucas put his original hand on Alisha's shoulder. "Don't worry, sweetie; they're not here for you."

Behind him, Erin said, "Phooey," and he was amazed that even with the small army on the sidewalk, she was able to keep it together in front of the kids. More of that magic that attracted him to her.

But he knew to avoid looking at her as he went to the door.

The bell rang, and he took a few deep breaths before opening the massive slab of oak and stained glass to the FBI's special agent in charge for Manhattan. Four overcoated clones came up the steps behind him.

Kehoe didn't say hello. Or smile. Or even extend a hand. All he did was ask, "Have you seen the news?"

5

Lucas unloaded the dishwasher as Kehoe went through his sales pitch. He didn't offer to take Kehoe's coat; he didn't want him to start feeling at home. Lucas didn't have anything more to give these people. Not unless they needed a little resentment.

Kehoe didn't start with an apology, and he didn't ask for one, and either would have been understandable. But a decade was a lot of time, and Kehoe wasn't an intellectually lazy man; he had no doubt worked out his own feelings on the way things had unfolded.

If he had any.

Of course, the net result was that none of it had been anyone's fault. There had been no meaning or purpose or even intent in what had happened. The universe had simply opened its arms and handed out one of those meaningless fuck-yous that history wouldn't even remember. All because they had been at precisely the wrong place at exactly the right time.

Kehoe put a diagram down on the table. It was a crime-scene mock-up with measurements and elevations penciled in, all in CAD-generated accuracy—more of that Kehoe efficiency. "The victim was westbound on Forty-second and got hit as he emerged from the Park viaduct. The shot came in from the south."

Before he could stop himself, Lucas put his aluminum finger down at the transept where the two routes overlapped. "Through this trough?" The diner under the overpass was one of the places he often took the kids for breakfast after their Sunday morning outing to the library. "Where, specifically, did the shot come from?"

"All we know is that he got hit in the intersection, and witnesses say the sound came in a full two or three seconds later."

Witnesses were notoriously bad judges of time, but the delay between impact and the sound wave had been big enough to be noticed, which meant that there was some distance in the equation. It also said that the shooter hadn't used a noise suppressor of any kind.

"Caliber?"

"The round went through the vehicle, and we haven't found it yet."

"You mean it went through the *window*."

"No, I don't. It went through the *car*."

Now he knew why Kehoe was standing in his kitchen.

Lucas thought about the corridor up Park, a trough of high-rises and windows that offered a million and one vantage points for a man with a rifle.

"A second victim was hit by the car after the driver lost control. She was with the New York Ballet. She's dead."

With each little Lego that Kehoe snapped into place, his motivations became clearer. This was the kind of event that could very quickly undermine the public's belief in the powers that be. And in a closed ecosystem like New York City, the implied social contract of the inhabitants was the only thing that truly prevented the experiment from descending into chaos.

"I see your problem but not how I can help. I was quit when you came in, and I'm twice as quit now," he said, doing a pretty good Rick Deckard impression.

Kehoe watched him for a few moments, and Lucas knew him well enough to know that he wasn't done. This was where Kehoe would try to get his fingers inside Lucas's head. So he waited for it.

"One more thing." The way Kehoe opened, Lucas could tell that this was the big sell.

Lucas stared back with his good eye. "I told you—I'm quit."

Kehoe reached down and picked up the elevations. He rolled them up, nodded solemnly, and looked like he was really about to leave when he paused and smiled sadly. "You should still know that the victim was your old partner, Doug Hartke."

6

Forty-second Street and Park Avenue

Lucas stood on Forty-second in the shadow of the Park Avenue Viaduct with the vector printouts. They were laminated and organized in a one-inch binder with the bureau's logo embossed on it. All neat and tidy and waiting for him when Kehoe's SUV came to a stop outside the big Blue Bird command vehicle parked at the scene. They were also very much useless.

Forty-second was closed in both directions, and Park had been shut three blocks south, tying traffic into a knot usually reserved for July. The street was upholstered in NYPD cruisers and FBI SUVs, the flashing lights bouncing off the snow and concrete and glass, giving the whole show a netherworldly disco effect.

It was freezing, and the wind funneled between the buildings, riding up Park Avenue and stirring up snow devils that at any other time would have been beautiful. The asphalt was covered in a dirty frozen crust that crunched like potato chips, and Lucas had trouble negotiating the uneven footing. His ankle always stiffened up in low temperatures. The prosthetic itself was mostly aluminum, but the joint pins were stainless steel and some of the other hardware was titanium or carbon fiber, and each alloy contracted at a different rate, which hampered mobility. To compensate, he added a hop to his good leg, giving his gait an idiosyncratic signature in the cold.

When they arrived on-site, Lucas asked about the food chain, and Kehoe pointed to a large crucifix of a figure near the evidence tent that he recognized as the unmistakable form of Grover Graves. He and Lucas had never hit it off, one of those bad chemistry dislikes that all the handshakes, smiles, and best intentions couldn't overcome. Graves was also the single known exception to Kehoe's rule of using only the best people, and having him in charge of a case of this import didn't feel like one of his moves.

After Lucas and Graves nodded hellos from opposite sides of the street, Kehoe told Lucas that Hartke had been working under Graves for the past few years, a detail that surprised him. Hartke had hated stupid almost as much as Lucas did, and Lucas couldn't see the man taking orders from Graves, no matter what the situation. But it was a possible explanation as to why Kehoe had Graves leading the investigation—it was making him take responsibility for his own people.

But Lucas wouldn't have to work with Graves. Or Kehoe. He was here as a favor to his old partner. Hartke was a lot of things, some of them not very pretty, but he had been a friend. Which meant that Lucas owed him. So here he was. Standing out in the street and waiting to slip into character.

The two agents Kehoe had sent with him were hanging back, near the corner, eyeing him with the preprogrammed disinterest of their kind. One of them was a typical bureau type who looked like he had been pulled from central casting—forgettable and bland; the other was a black chick who moved with the slow, deliberate patience of a badass. They were both quiet and professional, and they stayed out of his way.

After a few seconds of taking in the topography, he realized that he had moved behind a lamppost, which meant that his operating system was updating automatically. It was amazing how fast that kind of thinking became instinctive—and even more amazing how long it lingered after it was no longer necessary, like some phantom limb. After the hospitals and operations and rehabilitation and nightmares, it had taken him almost a full year to be able to walk through a crowd. It took time, but the fear had slowly dispersed into the ether. Until now.

But a little caution out here wasn't just smart, it was essential; when put into perspective, nothing was worse than hunting a man with a rifle in a city of windows.

"Fuck it," he said at church volume, and stepped into the intersection.

The victim—his former partner and onetime friend—still sat in his car. The vehicle was hidden from the world by a crime-scene tent, but Kehoe had walked him through, and Lucas would not forget what Hartke looked like. Taking the top off a human skull released a fountain of blood operating at 1.5 pounds per square inch with a reservoir of nearly two gallons. In an enclosed area like a car, that translated to enough bad dreams to last a lifetime. And Lucas already had a pretty good collection of those.

He hadn't sat down with Hartke in three years, but they'd exchanged Christmas cards and the occasional email, all embellished with the threat of visits that rarely materialized. Lucas couldn't blame the man; what had happened to him was simply too much of a reminder about just how wrong things could go in this line of work. And law enforcement people, especially old-schoolers like Hartke, were notoriously superstitious—even if he would never admit it, some part of his reptilian brain had to be worried that Lucas's luck might be retroactively contagious. So Lucas never held it against him.

He sighted up the street and took a deep breath, pushing the weather and the flashing lights and the army of men in blue and the giant Christmas ornaments and the tent hiding his dead former partner away.

Did he still have it in him? After all, if what everyone said was true, he couldn't really do the things he claimed. Not with a human brain.

There was only one way to find out. So he closed his eyes and waited for it to begin.

He thought about what he had seen back in the evidence tent. About the shattered car window and his friend's shoveled-out brain. About the dashcam footage Kehoe had shown him and that four-second window framing the round that had come screaming in. About where he was and why he had agreed to come.

Then he opened his eyes, and the world slipped into context.

Instantly.

Automatically.

And the street came to life in a way he hadn't seen in so long it felt like he had entered someone else's hallucination.

The world was suddenly reduced to an intricate geometry.

The smaller components of the city took on values—the bricks and blocks of stone becoming units of measure. These units connected to the larger planes—the windows and doors and lampposts—which in turn displayed their own numerical meaning, each relative to the others, and suddenly everything was one, and the city became a matrix of interconnected digits, a mosaic of numbers that stretched to the horizon.

Lucas stood in the intersection, lifted his arms, and slowly rotated in place, absorbing the city in a numerical panorama that pulsed and danced and flashed through his head. He took in the numbers around him, feeding the data into a series of instinctive algorithms that even he did not understand. It was an immediate process, fired up with an automaticity he could not explain. It was like being at the center of a vortex, and the lines of code carpeting the landscape swirled around him at a speed too fast to absorb in any conscious way.

By the time he had completed a single rotation, he could no longer see the buildings or sidewalks or police cruisers or flashing lights. He forgot the cop cars lining the street and the men and women in blue parading up and down the snow-covered pavement. All he saw, all he was able to relate to, were the numbers.

Everywhere.

Representing everything.

And then.

It was over.

He blinked and the circus shut down. All of it—the numbers, the geometry, the distances. All that was left was a frigid winter scene with too many cop cars and not enough traffic.

Lucas sighted down Park Avenue, and his mind connected the components. He no longer heard the honking of rerouted traffic, felt the mother-in-law's kiss of winter chill, or squinted into the snow coming down. All he could do was stare at the spindle of brick rising out of the earth like Kong's mountain home. It was the only building on the avenue that had been designed on a cant, its orientation offset by a ninety-degree twist. One of its corners reached out, towering over Park. It was 772 yards from the point of impact, give or take a handful of inches.

And perfect.

He turned to the woman. "What's your name?"

"Whitaker," she said, her friendly tone in direct contrast to her badass impression. The only visible features were her teeth hidden in the shadow of the FBI hood.

"Whitaker, tell Kehoe I know where the shot came from."

Lucas nodded at what he knew was a building in the distance but had turned back into a series of geometrical planes connected to the rest of the city by numbers. He raised his aluminum hand and pointed at the tower. "The roof of number 3 Park Avenue."

7

Although designed by the same architectural firm that had birthed the Empire State Building, number 3 Park Avenue possessed none of the grandeur of the company's crowning achievement. An unappealing monolith that rose precisely 556 feet into the Manhattan skyline, the building resembled a condo development. It lacked the chutzpah to be Trump ugly but still managed to look like it was trying too hard. It could have been built anywhere in the world and still not be nominated for any kind of an award.

The rooftop was the size of a football field, with two outbuildings housing access doors and various utilities, a water tower, and a bank of tractor-trailer-sized HVAC units that were running so hard the deck vibrated with their energy. The roof was set up like a medieval castle—or a prison yard—a twenty-foot wall enclosing the sky-high courtyard like defensive ramparts. Wind funneled down into the walled space, fueling an atmospheric turbine that created a self-contained snowstorm.

Everyone turned to Lucas, waiting for his magic powers to kick in. But there wasn't much to think about in the way of positions—the shooter had to have been close to the northwest corner, at the left-most edge of the massive heat pumps sending warm air down into the body of the building. A pair of tracks were carved into the thick carpet, but the wind had done its work; other than a rough gait measurement, they wouldn't learn much from the trail.

The footsteps led to the corner by the HVAC units, straight to the skeleton of scaffolding bolted to the wall—no doubt installed for repairs before the deep freeze put everything on hold.

There weren't a lot of ways up—the integrated ladders on the side were the only option: four levels to the ramparts. Whoever had used the scaffold wore gloves, so there was no worry about disturbing fingerprints or latent DNA, and whatever had been left behind in the way of trace evidence had been blasted past Hoboken by now. Lucas headed up the scaffold.

He had very little mobility in his prosthetic hand, and he had to hook his elbow over every second rung. His leg locked each time he pulled back his thigh, and this helped him Spider-Man up the frozen steel tubing, but it was a lot slower than someone with full biomechanics.

The wind had scoured the platform clean, and there were no immediate signs of a man's passing. Lucas pivoted and rolled up onto the deck.

Out there, high above the city, the wind became something to be feared. Coming up here required more than just motivation and determination—you needed to enjoy punishment. There were a thousand other places along Park or Forty-second that would have served all the tactical considerations better than this place.

So why here?

Lucas moved to the brick wall that rose three feet, then rolled out for another eight in a ledge before dropping out into space. He rose slowly, keeping his center of gravity low—the psychological hurdle of being forty-one floors up added all kinds of white noise to an already unsettling exercise. He wasn't afraid of heights, but you had to be a moron to not respect what gravity and pavement could do to a falling body.

Looking down Park to Forty-second was like staring down a long, narrow trench, which made the exercise seem easy. But when you took a figurative step back and examined the variables, this fucker had a lot of extra math involved: wind; shifting daylight; snow; reduced visibility; weapons adjustment (and possible failure); clothing choice; distance. And a narrow slice of time to line it all up. This wasn't a shot just anyone who knew their way around a rifle could make.

Lucas pulled out his scope and sighted down Park. Grand Central Terminal filled the reticle, and the intersection was a cacophony of flashing lights and cop cars—all for a single bullet that everyone was trying to go back in time to stop.

Making that shot from here would be like trying to thread a needle while riding a mechanical bull set to Motörhead. It would take the first half of the intersection to simply acquire the target. Which gave a tiny window to focus, take a breath, calculate the lead, and squeeze the trigger.

Close to impossible.

Lucas could think of maybe three men off the top of his head who could make it happen, and even then the statistics were against them.

But for their guy, it had been doable. Difficult and unlikely—but *doable*. All you had to do was ask Doug Hartke.

The deck was scrubbed virtually clean by the wind. There were no scratches or pigeon shit or any other marks on the engineered stone, either atmospheric or man-made.

Lucas turned back to the roof, back to the storm coming down and the city beyond the haze. Then he looked down at the forensics guys who would be doing all the heavy lifting in cataloging the million and one pieces of crap up here, very little (if any) of which would be useful.

He now had a developing picture of the man they were looking for. A guy like this hadn't been spawned in a vacuum; he had a life out there. He had done this before.

That was when Kehoe piped up above the wind. "Well, Page? What do you think?" he hollered from the rooftop below.

Lucas turned and examined him for a second; he had already given his opinion—he was only up here out of morbid curiosity.

"Bingo," he said.

8

Lucas was tucked into the corner under the spider-works of sheathed ducting that fed into the dead end behind the main service elevator. The coffee that Whitaker kept bringing him was better than the stuff they used to hand out in the field; evidently, the Starbucksification of America had spread to the FBI. All his parts had thawed out, and his prosthetics were loosened up.

But Lucas wasn't thinking about the coffee any more than he was worrying about the national debt; his mind was focused on what they weren't telling him.

Kehoe was definitely keeping something back. Lucas had no idea what it was, other than it was there, in everything he said and, more important, in everything he didn't. It was in the pauses and the little tick of time he used before answering questions. It was there when he looked Lucas square in the eye and in the way he watched him.

But the big tell was how everyone other than Whitaker was avoiding him. And it wasn't from discomfort; he was used to making people uneasy, but that was in the world at large—he wouldn't make a dent with these people. No, they were avoiding him because they had been told to.

Classic Kehoe.

He was on his third cup of coffee when Kehoe's tailored silhouette came around the corner, Grover Graves in tow. Agent Whitaker shadowed them but stopped short, near the corner by the elevator. Lucas was starting to like her, and it wasn't just because of her almost preternatural silence. He sensed that she was looking out for him, even though he was unable to articulate how. It had started back at the intersection of Park and Forty-second and had been amplified by the way she kept bringing him coffee.

Kehoe took off his gloves and blew into his fists. Even under the vent, Lucas could feel the cold wafting off him. Graves moved into the huddle, looking unhappy.

Kehoe filled a few seconds of airtime with a pause before saying, "You saved us a lot of time."

"You would have figured it out—"

"Yes, we would have," Graves interrupted, demonstrating that the old days weren't far away in his mind.

Lucas gave him a soft smile and finished with, "In a week or two."

Over at the elevator, Whitaker cracked a smile that she covered with a cough directed into her gloved fist.

Kehoe ignored the petty animosity but gave Graves a look that shut him down. Kehoe was one of those rare bureau people who was good at what he did because he was results oriented, not politically motivated. In an organization where ascension is as dearly coveted as results, divine protection would have been his had he stacked his boxed set with a pile of number-one hits. But his wake was littered with dogs—lost causes that no one else wanted. He was famous for it. And in the face of what appeared to be a direct desire to stay a field agent, he was nonetheless pushed up the law enforcement ladder by his superiors until now, almost three decades in, he was the acting senior agent for all of New York City. And one of the most respected in Manhattan's history.

Kehoe continued, "I'd like you to stay on with this one. As a favor to me and as a favor to Hartke. He would have wanted you here."

Lucas wondered if that had sounded as insincere to everyone else as it had to him. After mulling it over, he realized that these were no longer his people. And he would not let himself get manipulated. Besides, he had nothing left to give them. "No thanks," he said, heading for the elevator.

"Where are you going?"

"Home. We've got a new little girl, and she's not sleeping so well." He nodded at Whitaker. "And she's driving me."

Kehoe started to protest, but Lucas was already gone.

As they stepped into the elevator, Whitaker said, "You don't have a lot of friends, do you?"

Lucas reached out and hit the button with a green anodized knuckle. The doors slid closed, blocking out Graves and Kehoe. "What are friends?" he asked.

9

When Lucas walked in the front door, Erin was in the study, on the sofa between the fireplace and the new Christmas tree devoid of ornaments. She was staring at the fire, zoning out with a glass of sauvignon blanc and that crappy music that she liked and he thought belonged in the elevator at Saks—it sounded like the Smiths tonight. She didn't look up from the fire, and he hoped that she wasn't angry. He could deal with disappointment, but when she got angry, communication got reduced to slammed doors and silence.

He hung his coat up on the deco hall tree by the stairs, kicked off his boots, and went over to the love seat. He dropped into the tufted leather, his prosthetic straight out in front of him. "Hey, baby."

She didn't speak for a few moments, and when she did, all that came out was, "Are you going back?"

Erin was fearless—always—and when something rattled her universe, she charged it head-on. Now, with her face only a few feet away, he could see the anger twanging the muscles below her skin.

Lucas reached out, taking her little face in his hand. She closed her eyes and dug her cheek into his palm, and she felt warm.

"You look"—all emotion, except for disappointment, dropped out of her voice—"different."

He was going to ask her how, but he knew what she meant. He could also feel it.

Erin put her feet up on his lap, and he massaged the arch of her left with his good hand. She watched him for a few moments before saying, "You're not thirty-five anymore."

What she said had nothing to do with what she meant. Sure, the old him had both arms, both legs, and both eyes. But she was talking about herself and the kids.

"Just let me figure a few things out."

At that, she pulled her feet off his lap and reached for the bottle on the coffee table. "There's an *us* in this, you know." Erin filled her glass and stood up. "I'm going to go upstairs; I have an early morning with the kids."

He tried to kiss her good night, but she had already slipped away.

10

Lucas sat on the sofa for a while, cycling down the old machinery and nudging his OS toward hibernation. The adrenaline of being out there again slowly leached from his fibers, leaving guilt in its place. Erin was right—he'd have to be a complete and utter fool to forget what had happened the last time he had been out in the world with a badge clipped to his waist.

By the time the wheels in his head stopped spinning, the fire was reduced to a glowing mat of embers. The room was chilly, and his good leg was asleep. He gripped the armrest and pushed out of the sofa. The one positive thing he could say about his prosthetics (the arm and leg at least) was that they didn't suffer from fatigue; they never cramped up, and they didn't fall asleep. He stood there as the blood made its way into the lesser veins and capillaries of his good leg, and it felt like an army of ants were moving under his skin, chewing their way through muscles, tendons, and flesh.

He shifted his weight off the prosthetic as the imaginary neural insects finished off their feast. When they were gone, he headed down the hall to the kitchen and got himself a glass of milk from the fridge. He wondered how the kids were doing upstairs, what dreams were going through their little subconscious universes.

With Alisha added to the mix, there were now five children in the house, all kids whose biological parents had failed them and the system had given up on. Some had come from bad homes. Some had come from terrible homes. Some had come from no home. But somehow, magically, they had ended up here, with him and Erin. It didn't take a degree in Freudian therapy to understand that both of them were trying to fix the broken parts of their own childhoods. But now with Alisha joining the Merry Pranksters, it looked like they had reached critical mass. They had no plans to expand the ranks any more. At least that's what they had promised themselves.

Lucas counted the milk cartons in the fridge, making sure that there was enough for breakfast tomorrow; it was amazing how much milk kids could go through in a day. There were still six full half-gallon cartons, so he allowed himself another glass. Then he scavenged a piece of dry cheddar from the back of the meat drawer.

After he finished putting the dishes in the rack away, he grabbed an apple—there was always a big bowl of fruit on the island—and checked the back door. The lights were still on in Dingo's apartment, and on any other winter night he might have gone over; Dingo could always be relied on for a beer and a little conversation when Lucas couldn't sleep. But he needed to get to bed. After checking the lock for a second time, he headed down the hall.

The apple tasted like it had just come out of the fridge, and he stopped and adjusted the programmable thermostat. He inspected the front door and headed up the stairs in the dark.

He paused just past the pink elephant night-light on the landing. Laurie was camping out in Alisha's room, zipped up in a sleeping bag on the floor. Alisha was in the bunk with the dog, and the room smelled like canine farts and baby shampoo, but she looked at peace. She had taken to Lemmy, and if there was one thing that Lucas knew, it was that nothing helped a kid like a big furry friend who liked to lick you on the face. And Lemmy, even though he looked like a brute (the result of his Great Dane and mastiff genes), loved kids. He tended to gravitate toward the children who needed the most support, and Lucas and Erin had learned to watch how Lemmy approached newcomers to help guide their own advances—the technique wasn't gospel, but Lemmy demonstrated instincts that often bordered on mystical.

He then stopped across the landing, beside Maude's bedroom. She slept with the door locked, and it was an indulgence they allowed her for now. (She had agreed to let Erin keep a key around her neck.) He could hear her breathing on the other side, a metronomic rasp that was somehow in time to the house. The girl, now thirteen and already a young woman, had spent seven long months in an upstate institution before coming here. Preceding that, her years had been marked off in a middle-class home over on Staten Island—a place she was doing her best to forget. She was still uncomfortable around men, and Lucas never spent time alone with her; he didn't want her to feel even remotely uneasy, so he always waited for her to come to him. She had been with them for two years now, and he had worked hard to gain her confidence. And it was finally paying off. When they sat her down to ask if they could legally adopt her, she gave him a hug—a real hug—and nothing he could remember beat that feeling (not even that first big breath after he woke up in the hospital missing a few of his parts). It was one of the greatest accomplishments of his life.

He checked in on Damien and Hector, all tucked away and sleeping as if the world didn't have men with rifles in it. Lucas made sure that they were covered and kissed them both on the foreheads. It wouldn't be long before Damien became a surly teenager, and Lucas wanted to get all the kisses in before the deadline.

Back in their room, Erin was under the covers, and since Lucas had done a head count, he didn't have to make sure they were alone. Sometimes one of the kids snuck in at night. It was usually when they had a bad dream or it was the night before a court date or a thunderstorm was hammering the city outside, but every now and then, he found Erin in bed with a little hummock of blanket that was doing its own breathing.

He closed the bedroom door softly and padded into the bathroom. He needed a shower, but he doubted he'd be able to wash the day off; Kehoe and his world wouldn't be excised by something as simple as Irish Spring.

As he let the water heat up on its trip from the basement tank to the third floor, he stripped off the day's clothes and dumped them in the hamper. Taking clothes off was a lot easier than getting them on, but it still took a few minutes of practiced contortions and, as usual, the jeans were the worst. He hoped that the next fashion revolution would turn its back on straight-legged denim and maybe go baggy, giving him a few years of reprieve. After all, joy was in the little things.

When he was finally nude, the bathroom was filled with a thick weather system of steam. He took off his arm; it was a much more complicated construction than his leg, and the humidity built up in the joints and could get funky. But unless he wanted the added possibility of a somersault through a plate glass shower stall, he needed the leg.

He stepped into the travertine booth, the walls adorned with enough knurled aluminum handles to satisfy a rock climbing school. Back in the beginning, they had been indispensable, but now, starting his second decade as the mechanical man, they were there because he didn't feel like going through another bathroom renovation. Besides, as he got older, his shitty balance might make a comeback. And getting older looked like a real possibility these days.

The water was a shade below boiling, and he let it pelt his back. The scar tissue took a little longer to heat up than the rest of him, and as the warmth slowly spread through his system, he geared up for his end-of-the-day mental shutdown.

But this wasn't an ordinary day. Not by any sort of metric. He couldn't shake the image of Doug Hartke's gray matter splattered all over the vinyl dashboard in frozen chunks.

Or Kehoe's clumsy attempt at getting him back.

Lucas was no stranger to the machinations of the bureau, and he recognized a deeply flawed geometry in the way Kehoe had behaved. And if there was one thing he knew about Kehoe, it was that the man never did anything without a predetermined reason. There was always a plan.

What was going on?

And what wasn't Kehoe telling him?

Fuck it, he thought. *It's over. You're out.*

As the hot water softened his muscles and the steam cleared out his lungs, the night's storyboard faded, and once again he was just a university professor taking a shower.

He started to nod off under the steam, and he shut down the big jet and stood there, drip-drying his parts for a few seconds before stepping out of the tropical booth.

As he toweled off, he looked at the mirror, and his eyes did that weird thing that made everyone uncomfortable. His good eye somehow had perfect mobility, yet another of the thousand tiny miracles hidden inside the big one of him still being alive. But the orbit that housed his prosthetic had been put back together with a few titanium brackets and a beautiful ceramic insert, handcrafted by an artist in Okinawa. Problem was, it had zero motility, and whenever he shifted his gaze, he had to move his entire head; otherwise, the disjointed chameleon effect made it appear as if the tubes in his head were overheating, and it freaked some folks out—more rather than less. It was a party trick that he intentionally brought out only for special occasions, but every now and then it just kind of slipped by, and the result usually had someone looking for the exit. Which led to his habit of wearing sunglasses in public—inside and out. Lucas understood that a few of his new and improved physical traits voyaged well into the uncanny valley and began to scale the far side.

He was wrapping himself in a towel when there was a soft knock.

"Yeah?" he said, louder than he should have at this hour. Erin came in wearing her flannel robe and a grumpy face. "What?" he asked.

"Those assholes are back," she said and left the bathroom.

11

Lucas came downstairs in a clean pair of jeans and a concert T-shirt from a band he had stopped listening to a million years ago. He was still hot from the shower, and his Levi's weren't working with his damp skin, so he held the railing to make sure he didn't pull a Milton Arbogast; telling someone to get out of your house while lying in a heap at the bottom of the stairs lacked the required gravitas.

Kehoe and two field agents were in the living room. Kehoe still wore his coat, which meant he didn't intend on staying long. Or maybe he didn't expect to be *allowed* to stay long. His men flanked the arched doorway like architectural elements in an ancient temple. They seemed constructed from the same genetic building blocks, more of the infamous FBI sameness, right down to their off-the-rack suits and Mormon haircuts.

He bypassed Kehoe and his men and walked down the hall to the kitchen. Erin was standing over the coffee maker, watching it burp out liquefied caffeine.

"Go to bed," he told her.

She looked up and shook her head; it was amazing how much stubborn you could pack into a little redhead. "You're tired, and I know all the voodoo that this has to be doing to your head. You need a coffee. Actually, what you *need* is rest. But since I can't make you a mug of sleep, you get coffee."

Lucas planted a kiss on her forehead. "Go to bed. I'll take care of the coffee."

She took a step back and crossed her arms, making no effort to keep the volume down. "I took time off to help Alisha get used to us. You said that you'd be home over the holidays so we can get to know her and—*more important*—so she could get to know us. Right now, I'm starting to feel like I'm going to be single-mothering it. That's unfair to Alisha. And the rest of the kids. It's Christmas, Luke. Why are they even here at this hour?"

Kehoe was no doubt back to go at his head with an oyster shucker again. But Lucas had walked, and he intended to stay that way.

But he would be lying if he didn't admit to any sort of curiosity, even if it was purely academic. There were a lot of questions he wanted answered, starting with *What did Kehoe really want?*

Because Kehoe didn't need him. Not in any real capacity. He had the most efficient law enforcement organization on the planet at his disposal, Fox News pronunciations notwithstanding.

So why *was* he here?

"Let me work this out. Go to bed; the kids will be up in a few hours."

She looked up at him with an expression he didn't like. "I know that. Why do you think I don't want those men in the house?" she said, this time a little louder than before. "The kids don't need armed men in their lives. They need *normal.*"

They had a stare-down for a few seconds, and he added a *Please* to the equation to get her to drop it. She left him alone with the machine.

Lucas poured one mug of fresh coffee, filled a Japanese cup with boiling water from the teapot Erin had fired up, and dropped in two bags of Earl Grey.

Kehoe was the only man in law enforcement who drank tea.

Everyone else drank coffee—black—since cream and sugar were luxuries that tended to run out in the field. Two months into a job at the bureau, and every field agent Lucas had ever met switched to black coffee (the gourmet shit that Whitaker sprang on him earlier notwithstanding—which meant that maybe he was working with outdated information).

His spine felt like it had been transplanted a few hours ago, and all his limbs might as well have been borrowed. He had the mental stamina, but twenty hours on his prosthetic threw everything off; his body simply needed downtime that it wasn't getting. His remaining energy was being parsed out where needed most, and pain management didn't seem to be the application deemed important enough to keep online.

Lucas came down the hall with Kehoe's saucer on top of his own mug. "Coffee's in the kitchen," he said to the pair of FBI bookends.

Kehoe's briefcase sat on the big leather-topped desk by the built-ins, the antique brass catches open, the mouth of the bag spread wide. An orange file sat under the desk lamp, beside a grinning Play-Doh donkey with blue ears.

Kehoe was in front of the hearth, away from the window and the as-yet-to-be-decorated tree. He had loaded a few logs onto the grate, following the old fire-building adage of *one won't, two might, three will.* Evidently, his Boy Scout training had served him well, because the split hardwood had blossomed to life. The man stood in his suit jacket now, hands clasped behind his back.

Kehoe turned from the renewed blaze. "I'm sorry about that." He nodded at the ceiling above, where Erin's footsteps could be heard as she did the rounds, checking on the kids. Kehoe was still perfectly groomed, but the new day's stubble was coming in and his eyes were red; not even he could prevent exhaustion from making its mark.

"Why are you here?" Lucas handed the tea over.

Kehoe didn't reply. He simply gave Lucas a gracious nod and took a long, silent sip, pausing in the moment. Then he blinked as if the tea were laced with energy. "I need your help."

"So you seem to think."

Kehoe took another sip from the porcelain cup, then brought it back to the saucer. "I have a problem, Luke, and I don't have anyone who can handle it." At that, he glanced over at the file by his briefcase, and the gesture was pregnant with meaning.

Lucas followed his gaze, then went to the file on the desk beside the child's Play-Doh homage to Marino Marini. He picked it up and scanned the contents. It was a suspect file, the bulk of which had been assembled by French intelligence bodies—their versions of the Federal Bureau of Investigation and the Department of Homeland Security: the Direction générale de la sécurité intérieure and the Agence nationale de la sécurité des systèmes d'information. Lucas's French was nonexistent, but it was easy to see that it was a surveillance file on a French national named Philippe Froissant.

After flipping through a few pages, he looked up. "Who is this?"

"The man I have been told is our shooter."

"By whom, the Frenchers?"

Kehoe smiled. "I can say no to the French government."

And that's when it fell into place. He put the file back down on the desk. "What's going on, Brett?" He wanted to hear Kehoe say the words.

Kehoe turned back to the fire, and his voice dropped. "That file was forwarded to the DOJ from one of our liaison departments in the DHS, and the DOJ handed it down to me. Tonight. I was told that is our shooter."

Lucas dropped into the sofa. His lower back was lit up in ten shades of ouch, a reminder that all the computer-driven design on the planet couldn't compensate for a skeleton missing important muscle groups. Nothing a week of sleep and thirty painkillers wouldn't knead out. "And?"

For a few seconds, it appeared as if Kehoe were wrestling through some internal dialogue. Then his face switched back into business mode. "Take a look at the file."

"I don't read French."

"Humor me."

When Lucas began to stand, Kehoe picked up the file and handed it over—more manipulation disguised as kindness.

Lucas dropped back into the leather and flipped through the file. He couldn't understand any of the text, so he concentrated on the photographs. Froissant was young, maybe thirty, and obviously very rich. There was a shot of him in a dinner jacket—not off the rack—taken at a social function decorated with cocktail dresses, diamond tennis bracelets, and pretty blondes; there was another in the Formula One pits at Monaco, a bottle of champagne in his hand; one on a yacht, an expensive-looking woman kissing his ear, both of them holding cocktail glasses; another of him skiing in the Alps with an entourage—all wealthy and handsome and young.

The only shot that said he knew his way around a firearm was a single photo taken at a country club somewhere. He wore a tailored shooting jacket with a padded shoulder, and he was cradling an expensive Italian shotgun. It was not a sniper's weapon, and it most certainly did nothing to advance Kehoe's claim that this was their guy.

Lucas put the file down and made a point of not moving for a few moments. The coffee had edged out the exhaustion that the shower had hammered home, and his mind was cycled back to the point where he could hear the whine of the turbine in the back of his skull belting out the required rpm.

"And?" Kehoe asked.

"That's not the guy."

"How do you know?"

Lucas looked at Kehoe as if he had just asked if it were possible to land a spacecraft on the surface of the sun. "The same way you do."

Kehoe began a smile but killed it. "Humor me."

"This asshole looks like some rich French society kid who has too much time on his hands. Old money. I assume that he was bored and ended up making poor choices in either the friend or ideology department and ended up being flagged by French security. And they think he's radicalized." Lucas took a slug of the coffee and shook his head. "Maybe he can shoot, but there is no way this guy has the skill for what happened to Hartke. You don't learn skills like that on a manicured range. Besides, that's for skeet, not targets a thousand yards out," he said, pulling out the photo of Froissant in the shooting jacket.

Kehoe smiled, and Lucas realized that he had been sucked into playing the game after he had promised himself—or had that been Erin?—that he wouldn't. "Why are you here, Brett?"

"I want that cryptic computational wonder inside your head."

"Yeah, well, it's not for sale."

"I need your help."

"So you keep saying."

"That's not our shooter—the reasons you just—"

"Don't say *our*, Brett. It's your problem."

"Of course. Yes," he said, then picked up with, "The reasons you just mentioned are just some of the details that don't fit; but even the broad strokes don't mesh; I've been doing this long enough that I'm not wrong on things like this. Not anymore. But I've been told that Froissant *is* our guy, and I'm supposed to find him. Right now, the bureau is in a precarious position; this current White House administration is not exactly forward-thinking. They're myopic, and they're not very curious, which is a bad combination. They want us to hand them a Muslim terrorist because it fits their agenda—even if we *don't have* a Muslim terrorist to give them. It's confirmation bias, and it's a deeply flawed approach to solving crimes, but as you know, we live in a post-truth world where facts don't matter." He paused and finished his tea, then put the cup and saucer down on the mantel. "But they matter to me, Luke. I need someone I can trust who doesn't scare easily. And I need someone who isn't concerned about losing his job."

Lucas hated Kehoe using his first name. "Why aren't you using Hartke's death? Guilt is a wonderful carrot."

Kehoe's expression didn't even dent. "I already tried guilt; it didn't work."

"You've got Graves."

Kehoe eyed Lucas for a second. "Graves thinks what I tell him to."

"You don't need me. You are going to find this guy."

"Before we do, we are going to expend a lot of energy in the wrong direction so the people in the West Wing can slap each other on the back and proclaim what a swell job they're doing of keeping America safe from terrorists. While that is happening, what if this guy keeps going?"

Lucas examined him for a few moments, and by the way Kehoe's focus shifted around his face, he knew his eyes weren't lined up. "You think he might?"

When Kehoe answered, it sounded like his voice was coming from a different time zone. "I'm not paid to think in best-case scenarios."

12

Lucas locked the big front door behind Kehoe and went back to the study. He closed the glass panels on the hearth, pulling the vent open so that the heat would flow out as long as the fire kept emitting energy. Old Man Winter was in a particularly vengeful mood this year, and the front rooms all felt a little cold even though the insulation and windows were state of the art. Then he once again went through the preflight motions of locking up the brownstone to keep the lions and tigers and bears at bay.

He needed to wind down his mental machinery and get some sleep before he went down to Federal Plaza in the morning. *Jesus,* he wondered, *just how the fuck did I get roped into this?* But he knew. It wasn't really any kind of a mystery. He could blame Kehoe, and he could blame the man with the rifle, and, if he really wanted to, he could blame Hartke—but what it really came down to was that he wanted to do this in some way.

To prove that they hadn't taken everything from him.

To prove that his mind was still capable of the once extraordinary things that used to be easy.

Standing out on that street tonight, watching the world come alive in a living code that only he was able to see, felt better than the dreams he used to have where he was whole again.

But at the end of this, would he feel that same spiritual disappointment he always had when he woke up?

Fuck it, he thought. *Think about this tomorrow when you talk to Kehoe. If you don't like what you see, you walk away. Simple.*

Yeah.

Sure.

He put the three coffee mugs into the dishwasher and washed Kehoe's porcelain cup by hand, leaving it in the dish rack. Then he slipped his feet into the big boots by the back door and stepped out without a coat.

It was a little after 4:00 a.m., but the lights in the apartment over the garage were still on. Lucas knocked softly, and the door was opened before his arm was back at his side.

Dingo's expression telegraphed that he expected bad news; people rarely knock on the door at four in the morning in December to tell you the Powerball ticket you partnered had come through. Without a greeting, he waved Lucas into the small apartment before the cold made too much of a dent on the microclimate.

He was dressed as always, sporting a pair of board shorts, a T-shirt from his dojo, and his home prosthetics—carbon-fiber blades.

After he closed the door, he asked, "What be fucked, mate?" in a heavy Australian accent.

"I need a favor."

"You were here," he stated emphatically.

"What?"

"You need an alibi."

"For *what*?"

"I haven't got a clue. I'm not clairvoyant. You were out with another woman? Some hack from a posh Swedish school accused you of stealing one of his ideas, then died suspiciously? I have no clue. You're the one asking for an alibi."

"I'm not asking for an alibi. I'm asking for a favor."

"Oh."

"*Oh?* Sometimes I think you're a complete idiot."

"And sometimes you'd be right." He smiled. "As your own personal Kato Kaelin, I am your humble servant."

"You pay rent."

Dingo smiled. "I'm still happy to play Kato as long as you need me to."

Lucas and Dingo met at the hospital when it had been their mutual home address. They were wheeled into physical therapy one morning, and a friendly competition started up. Lucas, who was recovering from what he still referred to as *the Event,* started calling the Australian *Dingo* due to his relentless tenacity. He was a combat photographer for the BBC who had become a little too intimate with a land mine in the Sudan. The initial damage wasn't nearly as bad as it could have been, but what should have been a minor operation to set a broken tibia, clean out some shrapnel, and stitch up some severed tendons was complicated by local politics. Had he been able to get decent medical treatment, he most certainly would have kept both legs. But two days in the back of a pickup combined with no access to clean water had resulted in gangrene. By the time he made it to a South African hospital on a network jet, the doctors were worried about saving his life, not his legs. He lost both from just below the knee.

Lucas dropped down on the sofa facing Dingo's desk. "I'm taking a job."

"You have a job, mate."

"I'm going back to work."

At that, Dingo's expression flattened out. "The one that took your drumstick, wing, and peeper?"

Lucas was too tired to smile. "That's the one."

"And *I'm* the complete idiot?"

"Yeah. Well . . ." Lucas was too tired to argue—even with himself. "I'd be grateful if you'd watch over Erin and the kids a little."

"That's what friends are for. At least that's what the small print says. Besides, I've got fuckall going on at work right now. Product photos for one of the big-box landfill supermarkets." Dingo jabbed a thumb over his shoulder at three monitors displaying what appeared to be plastic lawn furniture. "Is this about the display of Second Amendment rights I saw on the news earlier?"

Lucas was getting too tired to think, and he realized that just getting out of the sofa was going to be a Herculean effort, so he simply nodded.

"I've been in this country for fifteen years, and I still don't understand the fascination with guns. I've never seen a bigger bunch of scaredy-cats."

Dingo—whose real name was Martin Hudson—was a Brazilian jujitsu master. He had a coral belt in the discipline and had trained for the Australian Olympic team in his younger days. He now taught the sport to other amputees, utilizing a unique approach that he had adapted to work within the framework of his new body. He had a hundred thousand Instagram followers and a Facebook page that went on forever. Dingo always had at least two extra pairs of prosthetics on hand because he kept breaking them at the dojo. Out on the street he usually wore his traditional prosthetics, but at home— as at the dojo—he preferred to use the blades.

Dingo examined him for a few moments before asking, "What *didn't* the news say?"

"The victim was my old partner."

"And?"

"Erin's not too happy that I'm going back."

"Neither am I. Which brings us to why *are* you going back?"

There were a lot of things Lucas could say, but he wondered if any of them would sound convincing, even to himself, so he opted for, "Because it feels like the right thing to do."

Dingo looked down at Lucas's leg, then shifted focus to his arm, then up to his ceramic eye. "If you say so."

13

The phone on Lucas's nightstand buzzed, and he had it in his hand before his wake command was fully executed. "Dr. Page here," he said reflexively, almost sounding like he were up.

"An agent will come by to get you in half an hour." It was Kehoe.

Lucas's software was up and running now. And so was Erin's. She sat up and flipped on the light, and Lucas stopped whispering. She headed off to the bathroom. "Who?" Lucas asked.

Erin left the light off in the bathroom but peed with the door open, and Lucas wondered if Kehoe could hear her.

There was a pause that could have meant a thousand things, which Kehoe ended with, "I haven't decided yet."

"Send Whitaker—she doesn't talk too much." He stifled a yawn, then said, "And tell her not to ring the bell."

"Of course." And with all pertinent information delivered, niceties over, and other things to do, Kehoe hung up.

Lucas looked over at Erin's silhouette against the night-light in the bathroom. She had her head turned to him, but he couldn't see her eyes in the dark and wondered if she was looking at him or not.

He placed the cell phone back on the nightstand and swung his leg around to the edge of the mattress, dropping his left foot to the floor. He never slept with his prosthetics at home; his body needed the break to reset tripped muscles and sore joints. And even though he hadn't had any bad dreams for a few years now, nothing ended the sweet and cuddlies like kicking Erin with a metal foot in the middle of the night. But he always felt a little incomplete—or was that vulnerable?—each morning before he snapped it in place.

Lucas reached for his leg leaning against the nightstand. All things being equal, he would have preferred to put his arm on first, but his leg was a bone-anchored transfemoral prosthesis, and attaching it was as simple as sliding the titanium rod implanted in his femur into the collar on the prosthetic where it locked into place, much like a speed chuck on an electric drill. His arm was a transhumeral amputation and had the same attaching hardware, but there was an extra harness and it took a little more time to maneuver into place—and the leg helped with balance as he twisted to get the arm on.

Erin flushed and stood up. "How long is this going to go on?" It was impossible to miss the accusatory tone.

"I don't know. Not long."

"Well, that's certainly vague." She walked back into the room and took her battered robe off the hook on the back of the door.

"This is temporary. I promise."

"I thought you hated them." She pulled the robe on—it was an old Pendleton blanket deal taken from her father's closet the day he died (and about ten minutes before her mother loaded every last one of his belongings into the family station wagon and dropped them off at Goodwill). "I'm sorry. That wasn't fair. I don't mean to be a bitch. I'm just—"

He could tell from the way she was missing the sleeve that she was tired.

"—tired," she finished.

"Don't apologize. But this is important." He wanted to tell her about Kehoe's little sales pitch but decided against it. "For them and for me." He stood up and headed for another shower; he'd put his arm on after. "It's a part of my brain that I never get to use. Not in any capacity that means anything."

"No. Of course not. You only have a wife and a family and your students and your work. Oh, and don't forget that you write best-selling books, go on Bill Maher three times a year, and NASA calls you when they have a problem. But you're right, your mental acuities are going to waste. You need *more*." Erin cinched the belt with an angry tug. "I understand." That part came out a lot like *fuck you*. "You want to be John McClane."

"I didn't say I need *more*. I have everything I want. But there's a part of my mind that only comes alive out there. I can't explain it, and I can't wish it away. Something happens to me when I do this, and I want to feel it one more time. Of all people, I'd think you would understand that I need to know how much I lost that day."

"I know how much you lost that day." She stopped at the bedroom door and nailed him with one of her looks. "I just don't want you to lose everything else."

14

The East Side

One by one, the lights in the terminal blinked to life in 1,500-watt increments, illuminating the tram floating motionless above the concrete floor of the hangar. The steam coming off the vents gave it the appearance of an alien craft hovering in the bay of the mother ship. The ice on the windows was slowly melting away as the onboard heaters cycled up. At peak capacity, the car could hold 110 souls and still manage a speed of eighteen miles per hour as it crossed the East River, a distance of more than three thousand feet. It was roughly half the size of a city bus, but there were only two benches—one at either end. Most of the occupants would be visible from the waist up through the large windows.

The tram hovered in the shooter's crosshairs, the image fading in and out through the visual noise of the snow. Mother Nature would add wind and cold temperatures to the equation, but these were simply more input. There was no thought, no analysis, of what would be done. This was not about magic or luck or even skill; it was about mathematics, patience, and experience.

And about putting another of those fuckers in the dirt.

15

Whitaker kept the patter set to zero as she threaded the black SUV through the snow-covered streets with patient determination. She had been kind enough to bring coffee and doughnuts, and the early-morning jolt of sugar combined with seat warmers and silence greatly improved Lucas's mood.

Whitaker was dressed the same as the night before with the only difference being that without the hood, her complexion somehow looked much darker. She leaned more to a large rather than medium build, but she offset this by being tall, and the impression that she wasn't someone you'd want to fight for the last seat on the lifeboat still held.

The post-storm world outside zipped by, looking only narrowly like Manhattan. And it wasn't just the snow or the wind or the lost cars that gave it a film franchise vibe; the almost complete lack of foot traffic drove home that the whole system was not operating on its usual frequency.

Ten minutes into the commute, she finally broke the silence. "So, do you enjoy teaching?" She had broad cheekbones and a small forehead that ended in an intricate hairdo held up in a tight dominatrix bun by a pair of polished black chopsticks.

The way she asked it emphasized that she couldn't see him standing in front of a class.

Then again, neither could he.

"Sometimes."

"Is your next sentence going to start with, 'Kids these days . . .'?"

He smiled. But he felt justified for his curmudgeonly outlook. Most of the studentry were addicted to phones and apps and all manner of digital bullshit that sold them on the communal delusion that they were interesting. The big problem was that their obsession with technology wasn't directed toward broadening their positively abhorrent knowledge base. "I just find it hard to fathom the lack of curiosity most of the students exhibit. And the ones who are curious love conspiracy theories. I had a student begin a paper by stating, 'I am not a conspiracy theorist,' then go on to proclaim to be a 9/11, Sandy Hook, and Boston Marathon Truther. If I were younger, I'd be petrified of getting infected by whatever brain-eating parasite these people have."

"Are there some good ones?"

"They're the ones who keep me getting up in the morning."

For the next few minutes, she expertly negotiated the sometimes-plowed, sometimes-not roadways of the city. She drove well, using third and even second gear to best harness the laws of physics. Lucas began to wonder where she had learned to drive in the snow like this.

Whitaker said, "Illinois."

"Illinois what?" He glanced over at her.

"You were wondering where I learned to drive like this." Whitaker's speech pattern was compact, with a slow, deliberate delivery.

Lucas knew there was no such thing as mind reading, telepathy, or clairvoyance, but he found her response a little weird. "If you say so."

"It's something I do. It helps with interrogations." Whitaker was on the younger end of the spectrum for this kind of work, but it was obvious that she had that particular mix of smarts, curiosity, and fearlessness Kehoe liked to groom in his people.

She pulled the Navigator through a southbound turn onto the West Side Highway, which was as deserted as the rest of the city. What was going on? Lucas had never seen New Yorkers scared off the streets. Not during 9/11; the big power collapse of 2004; or Hurricane Sandy. And he certainly couldn't believe that they were frightened by a little snow.

Lucas put more coffee into his system and felt the machinery get up to speed. Or at least as close as it could on so little sleep. "What's your—?"

"Anti-government militia groups," she offered by way of a preemptive answer, cutting his question off before he could say the word *specialty*.

Very few things impressed him, but that was a neat trick. "I see."

She glanced over. "In the interest of full disclosure, I want to tell you that Kehoe warned me about you."

He smiled at that. "That doesn't sound like Kehoe."

"He said that you were allergic to stupid." She hit the gas, pushing the big SUV through a drift that the wind off the Hudson laid across all three lanes.

"I take that back. That *does* sound like Kehoe."

"He also said you could be a prick."

Lucas sipped his coffee as his brain cycled up. "Eye of the beholder."

She answered with a shrug, and he was once again left with his own thoughts.

They passed the Lincoln Tunnel, and the closer they got to the FBI offices, the more distant home began to feel. And along with it a lot of the guilt he felt. Erin didn't mean to make him feel guilty; it was just a by-product of her protective nature. She always told him he was lucky, and when he looked at things from a practical point of view, she couldn't be more right. Things were good. At least right now. And he no longer thought about the Event. Not really. It had been the only thing he could focus on for so long, but like all hiccups in time, the things that had been taken from him slowly lost their meaning. Whereas he used to think of life in terms of *Before* and *After,* now he simply looked at it all as *Now.* And the *Now* was something Erin was worried he was taking for granted. And going strictly by his actions, it was not an unreasonable assumption.

But she had to know—had to understand—that every now and then, the monsters came back in a single sour surge. From the way his body had been taken apart to the Dr. Frankenstein months in the hospital to losing his first marriage and his job. Along with the rest of the broken architecture of what had once been enough to convince him that he was relatively happy.

Nancy had stayed with him for almost three of the thirteen months he spent being slowly bolted back into a functioning human being. Things with them were okay before. Not perfect all the time, but not bad all the time either. Then the Event interrupted their plans, and everything stopped. He spent forty-four days in a coma, plugged into as much medical hardware as was feasible. Nancy had okayed the cessation of artificial assistance on day forty-five. She signed the appropriate forms, initialed the important small print, assigned all salvageable organs for donation, and at 4:30 p.m. on an October afternoon—as witnessed by hospital officials—the medical appliances keeping his organs functioning were disconnected, and the wait for him to die began.

But like everything else associated with the Event, he defied the odds. In one of those weird happenings that the superstitious automatically label as miraculous, his heartbeat continued. And he began to breathe without the iron-lung rasp of the respirator. Seventeen days later, he woke up. Two days after that, Nancy came to visit. Then every second day after that. And once she saw he was going to live, she split. No good-bye. No final smooch. Just a visit from a bailiff and she was gone. He didn't hold it against her. Not anymore.

Not since that first time Erin had walked into the gym at the rehabilitation center and he learned that there was such a thing as unselfish love.

It had been an instantaneous attraction, one of the most powerful moments of his life. And by some miraculous intertwining of chemistry, it was the same for her.

She had been there to help one of the children she was fostering, a little boy named Kevin who had lost a race with a bus. He was eight but had an old soul and took to his prosthetic legs with determination and humor. Lucas and Kevin became pals. Soon followed by Lucas and Erin. And in a few days, it became obvious that Erin was timing Kevin's visits to the gym so she could see her new friend.

When they first met, Erin fostered children on top of her work as a pediatric surgeon, and he watched as she gave herself to the kids. She knew she'd only have them for a brief period, and she wanted to give them as many tools as she could before they went back into the world. He had never figured out how she kept her practice afloat with all the time she put into the kids, but he just wrote it off as more of the magic she was able to conjure out of thin air.

After they got married, fostering children became part of their life. But like anyone with even a modicum of compassion, they got worn down—seeing kids go back to places that they shouldn't became more and more difficult. And after too much heartache, they decided that the one way they could really make things better for the children who came through their lives was to adopt. So they started building a family.

The concrete of the parking garage swallowed the 4×4 and brought Lucas back from the past.

"Ready for your first day back at school?" Whitaker asked.

16

26 Federal Plaza

After checking through the security desk, Whitaker led Lucas through the core of the building with the flat, patient delivery of someone who didn't believe in surprises. The trip upstairs required two elevator rides and 309 footsteps. Lucas hadn't been in the offices for a decade, and it had gone through at least one big bout of plastic surgery and the underlying form of the space had been altered; whereas it used to resemble a press room in a seventies film, it now looked like a well-funded university with a straight dress code.

By the time they hit the right floor, night still hung in the sky and the office building directly across was pockmarked with squares of light. Without meaning to, Lucas did the math, counting the floors, multiplying it by windows per floor, counting the number of lighted windows per floor, and averaging them out. It was with these little automatic mathematical distractions that he often amused himself—a habit since childhood.

They headed down the hall, where Whitaker swiped them into a sally port. An instant later, the security doors opened and they crossed the line into the war room.

When they walked in, all work stopped, and a ripple of whispers rolled out.

Then everyone began to clap.

Whitaker slapped him on the shoulder. "Must be nice to be the cool kid."

Lucas looked around the room, picking out the few people he recognized and nodding a couple of hellos. Then someone hit the Play button, and the world started back up. "Swell," he said.

Flat panels were bolted to almost every vertical surface, each one filled with a news feed. Some displayed broadcasts from smaller stations that Lucas had never heard of, others were piped in from the larger networks, and there were many foreign news programs.

The staccato clatter of activity permeated the maze of cubicles, bureau personnel installed in overdesigned Aeron chairs—the ubiquitous government seat of choice since the early nineties. The space still wasn't sexy, but when you looked at the resources on display, it was hard not to be impressed.

Lucas finished the five-dollar paper cup of franchise blend and nodded at one of the FBI mugs peppering the room. "Where's the coffee machine?"

"Coming up."

As they plunged deeper into the war room, the pixelated presence ramped up with the heavy stockpile of computational firepower. Displays of every possible size, purpose, and permutation glittered, blinked, and hummed in a low-frequency choir that could keep a small country running smoothly. Outside, daylight was finally starting to seep into the sky.

Grover Graves spotted them and cut across the room. For some reason, he looked bigger without the FBI parka and hat, and his hair was little more than stubble on the sides. He had to be unhappy about Kehoe shoehorning Lucas into his playdate.

Graves stopped but didn't stick out his hand. "Glad you found the time."

Lucas nodded but didn't say anything.

"That thing you do is still pretty impressive." The little blip of incomprehension common to everyone who had seen Lucas work ticked over his features. "I thought that maybe"—Graves put his hands on his hips, pushing back the flaps of his wool jacket—"fame had worn down the edges, taken away a little of your smarts."

Lucas let the silence hang between them for a few seconds. "No, you didn't. You were wondering if having my head opened up has had an effect on my ability to outthink you." He smiled at Graves. "It hasn't."

Graves headed down the hall, walking fast enough that it was obvious he was trying to lose Lucas. "For some reason, Kehoe thinks you are an asset. I don't know why. He said I was to extend you every courtesy, but that doesn't mean I have to put up with your shit."

"Actually, Graves, that's *exactly* what it means."

The gray wool on Graves's shoulders hitched up with the shrug.

Lucas switched gears, opting for a topic that Graves could handle. "Have your people come up with anything?"

Without stopping or turning, Graves raised an arm, pointing to one of the screens up at the far end of the war room; a photo of the Frenchman Kehoe had shown him the night before smiled back from the plasma. "I thought Kehoe brought you up to speed."

"He did. But I'm not convinced you know what you're doing."

At that, Graves stopped, and Lucas had to put on the brakes in order not to ram into him.

Graves turned around and took a step toward him, closing the distance. "I know you've been gone for ten years; I know you were some kind of hot sauce back in the day; and I know your Wikipedia page paints you as some kind of latter-day Dr. Emmett Brown. But this is the here and now, and personally, I don't want to have to hold your hand. We know who did this. And we know why. So you can end with the speculation. I know you and Hartke went back, but this wasn't a personal vendetta against him. This was business. Hartke was a victim of opportunity. We got this." He started back on his way.

Lucas realized that bickering like kids wouldn't get them anywhere. "What is the signal-to-noise ratio in Hartke's file? He was on the job for what, twenty-eight years? That's a lot of time to make enemies. Have you cross-referenced his record against the parole registers? Gun nuts, ammo-sexuals, the regular gamut of crazies? Anti–law enforcement groups? Antiestablishment groups?" He hoped that straight-up logic wasn't too abstract a concept. "Anyone he collar fit the profile?" These were all obvious questions, but Lucas took nothing for granted with Graves.

"No one Hartke collared has the requisite skill set to do this. We've six-degrees-of-Kevin-Baconed it, and none of the cellmates or family members of people he put away fit the bill. As far as the rest of the spreadsheets go, nothing has come up. We've checked the parolees, social media ranters, and people who have sent threats to the bureau. He was just a random victim."

Lucas was put off by the narrow bandwidth Graves was using; he had made his mind up about too many things. "Has the NYPD given us any added value?"

Graves shook his head and opened a door to a glass-walled conference room where half a dozen agents were correlating digital imagery—the twenty-first-century equivalent of a corkboard. "We've got some solid ideas on this one."

"Such as?"

"Just take a look around."

Lucas reached for the tray in the middle of the runway-sized conference table and poured himself a mug of coffee. He walked around the room, taking in what they had. There was no mistaking how they were looking at this, and it was shortsighted. The Frenchman appeared to be the sole focus of the investigation, and Lucas wondered how this was possible if Kehoe were not behind the idea.

Graves began his monologue in a voice Lucas was certain he'd practiced in front of the mirror. "We didn't get much from the roof other than a gait measurement that suggests our guy is somewhere between five foot two and five foot ten, depending on long-bone length. Which fits with Froissant's height of five foot eight."

"Along with most of the people in the country over the age of thirteen," Lucas said.

Whitaker finally spoke up. "What about surveillance footage?"

Lucas realized that he had been focusing on Graves so acutely that he had forgotten about her. He had to start paying attention to that—he was back among people, not sequestered alone with his own thoughts all the time. Their effectiveness—and maybe even their lives—would depend on it.

"One elevator and four staircases lead to the access floor to the roof. We ran the footage back twenty-four hours in each stairwell and the elevator, and no one went up who didn't come down. No one we couldn't identify and no one who wasn't supposed to be there except some girl delivering lunch for a deli who grabbed a smoke, probably because it was too cold to go outside.

"Security guard did his rounds right on the clock. The only person who went up on the roof proper was a guy from maintenance to add fuel-line antifreeze to the generators. We checked him out, and he's completely clean and had nothing to say when he was questioned. We can place him on the ground floor at the time of the shooting; he's on camera in one of the hallways."

Lucas tried not to look like Graves was full of shit; someone had been up on that roof. "And in the two-plus hours between the murder and our arrival?"

"Nada."

Lucas turned to a portrait of Froissant pulled from a French society website. It was not dissimilar to many others he had seen. Froissant was standing on the steps to a theater or opera house or investment firm in a suit that cost as much as a nice vacation somewhere sunny. He had that natural grace of a man bred to inherit an empire, which he was. This was not the kind of guy who threw it all away based on the internal ravings that came from an invisible man in the sky. "And you're really convinced that this is your shooter?"

Graves sat down on the edge of the conference table, crossed his arms, and went back into condescending lecture mode. "French authorities saw a spike in his visits to extremist websites and Twitter accounts after the *Charlie Hebdo* attacks, and they started paying much closer attention. But the line between religious curiosity and budding terrorist isn't always clear, and by the time they realized he might be radicalized, he was gone."

"How'd the French lose him?"

"They didn't watch him all the time; apparently, they still believe in personal freedoms over there."

"I can't tell if you're joking."

"Neither can I," Graves said.

"I noticed you said, 'they believe' and 'he might be'; neither remotely approaches proof of guilt."

"Both the DHS and the DOJ believe; so does the administration in Washington—all of which are good enough for me."

Lucas knew that arguing with Graves was pointless. What could you say to someone who felt that belief was a component of truth?

Lucas steered Graves away from the circumstantial and focused on the concrete. "Did you ever find the slug?" After everything Graves said so far, he expected him to shake his head.

"That's where things get interesting. We dug it out of the sidewalk. It wasn't a PAR round. The slug was a copper-alloy-jacketed .300 Winchester Magnum with a ferrous core—"

Now Lucas understood why Kehoe had said the round *went through the car*—it was armor-piercing.

"The bullet was manufactured by Nosler, part of their AccuBond line—but the iron-alloy kernel is a modification."

Graves went to a screen and clicked up a page of text. "Kehoe wants you to take a look at this." Graves tapped the screen and read the report. "Metallurgy on the slug came back, and that ferrous core isn't regular iron or mild steel; it's an unusual combination—91 percent iron, 7.65 percent nickel, and an unusually high iridium content, a concentration of 11.3 parts per million." Graves looked up at Lucas. "What does that tell you?"

By the way he asked the question, Lucas could tell he thought it was a test. But there was only one kind of metal that could have properties anywhere near that, and it wasn't fabricated in some guy's workshop; it was smelted in the cauldrons that had formed the universe. "It's meteoric in origin."

Graves nodded, and it was hard to miss the disappointment in the action. "What does that tell you?"

"Does Froissant have any experience on long guns?"

"There's a photo of him with one in the file."

"That's a shotgun, not a rifle."

"Look, Luke, we've put a lot of time into—"

"That's *Dr. Page*. And *a lot of time* and *the required time* are two different things." Lucas thought back to the images of Froissant at the opera. "If he just wanted to kill a random citizen, why the theatrics? Why that rooftop?"

Graves thought about that for a moment before giving what was quickly becoming his signature move—a shrug. "I don't know."

"I can't see some billionaire playboy hanging out on that roof yesterday, balaclava or not. You don't learn to handle a weapons system in acutely humid subzero temperatures unless you spent a lot of time in a similar environment—not France."

Lucas took a sip of coffee. "Think about that round." The big payoff would be in the guy who modified the ammunition. Not many people could turn regular ammunition into armor-piercing rounds. And the ones who could would be expensive. "Making certain that Hartke died was important to him. He wanted Hartke dead. In *specific*."

Graves stopped going through the photos. "If he had hit a housewife from Astoria, would you be on board?" The sentence was still hanging over his head in a dialogue bubble when a junior agent ran into the room and asked for everyone's attention.

The hive stopped work for a moment as he said, "Someone with a rifle just shot a woman on the Roosevelt Island Tramway."

Graves was professional enough not to smile, but Lucas could see that it was a real effort.

17

Whitaker plowed east on Grand, pushing the big Lincoln through the still falling snow with the same combination of ease and aggression she had demonstrated on the ride downtown. Graves was in the lead car, alpha male in his rightful place, but it was clear Whitaker could outdrive him. The command vehicle, ambulances, and SWAT team were en route from their various dispatch points, everyone racing for the FDR, where they'd swing north to the tram terminal at Sixtieth Street and Second Avenue.

"What's between you and Graves?" Whitaker asked as she pulled the Lincoln up the ramp in a series of tight fishtails that she fought by stomping down on the gas and countersteering. "You sleep with his wife or something?"

Back out in the world, the snow reflected what little ambient light was able to reach over the skyline, and it looked later than it was. The twenty-first was the next day, and from there on out, every day they moved forward on the calendar would provide a few more joules of vitamin D.

Lucas watched the support vehicles in the mirror for a moment before answering. "Graves is a classic example of the Dunning–Kruger effect in action; if he doesn't know something, he thinks it's not important. At least he's diligent in his stupidity."

"Oh, good. I thought it might be something personal." She shook her head. "What about you and Kehoe? What's going on there?"

"I killed his brother."

She paused to take that in for a few moments. "You just can't stop yourself from making friends, can you?"

"I'm not here for my personality."

"No shit."

He turned back to the storm outside, thinking that it was smarter to keep his mouth shut. Or maybe he should just tell them to fuck right off.

Even though it was an hour-plus later than their trip downtown, the FDR was as deserted as the West Side Highway. The plows had done their job, but the storm was laying down more snow and very few cars were out. Instead of the usual field of taillights stretching into the distance, only a few red eyes blinked back through the haze.

Lucas checked the clock on the dash and did the math. Thirteen hours and ten minutes, give or take, since the previous night's killing. Which wasn't a lot of time if this was the same shooter. But Lucas could already feel the relationship building between him and the man with the rifle; it felt like the same guy. Hitting a moving target in a storm seemed to point to their boy.

Lucas kept turning the thirteen hours and ten minutes over in his head. A lot could happen in that time. But Hartke's killing wasn't the kind of demonstration most people could follow by getting up the next morning and doing it again.

Whitaker pulled off the FDR and followed Graves west on Sixtieth, their speed down now that they were off the expressway. Lucas could see the circus of flashing lights four blocks up, and the adrenaline hit him, manifesting itself in a low-grade fear that he was working with people who were making all the wrong choices. But the subtext in Kehoe's sales pitch had been pretty clear; Lucas was here because he would see things differently.

They slid to a stop with the rest of the vehicles in their procession, and Lucas was outside before Whitaker. Snow swirled around him, and for an instant the world was gone. He took a few steps forward and almost ran into Graves, who materialized like a big black ghost. A troop of FBI parkas developed behind him, more shadowy figures birthed from the snow.

"You," Graves said, jabbing a finger into Lucas's chest, "follow me."

The cops had closed the street, and the police cruisers that were there to quarantine the scene had to park away from the tram terminal building. There was a single path that cut through the square, a deep trough carved by one of the small sidewalk plows.

The building itself was a concrete engineering feat that rose through the static like an old-time dial-up internet image. A patch cleared near the walkway was occupied by an ambulance sitting at a steep angle, its nose halfway up a bright white snowbank. A paramedic sat in the driver's seat, the engine idling. Two uniformed officers stood at the back door. Everyone looked like the bogeyman had just visited.

The media crews were laying siege to the crime scene, and Lucas could see them testing the resolve of the NYPD officers who were in charge of keeping them out. There were hushed conversations, a few shouting matches, and a cameraman near the corner looked like he was a few harsh words away from getting shot.

The countersnipers had been deployed—after all, it was reasonable to believe that the killer wanted to flush out more game.

Lucas followed Graves up the concrete, making sure to use the handrail as he jumped two steps at a time when pushing off with his good leg, one at a time with his prosthetic. A police officer outfitted in a departmental parka and an AR-15 stood on the landing at the top of the stairs. He had the kind of face that belonged on the prow of a Viking longboat. His tag read *Sorenson*, and his big handlebar mustache—either light blond or gray—was covered in frozen perspiration.

Graves introduced himself with a badge and a curt nod. "FBI."

Sorenson nodded. "We were told." He then went into a quick report as he opened the door. "Passenger on the tram coming in from Roosevelt Island was shot. There were two officers on the car with her, but they couldn't do anything; it's all on camera."

Graves looked at Lucas, but his question was pointed at Sorensen. "A woman?" It was hard to miss the *I told you so* in his voice.

"Yes, sir."

Upstairs, the scene was as organized as anyone could hope for. Passengers were in the ticketing/waiting section of the terminal, giving statements, clouds of vapor rising into the frozen air. The low-frequency hum of shock was the only sound generated by witnesses standing around, looking like dejected models for Degas's *L'Absinthe.* A pile of cell phones lay on a tarp on the floor; crowd-sourced social media justice could destroy an investigation, especially when video was taken out of context—without facts or perspective, herd-thinking *digilantes* often railroaded innocent people with their ad hoc determination to assign blame.

Sorenson led Graves, Lucas, and Whitaker through the turnstiles to the tram car hanging in the bay. Two more officers with AR-15s stood by. Another pair of officers stood off to the left, both splattered with blood, looking defeated.

The art direction on the tram was straight out of an abattoir. The doors were closed, but it wasn't hard to see that someone's morning commute to the city had been irrevocably fucked. The center-front window had a fist-sized hole punched through at the five-foot mark and another drilled through the back window. Blood was sprayed over the broken glass, the cracks filled with black. A body lay on the floor in a wide pool of dark red smeared with foot- and handprints. The corpse wore what had once been a white parka.

Sorenson signaled the blood-spattered cops to come forward. Their names were Bolan and Washington. Both were with the Twenty-sixth.

Washington did the talking. "Yes, sir?"

"This is Special Agent Graves, FBI."

With the introductions laid out, Graves went to work. "What happened?" He tilted his head toward the tram.

Washington went into recall mode. "She was standing up front, facing west. My partner and I were off to her left, talking shop. About halfway through the trip, we took a rifle round through the front window. Hit her right in the face. The slug went right through her head and out the back of the car. Missed everyone else. Just fucking *boom* and a pitcher of blood." He held up his hands as if seeing them for the first time. They were caked with flaking red pigment. "The civvies went apeshit. She was dead before she hit the floor." He glanced sideways at the tram car. "Called it in thirty-five, maybe forty seconds after the shot. Everyone was on the floor, screaming, crying. We all thought we were dead." He looked out to where the river was beyond the storm. "By the time we got here, our guys had arrived." The sounds of more approaching sirens could be heard outside, rising above the whistle of the wind zipping through the concrete bay.

Lucas looked at the self-contained crime scene. The weather had probably saved some people's lives; on any other day, the tram would have been filled to capacity, and one of those nifty little armor-piercing rounds could have punched through half a dozen brainpans.

Behind them, the medical examiner's people rolled in with enough Pelican waterproof boxes to contain the instruments for a full-size orchestra. They were flanked by more federal agents.

Graves thanked the two cops, told them that one of the agents would take their statements, then steered Lucas to the tram car.

Up close, the murderous artwork was even more unsettling. Her legs were splayed at that awkward angle that those who spend enough time around the dead eventually get used to.

Lucas was doing his best to ignore Graves's posturing but the man wouldn't let it go. "Hartke in specific or Americans in general? Like I said, Hartke was a fluke. Especially since the next victim is a housewife from Roosevelt Island—I was wrong about her neighborhood, but same difference."

Lucas took a deep breath and waited for Graves to finish digging himself into a hole.

"Of course, going by your theory, it's possible that the shooter was aiming for one of the two uniformed officers standing beside her." Graves had the sarcasm dialed up with the volume of victory. "But I don't think so."

"Neither do I." Lucas crouched down and pushed back the flap of the woman's once white coat with an aluminum finger. A pistol in a pressure holster was clipped to her belt alongside a badge from the Bureau of Alcohol, Tobacco, Firearms and Explosives—both decorated with strings of blood. Lucas stood up and moved away so the medical examiner's people could take her away before she froze into a meat pretzel. "But it still makes you wrong."

18

Midtown

Connie had been waitressing at the Amphora Diner since her second week in New York, a little under three years now. She had earned prime hours on the good tables through a combination of hard work and occasionally letting Nick, the owner, fuck her face in the basement. Nick was a family man—the father of six little mustachioed girls—and after throwing it down her throat, he always made a point of stating that he was staying with his wife (as if Connie gave the tiniest little morsel of a fuck). She couldn't care less if fat old Nick decided to step in front of a snowplow as long as he left some postdated checks stapled to his suicide note. Nope, theirs was a relationship of mutual benefits.

Connie bused an order of blintzes and a chicken fat sandwich to the old Jews at table three and gave them an *I'll be back with your water*. She cleaned up the coffee cup and half-eaten BLT from table seven, along with the two singles he left as a tip, and headed back to the bar. She dumped the coffee cup in the plastic dish bin and wrapped the half sandwich in tinfoil; Kirby would be by on his way to work, and she liked to have something for him for lunch. Combined with the potato latkes she had saved from a drunk that morning, he'd have a decent meal today.

She checked the G-Shock on her wrist: Kirby would be out back in four minutes and fifteen seconds. Of all the things the army had hammered into his brain, nothing was as second nature to him as being on time. You could set the digital clocks in Times Square to the way he lived his life. Which meant he had learned at least one useful skill during his two tours shooting Hajis over in Idontgivea-fuckistan.

She took an order from a group of jamokes sporting hard-core midwestern mullets—three orders of bacon and eggs (all scrambled), toast (all white), hash browns, coffee, and juice. All on one check. She liked serving like-minded individuals; it was so much easier than dealing with people who made their own choices. As she spiked the order, she saw Kirby cross the street and walk by the side window to the back door.

She served the three coffees, then got Kirby's lunch from the counter. Nick was busy, and she slipped by the kitchen without him noticing; she and Kirby had a deal that the boss was never to see him. It would cause all kinds of trouble for her, especially if he knew she was feeding him—it didn't matter if it was with food that was des-tined for the dumpster.

Kirby was at the back door, bundled up in his old army parka and carrying that guitar case he never left home without. He smiled when he saw her, a shy farm boy who had seen exotic places but still looked like the Midwest mulletards at table five.

"Hey, baby," he said.

She gave him a kiss and held out the bagged lunch. "Half a BLT and some latkes."

"That them greasy pancake things?"

She nodded.

"You put in ketchup?"

"Of course." She crossed her arms. It was cold out here in short sleeves. "You left early this morning."

"I had something to do."

Nick called her name from inside. "I gotta go."

"Me, too." He gave her another kiss and headed down the alley, the guitar case and army jacket making him look like a Bob Dylan album cover.

For all their time here, he still looked like a farm boy in the big city. But what did she expect with a guy like Kirby? He wasn't good at change. She was just happy he didn't hit her too much.

19

The Queensboro Bridge

The wind whipping up the East River felt like it had been generated in a black hole, adding more cruelty to an already miserable experience. You would have to be insane or desperate to walk the bridge. So here he was, last man on earth, staggering across the frigid snow-scoured span.

The victim's name was Carol Kavanagh. She was a senior agent with the New York branch of the ATF. Lucas hadn't read her file yet, but like Hartke, she was a career law enforcement officer. She had been with the FBI in the Chicago office before switching to the ATF. Colorado before that.

The tram married mechanics with physics, ferrying Roosevelt Islanders to Manhattan. Four towers, strategically spread out over three thousand feet, supported the eight wrist-sized cables. Two cars did the duty, a twenty-hour schedule that started at six in the morning, seven days a week. Four massive General Electric turbines steadily pushed out eighty thousand pounds of torque, keeping the whole beast running.

Like the night before, no one could shake the specter of a shooter somewhere nearby.

And an exercise that should have been nothing more than basic geometry once again appeared to fuck with the laws of physics.

They had the exact time the bullet struck from the CCTV surveillance footage taken inside the tram, but that was all they really had. They knew that the round punched through the front window at precisely eleven seconds past 6:04 a.m., but there was no way to say where—precisely—the car had been at that exact tick of the clock. Which made reverse engineering the bullet's path impossible. The tram had been both advancing and descending when the bullet struck, so without knowing where the target was at the exact instant of impact, the margin of error in elevation was seventeen feet three inches. And when you factored in that both wind and temperature affected the speed that the cables moved through the massive turbines, the entire equation was pooched beyond any reasonable result. And all of that ignored the very real problem of intermittent visibility in this weather. So Lucas was out here walking the westbound span of the Fifty-ninth Street Bridge, Whitaker following thirty paces back in the big polished SUV.

He followed the pedestrian walkway that skirted the chain-link fence designed to keep jumpers from flinging themselves into the afterlife. He was coming up on five hundred feet when Whitaker pulled forward and opened the window. "What are you looking for?"

"The meaning of life."

"Oh. Sarcasm. Thank you."

Lucas ignored her. The world was reduced to windswept asphalt and snowdrifts and ice-covered girders. Eighty feet later, he stopped at a length of flagging tape tied to the fence. The ribbon was light blue, about a foot long. It reached north over the river, snapping in the wind. *That,* he said to himself and pulled the phone from his pocket, dialing Graves.

"Yeah, Page, whatcha got?"

Lucas could barely hear him over the wind. "Get someone with an evidence kit out here. Five hundred and eighty feet in on the north-side fence, you'll find a wind indicator. There are probably more up ahead, and I'd bet on a distance marker somewhere along here. I'll let you know when I find it." He hung up, took a few photos with his phone, then continued his fight across the polar span.

Whitaker rolled the window down again. "What was that?"

"Wind gauge!" he yelled.

Out here, with only two things to shoot at—him and Whitaker—the possibility of bad things happening was not lost on Page.

If you wanted to scare an urban population, few tools were as effective as a faceless man with a rifle. There was a long list of shooters who had exploited that particular loophole in the human fear department. Of course, most of them were short-lived spurts of violence that ended within hours. Lee Harvey Oswald and Charles Joseph Whitman belonged in that column. But they had effectively demonstrated how a man with a rifle could change the world. Both Oswald and Whitman were early prototypes of eventual archetypes. And both had irrevocably damaged the American psyche with nothing more than a rifle and a defective personality.

But the ones who scared Lucas were the other kind—the long-game types. Fast-forward through the wormhole to John Allen Muhammad and Lee Boyd Malvo, a tag team that had remained at large for twenty-three long, media-intensive, murderous days. Their kick (besides the obvious one of killing) was in spreading out the suffering. In a way, they had stretched time.

And now it looked like this guy most definitely had a long game planned. And he was fast. Which meant a lot of bad things could be on the way unless they could put him in a box—either the concrete or the pine variety.

The cold was messing with his mobility, and the wind kept pushing him against the fence. The far end of the bridge was lost in white, and the superstructure overhead disappeared into the snow coming down.

Exactly three hundred feet later, he found the second wind gauge. He called it in to Graves, took more photos, ignored yet another question Whitaker yelled from the Navigator, and continued.

The worst part of getting used to his new self had been the weird little neural jolts his phantom limbs threw at him without warning. The doctors said they were connected to literal muscle memory, but Lucas suspected that a deep-rooted denial about what had happened was the real culprit. It had taken a couple of years and a whole lot of determination, but he had finally scared them away, a bit at a time. Along with any desire to go back to his old life at the bureau.

Yet here he was.

The last marker was at 1,165 feet, and the shoreline of Roosevelt Island was barely visible below. This ribbon was bright orange instead of blue. He called it in, then turned back to the city.

Manhattan blinked intermittently through the storm, little more than a flashing series of shadowy blocks that looked like a geological formation. How the hell did you make a shot through the visual noise? You would need x-ray vision to peer through the weather—which was impossible. How had he done it?

This particular junction was where the tram—doing 17.9 miles an hour according to the maintenance engineer—dropped twenty-five feet in a few seconds. Lucas knew certified police snipers who wouldn't be able to make any kind of a meaningful shot in this weather, let alone at a tram car doing 17.9 miles an hour on an incline through a snow cloud above a river.

There was no other way to see it—this guy was intentionally trying to fuck with their heads.

Lucas pulled the scope out of his parka and turned, sighting Manhattan in the limited field of view. He had to wait for a window through the snow and just as quickly as the city appeared, it was gone, and all he saw was a wall of white. He dropped his arm and looked down at the marker. Then up at the tram lines.

How the hell had he made this shot? The weather had to cooperate at precisely the right time, down to a tenth of a second. Which required more than skill—it required luck.

He took a step back as the air pressure changed and a sudden surge of wind hammered the air. Visibility dropped to nil as a helicopter emblazoned with the call letters of a local news affiliate rose up beside him like some giant mechanical insect.

He wanted to give them the finger, but that was poor form. Where was a sniper when you needed one?

The downdraft kicked up the snow piled on every surface of the bridge and the whiteout must have interfered with their photography, because the aircraft banked away, bobbing up two hundred feet upriver. Lucas raised the scope back to his eye and sighted the tram station, visible for a second, then gone in the storm. There was a lot of math to do, and your timing would have to be better than perfect, almost preternatural. And the storm would have to cooperate, at least for a split second, which was something no one could depend on. All accomplished less than half a day after delivering death onto Hartke from the rooftop of an office building.

The image of Manhattan back in the distance flickered through the snowstorm. There were plenty of high-rises to take a shot from, so Lucas closed his eye for a second and filled his lungs with cold air.

Then he opened his eye and the city before him was gone, leaving a swirling tumbler of code pulsing in the storm.

He stood still, and the angles and geometry and distances in front of him snapped, crackled, and popped, morphing into a meaning that only he could see.

And then he blinked.

And it was gone.

With the chopper still hanging over the river, Lucas climbed the railing between the pedestrian path and the westbound lane. Whitaker reached over and opened the passenger door as he walked around the vehicle. He got in and cranked the heat up as far as it would go, looking for *11* on the dial.

"And?"

Lucas called Graves. When he answered, Lucas said, "There's an apartment building on Third and Fifty-ninth. It's the roof."

"You sure?" he asked.

Lucas hung up.

Whitaker spun the big SUV around in a tight arc and lit up her smile. "I could actually hear the bionic sound coming from your brain out there. You know, that weird springy *dit-dit-dit-dit-dit-dit-dit-dit-dit*. That's a pretty impressive trick in real life. If you're right, that is." Whitaker didn't sound convinced one way or the other.

Lucas held his left hand over one of the vents blowing hot air, and the needles in his bones began to thaw. "I'll make you a deal."

"Yeah, what's that?"

"If I am right, I never have to see your face again."

"It's not an act with you, is it? You really are a son of a bitch."

"It's the company," he said and shifted his focus to the news helicopter following them.

His iPhone buzzed with his home number, and he swiped the screen. "Yes?"

"Hey, baby. You busy?"

"I'm in the middle of—"

"The Queensboro Bridge in a shiny black SUV? Yeah, I know. You're on CNN."

He turned away from the window. "Fuck."

"They got some pretty good shots of you out there looking all John McClaney and stuff. Wolf Blitzer deducted that you—hey, stop laughing!"

"I'm sorry, but I can't picture Wolf deducting *anything*."

"Well, he did. Or at least his producer did. He said you were probably an FBI sniping expert judging by the highly sophisticated military optics you just used. That guy's a tool." Erin sounded angry.

Lucas preferred a good pair of Steiners, but binoculars weren't optimized for people with one eye; a scope was designed to carry a full optical load. Besides, the scope was a way to view the world the same way their shooter did, which was the closest thing to a Vulcan mind-meld he could manage; with this guy, every little bit would help. "I couldn't agree more. Call me if they get the shooter on film." And he hung up.

After a few seconds, he turned to Whitaker and said, "I don't want to see a chopper in the air next time. It's for my sanity, but the official line will be that it's for their own protection. Which it is."

"Next time?" Whitaker glanced sideways at him before turning her attention back to the empty bridge. "Why is it that you never have anything positive to say?"

"That *was* positive."

"Which part?"

"The part where I left out that he's going to shoot another law enforcement officer."

20

Manhattan

Kehoe and Lucas sat in the back of one of the dozen black FBI SUVs that peppered the streets in the space between the tramway station and the apartment on Fifty-ninth. Whitaker was up on the roof of the building, watching the forensics people cast their bones.

Kehoe had lost none of his intensity from the night before, and Lucas wondered how much of it came from having to answer to the men pushing wrong solutions across the table. He was a bureau man right down to a genetic level, and trying to get a crime to fit someone else's confirmation bias had to be bending him into a knot. No matter how you looked at Kehoe's position, there was no good way for this to finish; he'd end up looking incompetent, obsequious, or insubordinate.

Kehoe had changed his suit and shaved since the night before. Probably showered as well. But the scrub hadn't softened any of the stress fissures etched into his facial topography.

Lucas gave Kavanagh's file a reading as they talked. He flipped through the fresh printout, stopping every now and then on a random detail. Kavanagh had been a five-star asset to the bureau before she transferred over to the ATF. Lucas closed the file and looked over at Kehoe, who was silently sipping his tea and watching him for . . . what, exactly?

"And?" Kehoe said, once again taking reductionism to its furthest possible point.

"Be specific."

He nodded at the file. "Our victims."

"Hartke and Kavanagh were targeted."

"Why?"

There was something behind Kehoe's voice, something that Lucas couldn't place, and it bothered him.

"It's an awful lot of fancy footwork that has no understandable benefit."

Kehoe seemed to mull that over for a few seconds. "Is it possible this is a coincidence?"

"A man with a rifle shooting two random individuals who both happen to be on the job? Out of a city of nine million people with roughly fifty thousand individuals employed in law enforcement? It's such a long shot that it technically doesn't exist. One is a possibility. Highly unlikely, but possible. Two? No computer model would give you odds on it.

"Kavanagh and Hartke are connected; I don't think the only commonality is that they both carried a badge. I can think of a thousand easier ways to kill someone without having to go through these gymnastics. He's making a point."

"And the Frenchman?"

Lucas shook his head. "Without a message delivered to the media, this won't help a terrorist organization. It's off-brand."

Kehoe pulled his gloves off, one finger at a time. "And Graves?"

"He's nothing else if not consistent."

"You two getting along?"

"Graves and I will never be simpatico."

"Can you work with him?"

Lucas rotated his head just enough for Kehoe to see both eyes, and from the angle he knew that his prosthetic was doing that disjointed Marty Feldman chameleon thing. "I can work *around* him. But that's not the point, is it?"

"What do you mean?"

"You want to tell me what's really going on, Brett?"

Kehoe's focus went from Lucas's left eye to his right, then back to the left. "Since no one has claimed this guy, we don't know what he wants, other than depopulation. What's his mission statement?"

Lucas held up Kavanagh's file. "He's taking trophies. *Specific* trophies."

Kehoe's mouth pursed into a clenched fist for an instant, but before his eyes caught up to the expression, it melted away and he sank back into the seat, once again exuding armored confidence in a very nice suit.

"If I'm wrong, you still have a very big problem on your hands." Lucas nodded at the file in his hand. "But this isn't some jihadi. This is a man with a different message."

"Which is?"

"I'm sure you have qualified people who can give you educated opinions."

"I'm asking you."

Lucas locked Kehoe in another cockeyed stare. Right here, right now, there was only one thing he was certain of. "I don't know."

21

Whitaker stood inside the roof access door as the forensics team went over the scene. They operated on the directives of anal-retentive garbage pickers, depositing every scrap and morsel of detritus they could find into little polyethylene bags with gloved fingers, forceps, and tiny shovels. They were dealing with snow five feet thick in some places, looking for anything that might help point a finger at the invisible man with a rifle.

Graves had been certain that Page was full of shit, which was counterproductive at this point; especially since he had been right about everything so far, including victimology. What was it with those two, other than a double dose of toxic masculinity? Did owning a penis really reduce human beings to chest-thumping simians? Then again, Whitaker had worked in places populated exclusively by women before, and the takeaway was that they were just as bad at bickering—they were just sneakier and meaner about it.

When the SWAT ninjas popped the door and barreled out into the storm, they found a single path shoveled through the snow. It snaked from the door, around the staircase, to behind the pair of

HVAC pumps on the northeast corner of the roof—a position too high to be seen from any of the nearby buildings. It faced the river, and the tram, and when you were up here you realized it was the perfect spot for what had happened. Another mark for their shooter.

And for Page.

Whitaker wanted to believe all the things Kehoe told her about Page, but it wasn't an easy task. Whitaker was educated—a 3.7 GPA at UIC—and she knew better than to believe anecdotal evidence. So she had reserved judgment until she saw Bionic Boy in action. And those fifteen minutes on the bridge had certainly convinced her that there was something rare about Dr. Lucas Page, supreme grouchiness notwithstanding.

Very few people could stand out on the span for more than a minute and a half without their nipples turning into upholstery buttons. Along with the cold, there was the wind, snapping sleeves and pant legs like karate chops. If Page noticed the weather, he didn't show it. And the way he dialed into the environment and measured space pushed the whole exercise into voodoo territory.

Kehoe had described Page's *gift*—after all, what else could you call it?—as simple acute spatial awareness, nothing more than a very precise sense of comparison. Apparently, his intuitive understanding of geometry converted the landscape to numerical values. Combined with the awkward (which was really a euphemism for *nasty*) way he interacted with people, Whitaker would understand a diagnosis of Asperger's.

And what looked like a quiet anger could also be a litany of other things. Maybe he suffered PTSD. Maybe he was just a misanthrope.

No matter what it was, the way he handled numbers was spooky.

According to Kehoe, Page simply took a reference unit—something as simple as a sidewalk slab, a manhole cover, or even a brick in a building—and converted it to a unit of measure. So many units of measure from point A to point B. If deconstructed, so many bricks spanned a foundation stone, so many foundation stones a building. On and on, until everything in his visual path was simply a number in relation to all the other numbers his software generated. It was an instantaneous process, and Kehoe sounded more than a little perplexed when Whitaker asked him to explain it more clearly.

But when you started to read his file, his skills became less unsettling than his past, which read like a Thomas Hardy character sketch—minus the whimsy. You could look back in history at all the poor fuckers who had compounded a string of minor misfortunes into one major fuck-you at the Game of Life and not find a purer example of really bad things happening to relatively good people.

After the screaming was over, five people were dead—two of whom had simply evaporated from the known Newtonian universe. Page was in a coma, missing some of his long bones and one of his eyes. They had written him off. At least the realistic ones had. Yet here he was, braving elements, insulting people, and conjuring numbers faster than the most sophisticated software on the planet.

Whitaker watched the team at work, one of the techs scanning the snow with a metal detector. The wind blew straight in the door, and she realized that her shoulders were so tensed that her collarbones framed her jaw. She forced herself to relax, and a fistful of snow fell off her scarf, into her collar. She danced to shake it out before it melted, and Graves let out a little laugh beside her.

One of the techs came inside, interrupting the empty air that Whitaker didn't want to fill. He went straight to Graves with an ion mobility spectrometer. "The shooter was definitely here. In that northeast corner by the HVACs." He held up the sniffer and tilted the screen toward them. All the values were in the red. "The wind up here isn't helping our cause, but the snow on the ledge in the corner buried the needle. The signature is heavily degraded—like I said, the wind is murder—but I took six samples. Blowback is heavier on the lee side of the shot, indicating the same heavy crosswind. But it's definitely gunpowder."

The tech handed the scanner to Graves. Maybe now he would give Page a little respect.

Whitaker smiled. "I wonder if Page ever gets tired of being right?"

Graves concentrated on the screen for a few seconds longer before looking out at the rooftop and the city beyond. "Everyone gets lucky."

She thought about Page's file. "I guess," she said and walked away.

22

Whitaker and Lucas were stopped at a light on the way back to the office. Pedestrians crossed in front of the hood, a herd of bundled-up Michelin Men looking for someplace warm.

Whitaker thrummed the wheel with her fingers. "This guy doesn't even exist."

"Sure he does."

"He's shot two law enforcement officers. That's all I see."

"We know a lot more about him; we just don't know what any of it *means*." As he watched the people move by, wrapped in their protective insulation, he wondered what this guy wanted. What he was trying to say. Would he start sending manifestos to the newspapers? Or would he be one of those silent types? Kehoe's words at the tram scene came back to him: *mission statement*.

"Such as?" Whitaker didn't sound convinced.

"He has a message—political, social, or economic—there's just too many criteria in his selection of victims for him not to have a goal. There's a core slogan in this. A reason.

"Both victims are New Yorkers. We can pull focus to a macro view and find that they're both Americans, which is why Graves is sticking with the radicalized Frenchman idea. But go back to New Yorkers. Both were law enforcement officers; both were most likely killed with the same weapon and same type of ammunition; both were killed in extremely adverse winter conditions; both were shot through glass; both were murdered at rush hour; both were out of uniform. So we know the guy does his homework. He studies his victims. He works well under stress. And he's put a lot of planning into this.

"Then what do we know about his weapons system? If he was using a semiauto platform, it's easy to lose a shell with six feet of snow all around in poor lighting conditions and a lot of wind—a setting like that rooftop last night. So he's probably using a bolt-action rifle. Remington 700 is a good guess. And he's not using a noise suppressor, which says he's not concerned about sound.

"But most importantly," he added, nodding at the white world outside, "it's his choice of shooting conditions—this weather. Those deer-hunting rounds are second. This isn't some rich kid with a roomful of trophies next to his wine cellar. This is a guy who has spent a lot of time in the outdoors. In the winter. He didn't learn to shoot like this in the desert. He's comfortable in weather that scares Frosty the Snowman."

The light changed, and Whitaker eased forward with the rest of the traffic. "You mean like Siberia?"

"Nope." Lucas looked at the frozen world beyond the windshield and shook his head. "This guy's homegrown."

23

26 Federal Plaza

The bureau had a gag on the victims' names, and the news had resorted to a combination of gossip, hearsay, conjecture, and plain old bullshit. But they knew that the victims were in law enforcement, and all the major networks were running lead stories on the New York sniper. Without much to go on, they had reverted to tried-and-true journalistic gimmicks. CNN ran the same empty speculation on loop, coming up with very little in the way of real journalism; Fox had opted for the easy money, simply making shit up.

The shooter was a trending fixture on the social media feeds, generating a slew of hashtags and misinformation.

#nycshooter and #nycsniper topped the list.

But most of the hashtags were bereft of ingenuity or decorum.

#fuckfaceshooternuts

#dropdempigs

#eatleadcoppers

#youcanrunbutyoucanthide

#deathfromabove

Anti-government militia groups had birthed their own labels, singing the sniper's praises as he rose up against the tyranny of the government.

#nycriseupagainsttyranny

#donttreadonmebecauseishootback

But the social adulation was not an across-the-board phenomenon, and many were quick to label the sniper as a Muslim extremist.

#nycterrorist

#raghedsniper [*sic*]

Others accused him of being a black activist, intent on advancing a race war.

#jigaboowitharifle

#negroshooter

They generated clicks and followers and opinions and anger and trolling and finger-pointing and memes.

What they did not generate was any kind of meaningful discourse.

Kehoe and Graves were in a meeting when Lucas and Whitaker arrived. Kehoe was against the conference table, cradling an FBI mug of what had to be tea. He had a pile of papers at his hip. If one ignored the computer-pushing sales rhetoric of the last thirty years and looked only at the facts, the bureau generated more paper in a month than it had through any eight combined years prior to 2001. The leveling of the World Trade Center had propelled the bureau into its most paranoid and active period of data harvesting since the 1960s, and one of the office sayings was that the FBI killed more trees than suburban sprawl, Dutch elm disease, and IKEA combined.

Lucas folded himself into an Aeron and poured a coffee from the tray on the table. He slid it across the polished surface to Whitaker, who smiled a tired thank-you.

He poured one for himself and grabbed a plastic-wrapped sandwich without checking its contents. Then he sat back, took a deep slug of coffee, and willed the warmth to his leg. The stunt on the bridge had been an exercise in thermal masochism and had taken a toll he didn't expect. When it was really cold, the humid Manhattan kind that rat-chewed its way down to the major bones, the already lousy circulation in his left leg became less effective. That had been two hours ago, and his leg still felt borrowed from a corpse.

Graves took a seat on Whitaker's flank, across from Lucas.

Kehoe put the tea down. "What can you tell me? Start with absolutes, move down to certainties, and finish off with I-thinks—*strong* I-thinks. Where are we on our radicalized French national?"

Lucas watched Kehoe, searching for giveaways. All he saw was a supreme poker player at work.

Graves went through the broad strokes regarding what his people had put together, only going into detail when Kehoe asked a pointed question. Other than timelines and a list of investigative avenues that had turned up nothing in the way of relevant leads, he had little to offer. He gave a professional summary of both crime scenes and victims but not much in the way of deductions.

"The Frogs gave us a pretty solid folder, but we can't find Froissant. They have been monitoring his family members, all email, phones, and mail. The guy has stepped into the great unknown." Graves nodded over at Lucas. "We're canvassing anyplace he might hide out in New York. All the upscale hotels; with a bankroll of more than a billion dollars, our behavioral guys don't think he'd be in a Motel 6 in Jersey. That being said, they don't think he'll stay at the Plaza, either. This is the kind of guy who is used to buying security, so we went through all the upscale rentals citywide—starting at ten grand and moving up to a hundred and fifty K a month. So far, we've found nothing through the obvious agencies, including Craigslist and Airbnb."

Whitaker shook her head. "When you have a billion plus in the till, Airbnb probably isn't the obvious choice."

Graves shrugged. "Neither is killing people. If he's using his own money, he's carrying it with him. Or he's plugged into a network. We've gone back through the entire family's banking records, out to distant cousins and friends. Nothing points to money ending up stateside, not even if it's been hopscotched." The FBI could search almost any offshore bank via the DHS and NSA. The ones they couldn't audit had nothing to do with any form of refusal—any bank that said no to the United States government found itself slowly, but assuredly, smothered under a barrage of citations, audits, litigation, and other well-orchestrated negative pressure. No, checking every single bank was difficult because international money migration was a constant game of investigative Whac-A-Mole—in the speed-of-light economy of e-commerce, bank accounts opened and closed on a second-to-second basis.

"Our people have crunched the numbers a dozen different ways, and if he's bare-bonesing it, he needs half a million dollars, which is enough to show up somewhere. If he's going full tilt, it could be upwards of fifteen mil."

Kehoe raised a question. "Cryptocurrencies?"

Graves shook his head. "Only thirteen percent of terrorists and terrorist cells worldwide rely on cryptocurrency. But this guy wasn't raised in the backwoods of Carbombistan; he was raised with electricity and light bulbs—"

"Cut out the editorializing," Kehoe offered in an irritated voice.

Graves nodded in deference and continued, "We've checked anyone within five hundred miles of Manhattan who is capable of lending that kind of financial support. It's been short-listed to twenty-eight individuals, including two Saudi princes, one son-in-law to the Kuwaiti royal family, and an assortment of wealthy sympathizers. They're all on our scope. We're also watching all mosques in the area that are known for preaching what could be classified as radical views."

Kehoe turned to Lucas. "But you're not convinced that this is our guy."

By the way Kehoe phrased the question, it was obvious that he expected Lucas to speak up.

"No, I'm not."

"All because of a little snow?" Graves said.

"This is someone who was born shooting in this kind of weather."

That looked like what Kehoe had been expecting, and he nodded a thanks before turning to Graves and saying, "You focus on Froissant. Page is going to pursue his hunch with—"

Lucas spoke up. "It's not a hunch. It's—"

Kehoe cut him off. "Page and Whitaker will pursue his *hunch*. Give them what they need. But until this guy is in a cell, I want you functioning on a conjoined brain—as soon as one of you learns something, the other does, too."

Kehoe pointed a well-manicured index at Lucas. "You have any ideas where you want to go on this?"

"We start with ballistics. Very few people have the requisite know-how to convert a hunting round into an armor-piercing round. This wasn't a hobbyist; this was a little old guy with a mile and a half of machinist manuals in his skull."

Whitaker spoke up. "Oscar Shiner is a good starting point."

Even Graves nodded at that one.

Kehoe thought about it for a few seconds. "You and Page go put his feet to the fire."

Whitaker closed her notebook. "Yes, sir."

"And, Page?" Kehoe was still standing and he reached into his pants pocket, producing a leather security wallet.

Lucas didn't move. He didn't want to give in to the theatrics. But he knew what was coming, and he resented that he felt a little blip of adrenaline hit his system.

Kehoe held the wallet out. "You're officially back in; drop by HR and sign the papers."

Lucas unfolded the leather and examined the gold shield. It was identical to the one he had carried a lifetime ago, and seeing the eagle and the enamel letters brought back all kinds of emotions, none of which he was prepared for. They had used the photo from his passport, and he wondered just how they had managed that.

"All right," Kehoe said. "Get to work."

And with that, Lucas realized that they had been dismissed. He watched Kehoe for a few seconds, but he didn't see anything to indicate the thought process going on behind the controlled public image. Kehoe looked like all was fine and things were going exactly as planned.

Which was what bothered Lucas the most.

24

The Lower East Side

Bunny Morgan had moved into the nineteenth-century brownstone on February 21, 1947—the day after her marriage. It had been a nicer neighborhood then, but it had been her and Bert's home for half a century. He died of cancer in 1997, and she figured that she'd follow soon enough, but the wait had turned from months into years into decades, and by the time she realized she should have moved out, she was too old for any meaningful change. During that time, the area continued its steady, albeit incremental, slide into decay. Bunny Morgan, if pressed to remember the way things had actually been when she moved here as a young wife, would be horrified at the siege mentality she had adopted. Like the cracks in the limestone façade, newly refurbished when they had moved in, her survival skills had slowly broadened.

Over time, an increasingly paranoid obsession with her surroundings became the norm. And the first rule she had developed was to always keep her eyes on the Negroes—the ones on the street; the ones who lived next door; the ones who packed her bag at the market (especially the ones who packed her bag at the market—they liked to steal her sardines because she bought the good ones in oil).

But the pendulum of change was once again swinging back, and the neighborhood was succumbing to gentrification. At least that was what everyone said. But Bunny didn't believe any of it. Not as long as the Negroes and the Mexicans and the other foreigners were still around. You'd think that they'd want to go back to their own countries, but that was proving harder than you'd think. Which didn't make any kind of sense. Especially since the government would pay for them to go back—she had heard all about it on the news. Free rides to sunny places. Damn ingrates, if you asked her. They'd be smart to get away from the snow and the cold. Anyone would.

She didn't even go out in weather like this. And she didn't order in, either. Nope. She didn't want the Negro delivery boy knowing where she lived. Not a woman on her own. They liked white women, didn't matter their age. She paid attention to the news, and she knew what they were like. All of them. Except that Bill Cosby. He was the funniest. And Bunny Morgan didn't believe a word they said about him on the news. You couldn't trust anything out of Hollywood. The stations were run by a big Jewish propaganda machine, she had learned that. Actually, Bert had pointed it out the summer of 1969 when they faked the moon landing to drive up stock in batteries. And it worked. After that, everyone started getting cancer. Even Bert.

She had a little more faith in local news, but barely; again, too many Jews. But with the storm outside, there wasn't much to do. So she warmed up the roasted chicken from two nights back, cracked a bottle of good six-dollar wine, and plopped down in front of *Dancing with the Stars*. It was a rerun (a crappy one), but she watched it anyway.

When the commercials came on, she flipped through the channels and stopped on a news station where they were running a good local story about a Negro with a gun killing policemen. It was entertaining as heck. Of course, they didn't specifically say it was a Negro— they never did—but when they caught him, a Negro it would be.

Shooting policemen was one of their favorite things to do. And people wondered why they got killed by the police in return. All they had to do was be respectful. But the government was fixing all that. They would fix everything. They had promised.

Well, she wouldn't have to see any Negroes in real life. Not today. Not with the storm outside and the television inside. And her bottle of wine. After this one, maybe she'd crack another. Which would make what? Thirteen bottles in the past three days. Not bad—she was keeping it down.

Bunny took a munch off one of the two remaining drumsticks (she always ate the white meat first) and topped off her drink on the end table. As she poured, something in the distance, beyond the big window facing the final block of buildings before the FDR, caught her eye. Visibility was terrible, and she couldn't see past the roof-tops behind her—the river, two blocks away, was nonexistent in the storm—but someone was up there. Sneaking by the chimneys.

No, not someone—a *pair* of someones.

They were carrying . . . what were those? Shovels? Were they there to shovel the roof? In this wind, they'd fall off and kill their own damn selves. Maybe it was that spic landlord and one of his kids. That man was always complaining about her disposing of her wine bottles in his recycling bin. Damn Puerto Ricans, always causing trouble. Didn't he know that this was her country, not his? Bunny put on her glasses, and the figures came into sharper focus.

Holy Jesus. It wasn't the landlord. Or his son.

It was Negroes. Two of them. Bundled up in heavy winter cloth-ing, carrying rifles.

Bunny nearly knocked her wine bottle over when she snatched the phone off the cradle.

25

The Lower East Side

Officers Jason Lydon and Eddie Grozner were in a coffee shop two blocks from Bunny Morgan's house when the call went out. Lydon had been a patrolman for thirty-one years and had a record that he was sure he'd take to his retirement; Grozner had been in uniform for nine years but had amassed more street sense than a lot of officers ever gleaned from the blood and leather and concrete. They were good cops. And like any population under siege, they were aching to fight back.

Special Weapons and Tactics were on the way, but with the snow and traffic and generally shitty condition of the streets, it would take them half an hour to make the trek. By which time someone else might be in the ground.

So, in that nonverbal language that street cops develop, they came to an agreement—why should they wait for the men in tactical gear to do something that they could accomplish?

Grozner hit the lights, ignored the siren, and rocketed out of the parking spot in a cloud of white snow tinted blue with exhaust. They punched through the first light, barreled down the opposite lane in a haze of speed, and skidded through the second light, sliding around the corner and nearly taking out a stop sign in a perfect cinematic moment.

Lydon read off the numbers until they were half a block from the address the dispatcher had cited. Grozner slammed the car into a drive with *No Parking* strung across the entrance, breaking the chain and sending the sign flying off into the snow.

Lydon unlocked the shotgun from the mount on the transmission hump, and Grozner moved around the back of the car and popped the trunk, taking out the second Remington pump. They suited up and headed around the corner.

The building was a prewar five-story walk-up that had seen better times and would do so again with the wave of gentrification sweeping the area. There were no broken windows, and the snow covering all the horizontal—and some vertical—surfaces hid a lot of sins.

One of the tenants was coming out of the building as they mounted the steps, and Lydon gave her a keep-quiet signal by holding his finger to his lips. As they moved by, he leaned over and said, "Get someplace safe."

The woman—bundled up in an imitation fur coat and big red hair—took off, almost slipping on the steps.

They moved up the four staircases at a good clip, being as silent as five hundred pounds of human dressed in combat gear carrying shotguns can. They saw no one the rest of the way up, and the building was strangely silent in the way of ambient noise. The only sounds were their footsteps and a soft whistling from the wind finding its way through the structure's weak points.

When they hit the top floor, they had to check two doors to find the one to the roof. The passage was colder than the rest of the building, and light was shining in through the access door at the top of the steel staircase that stretched up into the dark like an antenna to some alternate world. Grozner, who was in better shape, went first. As he climbed, slush and other frozen shit fell off his boots and dripped down on Lydon.

There was a small landing at the top of the ladder, and the officers stopped, both trying to hear human-generated sounds above the whistle of the storm.

When Grozner opened the door, the blare of sunlight was drowned out by the blast of snow that funneled in, sucked into the tunnel and down into the body of the building. They burst out, teleporting to the surface of the moon. There were two sets of footsteps—now almost obliterated—trekking off to the east, toward the FDR.

They rounded the small support building that opened up onto the roof, and there they were. Backs to the officers. Rifles cradled in their arms.

"Drop your weapons!" Grozner screamed.

The figures spun.

Grozner raised his shotgun.

It was over and too late all at the same time.

26

Whitaker and Page arrived with the rest of the FBI entourage. By this point in the day, traffic was moving at the pace of plate tectonics, and it had taken them thirty minutes to get here. Which was good under the circumstances.

Police cruisers cauterized both ends of the block, but the news crews had yet to arrive, so there was still a semblance of order. Or at least it wasn't total bedlam. Two patrol cars sat across each intersection, nose to nose. Down the block, in front of the crime scene, an ambulance, a SWAT van, and two more cruisers lit up the snow with flashing lights, sirens silent. Even in the extreme cold, cops stood around outside, their dark uniforms in stark contrast to the white surroundings. Lucas could tell that it was more bad news from the communal body language; they were too late.

After a uniformed officer in a big coat took in Whitaker's badge, he nodded to one of the cruisers, and it backed away to let them through. She threaded between the two grilles, then wove down the street between the parked cars and snowbanks, stopping the 4×4 where it wouldn't get blocked in by more cars. Once again, they headed out into the punishing elements.

Graves, followed by another support vehicle from the bureau, entered the street behind them just as Lucas slid on his glove.

The snow squeaked underfoot and the wind off the river funneled between the buildings, freezing Lucas's ears and stinging the back of his neck. He wondered if he had gotten soft or old—back in the day, he wouldn't have noticed shit like this.

A few citizens stood out on their stoops, curious and cold. Faces were visible in windows but they disappeared behind dirty curtains or sagging blinds the moment Lucas turned to look at them. Several people were filming the goings-on with cell phones.

Up close, the scene was even more disheartening than it had been from a block away. Cops and SWAT team members smoked, talked, and drank coffee, the unmistakable look of defeat in their movements. If it were good news, they would have been doing their *we got a bad guy* dance instead of the depressed wallflower routine. The door to the building was open. A woman sat in a police cruiser beside the SWAT van, cradling a cup of something and crying. Two cops stood on the steps, guarding the entrance.

Whitaker once again flashed her badge. "Who's the OIC?" she asked.

One of the cops on the steps nodded at a big Suburban parked at a precarious angle on a snowbank just up the street. "There's a detective from the Twenty-first who you'll want to talk to. You guys want to go up? I can call her over."

"Yeah, we want to go up," Whitaker said, and they walked over to the Suburban.

A woman sat behind the wheel, a cell phone to her ear. Lucas couldn't see much through all the shit on the window other than she had a black pageboy. A big man whose face was equally obscured sat beside her. When the woman saw Lucas outside the window, she ended the call and got out of the vehicle. The man exited as well—SOP for partners.

She was in her thirties and looked like she had a mouth too wide for her face. "Yes?" she said as if Lucas were some great cosmic inconvenience. She was tall, six feet in her socks, and had the broad shoulders of someone who spent time in the gym. There was a mass of scar tissue on her jaw that Lucas recognized as reconstructive surgery troweled over with a skin graft. She also looked familiar.

Her partner was over sixty but had a curb weight and posture that Lucas wouldn't want to go up against. It didn't take a Ph.D. in body language to see that he was the strong, silent type.

Lucas held up the badge, and the move somehow felt natural. "Dr. Lucas Page, FBI."

Her demeanor didn't soften at all, one of the earmarks of years of dealing with humanity's finest. "Detective Alexandra Hemingway." She jabbed a thumb over her shoulder at the big man standing on the other side of the Suburban and looking unhappy. "That's Phelps."

"We want to take a look at the scene before the medical examiner's people get here."

Hemingway smiled at that, and the impression of too many teeth was confirmed. "Sorry, no one's going up there."

"We're not no one."

"Until my captain says it's all right, you are."

"Look, Detective, I don't mean to push things, but this is an ongoing investigation, and it's already been handed over to us." He symbolically tapped his wrist. "And we're losing time."

At that, Hemingway stood up a little taller and took a step toward him. "Until my captain gives you the go-ahead, it's fuck-off time."

Lucas was about to shift into combat mode when he realized that there was a disconnect here somewhere. "We received an alert that two individuals with rifles were spotted at this address. The ambulance is either for the shooters or an officer."

Graves came up behind them and put a hand on Lucas's shoulder. "We good here?"

Lucas nodded but kept his eye locked on the detective. "I think there's a mix-up."

Hemingway asked, "Which one of you is the big cheese?"

Graves stepped forward.

She pulled him aside, spoke a few hushed sentences, then nodded at the ambulance.

When the conversation was over, whatever she told Graves was enough for them to pull out. Graves rallied Whitaker and Lucas back to their vehicles. "Let's go before the news shows up."

On cue, a pair of news vans tried to honk their way through the police barricade. Hemingway glanced over at them, then turned back to Lucas, her irritation now a going concern. She zipped up her jacket and pulled on a pair of leather gloves. "Now, if you'll excuse me, I have to go talk to these assholes before they commence their fuckery." And she walked away.

When they were back at the pair of bureau Navigators, Graves pulled his people in. The information was delivered with a tone suggesting that there was a silver lining somewhere in the mix. "The call came in from a neighbor, an elderly lady who said she saw a pair of men with rifles on the roof. Two patrolmen nearby were first on the scene and decided to get a jump on the guys before they could execute their plan. The cops went upstairs and found two individuals on the roof. Those two individuals are dead."

"How do we know one of them wasn't our shooter?" Whitaker asked.

"They were kids, a nine- and ten-year-old playing with plastic rifles."

It was Whitaker who said, "Let the pants-shitting begin."

27

The West Village

After leaving Graves's convoy, they headed across the island to an
address off Jane Street. It was a three-story commercial building
from an age when form trumped function. The structure might have
been brown or red or even white at one point, but two hundred years
of pollution, acid rain, and disregard had incrementally patinated it
the color of an old smoker's remaining lung. The façade was a textbook example of Renaissance revival, intricately sculpted with time-
blackened gargoyles, flowers, and detailed arch work. Above the
door, cleanly chiseled into the capstone, were the words *Dempsey
Headstones*. All the windows on the building were barred, including the inaccessible ones on the top floor.

"Swanky," Lucas said, "in a Frank Lloyd Wrong meets Gomez
Addams kind of way."

Whitaker took a final loud sip from a travel mug and put the cup
back in the holder. "I know; it looks"—she followed his line of
sight—"a little run-down."

"Lady, the 375th Street Y looks a *little* run-down; this place looks
like archaeologists discovered it at the bottom of a petroleum de-
posit." He hooked an aluminum finger through the door handle.

"Before we walk in, would you care to tell me what we're doing at a headstone factory?"

"They haven't made headstones here for years."

"I was being sarcastic."

"You? Sarcastic?" She ratcheted the zipper on her parka up. "This is Oscar Shiner's place. He used to be a gunsmith for the bureau. Oscar's old-school, no CNC machines—everything is done by hand. He knows everyone, and he's worked for everyone. John Milius is a client. So was Dick Cheney. He used to do all of Idi Amin's pistols. And when Hussein was still an ally, Oscar is the guy who gold-plated and tailored his Kalashnikovs." She tapped the space under her coat where her pistol sat. "He retired from the bureau before I started; his daughter and wife were killed in a car accident, and he walked away. But a lot of the agents still come to him for porting or custom grips."

"And you think he might know someone who knows someone?"

"If it has to do with firearms, Oscar is the guy. Apparently, when you're good at your job, all kinds of people show up on your doorstep." She turned to him and smiled.

"And I'm supposed to be the mean one." He pulled on his fur-rimmed hood and stepped out into more of the same. Snow. Wind. Cold temperatures.

He climbed through a mid-thigh-high bank to get onto a sidewalk that was pockmarked with half-buried footsteps. Whitaker tried to follow in his path, but the stride was too wide, and she gave up after almost losing a boot. "I'm starting to think you're bad luck," she said.

"The feeling's mutual."

The iron door possessed the same carcinogenic complexion as the rest of the structure. It was outfitted with a litany of locks, and an intercom was fastened to the wall beside it, looking like it hadn't worked for a long time.

Whitaker reached out and pressed the small red button with a gloved finger. Then she looked up at the camera nestled into an alcove in the masonry.

A moment later, the locks went through their turns and the door opened. Whitaker was suddenly staring into the wide black eyes of a side-by-side twelve gauge.

"What the fuck you assholes want?" The words came from a voice mercilessly sculpted by cancer's familiar hands.

Whitaker dropped the hood on her parka. "Nice to see you, too, old man."

The barrel stayed leveled at her head. "Whitaker?"

"Hey, Oscar."

"Nice to see you." The old man's mouth shifted to what had to be a smile but in reality clocked out at less of a frown. "I think."

Oscar moved the double barrels onto Lucas and studied him for a few suspicious seconds, his eyes rotating from the Persols down to his anodized hand, then back up to his sunglasses. "And him?"

Lucas reached and placed the index and middle fingers of his aluminum hand in the barrels. He steered it away. "Point that at someone else," he said.

They stared at one another for a few heartbeats before Oscar nodded and snapped the safety home with his thumb. "Can't be careful enough these days. The neighborhood's gone to shit."

Whitaker let out a breath that frosted the air, and Lucas said, "Maybe it's the people who live here."

Whitaker gave him the stink eye.

Oscar waved them in. "Don't stand out there; I don't need the goddamned neighbors knowing my goddamned business."

After they stepped inside, Oscar slammed the door, snapping locks and dropping a thick piece of angle iron into place, sealing the building from interlopers. The room was completely black except for a single task bulb illuminating a metal lathe off in the distance. And by the way the sound bounced around the place, it was easy to tell that it was huge.

Oscar disappeared under the welded metal stairs that led to the office on the second floor and threw the breakers. The shop illuminated one section at a time, each round pool of gray-blue light coming to life with a loud *clack!*

In sharp contrast to the time-blackened exterior, the workshop was spotless and organized, as neat as any lab Lucas had seen. Gunsmithing tables sat alongside ancient brakes, lathes, drill presses, and two dozen other machinist's tools—all predating the computer age by an easy half century. There were a dozen felt-lined tables populated with firearms in various states of disassembly, surgery, and modification. The walls were lined with thousands of rifles, and felt-lined oak shelves filled up a good hundred feet of wall space, crammed with pistols of every conceivable make and caliber. Every firearm in the place was individually labeled with a bright yellow inventory tag. Lucas couldn't help wondering how many of these repairs and modifications would never get done; it was obvious that Oscar was losing his battle with sickness.

Oscar came out from under the staircase, and a small grunt morphed into a bout of coughing befitting a Volkswagen diesel that he punctuated by spitting into a handkerchief. "Cancer is a cunt," he said, pocketing the cotton square.

"Oscar, this is Dr. Lucas Page."

They shook hands, and Oscar said, "The astrophysicist?"

"The one and only," Whitaker answered for him.

Oscar gave Lucas an obvious up and down and nodded in approval. "Your piece on ballistics was excellent."

"Thank you." Lucas had written the book for a DOD think tank back when he still needed a way to pay for groceries. It made the rounds in various governmental agencies, eventually ending up at the FBI, where it became a standard manual. He had spent a good portion of his life wishing he never wrote it. Like now.

Oscar moved on, casting a sideways glance at Whitaker. "How's your shooting?"

She smiled at that. "First in the Law Enforcement Eastern Division, third overall."

"Third?"

She shrugged. "I had an off day."

"Yeah, well, we all—" And he was overtaken by another stretch of hacking that again ended with him spitting bloody mucus into a handkerchief. He wiped the corners of his mouth and nodded at the dark overhead. "Let's go upstairs. I need to take some medicine."

As Oscar climbed the welded metal steps to the office overlooking the workshop, Whitaker pointed out that he didn't advertise and he only accepted new clients on referral as long as they understood that there was a two-year waiting list just to bring a firearm in. And then there was still plenty of waiting to be done. Which once again hammered home the realization that work on many of the weapons in the shop downstairs would never be completed.

The office was large, with a twelve-foot ceiling. One wall was lined with shelving, one had a massive fireplace centered in it, and two walls were floor-to-ceiling windows that oversaw the shop. The space was covered with what looked like ten acres of Persian rug. Two big tufted leather chesterfields and a pair of club chairs flanked the fireplace, and there was a bar stocked with a good choice of scotches, from low-grade blends to expensive Japanese single malts. There was a good eighteenth-century portrait in a rocaille frame over the fireplace, a wall of reference books, a hand-crafted stereo, a small two-person dining set, a fridge, and an old leather psychiatrist's couch in the back corner. But the centerpiece was a taxidermied elephant's head, painted pink and staring down as if waiting for someone to turn on the television. There was a duffel bag on the floor, and a baby-blue sweater was neatly folded on top. It wasn't hard to figure out that Oscar spent a lot of nights here.

The old man put the shotgun down on his desk atop a pile of take-out menus, hung his apron on the antler coatrack by the door, then folded his glasses into a shirt pocket. After another short bout of coughing and spitting blood, he went to the bar. "Want a drink, Dr. Page?"

Lucas shook his head as he walked around the room, taking in the details. "Thank you, no."

The old man turned to Whitaker. "The usual?"

She looked at Lucas, letting him know that she knew she was on duty, then said, "Sure."

Oscar pulled a bottle from the forest of booze vessels and poured a couple of fingers of scotch into two simple glass tumblers. He handed a glass to Whitaker, then headed to his seat with the bottle in one hand, his drink in the other.

Lucas scanned the library, recognizing most of the books on ballistics, including his own. But the thing that caught his attention was the collection of cartridges on the mantel. He sighted down the long oak surface and did that thing he did with numbers, coming up with 2,461 separate rounds. The collection was organized from smallest to largest, eight rows deep, variances in length and diameter factored into the order. The first round in the forest of brass was a weird little caliber that Lucas didn't recognize, the last being a .50-caliber shell that might as well have been designed for shooting dinosaurs. The rounds were well thumbed, and would have taken Oscar years to put together, even with the contacts in his rarefied profession.

Oscar dropped into a leather club chair by the fire and said to Lucas, "If it's not booze, all I have is water."

"Not a problem. I just had lunch."

Lucas caught Whitaker eyeing him as she put the booze into her system. It was clear that she was wondering if he would blow this. Oscar didn't seem like the kind of man who relished having strangers in his place. Especially ones who didn't drink.

When the booze was away in his boiler, Oscar poured another and eased back in the tufted leather. "So, what brings you down to my humble place of business in the End Times blizzard?"

Whitaker bypassed small talk and went straight for the big money. "You heard about the killings?"

Oscar nodded and put another mouthful of single malt away. "Everyone's heard about the killings."

Lucas knew that a portion of the Second Amendment folks were a singularly minded group who interpreted every act of firearm violence as a newly minted excuse for the government to come after their guns.

Whitaker went on. "Our guy's a shooter. But he's not using military or tactical rounds; he's using a modified deer slug. Bench-load .300 Winnie Mag."

At that, Oscar shifted in his seat. "Good choice."

"But it gets weird after that. Copper-alloy jacket, lead-alloy core with a machined kernel of ferrous metal suspended in the mix."

That seemed to stop Oscar's internal machinery, and something blipped on his features. "Ferrous?" He leaned forward and poured two more fingers of medicine into his glass. "Which makes them armor piercing."

"There's more."

Oscar took another sip of booze. "Of course there is."

"The ferrous core isn't any sort of normal steel. It's meteoric in origin."

Oscar stared at Whitaker for a few seconds, and Lucas wondered what he was thinking. He hoped that Whitaker was doing that Amazing Kreskin Jedi mind trick of hers.

"Meteoric? As in *from a meteor*?" the old man asked, and his head swiveled to Lucas for a second. "A *space* meteor?"

Lucas didn't bother to nod. "That's the only kind there is."

Whitaker continued, "Whoever put those rounds together isn't some guy in a garage with a hacksaw and a drill press from Lowe's—this is a guy with a lot of experience. Either the shooter does his own work, or he has someone do it for him."

Oscar examined Lucas over the rim of his glass, then his eyes shifted back to Whitaker. It was obvious he considered her some kind of a friend and was weighing that against an unknown part of the equation—probably the shield hanging around her neck. "And what is it you expect from me?"

"Whoever this guy is, he is doing this for a reason. I don't expect you to ask around about the work and I don't expect you to ask around about the rifle, but I'm looking for anyone who might fit the ideals. Just ask a few questions."

Oscar polished off the scotch. "And you figured that I'm so close to death that I might sacrifice my principles to help you out."

Whitaker knocked back her own drink and leaned forward in the chair, hands on her knees. "Oscar, this guy is big game hunting my people in my city. All I'm asking is for you to think about it."

Oscar put his empty tumbler down on the coffee table. "I'll walk you out."

28

Midtown

The day had been busy on regulars but shy on walk-by traffic. No one wanted to go out in the storm unless they had to—all the checks today were for people who lived less than a block away. The every-day folks and the three-times-a-week people all showed up and had been generous with tips.

Connie was changing in the basement, behind the door of the rusty high school locker that Nick provided to all his employees, when Kirby knocked at the window.

She looked up through the bars and gave him the *I'll be up in a minute* sign.

He rolled his eyes and pointed at his wrist. He probably had a meeting with his buddies tonight, and he'd want her to go along. She'd refuse and they'd argue.

It wasn't that she didn't like his friends. She simply understood them better than he did. Sitting around an apartment arguing about how it was time for action. Angry at the world. Angry at everyone. They had a few valid points, but they only saw things in black and white. They called it patriotism, but it was really more of a low-level

Fascism fueled by a lot of anger that never translated to any kind of meaningful action.

She had experience with their thinking; she had been raised on it. Which was why she stuck with him. He was part of home, part of her past, and it made her feel a little more whole to have him in her life here.

She was finishing the tug on her zipper when she heard Nick at the top of the stairs. If she didn't hurry, she'd have to blow herself out of the basement, and after the day's shift, she really didn't feel like sucking the fat Greek's cock.

Kirby banged on the window with his guitar case, and she gave him the thumbs-up. *I'm coming!* she mouthed.

She hit the bottom of the stairs at the same time as Nick. "Where you goin'?" he asked, and by his tone, she could tell he thought it was blow job time.

"I got things to do," she said, and she ran by him before he could grab her arm.

29

26 Federal Plaza

When they got to the war room, Kehoe was already in full swing. SOP was an early-morning meeting followed up at the end of the day with a wrap (which served as the launching pad for that evening's workload). It was now almost four in the afternoon, and the sun was beginning to fade.

The entire team, now nearly seventy people, zeroed in on the need to know and the here and now. Kehoe paced in front of the screens, looking very much like a college professor giving a seminar. But in place of pie charts, graphs, and equations, the monitors displayed images of Philippe Froissant, the Frenchman that Lucas doubted had anything to do with the killings.

"We still haven't nailed down direct evidence to tie Froissant to these two killings, but information from French intelligence agencies combined with a recommendation from both our DHS and DOJ suggest that this is our suspect." When Kehoe saw Lucas, he stopped his delivery and nodded at him. "Which brings me to the mystery man you've seen walking around the crime scenes and our building for the past twenty-four hours. People, meet Dr. Lucas Page."

The forest of heads swiveled simultaneously, and Lucas nodded once and gave a small light bulb wave with his prosthetic hand so that there would be fewer surprises in the days to come.

Herd curiosity satisfied, the attention focused back on Kehoe.

"Dr. Page is filling the capacity of special investigator. He is an astrophysicist by trade, if you can call it that, and specializes in three separate branches of math that I won't pretend to understand. For our purposes he's here for projectile geometry. Dr. Page is partnered with our own Agent Whitaker, and I expect you to extend him every professional courtesy."

Introductions done, he returned to lecture mode. "On to ballistics." He nodded, and the screens behind him changed, now displaying images of the slug from the Hartke murder scene. It was mangled but in one piece, remarkable considering it had been dug out of frozen asphalt after punching through a human being and a car. It looked like a cast of some unidentifiable internal organ.

Lucas took up a position against one of the glass walls that bordered the hallway. Whitaker eased up beside him and leaned back, crossing her arms. "You missed the rundown on the French suspect."

"He's French—he likes wine, pretty girls with hairy armpits, and nice clothes—what's to know?" he whispered.

"You ever run out of sarcasm?"

"Sure. About twice a week."

Kehoe rocked up onto the balls of his feet—a new habit that Lucas hadn't seen before. "Our shooter favors very specific ammunition. He's not using off-the-shelf—these rounds are bench-loaded and have significant idiosyncratic properties; please check your in-boxes for a more detailed rundown when we finish here." Kehoe nodded at one of the screens, and a brochure photograph of a bullet popped up. "We've only recovered one round so far—from the scene of Agent Hartke's murder—but all evidence at the tram shooting indicate the same type of projectile. The slugs he's using began their life as off-the-shelf rounds manufactured by Nosler under their AccuBond line—copper-alloy jacket with a lead-alloy core in a .300 Winchester Magnum. This, in itself, appears to be atypical for our suspect. We expect him to use a military-grade anti-personnel round."

At that point, Kehoe's eyes went right back to Lucas, and for an instant they tried to communicate some unknown message. "These are modified hunting rounds, machined to contain a kernel of ferrous metal that is meteoric in origin." Kehoe looked at Lucas. "Dr. Page, do you see any tactical advantage in using such an unusual core?"

Lucas shook his head. "Over a man-made ferrous alloy? Not that I can discern. Before humans figured out how to smelt iron, many cultures used it as a material of opportunity. There are recorded instances of the Inuit using it in edged tools, and more recently, a knife with a blade of meteoric iron was found in King Tutankhamen's burial chamber. Both examples rely heavily on superstition, and that's the only benefit I can see—there's some imagined purpose or import to the shooter."

"How difficult is it to source?"

Lucas shrugged. "You can't buy it at your average scrapyard, but it's not completely uncommon. Specialty scientific and educational wholesalers are the obvious starting point. Mineral collectors. Finding a meteorite would be the most untraceable method. And since each meteor has its own unique mineral signature, it's possible that it comes from a known source."

Kehoe took back the reins. "We are checking with all mineral suppliers, mineral collector message boards, and other sources. Laterally, we're going after the initial off-the-shelf Nosler rounds. We have already sourced purchases."

In a state with lax or almost nonexistent gun laws, like Alabama or Tennessee, this would be impossible. But under the New York SAFE gun act, the acquisition of ammunition was a documented process; it was impossible to purchase powder, primers, slugs, cartridges, or ammunition without recording the transaction. Internet purchases were also monitored—it was against the law for any out-of-state seller to ship ammunition to a private citizen; it had to be shipped to a registered gun dealer, where it was recorded.

Problem was, ammunition and gun dealers were notoriously cagey when it came to talking to law enforcement; they tended to see it as an interaction with the very government whose tyranny they purported to be on the watch for. The laws helped, but their stoicism was a continual battle.

Kehoe once again nodded, and the image changed, this time to a page of text. "In the past three years, there have been six-hundred-and-thirteen shipments of Nosler's AccuBond to addresses in New York State, not including store purchases. If this guy's shooting skill and lack of trace evidence are any kind of an indicator of his personality, he got his ammunition some other way. Out-of-state dealer or gun show." Besides sifting through packing slips and delivery signatures, they'd move on to lateral databases, beginning with government records and working down to social media accounts; it was astounding what people posted about their lives—and their ideas—on social media.

Kehoe hit the end of his walk and turned slowly on his heel. "Out of six-hundred-and-thirteen shipments in the past three years, there are four-hundred-and-twelve individual buyers. Of those, thirty-eight have died." Another nod, and a screen changed again, this time coming up with a list of hard stats about the deaths. "We're looking at all of them."

Kehoe repeated his trick, and the screens behind him once again changed images, this time to an aerial photograph of number 3 Park Avenue. "The first crime scene is at the upper end of pedestrian surveillance, but there are no high-risk residents, so there has never been a need for top-shelf security. The elevators and stairwells are public access; the loading docks, service elevators, and maintenance points are all key access—Medeco commercial-grade registered keys. They are camera heavy, but it's not state of the art. One of their stairwells to the roof is not on feed, and it's not hard to get there if you know the building. But there is a camera monitoring the rooftop door, and this is where things get a little muddy.

"The access doors to the roof are monitored by IR cameras on a twenty-four-hour loop; it's impossible to step onto, or off, that deck without being filmed. We've gone over the footage, and no one went up during the full twenty-four hours before Agent Hartke's murder. More troubling still is that we have no footage of our subject leaving the rooftop. Imaging is taking the available video apart frame by frame, and we'll have an initial report in a few hours to see if it was manipulated in any way. We're also doing comparative counts with facial recognition software. We haven't placed the Frenchman in the city, let alone on-site."

Kehoe pointed up at number 3 Park Avenue. "Approximately 33,000 people circulate through the building each day. That is a lot of data to analyze. We identified one-hundred-and-sixty-one people with outstanding warrants against them. Most of those were for typical nonsense: failure to make child support payments, outstanding parking tickets, and the like. But we identified nineteen felons; all were in and out of the building hours earlier in the day. NYPD was able to locate eleven of them, and we're satisfied that they had nothing to do with the shooting. The other eight are still at large, but none of them fit the MO, although we're not writing anything off.

"We've employed a basic biometric registry for crowdsourcing, but when we factor in winter hats and scarves and balaclavas, we end up with a lot of dropouts. What we do know is that whoever killed Agent Hartke is on footage *somewhere*. But again—no Froissant."

Lucas watched Kehoe closely, paying attention to his inflection, body language, and delivery, and he couldn't shake the feeling that he was being used. Or was he just being paranoid?

"Which brings us to the second murder, committed from the Manhattan side of the Roosevelt Island Tramway station." Another nod, and the monitors brought up the second rooftop. "All the entry doors are monitored—both pedestrian and maintenance—but that's where it stops. With estimated traffic of a thousand people per day, it's a much smaller digital footprint to comb through. Again, no evidence that the Frenchman was there. The problem is the garage; the entrance is recorded, but it has sight holes. We've pulled footage from every camera in a two-block radius. Again, our suspect had to get there from somewhere. So far, no Frenchman."

Kehoe took a sip of tea and paused for a moment before turning to the victims. "As a precaution, we're looking at all law enforcement shootings over the last five years—both at home and abroad—to see if we have a similar MO or ballistics match. So far, nothing has come up."

Kehoe was silent for a moment before the screens changed again, this time to images of three sections of fence they had removed from the Queensboro Bridge. "The only physical evidence we have so far are three lengths of flagging tape left on the Queensboro Bridge as wind and distance markers. No prints or trace evidence of any kind. It's a popular PVC tape that can be purchased everywhere from Walmart to Bass Pro Shops. The only distinctive characteristic we found was that it was cut with a serrated blade. Simple knots were used. That's all that this guy has left behind so far.

"Which brings us back to our suspect." The screens lit up with a photo of Philippe Froissant. "We've got a BOLO out for him. He was born into a very good family—industrial fortune with manufacturing in North Africa, former Eastern Bloc countries, and China. There's a full bio accompanying the rest of this brief. I want you people to find this prick, and I want him brought in."

Kehoe's focus shifted to Lucas, and the monitors pixelated again, this time coming up with the dark silhouette of a man over a white background, a question mark in the middle of his chest. "We also have a second suspect—an unknown. This is off theory with the Frenchman narrative, but we're keeping our options open. Don't become myopic out there." And with that, he ended the brief.

The room shifted back into work mode, and Kehoe made a beeline to the back of the room, coming straight to Lucas. "You and Whitaker in my office. Now."

30

Kehoe sat on the edge of his desk, arms crossed over his chest, platinum Breguet gleaming under the cuff of the bespoke shirt. The guy made most of the younger agents look dumpy. His blend of body language and delivery had been honed at the best schools, and it was no secret that he was heir to a California agricultural empire that spanned three counties of the Golden State.

Kehoe pointed a fountain pen at Lucas. "One of the AccuBond purchasers—one of the *dead* AccuBond purchasers—bought enough ammunition to wage his own personal war. His name was Billy Margolis."

Kehoe picked a file up off his desk and handed it to Whitaker. "Mechanic. Lived on 142nd and Riverside. We went back three years in purchase records, and during that time, he bought enough supplies to load twenty-two thousand rounds of .300 Winchester Magnum."

Lucas did the math; the numbers worked out to just over 141 rounds a week. There were plenty of hobby shooters who put 500 rounds down the pipe every week.

Kehoe continued, "We took it back another five years, and during that time, Margolis purchased another twenty thousand rounds of the Nosler AccuBond, all in the latter two years."

Whitaker tapped the file. "I take it there's more than just a mountain of ammunition that put him on our to-do list?"

Kehoe simply said, "He was killed during a home invasion. The NYPD cracked his social media accounts, email, cell phone records, and hard drive during the investigation. It turns out that Margolis was a major player in the Patriotic Citizens' Militia of Manhattan."

"There's a militia group on the island?"

Kehoe nodded at Whitaker. "Ask our resident expert."

Whitaker nodded. "Same kind of assholes that took over the Malheur National Wildlife Refuge in Oregon. At least theoretically they're the same kind. Since oh-eight, when Obama took to the Oval Office, there's been a massive surge in militia enrollment. They all like to use words like *patriot, truth,* and *freedom,* but not a single group seems to have any kind of cohesive philosophy. Or even a very basic understanding of the Constitution. They like guns, say they hate the government but love America, seem to dislike people of color and the concept of paying for the infrastructure that they enjoy using. They call any kind of government intervention tyranny. And they complain. Constantly. Basically, they're pissed because people who are smarter than they are, or who work harder than they do, have more than they do. They spew a libertarian line about every man for himself and it's up to the individual to map their own path, yet they blame immigrants for their woes. Zero personal responsibility and zero self-awareness. What they're really pissed off at, but can't verbalize, is that the government isn't regulating things in their favor."

Lucas used the voice he reserved for the kids when they argued against some basic house rule. "They sound swell."

"They don't have that much backbone; a lot of these guys are wannabe cops or soldiers but can't pass the psych tests. A lot are borderline personalities with an unusually high percentage of addicts and depressives in their ranks. They think they're tough guys and they love gun culture, but they're classic bullies. You can thank irradiation by right-wing media for these dimwits."

Kehoe cut her editorializing off with a single blink of his eyes. "You and Page are going to talk to the investigating detective from the Margolis murder, a man named Atchison from the Thirteenth Precinct. I spoke to his CO earlier; he's undercover on a job, but they'll pull him in for us. It will be soon, but I can't guarantee a time. I want you to siphon his brain dry." He nodded over at a capital file on the table by the door.

Lucas examined the stained manila folder, then turned back to Kehoe. "Did they find Margolis's murderer?"

Kehoe shook his head. "And they didn't find a single round of ammunition in his home."

31

The Upper East Side

Whitaker stuck her hand across the console. "Not bad for your first day back," she said.

Lucas stared at the polished nails for a second, wondering how he should handle this. He stuck out his prosthetic and rotated his wrist, which forced the green fingers to assume a more or less neutral position that Erin called *karate chop mode*. Whitaker took it and shook like she had done it a thousand times. "Sorry for being—"

"A supreme grouch?"

"I was going to say *slightly irritable*, but under the circumstances, I'll give you that one."

She looked out the window at the house, at the lights inside the living room window. "I try not to be nosy when I'm off the clock, but how does a university professor manage to own what has to be an eight-figure chunk of real estate in such a swanky neighborhood? Unless the pay is better than I imagine, that is."

"Can't you just do that thing and divine the answer out of thin air?" He gave her an irritated look.

Whitaker smiled and shrugged. "I can only do that with questions, not answers."

"I won the lottery," he said, pulling the handle. "I'll see you to-morrow," he added as his boots touched the snow. He closed the door, sealing the big 4×4 with a hermetic *thunk*.

Erin opened the door before his key was at the lock, and she pulled him inside. She wrapped him in a hug and kicked the door closed in a well-choreographed move that was mindful of his balance. His stance was always solid, and his prosthetic was better than a natural leg when it came to tensile strength, but it had no give, requiring a cantilevered weight distribution. He could throw it around, but if someone else did, the whole house of cards could come down.

"Did you catch him? Did they get what they want? Are you home to stay?" she asked, punctuating each question with a kiss.

He kissed her back and realized how cold his skin had become on the short walk from the car to the door. In what—thirty seconds?—twenty-five? It took hardy genes to spend time outside in weather like this; it couldn't be learned. "No," he said. "No. And no." He wondered what the hell he was doing, running around on frozen bridges when he had a warm place to be. Where no one was getting shot.

The kids were in the study, decorating the tree. He could smell the pine and hear ornaments clinking. They finished kissing, and Alisha came barreling over, Lemmy following in a slow-motion trot, her silent wingman. "Mr. Lucas! You back!"

"Hey, Alisha. Are you sure the dog isn't bothering you?" Lucas and Erin unclenched, and he did his best to crouch down. He took off his sunglasses and kept his head straight so his eyes wouldn't misalign—his line of sight weirded out most kids, and Alisha was still new to their little world.

Alisha skidded to a halt. Behind her, Lemmy hit the brakes, but he was just too much weight moving too quickly, and the carpet bunched up under him. The Persian runner surfed under Alisha, and she toppled sideways. Lucas reached out and caught her.

"No, sir, Mr. Lucas. Lemmy is the most best. We're friends. As long as I don't feed him no chocolate." She glanced up at Erin.

Lucas turned his head, following the little girl's gaze up at Erin. How the hell did she manage to pack so much learning into each day? "Well, that's good advice. Chocolate is very bad for dogs. I wonder if it's good for little girls?"

She clapped her hands. "Oh yes, Mr. Lucas. It's the most bestest, too!"

"Well, I know where we keep the Hershey bars."

Four voices from the study piped in with a pretty good harmony of, "Me, too, please."

Erin threw him one of her looks—first off, it was too close to supper; second, she hated when he bribed the kids. "So, just what *are* you doing home?"

"It's the end of the day. I need some rest. There's nothing else I can do right now; it's up to the regular bureau people to do what they were trained to. Me? I'm going to relax with my family."

"And to hand out some Hershey bars!" Maude hollered from the study.

"Did Maude get her algebra test results yet?" Lucas whispered to Erin.

She shook her head. "She's been checking her phone every three minutes. They're posting them tonight."

Maude was having a particularly difficult time with algebra, and Lucas had been tutoring her. She was working very hard to break its back but it was a difficult process for her; she was a very artistic child but math was just not a natural talent. In absolute terms, Lucas didn't care if she passed or failed—not in any real sense. But he hoped that some of what they had worked on had stuck in that she could use a little confidence right now. *Especially* right now, as she was making the transition from girl to young woman.

Erin headed off to the kitchen as Lucas moved to the deco hall stand by the door to the dining room and began to take off his boots. His gait had changed the instant Kehoe handed him the shield—it felt as if they had returned a piece of his body. There was something unsettling about the sensation, as if maybe he wasn't more than the sum of his parts. Was that all it took? A piece of brass-plated nickel? Had he really been craving the recognition that much? If so, what did that say about the strength of his character? His self-worth?

The kids had pimped out the tree with enough decorations to shame a Mardi Gras float. Maude was working on the lights while Hector and Damien put ornaments on the higher branches. Laurie was by the fire, eating a clementine and holding a fistful of tinsel.

Erin had lugged the Christmas Tupperware containers upstairs, and they were open, red and green and silver and gold spilling out. This year they had the gnomes out, a little bearded army of ZZ Top members; all that was missing were the Marshalls and groovy dance moves. The change in the room from the night before was startling, and Lucas realized that he needed to finish with Kehoe's people and come home. Christmas was one of the few times where he could spend more than a day or two with the kids. And he had promised a full two weeks this year.

Erin came back, followed by Alisha and Lemmy. She had a stack of Hershey bars in her hand. She handed one to each of the kids and gave the last one to Lucas. "Just because I love you," she said as she pressed it into his hand.

"You know I don't eat chocolate."

"It's for your new partner."

"I don't think she eats chocolate." He dropped one of his boots onto the tray and went to work on the other one.

"Is she a woman?"

For a second, Lucas thought it might be a trick question. "I believe so, yes."

"Then she eats chocolate."

He didn't want to argue. "Okay. You win."

He was about to kick off the other boot when the doorbell sounded, a loud musical *bing-bong* that all the kids—including Alisha—mimicked with operatic cadence.

"It's the woman who just dropped you off," Maude said from the front window.

Lucas shrugged as Erin gave him another one of her looks—the kind he didn't like.

Lucas walked over, the boot still on his prosthetic throwing his gait into *clonk-clonk-clonk* mode. He opened it to Whitaker trying to look like it was good news, which, he knew, it wasn't.

"We got that meeting with the detective from the Thirteenth."

Lucas looked at his wrist. "Now?"

"He's got an hour window, so it's now or never."

Lucas turned to Erin, who was coming to the door with his other boot. "Supper's at seven if you can make it."

He tried to give the kids his *I'm sorry* shrug, but they were too engrossed in peeling chocolate wrappers.

He put his boot on as Whitaker walked down the steps to the Navigator.

When he stepped back outside, it felt like Mother Nature had turned down the thermostat and the snow was dialed into optical illusion mode. Lucas handed Whitaker the Hershey bar as he climbed into the Navigator.

"Holy fuck, I *love* Hershey bars!" she said, and she went at the wrapper with her teeth.

He wondered how Erin was always right.

32

Lucas and Whitaker met with the investigating detective from the Margolis case at a diner on Fifty-eighth.

The holiday decorations looked like they hadn't been taken down since last year and were all the cheap dollar-store variety. There was a picture behind the cash register of Hans Gruber posing in front of a Christmas tree at Nakatomi Plaza, and Lucas couldn't help smiling as they walked by.

Like everyone else in the city, Atchison was bundled up in arctic finery. He had one of those faces dictated by the wires pulsing just below the skin, and nothing about him said cop except for the thousand-yard stare that was one of the standard upgrades that came with experience.

They shook hands all around, and Atchison seemed focused. "Thanks for meeting me here. Traffic's a bitch, and you saved me an hour that I don't really have." He gave Whitaker a once-over and there was something unpleasant, almost reptilian, in the gesture that Lucas didn't like.

Without discussing it, they chose a booth at the back, away from the windows. Atchison slid his briefcase onto the seat. They shed their parkas and sat down. Lucas placed the Margolis file Kehoe had pulled from the Pearson Place Warehouse on the table. Some of the old coffee rings decorating the manila had no doubt happened during Atchison's work sessions.

Atchison saw the folder and put his hand on it as if saying hello to an old friend. He nodded at the white world through the rectangle of window at the front of the diner. "Only thing that scares people off the streets in this city is weather. I don't think they even care about the guy with the rifle."

There was a break in the storm that Lucas knew wouldn't last long, but it gave the illusion the cleanup crews might have a chance at restoring general order—in about two months. Cars were only identifiable by their regularly spaced humps along the street; the sidewalks were trenches hacked out by city workers and citizens alike; wind screamed up the street.

Lucas didn't agree. Weather didn't scare New Yorkers because it was too much of an abstract threat. And a man with a rifle wouldn't scare them either, especially if he was a foreigner. Not in a million fucking years. This city would eventually drink his blood. No, the only thing New Yorkers collectively fear is other New Yorkers because they know they have the staying power.

The waitress brought three mugs in one hand and a pot of steaming coffee in the other. She laid out the cups, filled them, and walked away with a nod at the menu and a "Let me know if you need anything." Evidently, she had been at this long enough to know that good service sometimes meant leaving customers alone.

The diner was empty to the point of distraction. There was one single patron near the door, a kid in his twenties working on an egg cream and a Reuben. That was it.

Management had two televisions spitting out opposite ends of the almost-information spectrum, CNN on one, Fox on the other—volume off, subtitles on. The bureau had yet to release victim names, but the law-enforcement-agents-as-targets storyline was letting them fill in the blanks with all manner of straw-grasping. The screen in the corner above the cash register displayed a smiling newscaster at direct odds with the graphic of crosshairs superimposed over an old-fashioned sheriff's badge. It was a powerful graphic, and Lucas knew that he'd be sick of seeing it by the time this was all over. The flat screen in the other corner—above the glass display wall of wax pies, plastic cakes, and resin sundaes—was tuned in to the blond porn star brigade, and one of the actresses was wondering aloud that if this wasn't a jihadist plot, could it possibly be the work of Black Lives Matter militants? Even on mute, their hope was hard to miss.

Lucas wrapped his good hand around the hot mug of coffee as Atchison leaned back in the booth. His sports coat crept up, exposing a shield on his belt that looked like it had opened an army of beer bottles. "What—in specific—can I help you with in regard to the Margolis case?" he asked in the to-the-point diction of a man who had a lot of things to do and not nearly enough time to do them in, an affliction that affected 100 percent of the police officers Lucas had ever met.

Whitaker shifted into agent gear. "This is all official, and we control this information. Anything we discuss here becomes public knowledge when and if we say so."

Atchison took a sip of his coffee and sounded a little defensive when he said, "This isn't my first time doing this." He put the coffee down.

Whitaker said, "The slugs we pulled from one of the scenes is a custom-load round. Modified Nosler AccuBond in a .300 Winchester Magnum."

"I see."

There was something in Atchison's response that Lucas couldn't read, and he wondered if it was simply the obvious dislike he had for Whitaker or if it was something else. Regardless, the needle moved, and Lucas consciously started paying attention to his body language.

"Which was Margolis's round of choice," Whitaker added. "So you can see where we're going with this."

Atchison signaled the waitress with a snap of his fingers before turning back to Whitaker. "All of Margolis's rifles were accounted for."

"But not his ammunition. He purchased nearly fifty thousand rounds in the last five years before his death; how much of a shooter was he?"

Atchison tapped the file. "These militia types are serious about shooting. They're civic minded and have a belief that they will be the ones to save America if things go south." He made it sound like they were the swellest bunch of guys around.

Whitaker locked him in a cold stare. "The bureau lists *these militia types* as the single-biggest threat to our nation's security, *much greater than* Muslim terrorists and Russian cyberattacks."

"Everyone is entitled to their opinion." Atchison shrugged as the waitress arrived. He ordered two cheeseburgers with bacon, onions, and mustard along with a load of fries. In the midst of ordering, he turned to Whitaker and said, "You should try the fried chicken; it's the best in the city."

"I just ate." Her voice had a frost in it that Lucas hadn't heard before. "But knock yourself out."

Lucas was amazed at how Whitaker didn't reach across the table and choke the guy. Lucas wanted to say something, but Whitaker had been firm in her instructions on their way down here—Lucas was supposed to follow her lead. So he swallowed it.

"Suit yourself."

When the waitress asked Lucas if he wanted anything, he shook his head and said, "Privacy," and waved her away with a twist of his aluminum hand. He wanted to make it back home in time for supper—maybe undo a little of the damage skipping out had done.

After the waitress was back at her station, Whitaker picked up with business. "What happened to his ammunition?"

Atchison thought about it for a few seconds, and the action was now becoming familiar; he liked to think about his responses. He eventually put his hand back on the file. "We ran this case down. I mean we followed every fucking lead you can think of. I went back in his phone records and email, credit cards and bank accounts—what little there was. I checked out his magazine subscriptions and looked through his bookshelves. Social networking accounts and his favorite websites. I interviewed his friends and the guys he worked with, his clients and neighbors. I can't tell you how many interviews I had with his militia buddies. And after months of running around, that was that."

"Suspects?" There was nothing in the file to suggest they had found any, but that didn't necessarily translate to real-time information. There was always background chatter that never made it into a file, pet ruminations and biases that no one put down on paper.

Again, Atchison mulled the question over for a few ticks of the clock before shaking his head. "I'd have run him to the ground by now."

And again that weird needle on Lucas's meter moved.

Whitaker went back to the obvious. "What about his militia friends?"

Atchison leaned back in his seat and crossed his arms over his chest. "I told you, these are just a bunch of guys trying to be part of the solution."

Whitaker held up her hand at that one. "Like their support of Operation Jade Helm?"

Atchison nodded. "Sure. They saw it as a way to protect their country from an overreaching government."

"As opposed to seeing themselves as traitors?"

"How do you figure?"

"Really?" she said, and Lucas could tell that she was starting to get pissed off with his attitude.

"Really. I'd like *specifics.*" As a matter of form, he added, "Please."

Whitaker nodded. "Our main theater of war for the foreseeable future will be in the Middle East. And where would we find an arid environment that mimics that particular chunk of geography, where we could train our troops? I'm thinking Texas. And these guys want to record and report on the maneuvers? Sure. Let's give our enemies as much information as possible. Not very forward-thinking, if you ask me. If a truckload of Muslim American men hung out near the operation and broadcast the comings and goings on Al Jazeera, those same so-called patriots would bust a nut and call for their execution. They aren't part of the solution; they're most of the problem."

Atchison looked at her for an angry moment. "You're missing the point."

"No, *you're* missing the point," she said.

"Again, everyone's entitled to their own opinion." Atchison took in another mouthful of coffee, then asked, "You guys have any leads?"

Whitaker put her hand on the file. "We've interviewed a few local gunsmiths, and we've got some feelers out, but nothing has come in. Which is why we are here with you."

Atchison's food arrived, and the waitress dropped it without looking at Lucas. When she was gone, Whitaker opened the conversation back up. "Can you see any of these militia types killing federal agents?" she asked.

Atchison took a bite out of his cheeseburger, and it was hard to miss the wheels spinning behind his eyes. "Not as things are now. But if society starts to collapse, which anyone with a brain thinks is imminent—"

Lucas held up his hand. "Did Margolis have a girlfriend?"

Atchison washed the mouthful of cheeseburger down with some coffee, then snapped his fingers at the waitress and asked for a Coke.

Whitaker leaned forward. "Do any of these guys have girlfriends? You know, *real* girlfriends?"

Lucas thought that she was intentionally baiting him now.

"He had a girlfriend, or at least a woman he saw on a more or less regular basis, but I couldn't track her down. She was younger than him. And quiet." Atchison tapped the file. "One of his mechanics remembered a brunette coming by the shop a couple of times—young, thin, pretty, freckles. His neighbors saw a woman come by a few times, too—probably the same chick—same description. Coulda been anyone, but I didn't find anything in his phone or email records. Coulda been something. Coulda been nothing."

"So what are we missing with Margolis?" she asked.

"Nothing." Atchison wiped his hands on a paper napkin that went clear with grease. He tapped the pregnant briefcase beside him. "I brought you copies of my notebooks and personal files." He nodded at the folder still on the corner of the table. "And you've got a copy of everything. I'm not big on leaving shit out." He placed his hand back on the file in that weird little act of repeated intimacy, then he looked over at Lucas. "You read the Bible, Dr. Page?"

"I've *read* both." Lucas took off his sunglasses and rubbed the bridge of his nose.

Atchison nodded as if that were an admission. "Remember Samson? He slew a thousand Philistines with nothing but the jawbone of an ass."

Lucas cranked his good eye over, and by the way Atchison ticked, like one of his cylinders had missed, he knew he was doing that amusement park thing with his eyes. "What's your point?"

"Imagine what he could have done with a rifle." Atchison jabbed his thumb at the silent city behind them, through the front windows. "A handful of bullets and a little don't-give-a-fuck go a long way. You have to admit that it's a hell of an effective way to wage a war."

"Against what?" Whitaker asked.

Atchison looked at her for a moment before saying, "Name it."

33

The Upper East Side

Lucas had Whitaker drop him off in the alley behind the garage. He got out of the Navigator without using the holy shit handle, a feat that had taken a lot of practice over the years. As the door closed, hermetically sealing her in the rich leather interior, Lucas heard the music come on inside. The big 4×4 pulled away, spinning its tires and fishtailing up the alley, "Cult of Personality" by Living Colour shaking the vehicle.

Dingo was keeping up with the shoveling. He had chopped neat furrows through the new snow, clearing the two garage doors and the gate, and Lucas could see the telltale rectangular imprints of his outdoor blades, the impressions crisscrossed with the heavy tread that kept him from taking a dive. Lucas unlocked the door to the garden, and as soon as he stepped inside, he heard the screams of the kids playing in the house. As usual, Erin had shit under control. Which almost mitigated some of his guilt in taking on Kehoe and his puzzle.

The path beside the carriage house was perfectly sculpted, and Lucas counted the footsteps in the snow. While he was gone, Erin had taken the kids out for a little R&R, and judging by the freshness of the tracks, some of them were probably still fighting off boots and snow pants. He pushed up his cuff and checked his watch—still twenty minutes until dinner.

Before heading up to the kitchen, and with no real plan, he turned and climbed the wide steps to the apartment above the garage, standing there for a few moments, wondering why he wasn't going to the house. Did he want to wind down before he saw Erin? Put on a poker face? While he was cycling through these questions, Dingo opened the door.

He was in his usual outfit of shorts and a T-shirt, again sporting carbon blades instead of the traditional prosthetics that usually substituted for his original hardware out on the street. "Come on in." He pulled the door wide and stood back.

Lucas kicked off his Clarks and negotiated his way to the sofa facing the fireplace. Dropping into the cracked leather seat nailed home that he wasn't nearly as tired as he should be. His back should have felt like a lightning rod crackling with irregular current, and he wondered if the pain would set in later or if he had somehow escaped it.

"What are you smiling at?" Dingo said as he headed across the loft to the kitchen.

Lucas watched him until his line of sight caught the television in the corner dialed to the news. The footage was from that morning, a newscaster standing in front of the tram station delivering details with just the right mix of gravity, authority, and brevity. "I don't ache nearly as much as I should."

Dingo crouched down in front of the fridge, a hand touching the floor in one of those balance trade-offs that were necessary to compensate for missing muscle groups. "That's an odd complaint, mate." He came away with two gold-necked Modelos and closed the door with a gentle horse kick.

Lucas's sight migrated to the fireplace when Dingo placed a beer in his hand and dropped into the club chair. He raised his bottle in the salute favored by drinkers since time immemorial and took a big pop off the top. "So, have you decided to quit, or are you going back for more abuse?"

That was a good question. Maybe even a great one. "Both."

"You, my friend, are a slow learner."

Lucas raised his bottle and mimicked Dingo's accent with a, "That's the first time anyone has given me that particular label, *mate*." He took a sip and realized that he didn't want the beer. What was he doing here? He should be inside with Erin and the kids. He put the bottle down on the side table and let the fire hijack his attention. After a few moments of nothing but the sound of the hearth offset by the voice of the television, he let out a long, loud groan. "Thanks for shoveling," he said. He lifted his head to see Dingo staring at him. "What?"

"You're sitting there smiling at the fire. It's a little weird."

And with that, he knew why he had come. After the day he'd had, he should have been grumpy and more than a little tired. Yet here he was, not needing a beer and enjoying the sensation of work rinsing through his gray matter. Is this what had been missing all this time? Stress? "Shit," he said, drawing it out.

Dingo raised his bottle again. "Yeah, shit. You'd better not go in the house grinning like you just won a subscription to the jelly-of-the-month club."

After the Event, Lucas had spent a lot of time putting a candle to his head to cauterize all the psychic short circuits. One of the take-aways from therapy was the very real possibility that PTSD wasn't a retroactive stress from past experiences but the loss of stress in the day-to-day—and he somehow missed it. And the way he felt—energetic, calm, and maybe more than a little pleased—suggested that the head shrinker might be right after all. "I'd better get home," he said, rising from the sofa. "Sorry about the beer," Lucas said as he slipped his boots back on. The snow still hadn't completely melted off the leather.

Dingo stood with his hand on the hilt of a sword rising above the forest of ski poles and walking sticks in the umbrella stand. "Don't worry, I'll finish it."

Lucas nodded down at the big weapon. "What the hell is that?"

Dingo pulled it out, modeling it for Lucas with a classic attack pose. "Found it in the garbage. It's a Conan sword, man. Cool, huh?"

Lucas smiled. Then laughed. "You are nothing else if not consistent."

"You really know how to hurt a guy." There was something he wasn't saying.

"What is it?" Lucas asked.

Dingo looked as if he were deciding whether or not to share a secret. Then he put the big broadsword back in the umbrella stand and said, "I haven't seen you like this before."

"Like what?"

Dingo nodded at the Arts and Crafts mirror beside the door. "Peaceful."

Lucas glanced at the oak-framed image of himself, then turned back and stuck out his hand. "Thanks again for shoveling and checking up on Erin and the kids."

Dingo shook in the sideways grasp they had developed and, with a serious tone, said, "Just try to look a little tired when you go inside."

Lucas slipped back out into the cold.

Going down icy steps was always more difficult than going up, and he was glad he hadn't put the Modelo away. The one thing that messed with his balance was booze. Not that he couldn't function after a few drinks, but all the spills he had taken with the new leg had happened under the influence. And of course a little Johnnie Walker Black Label was responsible for the course he was now famous for. So he tended to lay off the sauce these days. He had never been a boozehound, not even back in his salad days, so it wasn't something he missed all that much. Every now and then, he and Erin had a beer on a summer evening. And a couple of times a year, they actually finished a bottle of wine. But other than those few anomalous blips, he lived in a dry county.

He unlocked the back door with the security key, and Lemmy came ripping down the hall, a windmill of too much enthusiasm and not enough self-control. Lucas leaned forward, putting his weight on his left leg, and absorbed the dog's impact. "Yeah, yeah, yeah, I missed you, too, dummy."

"Lemmy not a dummy," a tiny voice said.

Lucas lifted his vision, making sure to move his head so his eyes would stay in line, to see Alisha coming toward him. Erin and the rest of the kids were behind her—his personal army of cheerleaders, big smiles, and happy faces. Even Erin looked happy. "Hey, guys."

"Hey, yourself, Mr. Man," Erin said, and the kids rushed forward to hand out hugs. Even Maude gave Lucas a quick tentative squeeze, and the significance wasn't lost on him.

Erin stayed in the doorway to the mudroom, leaning against the doorjamb, her hip popping out. She was happy about something. "We were waiting for you to order in some supper. We thought Chinese would be fun."

"China-eeze! China-eeze!" Alisha hollered and gave the side of Lemmy's snout a big kiss. "Lemmy love China-eeze, too?"

"You betcha, kiddo," Lucas said. He finished kicking off his boots and hung his parka on an empty hook amid the children's candy-colored snowsuits, pants, and jackets. "What's the special occasion?" He hoped it was Maude's exam results. Anything better than an F was worth celebrating.

Erin's crossed arms dented her breasts and added another jolt of femininity to the equation her popped hip had started. She nodded at Maude. "Guess who aced her math exam today?"

"Congratulations!" he said.

Maude started an embarrassed smile and looked down.

Lucas wouldn't let her go into herself on this one. She needed encouragement. "That's the best news of the day. Chinese it is."

"It was only a B-plus." Maude kept her eyes on the floor.

"Are you kidding? Awesome," he said, pulling out a word he usually detested. "Do you know how many people would love to get a B-plus in math?"

She looked up. "You really think so?"

Lucas wanted to sweep her up in a bear hug, but he kept his distance. "Maude, I am so proud of you! This calls for extra wontons and that peanut sauce you love so much."

"And sesame beef?"

"And sesame beef."

She gave Lucas a hug, and as quickly as it began, it was over. She moved back beside Erin.

"What do you say, Alisha? Should we go order some Chinese food?"

Erin went to dig out the menu while the kids began to sing, "China-eeze! China-eeze!" in a dinnertime chant.

34

Rikers Island, New York
The Robert N. Davoren Complex

Across the bay, LaGuardia was unusually busy, even for a Friday night. The increase in traffic was no doubt to make up for lost time that the ice age was eating up, and the tower was using the break in the weather to launch as many flights as possible. It had been stop-and-go like this all winter, but it had been insane for the past hour with both passenger planes and private jets alike in constant rotation—landing, taking off, and taxiing around the snow-swept circuit board of runways and lanes. The deicing crews were in full swing, and even from this distance, the steam from their high-pressure guns was louder than the takeoffs and landings. The sky overhead was dappled with lights.

Mark Lupino, the tactical squad leader for the prison, turned away from the airport, bringing his attention back to the interior of the guard tower. There were a few cheap decorations in the booth, including a three-foot light-up plastic Santa that one of the guards had brought from home. The rest of the stuff was broken and sad. Then again, maybe it was just his mood. Lupino had enough shit to do without having to orchestrate drills to demonstrate the readiness of his men. And the apex piss-off in the whole deal was that this was nothing more than a bid to earn his warden a few gold stars from a pencil pusher whose ultimate goal was to be named the security chief of New York City. It was impossible to work for the Department of Corrections and not get roped into the political tug-of-war that was as intrinsic to the prison island as its despair, violence, and destroyed opportunity.

Thing was, if Lupino didn't want to round out nearly ten years of work with a dead-end clerical position in the bowels of the administrative offices, he had to keep his warden, Arnold Rosenberg, happy. Which, when he thought about it, was the basic operating system on Rikers; everyone had to answer to someone higher up the predator ladder. It started with the fags in the block who had their teeth knocked out and were forced to wear mops on their heads and ended with the wardens, who only answered to the chief of security for the island.

Here, the pecking order was carved in bone. And since Warden Rosenberg was smart enough not to bother showing up for mind-numbing crap like performance drills in the snow, it was left up to Lupino to put on his dancing shoes and boogie to whatever tune they needled up on the jukebox. So here he was, locked in the tower with a guy who had his hair arranged into one of those architectural marvels popularized during the last presidential election. Life was grand.

He checked his watch and wondered when the security stooge—whose name was Mickey Cardel—would give the nod. The unusually frigid temperatures were wreaking havoc with all the HVAC systems on the island, and the guard tower felt like a good place to store raw meat. Lupino took a sip of his coffee before the top skinned over with ice and he'd have to go at it with a screwdriver. At least it wasn't snowing.

And then the snow started back up.

"Mr. Cardel, would you like to get started?"

Cardel looked up, let out a sigh, and nodded a *might as well*. "I guess." His delivery was as bland as his appearance—resting firmly in the transition between boring and nonexistent.

"May I take that as a confirmation?" Lupino was used to asking bureaucrats to sign off on their orders; in the public sector, the one thing you could always count on was finger-pointing if things went wrong. And if there was one certainty, it was precisely that—things going wrong.

Cardel checked his watch, thumb-tapped some notes onto his iPad, and nodded with the even lack of enthusiasm that permeated his every action. "Sure."

Lupino wondered how the guy got laid, if at all.

He turned to the security camera recording in the corner and said, "Countdown to start"—he reached for the emergency alarm—"now," and he dropped his gloved palm onto the big red button. He turned back to the fish tank window facing the concertina wire encircling the yard.

The entire prison lit up in a Japanese karaoke bar cacophony of epileptic seizure–inducing strobes accompanied by sirens.

Lupino eyed the clock; the entire exercise would ultimately come down to a few seconds on either side of a pass/fail line. The drill was no secret; state regulations mandated that every security institution conduct a live drill once a month.

The inmates had shoveled the yard twice that day; if they wanted the privilege of outdoor time, they had to work for it. The last crew had been ushered inside an hour ago, and Lupino had spent the interim answering questions from Cardel's checklist. The center was host to the island's juvenile offenders—roughly a thousand kids who decided that bad decisions were better than difficult ones. The complex didn't have a yard proper, at least not like seven of the other eight prisons on the island, and tonight's drill was focused on the triangular patch of asphalt that bordered the main wall—a stone barrier that faced LaGuardia across the bay.

The drill wasn't an entirely empty gesture; every time his squad went through the motions, they got a little better. It wasn't that he disapproved of the exercise—it made sense on all kinds of levels—but he found it too simple a test; telegraphing that they would have a drill defeated the purpose. But the suits in the upper echelons of the DOC had decided that advance knowledge was the most effective way to ensure good grades.

The manual stated that his men had to be suited up and out on the field in less than five minutes even.

There were two things that made tonight's drill unusual. First, Cardel was present (which meant that things had to go well); and second, the tactical squad would be armed with the new departmental AR-15s. Contrary to popular belief, there are very few firearms on regular duty in prisons, and even during riots, they are rarely employed. The fallback tends to be shotguns with rubber bullets, and those come out only after tear gas, shields, and nightsticks have failed to be persuasive. The last thing any corrections officer wants is a loaded firearm falling into the hands of a rioting inmate. But the politicians were well into a might-makes-right approach to prison reform, and Lupino's budget had been massaged accordingly; hence the arrival of assault rifles to their violent little corner of the world.

A big jet, this one an Air Canada 737, came in low over the yard, vibrating the coffee in Lupino's hand, reminding him to take a slug. It was cold and bitter, and he spit it back into the mug. What he wanted was for this to be over so he could get back to the nuts and bolts of his job. After that, he'd head home, maybe stopping by his girlfriend's place for a glass of wine and a little dirty talk. Eva was no rocket scientist, but she was fun and shaved her good parts. And she smelled a lot better than this place.

The big orange second hand on the clock above the window swung past the four-minute mark, and Lupino dropped his eyes to the double security door that opened onto the yard. His guys had sixty seconds to open the door or they'd get a fail; two fails in a year and Lupino would have to sit down with a review board. More stooges. More questions. More fucking drills. More lost time, cold coffee, and boredom.

Eight seconds had ticked off when the block opened its mouth and the tactical unit burst through, splitting left and right, their big polycarbonate riot shields linked like Roman centurions. The men spilled into the yard in perfect formation, each man protecting the flank and back of the one in front, two rows of eighteen ballistic-nylon and Kevlar-clad gladiators ready to face destiny.

Lupino noted the time, looked over at Cardel, who was nodding in approval, and picked up the phone. A voice from the guard station answered, "Security desk."

"Kill the alarm." And before the phone was back in the cradle, the lighting and siren faded out in one final quack.

"Four minutes, twenty-seconds," Cardel said in even monotone.

Lupino hit the breakers on the switchboard under the window, and the yard went supernova with bright halogen floodlighting, turning the space into a bubble of daylight within the storm. The light bounced off the snow coming down, and if you forgot you were in a prison, the view was almost relaxing. Lupino snapped the top button of his DOC parka and stepped out onto the walk.

The cold hit him like a small heart attack, and his eyes watered. He rubbed his sockets with gloved fists and stepped to the edge of the catwalk, nodding down at Don Sweeny, leader of the tactical squad. Sweeny's men stood behind him, still in formation, their shields locked in place, rifle muzzles covering imaginary rioters. Lupino didn't know another human being he trusted more in the joint than Sweeny; he was small, but he made up for it with a complete lack of fear. More than a few inmates had misinterpreted his size as weakness and ended up in the infirmary; a few who wouldn't take no for an answer ended up in the subway-tiled morgue in the basement. Lupino had been around guys like him for years. Back when he had been with the ATF, traipsing across the country in a never-ending war against homegrown zealots, guys like Sweeny had been the mainstay. Eight years of a backward-thinking government had stifled some of their power, and they were put under the heading of old-school, their tactics frowned upon. But once the Democrats had been forced out along with their politically correct tunnel vision, things had begun to swing back, and shit was once again getting done.

"Four twenty!" Lupino yelled down and gave Sweeny a thumbs-up.

Sweeny raised his hand in the stand-down signal. The forest of rifles behind him dropped, and he heard the mechanical clatter of safeties clicking on.

And that was when the dome of Mark Lupino's head detonated.

With his brain removed from the equation, his body slumped forward, over the rail, and slammed into the icy yard with a big splat. Whatever gray matter was still clinging to the inside of his skull puked out into the snow in one big steaming glop.

Then the sound came in, a high-pitched *crack!* like a jet engine blowing its rivets.

Inside the tower, Cardel watched Sweeny's men rush forward. He snatched up the phone and barked, "Officer down in the yard! Accidental weapons discharge. We need a stretcher and a doctor! Now!"

35

The Upper East Side

When the kids finished chewing, singing, and talking their way through twenty-one folded cardboard takeout boxes and six Styrofoam soup containers, they chipped in with the cleaning. The younger ones collected the trash, and the older ones divided up the recycling before stuffing plates and milk glasses into the dishwasher. Once the subway-tiled galley was spotless, Maude and Damien got into a light saber fight with the chopsticks, and on any other night this would have been all Lucas needed. But he had too many distractions. He would usually have been planning his workload for the university; his TAs had to give the final papers an initial reading, and that would float him three days. He'd give it one full day and the year would be done. He didn't anticipate many problems; the entire semester had passed without a single indication that any of his students were either extremely dumb or extremely smart, and the middle-of-the-road types very rarely surprised him. And his grad students were all of the self-sufficient variety, which was some kind of a miracle. No, the problem that was taking up a lot of his RAM was Kehoe.

What Lucas couldn't understand was how Kehoe was letting

politics shape the investigation. It was no secret that the current government wanted the world to be like they imagined, not as it actually was. But pushing this terrorist narrative simply because it fit their worldview was setting them up to look like fools. Not to mention wasting resources. And possibly lives.

Which brought him back to the man with the rifle. And his message; you don't begin hunting human beings with the precision of an Apple product launch without having a core message. Kehoe was right about that. But no matter how individual the shooter thought himself to be, in the end, it would be a variant of the same boring formula: refusal to accept that there is no such thing as fair.

He was brought back from the ether when Damien stabbed Maude in the stomach, complete with a million-watt sound effect. Damien danced around, a cosmic gladiator relishing the coup de grâce. But while he stood there, arms up and unable to defend himself, Maude lashed out with one of her chopsticks, dealing a final death blow to the heart. Damien's expression turned from victory to shock, and he dropped to the floor in the throes of mock death, coughing, groaning, and trying not to laugh.

Lucas wanted to be here with the kids, in the now, not frozen between fear and what-next? Yet here he was watching the fate of the universe get decided—which, no matter how you looked at it, had to be a big deal—and thinking about the shooter.

"Okay, okay." Lucas stood up, and Alisha froze, absorbed in Lucas's prosthetic hand. "Before we all die of chopstick poisoning—"

"They're not chopsticks! They're light sabers!" Damien hollered from his deathbed.

"Chopsticks, light sabers, it doesn't matter. You're dead, and Maude feels bad about it." Maude tended to get overemotional about any kind of wrong, even pretend ones. The guilt over murder—or was it that sneaky parry?—was setting in on her face. "I've been gone all day, and I could use a little walk. Anyone want to go for a walk?" At that, the dog began to dance in circles. "Except Lemmy, that is?"

Five hands shot into the air.

"A walk it is."

Lucas's booted foot had just hit the snow-covered sidewalk when the street went electric in red-and-white flashing lights.

The dog was growling, and Lucas turned to the kids. "Come here, guys."

Alisha turned around, put her hands on her knees, and yelled, "I ain't no *guys*!"

The stereo of lights went quadrophonic, and the falling snow pulsed with visual feedback as a fleet of black SUVs pulled down the block, a caravan of police cruisers behind them.

Vehicles skidded to a halt. Doors opened. Men in fur-rimmed parkas emptied out into the storm.

Whitaker stepped out of the static and said, "Hello, everyone," in way of a greeting. She smiled at the kids, but you didn't have to be James Lipton to see the stink in her performance. "Dr. Page, you and I have some work to do."

Lucas turned back to the house, and Erin's unhappy shadow filled the doorway. She flashed in the red-and-white Lite-Brite display, and it did little to soften her features.

Lucas turned and ushered the kids up the steps. "Sorry, guys. This will have to wait." He looked down at the dog, then turned to one of the overcoated clones who had spilled from one of the SUVs. "Since I am the only one who can do what I do, you get to walk the dog. Don't forget to pick up his poop. Here's a bag," he said, and he handed off Lemmy's leash and a Saks shoe bag from his pocket. The agent looked like he was about to complain when Lucas hit him with, "You say one word and you people can simply fuck right off."

The agent took the leash and the bag.

"And rub his feet if they get cold," he called after him.

Then he turned to Erin, who had corralled the kids behind her in the doorway, and mouthed the words *I'm sorry*.

Erin nodded like she didn't believe him and slammed the door loud enough that Whitaker looked back.

When Lucas got in the Navigator, Whitaker asked, "How did that go?"

"Pretty good; you should see her when she's pissed."

Whitaker smiled and pulled out.

After a few minutes of cutting through the maze of snow-filled streets, she cracked the silence with, "I have a kid. A boy. Stan, the Little Man." Her voice carried a cadence he hadn't heard in it before.

Lucas didn't really care. As far as he was concerned, Whitaker was part of the problem. She had ruined the vibe at home twice in one night, and he wasn't in a forgiving mood. He didn't say anything even though she probably expected him to.

"He stays with his father. Mostly. I get my two weeks with him in the summer. And every second Christmas. I get along with my ex. It's not like I sneak into his apartment and hold a gun to his skull while he's sleeping." She glanced over and smiled. "At least not anymore."

She had a kid. Great. Huge accomplishment. She had been married. So were a lot of people. He could have asked how old the boy was or about his favorite comic. He could even have asked what caliber pistol she pressed to her ex's head on those special evenings. But he wasn't interested. "Where are we going?"

The question killed Whitaker's big personal moment.

"A corrections officer was shot on Rikers."

"A guard?"

"A corrections officer."

"Do prison guards have social justice warriors on their side now? Like the guy at the supermarket tripping over himself to make sure the aisles are clear for me when I walk in wearing shorts after the gym? How about people mind their own fucking business."

Whitaker nodded. "You're right. Fuck 'em. All of 'em." She paused. "Just who am I cursing at, specifically?"

With that, Lucas smiled, if only a little. "I guess I am a little prickly."

"Gore Vidal was a little prickly. You, my friend, are mean. There's a distinct difference."

The reference was an odd one coming from an FBI agent. The bureau was a preppy gun culture to its core, but its employees were all college graduates; Lucas wondered what Whitaker's major had been. Five minutes earlier, he would have gone for ass-kicking, but after the Gore Vidal comment, he was leaning toward a liberal arts major.

"I have a BA in political science and an MA in anthropology," Whitaker said, once again answering the question before it was asked.

"That's a pain in the ass," Lucas offered flatly. "And you should stop it."

"You're not the first person to say that."

"I'd like to be the last."

"You're not much fun at parties, are you?"

"I don't go to parties."

"If you were nicer, maybe you'd get invited to some."

Lucas leaned back in the big expanse of the leather seat, and the side-view mirror lit up with the fleet of flashing lights behind them. He wondered if Erin would get any sleep. And if she did, would she be a little less angry with him tomorrow?

But she had to know he didn't really have a choice in doing this. It was how he was wired, and there was no undoing it. And like any immutable personality trait, it could be traced back to his origin.

He had started life out with as few advantages as can be found in the wealthiest country in the world. He never knew his mother, and what he did know he got from the adoption files years later, well after he had grown into a man, by which point she was dead.

His mother had been an upstate farm girl who had come to the big city to find her future. She had probably started out with typical ambitions involving a job, a nice apartment, a husband, and a few other basic hopes. But whatever had fueled her dreams of a life in the city eventually gave way to the reality of bad decisions, and she gave Lucas up for adoption when he was eight months old.

He started out with statistically bad luck in not finding a family while still a baby, and the lost window of opportunity destined him to years of playing musical chairs at a series of foster homes. He was a bright boy, but the people he passed his time with were not equipped to look for attributes above the usual; like everyone else, they were just trying to get by. But a small gift from a social worker changed the course of his life.

It was a month before his fifth birthday, and Lucas was at his eighth foster home. The Pottses were middle-of-the-road working-class people from Nyack who believed a little in God and a lot in hard work; John Potts was a barber and his wife, Rose, was a full-time mom who did laundry for other people. They were uncomplicated, kind, and served watermelon every day in the summer. They grew them out back and enjoyed watching the kids go at them with that particular relish that disappears with age.

Lucas shoehorned into the household, by now adept at keeping his head down, eyes averted, and mouth shut. He was old enough to know that the routine wouldn't win him any friends, but, more important, it was less likely to earn him slaps, punches, or worse.

By the time of the first-month inspection, Lucas had already found a rhythm in the house. It wasn't a particularly exciting place, but the Pottses were good people who didn't make him feel unimportant. They had a lot of magazines with all kinds of hairs—from short and red to long and gray—hidden in the pages; an occupational hazard for a barber who brought old magazines home from work. Lucas flipped through them, absorbing the photos and wondering how the text worked.

This particular visit was different from the previous ones in that the lady, a handsome black woman named Miss Odia Clark, asked *him* questions. They spent time together on the porch of the little postwar bungalow. It was a cool fall morning, and the garbage can by the curb was filled with watermelon rinds and some broken wooden seats from the swing set out back that Mr. Potts had replaced with new ones, painted a glossy red.

Miss Clark asked him if he was hungry or if he had any bruises or if he had any chores, and he gave her carefully tailored answers, at least as carefully tailored as a five-year-old is capable of. She recorded his responses in her notebook, and Lucas realized that she was creating text by hand—just like in the magazines. He was fascinated by her writing—it was an activity he had never seen before in any detail.

Lucas asked her questions about the letters, so she gave him a very quick lesson that was basically no more than a rundown of the ABCs followed by the numbers, using her fingers to explain one through ten. He asked about addition and subtraction, two concepts he had already labeled as *bigging* and *littling* in his limited lexicon. It was not a long lesson, but those few precious moments that Miss Clark took from her too-busy day were the most important of young Lucas's life. When she was done, he asked to borrow her pen and proceeded to write out a math problem that he had been lacking the scientific vocabulary to complete. When he was done, he asked if he could have the page, and Miss Clark tore it out for him. But not before looking at it. Then she gave him a notebook of his own, along with the first compliment of his life. She also gave him a blue Bic.

Miss Clark had a talk with Mr. and Mrs. Potts at the kitchen table while Lucas sat in the living room, working in his new notebook. He didn't think he was in trouble, but he wasn't certain. If life had taught him only one lesson so far, it was that people did not all react the same way. There was always a chance that he was in trouble, and he hoped they weren't hitters.

After Miss Clark left, Mr. and Mrs. Potts stood over him in the living room. Mr. Potts had his hands on his hips and slowly shook his head as if he had just won a set of Greek encyclopedias. "So, what you wanna learn?" Mr. Potts innocently asked, stretching his abilities on teaching to the breaking point.

Lucas's focus shifted from Mr. Potts to his wife, then back. Then he lifted his arm and pointed out the window at the only constant he knew: the sky.

That night, as Lucas was getting ready for bed with the other children, Mr. Potts came to get him. He packed a sweater from Lucas's little bag (he had accumulated a handful of personal items at this point, all hand-me-downs). Then Mr. Potts ushered the boy out to the car and drove him off into the night. As he had done so many times before, Lucas waved bye-bye to another house.

Mr. Potts drove Lucas far out of town in the big Country Squire station wagon. He helped him out of the backseat, and Lucas stood there in the dark, worried, wondering what was happening as Mr. Potts set up the two lawn chairs. Lucas had never been out in a field at night before, and it wasn't until he became an adult that he understood how hard Mr. Potts had tried to help. He wasn't an academic, and he most certainly wasn't an astronomer, but he opened two lawn chairs, bundled Lucas up in his sweater, wrapped him in Mrs. Potts's old quilt, and handed the boy a pair of binoculars and a tattered astrology—not astronomy—chart torn from an old *National Geographic* magazine. (Lucas still had that chart, taken from the August 1970 issue—it was titled *A Map of the Heavens*, and it was framed and hung over his desk in his office at home.) "So you can see them stars," was how he put it, and he gave Lucas a quick rundown on how to adjust the focus on the cheap binoculars.

Mr. Potts sat down beside him, handing the boy a bag of peanuts and a little metal thermos filled with hot chocolate. "Let me know if you need anything," he said, and he plugged the tiny transistor earpiece into his head, piping in a ball game from Dodger Stadium.

Lucas sighted through the binoculars and played with the knob until the sky overhead came into focus, a silent symphony of lights. He had never used optics before, and the newfound power amazed, delighted, and humbled him.

He sifted through the barrage of information, methodically mapping the sky in a manner he would never understand. He memorized the patterns, embedding constellations into a mental library where one image connected to—and was relative to—all others.

When Lucas finally put the binoculars down, his fingers had frozen up, his nose was red and cold, and Mr. Potts was dead asleep beside him, head back, snoring. The sun would soon be up.

On the drive back, he fell asleep, and when they got home, Mr. Potts carried the boy inside, then showered, changed his clothes, and went off to work.

And that was where the notebooks began, a habit that he would carry with him the rest of his life.

When Miss Clark came to visit the following week, she asked Lucas if she could borrow his notebook. As a bribe, she offered him two empty new ones—and they were thick!

Miss Clark showed his star notebook to her brother-in-law, a science teacher at the Rufus T. Firefly High School on Staten Island. He refused to believe that anyone younger than a graduate student would be able to put such a journal together. He made a copy and sent it to a friend who taught physics at Columbia. More incredulity. More questions. More curiosity.

Then one night just after Halloween, a car pulled up in front of the home. It was a long silver automobile with big bug-eye lights driven by a man in a uniform. The car was almost as long as the front yard, and when the vehicle stopped, a ripple of excitement went through the children. As in any foster home, most of the kids had been in the system long enough that they all ran to comb their hair and do their best to look like well-behaved little people. Lucas stood at the window and watched the driver get out and open the back door. Lucas expected a king to step out. But a small man who looked stranger than anyone he had ever seen emerged from the interior.

Mr. Potts seemed to be expecting him, and they sat in the living room for half an hour while the children played outside (and Lucas worked in one of his notebooks). The driver stayed with the car, smoking cigarettes and polishing the chrome with a quiet patience.

After a while, the Pottses and the man came outside to watch the children. Lucas could sense their focus directed at him. The man was small and wore a well-tailored suit in dark purple. But the thing that struck little Lucas as his most idiosyncratic feature was his hair—it was wild and bushy, growing into a big bushy beard that covered most of his face and made him look like a Muppet—the one who played the drums.

Since Lucas wasn't sure as to how he should behave, he sat quietly in the shade of the tree, working out one of the "sky problems," as Mr. Potts called them. To Lucas, these problems were nothing more than maps that moved, and he was happy that he finally had a way to record them. He wondered if the social worker would bring his other notebook back—she had promised to return it. But he knew that people didn't always keep their promises. Not even adults.

Mr. Potts brought the man over to the shade of the big tree and introduced him as Mr. Teach. He seemed nice and asked Lucas some questions. They spoke for a few moments, then he said good-bye and that he hoped to see Lucas again sometime.

A few days later, when the children had forgotten about the visit, Mr. Teach returned in the big silver car. Before he was even out of the vehicle, Mr. Potts called Lucas over and, with tears in his eyes, gave the boy his binoculars as a present. Mrs. Potts hugged him, kissed him, and bundled him into his coat before bringing his little suitcase to the door. And Mr. Teach took him away. To meet an old lady who lived on top of a hotel.

36

The Upper East Side

The Grand Cherokee had been parked on the street for an hour now, and the heat radiating through the metal skin melted the snow coming down into an uneven camouflage. The vehicle was lopsided, one of the back wheels jacked up on a block of ice left by a plow. Two men sat inside, sipping coffee and dialed into the silent zone out of habit. The snow on the windshield melted, giving the occupants a fragmented water-dappled view of the brownstone across the street. But they didn't use the wipers.

Someone in the house began snapping the lights off, one room at a time; no doubt little ones being put to bed. First the main floor, then the second, and finally the third—life support cycling down in increments.

Detective Michael Atchison finished the last of the coffee and slipped his cup into the holder before cracking his knuckles in a series of moves that looked like he was changing fingers. He finished the exercise with a stretch that had all his muscles twanging in opposite directions.

Atchison's partner, Detective Alex Roberts, sat in the passenger's seat, repeating a similar set of adjustments with the extra moves of cracking his neck and jaw. Then he took a deep breath and nodded.

Atchison fired up the engine and pulled out into the street with a little more gas than he wanted, revving the engine with that particular growl native to winter. No one noticed them pull into the alley behind Lucas's house.

37

Rikers Island

The long arm of the bureau had reached the island well before Lucas and Whitaker arrived in the black multi-SUV centipede. The prison was under double lockdown; one for inmates, enforced by employees; one for employees, enforced by the bureau. Every light in the complex was on, and the falling snow felt like a witch's curse focused on the island.

The usual sign-in process was forgone in lieu of expediency: the SUVs were waved through the big double-gated sally port and directed to the loading bay. The on-site coordinator was in the midst of issuing passes. There were approximately thirty bureau people already there.

Lucas stepped out into the concrete hangar, and the double doors ratcheted down, sealing the space with an ear-pressurizing clang. He slipped his sunglasses on and took a deep breath, setting his internal controls to work mode.

Whitaker came around, and one of the field agents walked over from the dispatch desk already set up. "Whitaker, Dr. Page, this corrections officer will show you to the crime scene," he said, forgoing any form of a greeting and ushering them past the briefing point after handing them security passes.

A corrections officer named Dominguez who wore sergeant's stripes speed-walked beside them, giving a quick procedural drill. "Please keep your passes on you at all times. We've got all corridors leading to the yard locked down, but don't move around by yourself. If you need to move between here and there—to get your equipment, make phone calls, that sort of thing—have one of the corrections officers with you. Do not put anything down that you might miss if it were to disappear. You shouldn't see any inmates who aren't in their cells, but if you do, do not give them anything. Since you're law enforcement, I'll forgo the usual emphasis that I mean *anything*." Dominguez then went silent.

The interior resembled a Cold War Iron Curtain airport, circa 1961, but in need of more repairs. Accelerated decay seemed to be built into the genetics of the prison, and it was impossible to miss the architectural progeria that rusted metal, ate concrete, and chipped paint much faster than in the outside world. The general taste of defeat was hard to miss, even with the holiday ornaments Scotch-taped up here and there. There was a red-and-green foil banner above the entrance to one of the wings that read *Mer y Ch is mas*. The building was the saddest place Lucas could remember, save one.

Lucas and Whitaker followed Dominguez into the heart of the prison, navigating its arteries through sally ports, riveted steel doors, and a dozen barred portals that opened up onto yet more hallway bathed in harsh whites generated by a mile of conduit-connected overhead fluorescent fixtures. Dominguez explained that they were using the service, maintenance, and transport passages.

Whitaker walked in step beside him, and he realized that his initial judgment on her still held. Besides looking like she spiked her kombucha with cartridges, she was professional and generally not very nosy—both top-tenners.

After a few moments of silence, Dominguez said, "Afghanistan?"

"No."

"Iraq?"

Lucas wanted to ignore him but decided he would be of the persistent variety, so he simply gave him another curt, "No."

"Gonna tell me?"

"No."

After a few more moments of silence, Dominguez changed his approach. "What's the *Doctor* stand for?" he asked. "You some kinda coroner? 'Cause we got a doctor here."

"Astrophysicist."

"A scientist?"

"Apparently, yes."

"Never heard of you."

"I can't see my work being relevant in prison guard circles."

"I'm not a prison guard, I'm a *corrections officer.*"

"People who install air conditioners are air conditioner installers, not refrigeration engineers; people who work at the checkout are cashiers, not sales associates. There's nothing wrong with language being succinct. Guarding prisoners makes you a prison guard."

"What would you do if I called you *science guy*?"

"You're a prison guard; I'd expect it from you." Which effectively ended conversation.

Whitaker eased up beside Lucas and whispered, "Remember what I said about being invited to parties? Well, that wasn't what I meant about being nicer."

A hundred paces later, Grover Graves came into view, waiting for them on the other side of a sally port, hands on hips, an overcompensating intensity in his posture.

Graves nodded a hello as they buzzed through. "Dr. Page, Agent Whitaker." He looked down at his watch. "You made good time." Then he nodded at some unknown point through the walls up ahead, no doubt in the direction of the dead. "The tactical squad captain was killed during a drill. They thought it was an accidental discharge by one of their men, but when they got him inside, the doctor realized that the victim was shot from behind, meaning from outside the prison. They have the body downstairs for now, but—" He checked the big Seiko on his wrist. "It will be heading off to the morgue in a few minutes. You need to see it?"

Lucas shook his head; his specialty was geometry, not dead people. "Where was he shot?" he asked, half expecting Graves to say, *In the head.*

"Catwalk outside. The scene was scrubbed by the storm before we got here. The forensics team wasn't able to grab blood spatter from the snow; it's a mess out there, so we don't really know where *exactly* the victim was standing when he died."

"What can you tell me in the way of details?"

"Six-foot-one man in a one-and-a-quarter-inch heel standing on a walkway that is twenty-five feet six inches above grade; fifty-seven feet three inches above sea level. Large-caliber round hit him at the base of the skull. His head is too much of a mess to figure out specifics, at least until we get him to the medical examiner, but even then, I don't think we'll get much." He held out the tablet, showing Lucas an image of what used to be a man's head but now looked like a sea creature that had depressurized on its ascent from the ocean floor.

Lucas turned away. "Anyone find the round?"

"We're working on that."

Three minutes later, Lucas stepped out of the guard tower onto the catwalk where Lupino had spent his last few moments as a living, breathing human being. The snow was coming down in full IMAX 3-D with the wind off the bay adding a little extra misery to the equation. Across the water, LaGuardia was an animated scale diorama. Planes, baggage carriers, deicers, snowplows, passenger buses, runway maintenance vehicles, and all manner of transport motored about in an improvised dance focused on the simple goal of keeping people moving.

The forensics team combed the yard below, searching for the round with the slow, deliberate actions of grazing farm animals. Everything from metal detectors to density scanners were being utilized, and the sections that had already been searched were being shoveled clear, the snow going into plastic bins that they would go through later if they didn't find the round on the first sweep.

The bureau's trajectory tech was set up on the walkway, the same guy from the night before on Park. Like everyone else Kehoe kept around, he knew what he was doing. Only problem was, you couldn't string a sniper shot like you could a handgun shot. A crime-scene mannequin was set up where Lupino had likely stood when his clock had stopped, and Kehoe's man was calmly scrolling through the settings for the electro-optical range finder set up on a tripod beside the dummy. Snow frosted the mannequin. He nodded a hello that wasn't returned.

The first two victims had kept moving after they died, one in a rolling automobile, the other in the cable car. But Lupino had flopped over the railing, basically dropping where he had stood, which should have provided all the data they needed to reverse engineer the bullet's trajectory. Except they had moved the body, and the snow coming down had wiped out Lupino's footprints, so figuring out exactly where he had been standing was impossible. And the snow had mixed with the blood spatter, absorbing it and turning it into a pink slush that told them nothing but Lupino's blood type.

The catwalk was at the outer perimeter of the complex but inside the final span of concertina wire. Beyond the razor fence, there was about two hundred yards of open terrain that ran to the rocky shoreline, the only feature interrupting the bare ribbon of land being a single plowed road near the water. There was nowhere to hide out there, not unless the shooter had lain buried in the snow, which made no kind of practical sense at all.

Lucas scanned the far shoreline and the airport across the water, then pulled the Leupold scope from his pocket for a closer look. The circular field of view lit up in harsh blue light filled with the visual noise the falling snow added. The bright airport was overexposed compared to the dark shoreline, and Lucas saw nothing but an empty ribbon of land that could hide a thousand different dangers.

He panned along the bank and was about to swing back when something below the bright canvas of the airport caught his eye. A pair of electric generators were removed from the hustle of the runways and the bustle of the maintenance roads, offset from the airport proper near a maintenance dock at the northwest corner of a runway that pointed straight at Rikers. The generators were each roughly the size of a school bus. And the narrow alley between them offered protection from the wind.

"Put that away," Lucas said to Kehoe's man. "He fired from between those two generators."

38

The Upper East Side

The place had been dark for an hour now, which meant they should all be asleep. There was no guarantee, of course, but most people were so run-down from chasing the ever-receding American dream that their brains shorted out the minute they hit the Posturepedic. And if the stress was of the insomniac variety, there were all kinds of remedies, running the gamut from Seconal to Jack Daniel's to OG Kush to whatever the fuck they used to pump into Michael Jackson's veins.

Detective Atchison checked his watch. "It's been an hour."

Roberts grunted in what could have meant *yes, no,* or *maybe* and reached into the duffel on the floor in the backseat, lifting out a Colt M4 Commando. He passed the small carbine over the transmission hump to Atchison and took a second one out for himself.

Both men checked their weapons, making sure the magazines were properly seated before chambering rounds.

Atchison said, "Remember—*everyone.*" Then he climbed out of the Jeep.

39

LaGuardia Airport
Beside Runway 13-31

Lucas had to squint when he turned back to the airport over his shoulder. The lights were beyond blinding, and he wondered if he were actually feeling their heat from this distance. Then a gust of wind off the bay kissed his neck, and he realized that it was just hopeful projection.

He turned back to the shoreline below, a snow-swept filigree of land that was sloshed over with ice that formed from water the wind threw against the break wall. Spending more than a few minutes out here was an exercise in masochism. Very few people could do it.

Whitaker stood at his side, dialed into general Girl Friday mode, while Graves's men went over the terrain with the patience of diamond hunters.

The shot had definitely come from the space between the two massive generators. The spectrometers had picked up gunpowder residue on the snow, but it was minimal—in this weather, they had been lucky to find any trace evidence at all.

Even a cursory glance at Lupino's file gave Lucas everything he needed to make the judgment call; same general victimology. Lupino had been with the ATF for sixteen years before coming to the DOC a decade back. The file was by no means complete—that was still a few hours off as the bureau ran down all his postings—but it painted enough of a picture to see that he was the same basic phenotype as Hartke and Kavanagh.

The wind walloped Lucas in the face with another blast of shivers, and his shoulders instinctively tightened. He realized that he was suddenly very hungry, Chinese food a few hours ago notwithstanding. Which led him to the next realization that his wife and kids were at home, dreaming Kodachrome dreams, while he stood out here on the LaGuardia peninsula freezing his parts off and thinking of food.

Whitaker reached into her pocket and pulled out an apple. She held it up.

He was about to ask her how she knew he was hungry, but he just let it go. "Thanks," he said and took it from her gloved hand.

They didn't need him, not with three kills under this guy's belt. They'd find him; there was no way they wouldn't. It was what the bureau did. Period. Even if the people running the country wanted different results, fantasy would crumble when put up against reality.

Just then, Graves's body language changed, and he reached into his pocket, pulling out his phone. He took off his glove, swiped his thumb across the screen, and cupped the phone to his ear, trying to block out the screech of the wind and jet engines in the background. He turned his back to the bay, to the wind tearing in. He yelled into his phone, and the call lasted no more than forty seconds. When he was done, he came over to Lucas and Whitaker.

"They found the round, buried in a wall about eighty feet from where Lupino was standing when he got hit." He pointed out over the water at the prison island across the East River. "Same caliber."

Lucas looked down at the apple in his hand, at the sticker from the orchard in California, and everything suddenly fell into place.

"So now you know."

"Know what?"

"That his hate-on is specific, not general. Hartke, Kavanagh, and now Lupino were chosen for a reason. They're not blind targets."

"How do you know that?"

Lucas nodded at a jet taxiing down the runway. "Because he would have made a much bigger splash sighting down a 737 and taking out the pilot." He pulled out his badge and held it out. "You don't need me anymore."

"What the fuck is that?" Graves said.

"Most people would be able to identify a badge."

Graves looked at him. "And most people wouldn't be a sarcastic prick when it's unnecessary."

"You're right. But I'm still leaving."

He decided that he needed to clarify things so that there would be no misunderstanding. "You don't need me on this. Not anymore. I have had enough, and I quit."

"Quit?"

"Did I stutter?"

"You can't quit. Kehoe will—"

"Kehoe will understand." Lucas stared Graves down. "And let's not pretend that you and I will miss one another. Just take this shit from me before I pitch it in the river."

Graves's mouth pursed up, and he took an audible breath. "You can drop it by the office," he said and stepped back in a combined effort to save face and be dismissive.

Lucas didn't bother arguing; he simply dropped the shield and walked away.

When Whitaker followed, Graves called out, "And where are you going?" at her.

She jabbed a finger at Lucas as she ran after him. "I'm his ride home."

Graves said something, but it was swallowed by the Led Zeppelin rumble of a jet taxiing by.

40

The Upper East Side

Dingo woke up on the tufted leather chesterfield. It was late; the three iMacs were dark, which meant he had been out for at least two hours, the automatic sleep time for the machines. How had that happened? His iPod was still on, N.W.A's "Fuck tha Police" playing not nearly loud enough.

With the deep freeze and storm, he had canceled his classes at the dojo, using the extra time to wade the drifts out in the science fiction landscape, taking photos. Dingo augmented his income by selling his work on online stock photo services. The market forced him to use his eye in a different way, an exercise that was slowly beginning to undo all the years spent in combat zones, framing war's insane art.

So he had come home, taken a hot bath to thaw out, and started postproduction. A few hours of staring at the screen required a beer, and the beer turned into supper, and after he ate, he needed a nap. And now it was . . . he checked the clock on the microwave across the little apartment above the garage: 2:11 a.m.

In the old days, the love seat would have been too short to sleep on, but since the amputations, he took up a little less space. Not much in the way of an upgrade, but for this particular application, he was willing to take it.

He reached down and picked his legs up off the carpet. He snapped the carbon blades home and yawned, tasting his breath of beer and Top Ramen. Dingo usually treated his body well—his view was that it was the only one he had—but once in a while he allowed himself a little booze and comfort carbs. Maybe a joint and bag of M&M's. But most of the time, he walked the walk.

He got up and stretched and for a brief second teetered on the edge of his balance—which happened sometimes after sleeping, as if his muscle memory reset and needed tweaking. What to do, what to do? Go back to work? Or go to bed? He yawned again, and the action drove home that he was now awake. And that he needed to brush his teeth. Or get another beer. After thinking through the options, he decided on another Modelo and headed for the fridge.

It was dark out, but the snow that blanketed the city reflected the ambient light cast by the lamps in the alley, adding a softness to the scene. The world was somehow both bright and serene, the snow drifting lazily toward the ground ramping up the Christmas card effect, and though he had been out in it all day, the sight was still mesmerizing. Maybe grabbing his Leica and heading out into the storm was the thing to do. He loved the city, or at least the neighborhood, at night, and the abandoned streets might make for a good palette.

He had looked out the window thousands of times, and his eye always framed the scene, an instinctive habit that work had hammered into his way of viewing the world. The back fence headed off at an angle, joining the neighbor's garage twenty-three feet away, giving the image a nice strong line to build around. The alley was crisscrossed with drifts and ruts that gave the scene texture. And the footprints leading from the Jeep Grand Cherokee across the alley to the gate were—

He ran to the back door, keeping to the carpet so his blades wouldn't clack on the hardwood, and peered into the backyard.

Two figures stood just under the balcony, but he couldn't make out any detail in the shadows.

What the fuck were they doing here? Were they Lucas's new friends? Were they with the FBI? Did Lucas know they were here? Were they supposed to be here? Where was Lucas?

He was trying to decide what to do when they stepped from the shadows, dressed in the typical paramilitary garb that American outdoorsmen seemed to find stylish. But it wasn't their clothing that made Dingo's mind up for him; it was the assault rifles they carried.

He wanted to call Erin—to warn her. But she might turn on a light and these two would up their timetable. As things were now, they were moving slowly.

And if he called Lucas, what good would that do?

Dingo dialed 911 without losing sight of them. They moved around the balcony and up the steps to the back door.

The phone rang three times before the monotone voice of the police dispatcher answered. "Nine-one-one, what's your emergency?"

"There are two men armed with semiautomatic weapons breaking into my neighbor's house."

"What is your address, please?"

Dingo gave her the address, repeating it.

"With the weather conditions, it may take a while for—"

"Tell them not to shoot the guy with the prosthetic legs—that's me." The adrenaline had bellowed into a furnace in his stomach, and he felt his core heating up. Erin was alone with the kids.

"Sir, I need you to stay on the line—"

The man working on the door got it open.

And Dingo hung up.

He pulled his hair back behind his ears and slipped on his Yankees cap. He locked the brim on backward, took a breath, whispered, "Fuck the police," and pulled the massive Conan sword from the umbrella stand.

He then stepped into the storm.

41

The lights were off, and the snow coming down beyond the big bay window looked like volcanic ash. Erin couldn't sleep. And she knew she wouldn't be able to until Lucas came home—*if* he came home. And that pissed her off because if she didn't get any sleep, the kids would suffer. All because the people Lucas used to work for weren't happy with the pound of flesh they had taken—they wanted all of it.

She hadn't been feeling okay since Kehoe and his bodyguards—or whatever the gorillas in the matching suits were called—had shown up. And now Lucas was back out there, surrounded by bad people who had worse ideas all because they couldn't develop the technology to replicate the very unusual thinking he was capable of. Which made her both proud and angry at the same time.

And she was self-aware enough to realize that she was feeling short-changed by recent events. She had wiped her slate at the hospital, handing off all her surgeries for the next two months, so that she could be here for Alisha. She would never ask Lucas for that kind of commitment—not that he wouldn't have agreed, but because he needed to work; it was the only thing that calmed the monsters in his skull—but she expected him to keep his word about the holidays. Was that really too much to ask?

Erin rolled onto her back, then up onto her elbows. Maybe tea would help her sleep.

She quietly opened the bedroom door and stepped out into the hallway, avoiding the noisy third board from the sill; if the kids heard her, they'd start with the *I'm thirsty*s and the *I've gotta pee*s, and a five-minute foray to the kitchen would end up taking an hour.

The hallway glowed with a pink light thrown off the little elephant night-light at the top of the stairs. She took a step and then stopped. Something was wrong. She could feel it.

No. Not feel it.

She could hear it.

Someone was downstairs.

42

The Robert F. Kennedy Bridge

Whitaker kept the chatter dialed to monastic levels as she drove. Lucas couldn't see anything beyond the hood—the world outside looked like a television dialed to static, and he wondered if she actually saw the road or if she navigated using some vestigial perception that he lacked. Whatever it was, they were firmly planted in the passing lane of Grand Central Parkway, and Manhattan ahead was completely painted over by the snow coming down. She passed what few drivers were brave enough (or was that stupid enough?) to be out, and whenever she came up behind someone sitting in the passing lane, she hit the asshole lights—as she called them—and they moved over.

Lucas was tired. And grumpy. And pissed that he had let Kehoe bait him into coming back. What the fuck had he been thinking? But if he really thought about it, he knew *exactly* what he had been thinking: that going back would, in some intangible way, mitigate what he had lost.

Which made him the one thing he had fought his entire life not to be: foolish.

There was no getting it back any more than it was possible to bend time. Fuck Faust and fuck Stephen Hawking. Once the second hand moved on, past events became immutable, completely resistant to bargaining. Human emotions? Much less so. He had fallen prey to the saddest of wants: to turn back the clock of life. It was embarrassing.

The lights of Manhattan finally peeked through the snow, distant and almost unreachable, and Lucas was somehow drawn back to his childhood, to the day he left Mr. and Mrs. Potts.

The big Bentley pulled up in front of a stone building that stretched up into the sky. Little Lucas had never seen anything like it, and for the rest of his life, every building that impressed him would be compared to it.

A man in a green uniform with lots of buttons came to the car and opened the back door. Mr. Teach stepped onto the sidewalk and held out his hand, helping the boy to the sidewalk. Lucas's feet touched the concrete, and he took a few steps, his neck craned up at the edifice.

The big gold letters over the three entrances were framed by two beautiful couples sitting on chairs, children at their feet. The letters spelled out *The Waldorf-Astoria*, and Lucas did his best to sound it out. Combined with the images of happy couples sitting with their children, he realized that it must be some kind of orphanage. Or at least a place where children were brought to meet their new families. Maybe the Pottses had sold him; some of the older children said that went on all the time.

The driver took his suitcase out of the trunk and handed it to Mr. Teach. Lucas kept his notebooks clutched to his chest and took Mr. Teach's free hand and followed him inside.

There was a big clock in the middle of the lobby that grew out of the floor like a tree. Lucas had never seen one like it, and as they walked by, he tried to hear it ticking. It didn't make any noise, and he wondered if it even worked.

He had never been in an elevator before, and when he became heavy and his ears popped, he was afraid. He tried very hard not to cry by holding his breath, and the car stopped and the doors *bing*ed open onto a carpeted hallway that had five doors, all with big brass numbers on them.

Mr. Teach led him to a door at the end of the hallway and crouched down, fixing Lucas's hair with a comb from his pocket (which even little Lucas found ironic). After flattening the boy's lapel and straightening his placket, he asked, "Are you ready?"

Lucas didn't want Mr. Teach to be upset, so he said, "Yes, sir," even though he had no idea what he was supposed to be ready *for*.

"Well, then, I have someone who wants to meet you," he said and knocked.

A man in a black suit with a little black tie that looked like a butterfly answered the door, clicking his heels as Lucas and Mr. Teach walked by. Mr. Teach handed Lucas's suitcase to the man, and Lucas wondered if he would get it back. Maybe they would sell that, too.

The room was the largest Lucas had ever been in. Much larger than the church Mr. and Mrs. Potts had taken him and the other children to every Sunday. And it was filled with shiny, curly gold furniture that looked like it belonged in a fairy tale. Maybe even a castle. There were paintings and candlesticks and carpets everywhere.

As they passed one of the three fireplaces in the space, the regal woman in the painting above the mantel watched him, her eyes swiveling in their sockets. Even little Lucas could tell that it was an old picture and that the woman was very special, maybe even a princess. She was young, with a long neck, pale white skin, red hair, and a shiny pearl necklace.

Mr. Teach led Lucas to a pair of doors that opened onto an enormous balcony overlooking the city. Lucas had been impressed by the sheer volume of people, streets, and big buildings on the drive in, but up here, looking over the skyline, he was awestruck. At the far end of the balcony, past a fountain decorated with a statue of the devil playing a flute, an old lady sat at a big stone table in the sun.

The woman was small and possessed a poise that even at such a young age he recognized as elegance. She looked like the woman in the painting, but she was much older. And her hair wasn't red—it was white. She was wrapped in a fur blanket that was the most intense black he had ever seen. But what hijacked his attention was the notebook on the table in front of her; it was the one Miss Clark had borrowed.

Mr. Teach introduced Lucas to the woman. "Lucas, this is Mrs. Page."

The old lady stared at the boy for a few quiet seconds before smiling. "Lucas, it is a pleasure to meet you."

Lucas didn't know what to do, so he said, "Yes, ma'am."

She gestured to the seat to her left, and Lucas walked over. Mr. Teach pulled the chair out for the boy and said, "Will there be anything else?"

Mrs. Page smiled at Lucas and asked, "Perhaps some lemonade?"

Lucas liked lemonade very much, but he didn't want to be a problem. He was silent for a minute as he figured out if he should say yes or no.

While he sat there, Mrs. Page said, "Yes, bring us *two* lemonades, Mr. Teach."

And with that, Mr. Teach disappeared, leaving Lucas alone on the balcony with the old lady in the sunshine.

"How was the ride into town? Long?"

Again, Lucas wasn't sure how to answer the questions, so he said, "One hour and three minutes, ma'am." He had just learned to tell time (Mrs. Potts had patiently explained how to read a clock), and he was proud to show off his new talent.

"One hour and three minutes?" She smiled at that. "What a precise answer."

Lucas tried to keep focused on her, but his attention was drawn down to his notebook.

"Do you like Mr. Teach?" she asked. "I know he certainly looks very scary. But I trust him. And you can, too."

"Yes, ma'am." He couldn't take his focus from the notebook in front of her.

"I suppose you are wondering who I am and why you are here."

The little boy nodded, then pointed at his notebook. "And why you have my star book, ma'am."

Mrs. Page looked down, and it appeared as if she were seeing the notebook for the first time. "Your star book is why you are here."

And with the change in the tone of her voice, Lucas began to worry that he was in some sort of trouble.

His fears must have colored his expression, because Mrs. Page said, "You are not in trouble, Lucas. Far from it. I was hoping that maybe you and I could talk. Like friends." She kept her hands on top of the notebook. "Mr. Teach said you are a very curious boy."

The tone in her voice lent an import to the question, and Lucas thought about it before answering, "Yes, ma'am."

Mrs. Page smiled at the short-form answer. "Lucas, there are no right or wrong answers with me. Mr. Teach likes you very much. He said you are kind and polite and smart. *Very* smart."

"Yes, ma—" He stopped as Mr. Teach came back out with two tall glasses of lemonade on a fancy silver tray.

Mr. Teach put the glasses down without clinking them on the stone table, then disappeared.

Lucas was very impressed by Mrs. Page; she had to be an important lady to live at the top of the building and to have people serve her lemonade when it wasn't even lunchtime.

The boy took a sip of the lemonade, and it was cold and sweet and sour all at the same time, and his mouth puckered up.

"Do you like lemonade?" she asked, giving the drink a sip and making her own sour face that made Lucas laugh.

"Yes, ma'am. It's my favorite." He took another sip. "Along with root beer."

"Root beer? I'll remember that."

They spent the rest of the afternoon talking, and it was the third time Lucas could remember an adult treating him like something other than a nuisance or a responsibility. They didn't discuss anything of import, simply a little back-and-forth between two people trying to get to know each other. They talked through two more glasses of lemonade each, even going on through a soup, a salad, and the tiniest little roasted chickens that Lucas had ever seen.

And just like that, it was the end of the day. Mrs. Page apologized that they had to end their conversation—which she said she was enjoying very much—but she was old and tired and ready to lie down. Lucas climbed out of his chair and walked around the table to say good-bye to his new friend. He said he had had a nice afternoon and he hoped that they would see each other again. He said that maybe she could come to visit him at the Pottses' house.

And that's when Mrs. Page said, "How would you feel about moving in here with me?"

43

The Upper East Side

Dingo stood on the back porch for a few beats of his heart, gearing up for war. The Christmas lights overhead blinked, casting weird shadows in the snow and tinting the blade of his garbage-found sword red, white, and green. He took a deep breath to push the adrenaline into some kind of a usable fuel, eased the door open, and slipped inside.

He moved forward, testing out his wet blades on the floor. They were good for his apartment, which was mostly carpeted, but on the ceramic he knew they could be a little iffy. The movement gave him a good feel for the place, and the rubber contacts seemed to be both quiet and solid. He stopped and listened.

They were doing their best to be silent. And they were doing a decent job. But they were somewhere to the front and left, probably near the door in the dining room. Which meant they were on their way upstairs.

Fuck these guys and their guns. Good old-fashioned muscle and a ten-pound broadsword had a lot more history.

Dingo raised the massive slab of garbage-found steel in a classic two-handed attack position and stepped into the hallway, into the darkness.

It was time to walk the walk.

Fuck the police.

44

The alarm bells in Erin's head were clanging her teeth loose as she crawled on the carpet. They were being very quiet, but she knew the sounds of the house. There were little tentative noises that didn't belong.

She peeked through the spindles of the banister to the U-shaped staircase.

The only discernible details other than *human* were the ugly silhouettes of assault rifles that grew from their outlines. Those weren't burglar weapons; they were murder weapons.

She scuttled sideways, racing along the banister above them, keeping low so the little elephant light at the top of the stairs wouldn't throw her shadow.

All she heard was the adrenaline-fueled twelve-cylinder scream of her heart as she hit the end of the Persian runner and turned left, making sure not to kick over the little table in the corner.

Erin reached Maude's door and wrapped her fingers around the knob. It was slippery with her sweat, and she had trouble getting a grip on it. When she finally got it to turn, it was locked.

Erin lost a second getting the key off her neck, but it magically went straight into the hole. She turned and slipped into the dark room.

Maude was up at the edge of her bed. She didn't say anything, and Erin knew that her instincts would kick in—fight or flight; this girl was an expert.

Erin whispered, "We have to get out," and the girl was on the floor beside her.

Before they went out into the hallway, Erin cradled Maude's face in her hands. "You get Laurie. I'll get the boys and Alisha." Erin kissed her, and they scampered out into the hall.

Maude moved left, Erin across the hall, straight for the boys.

Before entering the room, Erin glanced at Alisha's door, working out how to get her. Three steps down to the landing, an eight-foot span, then three more up, and another five to her door.

She couldn't do it. Not without being seen.

She didn't try to hide the fear in her voice with Damien and Hector, and that woke them up. They all slithered out into the hall. Maude and Laurie were there, and they all crawled into her bedroom.

She closed the big oak door, and the final sliver of film to flicker out in the hall was of the men cresting the landing and turning toward Alisha's room.

Erin closed the door.

And quietly locked it.

45

FDR Drive

Whitaker pushed the SUV in the outside lane, using momentum to compensate for a loss of traction. Theoretically, they were in no rush, but Lucas now knew Whitaker well enough to understand that she only had one way of driving.

They were making better time than most of the other vehicles desperate enough to be out in this soup. Somebody in a blacked-out Porsche Cayenne had passed them about two miles back, and other than that one incongruous mental case, they were passing everyone. Whitaker had to go around a few people, and she had resorted to using her asshole lights a handful of times to convince the unobservant to move over. The dangers of passing were compounded by the trucks sitting in the middle lane, throwing up an icy wake that had all the give of a wooden fence.

She was changing lanes to overtake an eighteen-wheeler when the car phone rang, cutting into the ambient noise via the SUV's Bluetooth system.

Lucas checked the clock on the dash: fourteen minutes since he had dropped his badge on Graves; this had to be Kehoe.

Whitaker thumbed a button on the steering wheel, her eyes locked on the shifting road and the optical illusions being conjured by the snow.

Kehoe's disembodied voice came on in remarkably clear and calm Dolby THX. "Is Page with you?"

"Yeah."

Kehoe went straight by the greetings with, "Nine-one-one got a call regarding your address twelve mikes ago. Something about armed intruders. A pair of NYPD cruisers are on the way, and I've sent a tactical team. ETA: six and a half mikes."

Lucas felt the big V-8 growl as Whitaker pushed down on the gas and hit the disco switch, lighting up the claustrophobic world outside in a dancing red-and-white heartbeat.

Lucas tried not to scream.

46

The Upper East Side

Erin was running on full shakes now, and all she could hear was the pounding of her fear as she lifted the sash on the window. The kids were a warm spot in the darkness behind her.

The window locked open, and a gust of snow blew in, yanking the curtains back. She hoisted the aluminum-and-nylon escape ladder out from beneath the bed and hooked the rubber-coated brackets onto the sill. She tried to keep it away from the wall so it wouldn't clatter against the brick as it unfurled into the night.

The kids huddled behind her, a lump of pajamas and wide eyes.

"Out. Out," she whispered.

They had gone through fire drills without ever actually using the ladder, but the children knew the routine—the older kids went first, followed by the others. She'd wait inside until they were all down.

As Damien went over the sill, she whispered, "Get them to the market on the corner. Tell them to call nine-one-one. And keep out of sight until I get there."

"I know. I know." He looked all grown up for a moment. Then he nodded solemnly and slipped over the edge.

Erin fed Maude over next, followed by Hector, then Laurie. And then it was her turn.

Erin watched Damien hit the small courtyard to the basement door, then reach up for Maude. The kids would make it. They would be fine. All of them except Alisha.

But she couldn't leave the little girl.

She waved Damien away. He put his arm around Laurie, and they all ran for Madison.

Erin tried not to cry as she turned and went to the bedroom door.

47

Alisha was getting used to sleeping in her new home, and she was far across the slumber frontier, dreaming little girl dreams and breathing little girl breaths. There were no people or animals or rainbows in her head, only colors and music, but it was enough to keep the machinery moving. She was gone, unaware of anything. And then a low-level rumble began to shake her skeleton.

She opened her eyes, and the rumble grew from an indistinct but personal noise to a full-blown growl coming from the big furry rib cage in the bed beside her. She had her arm over Lemmy and her face was stuffed into his collar and all she could smell was dog. And all she could hear was his growl coming up.

The little girl sat up in bed and rubbed her eyes. The dog rose beside her, his snout aimed at the door. She could feel the heat rising off him. Someone was out in the hallway; she could see the shadows under the door. Was it Mrs. Erin? Mr. Lucas? She wanted to call out, but something stopped her. Maybe the dog. Maybe the movement out in the hall. Maybe the dark. Whatever it was, it was enough to keep her quiet.

The door opened a crack.

The dog stiffened.

Alisha was small, and she didn't have a lot of experience with the world, so she went with what she knew. And she knew how to hide; she used to play hide-and-seek with Mommy's friend, Uncle Quincy. She was an expert at the game. When she closed her eyes, no one could see her.

So as the door swung silently in, Alisha closed her eyes and stayed very quiet. She knew they couldn't see her.

It felt good to be safe.

48

Dingo stopped at the bottom of the staircase, beside the newel post, and shifted the sword in his grip. He took a deep breath to power his blood, then headed up into the dark.

The carpeted steps dampened his footfalls, and the only sound he made was generated by his left blade where it flexed at the footpad; the slight torque caused an almost imperceptible squeak that it took him three steps to correct.

He stopped on the landing, in the shadows of the stairwell, balancing on the thick carpet. Above him, the oak paneling and spindles wound up into the dark. The sword vibrated in his fist, and he tightened his knuckles around the leather-wrapped hilt.

There was a little pink night-light on the landing above, and the men were there. In front of one of the kids' doors—the little girl who had arrived a few nights back.

The two men looked virtually the same in the dark. Medium height and medium build.

He skirted the wall on his way up the steps, keeping below their line of sight in the dark. He was two steps away when he heard one of them turn the knob on the little girl's room.

Dingo rushed the last few steps.

49

The clock slowed, and time unfolded in perfect CinemaScope slow motion. They were miles away. Distant points in the darkness. Erin ran forward, her screech lighting up the air in a siren of rage.

As Alisha's door swung in, the men spun, their muzzles coming around in unison.

Erin knew that in a few more seconds she would be dead. But between now and then, she would fight.

Their weapons came around in a tight arc.

And . . . then . . . a shadow sprang out of the staircase, screaming.

Some primitive part of her recognized Dingo, and with that, her rage increased. *These were her children!*

Her fucking children!

In her house!

Dingo shot up out of the dark. And he was swinging a . . . a . . . was that a *sword*?

There was the sound of the blade cutting the air. And the meaty *thwack* of steel connecting with human. And the thump of two arms and an assault rifle hitting the floor.

The man fell back, bloody stumps painting the air in a black mist delivered on a scream.

The second man spun on Dingo.

There was a thud as they connected.

His rifle fell to the floor.

Fist and elbow connected with bone.

The swish of a pistol coming out of a holster.

There was a grunt. And a snap. And the knot of men tumbled down the stairs, taking out spindles, and crashing into the table on the landing.

Lemmy bounced out with a roar and grabbed the armless man by the throat, punching him back into the banister.

Erin ran into Alisha's room.

The little girl had her eyes squeezed tight. Erin scooped her up with a quick, "It's me."

Back out in the hall, Lemmy was making horrid, monstrous noises, and the man without arms tried to scream.

He punched at the dog with his bloody stumps, but each movement had less vigor than the last as he lost consciousness. Lemmy tore at him, pushing him down as a horrible squawk bubbled up from somewhere deep within him.

Downstairs, Dingo and the other one were kicking the everloving shit out of each other. Punches snapped in the dark. Grunts. Kicks. More broken furniture.

Erin locked the bedroom door and carried Alisha to the window.

She wrapped the girl in a throw from the chair in the corner, then looked down at her. "You hold on to me, okay?" She had to say it twice—the little girl was shaking, frightened by the sounds of violence beyond the door.

Alisha nodded.

Erin climbed out the window, first sitting on the edge, then rotating until her stomach was on the sill, and Alisha was under her arm like a football. She shifted the girl to her front, then began to Tarzan down the ladder.

It was freezing out, and the metal rungs stung her hands, but she kept moving.

One hand at a time.

One foot at a time.

One rung at a time.

Below her, the street was deserted.

She hit the snow-covered ground beside the trash can and gave Alisha a comforting squeeze.

Then, from inside the house, she heard the ugly punch of gunfire—four rounds in tight succession.

Pause.

A fifth.

Silence.

Erin ran for the corner.

50

The Upper East Side

Whitaker swung the SUV around the final corner in a four-wheel drift that crossed three lanes. She hit the apex of the skid, and the tail knocked through a snowbank, taking out a mailbox in a loud display of Newton's third law of motion. The blue metal can flew into a lamppost, wrapping around it like a wet sock.

She punched up the street and rammed up onto the sidewalk, murdering a family of garbage cans.

The house was dark, and all Lucas saw was the ladder hanging from the window, billowing in the wind like a disconnected spinal column that didn't know it was no longer alive. He hit the sidewalk before the truck had even approximated a full stop and took a single step when Erin's voice cut through the screaming in his head. "Luke!"

He turned to the direction of her voice and almost lost his balance as he torqued his prosthetic ankle on the ice.

Erin was two houses down the block, headed for the market on the corner of Madison. "Luke!" she screamed. "Run!" She had a bundle that had to be Alisha clenched to her chest in a running back's grip.

Lucas ducked around a boulder of snow that used to be a car, picking up speed with his idiosyncratic hop. She reached out and he pulled himself into her and Alisha, almost losing his footing. She was sobbing and shaking, and he tried to get her to Whitaker's SUV.

She pulled for the corner. "The children! They're at the market."

"My kids are in the market on Madison!" Lucas yelled to Whitaker.

Whitaker unclipped her pistol and ran for the corner.

Lucas tightened his grip on her. "What happened? What's going on?"

"T-t-t-two men. With m-m-machine . . . guns. I think D-D-D-Dingo killed one, but there were shots and . . ." Her speech was skipping like her reader had malfunctioned, and Lucas suddenly realized that she was only wearing her bathrobe and slippers.

"Is someone still in there?"

"I-I don't know." Erin shook her head. "Dingo. Dingo's in there!"

Lucas grabbed her by the shoulder and pointed her toward the market. He was about to give her a shove when the tactical van rounded the corner, two police cruisers on its back bumper. As the support vehicles rocketed up the street, fishtailing in the not-yet-plowed snow, the red-and-white lights turned the night into an epileptic fit–inducing tunnel.

Lucas pointed at the corner of Madison. "I'll get Dingo. You need to—"

The front door of the house blew open, the oak slamming into limestone and shattering the colored window. A man stumbled out—Detective Michael Atchison. Blood vomited from his mouth in a black rope.

He had a good foot of sword sticking out of his chest.

And an assault rifle in his hands.

He saw Lucas. Saw Erin. And drunkenly swung the murderous muzzle toward them in what looked like stop-motion animation.

Lucas heard the van carrying the tactical team slide to a halt behind them. But they were too late. Everyone was too late. This fucker had them.

Lucas threw his arms around Erin and leaned into a turn.

The doors of the van slid open, and all Lucas could do was hope.

And that was when it came whistling in. A supersonic pulse that bent the air in a high-octane hiss.

For one last tiny instant, Atchison still had a bead on them.

And then, as if Satan reached out with a big wet kiss, Atchison's head disappeared.

He hammered back through the door, landing with one foot out on the stoop.

Brains and blood hung in the air in a black mist.

There was an awkward silent second that Erin ended with her scream just as the *kaboom* came cracking in.

Someone screamed, "Sniper! Sniper!"

Lucas pulled Erin down, covering her and Alisha with his body.

And waited for a shot to take his world away.

51

Lucas held Erin down on the snow-covered pavement. Alisha was clamped between them, and he could feel the little girl's heartbeat above his own.

Erin kept screaming that Dingo was inside.

He was scared. Then fear morphed into terror. And terror gave way to anger.

Behind him, in the dark, the SWAT men kept whispering, *"Sniper. Sniper. Sniper."* Over and over—a serpentine death mantra.

Lucas knew it was the man he had been hunting—the question mark with a rifle out in the storm that he had tracked to two rooftops and a windswept shoreline at LaGuardia.

He was here.

On top of them.

Lucas lay on Erin and the girl, waiting for a round to come in.

A second turned into two.

Into five.

Into ten.

Then thirty.

And there was nothing but silence and the ambient sounds of the city beyond his little universe of fear.

The shot had come from the east.

And the lag time between impact and the sound rolling in had been significant—an easy second.

Which meant a thousand yards out.

And there was only one building in that direction with a clear vantage of his front door that timed out at more or less a thousand yards.

The cops across the street were calling for backup. The SWAT team wasn't so patient; two men with sniper shields crab-walked toward Lucas, Erin, and Alisha.

Lemmy came to the door and sniffed the dead man in the snow. The dog's snout, front paws, and chest were a different color now—a deep pink—as if he had been feeding on a corpse.

Lucas heard the cops behind him shoulder their weapons. "No!" he yelled. "That's my dog!"

He snapped his fingers, and Lemmy bounded down the stairs.

The dog reached him and gave him a big lick on the side of the face that was slimy with blood. Lucas pulled him in just as the armored men reached them. He grabbed the one with sergeant's stripes on his shoulder. "The shot came from two blocks east. Off Park. The high-rise. Check the roof."

The man looked at him as if he were nuts.

"Trust me," he said. "Now get my wife and little girl to safety." He gave Erin a quick kiss before she was pulled away. She called Lemmy, and he disappeared with her. "You," Lucas said, pointing at the second man with the shield, "come with me."

"It's not safe, sir!" The man shook his head.

The shooter was gone; if he'd wanted anyone else dead, they'd be Sleepy Hollowed all over the snow by now. "Then stay here." Lucas stood up.

The clock was on Pause, and it felt as if he were moving slower than he ever had in his life. His limbs felt like they were weighted down, and the adrenaline coursing through his tissue was acting as a coagulant, not fuel. His reasoning said that the sniper had jackrabbited—it made no sense to hang around. But that tiny little primitive part of his mind that ran the fear generator wasn't as certain.

He heard the SWAT man come up behind him, waving the shield like it meant something against their guy and his magic bullets.

Lucas hit the steps and moved up, his hand out on the stone rail for balance, concentrating on one stair at a time. When they hit the landing, they had to step over Atchison's body and Lucas tried to ignore the brains and blood steaming in the snow. Once they were inside the house, he felt the clock power back up.

Dingo was on the landing at the top of the first flight of steps, sitting on the blood-soaked Persian rug. His back was against the wall, and his legs stuck straight out in front of him, one of the blades snapped off and hanging by carbon fibers like a broken cigarette. He was hugging himself, his hands over his stomach and chest. Even in the dark, Lucas could see blood thudding out between his fingers.

Lucas snapped on the light that was knocked over and kneeled, the only movement he could manage to get closer to the floor without sitting or lying down. He took Dingo's hand. "Dingo?"

Dingo didn't move.

Above them, sprawled out like a doll that had been abandoned, was the other intruder. One of his arms was on the bottom step; the other was wedged in between the rungs of the banister. There was no questioning that he was dead as fuck—his throat was torn out, and his face was twisted into a frozen mask of pain. Unable to override his training, the SWAT man checked for a pulse. Then he moved past to clear the rest of the house.

Lucas scanned Dingo's wounds and put his good hand over two holes in his chest to stop the awful sucking sound he heard. With that, his friend coughed. It was a small, tentative action, barely a breath, but it said that he was still alive.

The SWAT man ran through the floor, clearing the rooms, while Lucas tried to stop the bleeding.

Dingo looked up at Lucas and smiled a mouthful of blood. "Erin . . . and the . . . girl?"

Lucas kept the pressure on the mass of chest wounds, and his eyes filled with tears. "Everyone's safe. You saved them."

Dingo coughed. "The sec . . . ond . . . asshole? I heard . . ."

"They're both dead."

Dingo managed a bloody smile that sent a little stream of black down the stubbled terrain of his chin.

The SWAT man came back, and by now his friends were charging through the downstairs, calls of *Clear! Clear! Clear!* echoing in the dark. More sirens outside. More diesel engines. More personnel.

Back at Lucas's side, the SWAT man got on the horn. "We've got a man down in here. Multiple gunshot wounds."

Lucas still held Dingo's hand. He didn't know what to do, so he said, "Thank you."

But Dingo was just staring off into the distance.

SWAT men poured up the stairs with a pair of paramedics in tow.

They went into lifesaving mode, probing wounds, checking vitals, and administering the appropriate mix of painkillers, blood thickeners, and assorted syringed voodoo. Lucas stood back while they worked, but he kept his eyes locked on Dingo's. He didn't see any fear or pain, and all he could think was that Dingo was going to die.

They got the stabilizer board under his body, strapped him in, and hoisted him onto the stretcher. Lucas kept with them all the way downstairs, and when they got to the doorway, the street was lit up with the barrage of headlights, emergency lighting, and task lighting that, when reflected off the snow, magnified to the point that it looked like daylight out. Vehicles of various form and purpose—both marked and unmarked—decorated the street. The scene was interlaced with SWAT and police doing their best to be effective in the cold.

Lucas followed Dingo's stretcher down the front steps and across the sidewalk to the ambulance. The pair of EMS techs had to ford the narrow path chopped through the snowbank before they could drop the wheels for the few feet it took to get to the back doors of the vehicle.

Whitaker and Erin were across the street, beside a police van. Erin was wearing a big police parka and fireman boots, and Whitaker was on her cell. The kids were in the van, and when they saw Lucas, they waved, but there was nothing joyous or festive about the action; they were just searching for something familiar.

Erin crossed the blocked street, negotiating a zig, then a zag, between a cruiser, an unmarked SUV, and two SWAT men decked out in what looked like assassins' gear.

As the wheels came up and the stretcher slid into the back, Dingo tried to say something, and Lucas leaned in and put his ear to the oxygen mask covering his mouth and nose. "Don't forget to . . . oil the sword and . . . feed the horse," he whispered. Then he passed out.

Erin began to cry.

The techs closed the doors, and the siren spun to life. As the ambulance headed off, Lucas and Erin stood in the shadow of a building, away from the lights. "How are the kids?" he asked.

"In shock." She dug her face into his collar.

"And you?"

"I can't tell." They stayed like that for a handful of heartbeats before she pulled back and looked up at him. "What are you going to do?"

He held her at arm's length in the middle of the street as the snow came down and the various branches of the Manhattan law enforcement community scuttled about in their tasks. "I quit."

"You can't, Luke. If you do, I'll never sleep again."

"I already did. I handed in my badge. I promised I'd be home for the holidays. I promised that you wouldn't go at it with Alisha alone. They"—he nodded in the general direction of the flashing lights off to their left—"don't need me. You and the kids do."

It was hard to miss that she was a little pleased with that. But then her features tightened, and she said, "You can't quit now. I understand why. And it's not just Dingo. It's you. You need to do this. And now I need you to do this. So I'm screwed no matter how I look at it. You go after this guy and you find him and you lock him up."

He was still staring at her, wondering what specific magic had brought her into his life, when Kehoe's SUV hit the roadblock on the corner and the duty cops the bureau were now using as support personnel waved him through.

Lucas told Erin to go be with the kids as the Lincoln moved slowly down the street. It pulled up in front of Whitaker's vehicle, nosing into the spot where the EMS guys had loaded Dingo into the ambulance. Lucas walked over, his processor trying to find a logical route out of all of this. He didn't have a lot of options. Not if he wanted to stay true to the man he had fought so hard to become.

Kehoe got out and, even after a day of madness, still managed to look like he had been plucked from the pages of a men's style blog. He walked over and took up a spot beside Lucas, against the hood of his SUV—which was an easy way to keep the warmth up.

"What happened here, Page?"

Lucas looked around. The media had set up shop on both ends of the block, prying into events with their lights and curiosity. "Detective Atchison and another man broke into my house and tried to kill my family. My friend stopped them with a fucking sword and is now probably going to die. Atchison had enough life in him to come after my wife and my little girl, and when he stepped outside, our shooter took his head off." That was as short and sweet as he could come up with. The adrenaline had leached from his pores, and he was feeling the chemical letdown replace it.

The FBI's crime-scene boys and girls were going through his brownstone, applied FBI particle theory in action. The snow was still dropping from the sky, and it wasn't making things even a tiny bit better.

"I'm sorry, Luke." Kehoe removed his gloved hands from his pockets and crossed his arms over his chest.

Lucas thought about that. "I'm still too angry to be sorry."

They watched the cleanup boys bring a body out on a stretcher.

"Whitaker and I spoke to Atchison last night. What the fuck is all this about?" Lucas watched Kehoe for signs of movement behind the machinery. There weren't any. "What did I do that would make the guy come after my family, Brett?"

"We'll find out," Kehoe said. There was genuine concern in his voice. Or at least more well-orchestrated manipulation.

"Why was the shooter watching my house?" Lucas had a mix of emotions swirling around in his head over that one. It was hard to miss the bittersweet reasoning—because of the shooter, Erin and Alisha were still alive. He, too.

Graves's vehicle was waved through the roadblock at the end of the street.

Kehoe looked over at the van where Lucas's family were. "How is Erin?"

"A man with a sword sticking out of his chest had his head blown off in front of her kids, Brett. That's how she is."

"She knows this isn't your fault."

"No, she doesn't. Because it is. If I hadn't gone back to work for you, we wouldn't be standing here having this conversation while dead men are being wheeled out of my house in pieces. She has every right to be angry."

"What can I do?"

Lucas looked over at him. "Dingo has been in immigration limbo for three years. Punch it through."

"Look, I don't think—"

Lucas cut him off. "I'm not done."

Kehoe stopped. After what had happened, he owed it to Lucas to at least listen. "Of course."

"I want you to get Dingo his citizenship. And I want Alisha's adoption cleared. After tonight, I doubt the courts are going to find us to be safe guardians. Erin will be crushed. It's not a complicated case, Brett. Her father will be in prison for the next five decades for killing her mother. She has no aunts or uncles or grandparents, and that poor kid spent three days alone with her dead mother lying naked on the bedroom floor."

Graves came over, nodding a lackluster hello to both of them.

"I'll see what I can do," Kehoe said.

Lucas turned to him and stood up to his full height, a good four inches over the man. "No, you won't. You want me to come back? You want to catch this guy? Then you fucking get this done. Otherwise, you can hand this over to Graves here and see what happens. I want both those things taken care of by breakfast. I don't care how you do it, just get it done."

Kehoe nodded. "I will do my best."

Kehoe was a lot of things, but he wasn't a liar.

"Give me back my badge."

Graves reached into his pocket and pulled it out. "Kehoe told me to deliver it."

Lucas shook his head. "I hate being predictable."

52

Columbia University Medical Center

The surgical ICU was relatively quiet during the early hours of the coming day. The room was round, with a nursing station in the center. More than two dozen beds were parked against the curved outer wall, chariots designed to not deliver occupants to the afterlife. Five nurses attended to the nuts and bolts of the surgically reassembled humans, and a single uniformed officer stood watch over Dingo's bed. Other than Lucas, there were no visitors.

The cop took a break to give him a little privacy with his friend. Not that his presence here did any good. Or bad. But the act of being here somehow calmed the old demons clawing out of the locked closets in his head. And maybe Dingo was absorbing some of the hope that was being sent his way.

Dingo did a pretty good impression of a human distributor cap wired into a bank of NASA diagnostic systems. The collage of monitors displayed every possible numerical value his body was capable of producing, some of them represented on more than one screen. He was doing an effective job of looking dead. The surgeon who plucked the five copper-jacketed .45 rounds out of his sternum said that a lot of things needed to line up if he was going to make it. But he was fit and obviously no stranger to punishment, which were both pluses. The surgeon gave him a one-in-three chance of making it through the next twenty-four hours, a one-in-two chance in making the twenty-four beyond that, by which time, he would fall into the likely-to-survive category. The good news was that as of now, all his major organs were online and enthusiastically working toward the single goal of keeping his body on the green side of the grass.

Being back in a room like this was doing all kinds of black magic on Lucas. It was the Ghost of Christmas Past mixed with the Ghost of Christmas Future, and neither the memories nor the possibility were places he wanted to visit. Doing this once was more than enough for anyone. That Dingo was lying there felt like letting someone else go to prison for a crime he had committed.

The whole exercise drove home that he was too old for this business. It wasn't just the damage to his body—he could get used to that. No, it was the beating his mental state was taking. He was having trouble seeing the forest for the trees, and that never happened to him. And that he was thinking about himself more than Dingo made him ashamed.

Lucas watched the numbers dance across the bevy of monitors, and he couldn't help but fit them into a pattern. It had no real value as a diagnostics tool, not in any way he could understand, because some values were rising while others were decreasing. But it enabled him to build a short-term model of how a human being came back online, even if he knew nothing about what was happening. He trusted the software—and the nursing minions moving noiselessly through the ICU—to do that. But he couldn't turn off what he was built to do—see patterns.

In the patterns, there was direction. Order. Predictability.

Kehoe's men found the shooter's lair right where Lucas had said they would. Another rooftop perch where very little had been left behind. In this case, as in the others, *very little* meant *nil*. Which was some kind of a miracle because less than six hours before, the shooter had been hiding between a pair of backup generators at LaGuardia.

While Dingo was in surgery, ballistics came back on both of the night's victims—Lupino and Atchison—and it was that same weird bullet. A copper-jacketed hunting round modified to contain a morsel of the building blocks of the universe.

Which meant that Lucas was on the guy's radar.

But the shot that had taken out Atchison was different from the others in that there had been no surveillance involved. There hadn't been time. The building where the shot had come from was a last-minute choice.

Until now, Lucas knew the shooter put a lot of time into surveillance. He had mapped out Hartke's and Kavanagh's and Lupino's schedules—which meant he had months of footwork into this. But taking Atchison out had proved that he could do this on the fly. Which elevated his threat factor by orders of magnitude.

And that brought Lucas to the next set of questions. Had Detective Atchison been on the killer's shopping list before tonight, or had he been an addendum? Was this tied to the Margolis murder—where a truckload of ammunition disappeared? With Atchison being the lead detective in the Margolis case, the power of coincidence seemed a little overstated. Or was Atchison added to the list simply because he was part of the law enforcement gene pool? Had the shooter been protecting Lucas? His family? Or had he simply been making a point? And if so, what was said point? That he was everywhere? All-knowing? All-seeing? Unstoppable?

Because, if Lucas really thought about it, the shooter looked like he was all those things.

Only he wasn't.

He was a human being. Which meant he had a flaw somewhere.

Why had Atchison come for him? It made no sense from any kind of a logistical standpoint. Lucas was only involved in the periphery of the investigation. If they wanted to try to scare investigators away, they should have gone after Graves or Kehoe. Hell, any of the other agents would have made a bigger splash than Lucas.

Lucas stood up and put his hand on Dingo's arm. He felt cold. Lucas leaned over and gave his friend a kiss on the cheek. "Thank you."

Out in the hallway, Whitaker was thumbing through email. She stood up and pocketed her phone. "How you doing?"

"The man who saved my family is an inch away from dying. That's how I am."

As they headed to the elevator, Lucas put a hand on her shoulder. "I'm sorry about that. I'm tired."

"So how about we get you some sleep?"

"That's the best suggestion I've heard in a while."

53

The Park Lane Hotel

Lucas had managed a little more than two hours of sleep before the monsters in his head started picking the locks. He woke in the dark, and it took him a few seconds to gather the strength to push himself up in bed. The hotel was a mid-priced joint that checked all the boxes and had the added plus of being not far from either his house or the hospital where Dingo was facing down the reaper, which somehow offset the feeling he had entered the witness protection program. Erin and the kids were at their beach house, where they'd stay until this nightmare was put to bed.

He stretched, knowing he needed more sleep but understanding that it was a lost aspiration. He kicked off the covers and had to manually untangle the top sheet from his prosthetic before he swung his legs over the side of the bed; he always left his leg on when he slept away from home. His head felt crammed with warm ball bearings, and his eye felt as if it were being held in with roofing nails. But at least he could stand.

Lucas peeled back the curtains and stared out at the still-dark city, buried in what looked like a hundred feet of winter. Everything was under snow, a component that time, patience, and tens of thousands of man-hours would eventually dent with New York's basic nature: sheer relentlessness. But until then, it would be an eerie in-between world that looked almost deserted. People were out, but nowhere near the usual pedestrian time-lapse that he was used to. Vehicular traffic was running at a weak 30 percent, cabs and Uber drivers doing their best against the deep drifts in a competition with errant SUV owners.

Even from four floors up, it was apparent that no one on the street texted or yakked into cell phones; it was just too fucking cold.

After a coffee, he texted Whitaker to let her know he was awake. If she was up, she'd call. If not, he'd grab a cab down to Federal Plaza.

He was sitting there, wondering if he had the strength to stand, when the phone rang. It was Whitaker.

"What did you find out about the second man at my house last night?"

"Good morning to you, too."

"Sure. Sorry. Whatever." He resented feeling like the life he had ordered was out of stock, but it was too early to be rational. At least until he pumped more coffee into the tank.

She switched to business mode. "The guy is—*was*—Atchison's partner, Detective Alex Roberts."

"He was in on the Margolis investigation."

"That's the one."

"Any idea why he came after my family?"

"Not yet. But we tossed Atchison's house, and it fills in a few blanks."

From the tone of her voice, he could tell it was more of the same— pieces of a puzzle that were facedown. "When can you be here?"

"Fifteen minutes."

"Make it twenty; I need a long shower."

"No problem. Are you all right?"

He had been ready to walk away from it all. Take his wife and kids and head to Bimini until the FBI collared this asshole. But Erin didn't trust anyone like she trusted him, and she'd only start sleeping better when this guy was out of his head. So he had sent her and the kids out to Montauk.

The kids liked it out at the beach, even in the middle of winter. And Kathy, their neighbor out there, would help Erin pick up the slack left in Lucas's wake—she was a retired schoolteacher (and the beneficiary of a very healthy life insurance policy from a very unhealthy third husband) who loved the kids as if they were her own.

After getting Erin and the kids off to Montauk, he spent some more time with Kehoe, followed up by his visit with Dingo. "I'm good. But I need to stop listening to both Kehoe and Graves; the signal-to-noise ratio is too interbred. I have some ideas that I want to pursue, but I need a little help."

"You going Johnny Utah on me?"

Lucas thought back to Erin's John McClane comment and wondered how come the people who came into his life always had the same worldview. "I'm just not willing to waste time pursuing avenues that will be nonproductive."

"Kehoe wants you to see Atchison's place over in Hoboken."

"What about the Frenchman?"

"He said Graves could take care of that."

"Graves couldn't sink a canoe with a hand grenade." Lucas stood and walked over to the coffee maker. "I need all the files on our victims." The coffee filter was a commercial single-portion tea-bag affair encapsulated in a heat-sealed plastic bag. "Sorry, can you hold on?" he asked and put the phone down. Things like opening little plastic sachets were impossible without two hands, and using his metal prosthetic required a little attention or he'd end up with coffee all over the floor. When he was done, he plopped it into the little machine and added a bottle of water from the tray on the table. He hit the On button and picked the cell back up. "I want *everything* our people can dig up on the victims. All of it. From junior high records right up through last pay stubs. Credit card statements, phone bills, bank statements, loan applications, insurance claims—every last fragment of data that you can get your hands on. Go back as far as you can."

"That's a lot of information."

"We also need to look at the FBI's National Data Exchange."

Whitaker interrupted him. "We've run this through N-DEx ten different ways and come up with nothing. This guy hasn't—"

Lucas cut her off. "I'm not interested in the similar crimes we've found; I'm interested in the ones we *haven't*. This isn't his first time doing this; you don't make those four shots without a lot of experience. He's done this before; we just don't know where."

The coffee maker was farting and burping, and Lucas turned back to the view of the park. He was enjoying the scenery until he realized that he was standing in a window. "How many law enforcement agencies are there in the U.S.?"

"About eighteen thousand, including local PDs, sheriff's offices, official state agencies, and other miscellaneous organizations."

"With that many sources, some crimes aren't getting reported. There's bound to be data loss—we just have to find it. I bet there are a few small local PDs that just don't have the time or the budget or the inclination to report to the federal government."

"You want us to call eighteen thousand law enforcement agencies and ask if they haven't reported any crimes? That's insane."

The coffee maker wheezed out one final sputter, and Lucas lifted the mug. "We won't have to. We're looking within a very specific set of parameters. We need someplace with a harsh winter and a largely rural population, someplace without a lot of incentive to report their business to the feds." He took a sip of the coffee and walked back over to the window. "We're looking for a law enforcement agency that doesn't have the resources to file with the database—they lack the interest, or they don't understand the process. They won't be regular contributors."

"That's still a lot of work."

Lucas turned away from the city. "Which is what they are paying us to do. Just put the victim files in motion, then come and get me," he said. "Besides, we're not going to do the sifting—I have someone who will."

"Are we allowed to—"

But he stopped listening and hung up.

He poured the rest of the coffee down his throat before reloading the machine with another packet of hotel-brand dark roast. Then he fired up the shower.

54

New Jersey

The neighborhood was a no-nonsense example of postwar America; nice single-family dwellings with two-car driveways and perfect backyards for weekend barbecues. It was a working-class haven, houses decorated with too many Christmas lights, plastic Santas on stoops, and inflatable decorations from Costco dancing in the wind. The massive elm, oak, and chestnut trees that lined the street reached into the sky, their branches bare as they slept through what had to be the hundredth winter for some. If you squinted, you could see back in time, and through the lens of history it had once been a place like many others across the nation—a life to aspire to. Now, if statistics were to be believed, it was a place where the majority of households were barely hanging on to the American dream, their lives controlled by too much debt and not nearly enough sex.

If not for the cop cars, black SUVs, government sedans, and the large armored cube van, it could have been just another morning in Jersey.

Lucas and Whitaker walked up the shoveled path to the front door. They were insulated from the curious being held at bay behind a spiderweb of evidence tape that the Hoboken PD had strung around the property before the bureau arrived the night before. The FBI's investigative team was still going through the place.

As they approached the house, two bureau men in matching windbreakers came out with what looked like a waterproof plastic coffin. They didn't bother nodding a hello as they slipped by Lucas and Whitaker on the narrow path, taking the case to the armored van.

Whitaker was bringing Lucas up to speed. "The Jeep we found in the alley behind your house was stolen from an apartment garage about three miles from here. We figured out who Roberts was by running his prints. Incidentally, your sword-happy friend made our job of inking him a lot easier."

Lucas shook his head at that.

Whitaker snorted once, then grimaced, obviously embarrassed at her laugh. "And the medical examiner said that he looked like he had been attacked by a lion. You know where I can get a dog like that? I would like to give it to my ex as a Christmas present."

That brought a small smile to Lucas's lips. "I'll rent him to you."

"Look at you, all smiley and shit." They hit the stoop, and Whitaker held the door open for him. "Both Roberts and Atchison were exemplary officers. Zero on-the-job complaints. Atchison had one civil case involving a land issue with a neighbor. The owners of that house," she said, nodding to the left. "He's got an ex-wife in Pittsburgh and two grown kids, both out of state; one's a pilot for Alaska Airlines, the other's a nurse in California."

Whitaker followed Lucas as he went through the house, room by room. Agents were dissecting the residence one piece at a time, but they were being relatively neat. A few drawers were open; things were taken off shelves and left on tables; closet doors were open. But nothing a couple of hours of tidying up wouldn't fix.

The living room and dining room offered up nothing that hit Lucas as noteworthy. Typical nondescript big-box store decorating along with all the little bells and whistles that television convinced people they needed. There were a few photographs over the mantel—grade- and high-school photographs of Atchison's daughters in various stages of awkward development, ending with two wedding photos. It could have been anyone's living room. Anyone's dining room. Anyone's life.

One of the upstairs bedrooms still had kids' furniture and a closetful of clothes that were probably from when his daughters still lived here. There were jeans and sweatshirts and a tech hunting jacket in mossy oak and a dated blue-and-white waitress uniform. Some sneakers and a pair of winter boots. Nothing Lucas didn't expect to find.

The master bedroom could have been a hotel room for all the personal touches present. The only things that denoted individuality were a pair of prescription reading glasses and a book on the coming race wars.

The master closet contained a lot of work shirts and jeans along with three off-the-rack suits—Atchison's detective garb. But the room itself could have been staged for a television show. "Pretty boring guy," Lucas said as they finished upstairs.

Whitaker shook her head. "You haven't seen the basement."

They headed down the carpeted stairs, rounded the wall, and cut through the house to the basement stairwell off the kitchen. The door had two security dead bolts and an electronic push-button lock that had been drilled out. "Took our guys half an hour to crack these," Whitaker said.

The basement staircase was decorated with a patchwork of cheaply framed photographs of Atchison that dated back at least three decades judging by the creeping male-pattern baldness. Each picture was identical in that Atchison held a rifle, albeit in varying format, caliber, and purpose. The majority had been taken at target ranges, but a few were hunting shots, Atchison proudly standing, kneeling, or sitting with freshly killed game. Mostly deer and bear with the odd moose thrown in. Nothing exotic. Nothing that couldn't be found within a six-hour drive of the city; no elk or bighorn sheep or wild boar. Not one of him in uniform. Again, it could have been any staircase in the country.

But Whitaker was right; the big payoff was the basement itself.

The large room was finished in wood paneling from some time in the eighties, judging by the style. There was a small office in the corner that consisted of one old oak desk, a small two-drawer filing cabinet, and a keyboard that was missing a computer—no doubt ferried off to the FBI's lab for probing. There was a Rhodesian flag hanging over the desk, flanked by larger American flags.

The walls were lined with hundreds of rifles of every conceivable type, both restricted and non. Everything from shotguns to bolt-action hunting rifles to tactical arms was represented several times over, all oiled and dusted and neatly displayed like a store. It was impossible to miss the emphasis on assault weapons—a good 70 percent of the stock was designed to kill the maximum number of warm bodies in the least amount of time.

Four agents were at work, inventorying the stock. It appeared as if they had made a 10 percent dent in the weapons; they were taking each one down, photographing it, recording the serial number, labeling it, placing it in a long polyethylene bag, then stacking it in a plastic coffin-case like the one Lucas had seen out front.

"Any of these registered?"

"Not so far," Whitaker said. "They ran some random serial numbers, and a few turned up as stolen. We found sixty-one .300s."

"Do I need to ask the next question?"

"You want to know about ammunition."

"I'm starting to like the way you do that."

Whitaker led Lucas to a door in the corner that could have been to the furnace room or a small bathroom. Whitaker opened it, cracked the light switch, and stepped back to let Lucas through.

Once inside, Lucas fell back onto Maude's standard response whenever presented with something in gross violation to the norm. "Wow."

"My exact thoughts when they brought me in here," Whitaker said.

The room was as large as the main body of the basement and filled with lines of heavy-duty metal shelving. Ammunition of every conceivable make and caliber filled the space, from small boxes of Winchester .22 Long Rifle to crates of Chinese 7.62. There was, quite literally, enough ammunition in there to start a military action almost anywhere in the world.

"Any armor-piercing Nosler rounds?" he asked.

Whitaker walked him down an aisle and stopped near the end at an empty shelf. The label on the lip was handwritten in neat noncursive and read: *.300*. Several photographs—stamped with the FBI evidence logo—sat on the shelf. Lucas picked them up and flipped through. They were shots of the same shelf, only in the photos the space was efficiently packed with unmarked blue plastic containers that looked roughly the size of shoe boxes. Three of the containers were white.

"There were eleven thousand rounds of standard bench-load incorporating Nosler slugs here. Those three white containers you see had modified rounds in them—they're at the lab, and so far, they match our guy. We don't have metallurgy back yet, but on every other front they're the same—including a ferrous kernel."

Lucas nodded as he examined the pictures. "And now we have powder load as well as cartridge and primer manufacturer." He placed the prints back on the shelf and looked around the storage room. "So riddle me this, Special Agent Whitaker—"

"Why would a police detective who also happens to be an arms dealer—the same officer who investigated the Margolis murder that we interviewed yesterday—come after your family?" she interrupted with one of her preemptive question hijacks. "I'm the question guru; you're supposed to be the answer guy on the team."

Back in the main room, he took in the massive amount of firepower and continued thinking out loud. "How does a guy like this stay under the radar? This is on an industrial scale."

Whitaker nodded up at the Rhodesian flag. "He obviously had white supremacist leanings but managed to keep them to himself."

"Fried chicken comment notwithstanding," Lucas offered.

"He didn't have an online presence. But he was definitely selling arms. Roberts, too, judging by what our people found in his garage. Not as big a cache as this, but about two hundred small arms, mostly machine pistols." She picked up a battered Thompson machine gun, turning it over in her hands. "St. Valentine's Day typewriter. Hard to go wrong with this thing."

"Selling them to whom? He was a cop."

"Like I am fond of citing, patriot militia enrollment has gone up by about fifteen thousand percent in the past decade, coinciding with the election of the country's first black president—remember?"

"Coincidentally, of course," he said.

"In all models, these groups are the greatest threat that exists to American security. They think they're above the law because they're white. And most of their members lack the critical-thinking skills to figure out that their belief systems are anti-American." She waved a finger around the room. "Atchison had a good record and didn't raise any red flags."

Lucas looked around, and it was hard to miss the paranoia. "Any financials?"

Whitaker put the old blued Thompson back in the rack and shook her head. "Guy was pulling in a little over seventy-five K a year and, other than what you see down here, didn't have any expensive habits. A Sam's Club card and two Visas, never spent more than fifteen hundred bucks a month on his plastic. Mortgage was paid off three years ago. His truck is eight years old, and he bought it used. He's got a little over eighty grand in his savings account. Safe in the corner over there contained a hundred and fifty grand plus change, all in hundred-dollar bills. That's pretty much his life story."

Lucas took a look around the room and shook his head. "No, it's not." He walked over to the desk and sat down.

Whitaker said, "His hard drive is encrypted. It's basic software for Mac, but it will take some time for our people to crack. Apparently, Detective Atchison was relatively careful with his data."

Lucas went through the desk, but the drawers were empty. He was going to ask what the bureau had found in them but waited for Whitaker to do her thing.

She turned to the men cataloging the weapons. "You have a list of the contents of the desk?"

Without breaking stride, one of the agents nodded at a tablet atop one of the kit bags on the floor. "Right there."

Whitaker passed it to Lucas, and he flipped through the high-definition photographs. After a few images, he realized that Atchison had been a careful man; there wasn't much in the way of incriminating evidence. There were no phone books or customer lists or invoices or any other information that had immediate value. The desk had contained a few manuals for different weapons systems, a dozen catalogs from survivalist supply stores, three binders of brochures, and a handful of takeout menus. The rest of the contents could loosely be classified under the dual heading of office supplies/drawer shit.

Lucas pushed back from the desk, and the chair caught on the carpet beneath, pulling it back. There, on the floor, was a small yellow tag that had obviously been meant for the trash can. He stared down at it for a moment and felt the tumblers in his head go through their turns before they clicked in place. "Son of a bitch," he said and picked it up. "It's an inventory tag from a gunsmith." He held it up so she could read it. "Your friend Oscar."

55

The West Village

Lucas and Whitaker sat in the Navigator while the SWAT team took the door off its hinges with a grinder. The heat in the SUV was dialed to full strength, but the windshield still fogged up without the grille to push extra air from the block through the vents.

All efforts to contact Oscar via telephone and doorbell had been unsuccessful, and going by his unknown affiliation with Atchison, they were under the assumption that he wasn't interested in playing footsie.

The SWAT team slipped into the building, assault rifles at the ready, adrenaline and testosterone at peak levels. Lucas started counting off the sand in the hourglass.

The subzero temperature was slowing everything down, from the SUV's heater to time itself.

"Graves is convinced that Oscar, Atchison, and Roberts are not related to our sniper. They're collateral."

Lucas kept the timer in his head going as he answered her. "You know how I feel about Graves and his critical-thinking skills." The loop of Atchison's head disintegrating as he blew back over the sill of the door filled his mind like a scene out of a Tarantino script.

"You have any ideas?"

Lucas shook his head but kept his eye on Oscar's door. "You mean other than Oscar's dead inside?"

"Jesus!"

By the way she said it, he could tell that the thought upset her. Lucas just shrugged. "Things are starting to make sense on a certain level."

And that's when the squad captain came out and waved an all clear. Whitaker and Lucas stepped out into the cold.

When they were inside the building, the squad commander pulled them aside. "We found a body upstairs. A man." His face played around with a few different expressions—none of them good. "Someone took their anger out on him."

The commander tried to stand in front of Whitaker, and Lucas could see that he didn't think she could handle what had happened upstairs.

She took a step closer to him and ramped up what looked like a snarl. She had a presence, and even in tactical gear, it was obvious that the smaller man didn't want to go up against her.

All he offered was, "You shouldn't go up there."

Whitaker looked up to Oscar's office above the machine shop. "No one goes up until the forensics team is done."

"We need to—"

Whitaker cut him off. "I'm senior agent here. You do nothing until our people go through the place. Now, get your men out of here. I don't want you fucking up my crime scene."

The squad leader stared at her for a few seconds before nodding. "Yes, ma'am."

"It's *Special Agent,* not *ma'am.*"

"Of course, Special Agent Whitaker."

As they walked away, Lucas slapped her on the back. "And you said *I* don't make friends."

"With you, it's personality. With me, it's good old-fashioned racism."

The CSI crew showed up, two vehicles filled with all manner of equipment meant to pull answers from the dead.

Lucas was about to ask how long the caravan of death would take when Whitaker preemptively answered, "Two, maybe three hours."

He didn't bother with the second question; he just waited for her response.

She held up the hard drive he had asked for. "Have I failed you yet?"

He tried not to smile as he said, "I need you to take me somewhere while the ghouls do their job with Oscar."

56

Columbia University

While they waited for the forensics unit to finish in the West Village, Whitaker and Lucas hit his office on campus. The school had settled into that between-time after exams and before Christmas where the only people on-site were those with something specific to do, someplace specific they didn't want to be, or both.

When they walked in, Debbie was at her permanent perch behind the desk. She uncharacteristically stopped her work and looked up at Lucas, ignoring Whitaker. "Dr. Page, how are you?" And by the way she said it, he could tell that even she had been rattled by the news of what had happened at his house the night before—the media was going bananas with the story.

"I don't want to talk about it."

"Not a problem."

He turned to the three twentysomethings sitting on the leather sofa he had insisted the university provide; if he was going to have students bothering him, he needed somewhere for them to sit. It was also useful when he kept students waiting when he wasn't in the mood to speak to them. Another of those win-win situations the school was so fond of pushing these days.

Manuel Muñoz, Caroline Jespersen, and Bobby Nadeel were three of his grad students. Manuel was a tall, thin kid who Lucas strongly suspected had never seen a woman naked, at least not on this side of a computer screen. He was also one of the brightest systems modelers ever to have come through Lucas's class. Caroline was completing her master's and Ph.D. simultaneously because her scholarship was running out and she wouldn't be able to afford any more semesters in school. She was curious and smart and funny as hell. Bobby came from a family that had pushed all their kids academically, and he had two dentists and a cardiologist as siblings—the pressure was most definitely on him to perform. He was on full scholarship, and the school had had Lucas approach him personally as an enticement. Bobby had that all-too-common combination of brilliance and dislikability that made him the perfect candidate for academic greatness. He was also smarter than almost anyone in the department—faculty or student.

"Thanks for coming," Lucas said to the group. "Now, grab your shit and follow me."

He made the introductions on the way to the subterranean lab. Everyone was duly impressed with Special Agent Whitaker, and a few seconds into their walk, Lucas was certain that they'd do anything he asked of them. It was also obvious that they were aware of what had happened the night before by their body language and sideways eye contact.

"Regardless of what you saw on the news, nothing really happened last night." And even as he said it, he realized it was the single-largest understatement he had ever made. "I'm fine, and the bad guys are dead."

Nadeel snorted in way of a laugh. "No shit. Didn't one guy get chopped up with a sword?"

Lucas ignored the remark and went into his disclaimer as they hit the staircase. "I need your help. Hear me out before you say yes or no, and if you walk out, I won't hold it against you. If you stay, however, it will impact your mark in a positive way, regardless of results.

Not that any of you need academic handouts, but I want you all to know that I appreciate you coming down here on Christmas and doing this."

"Dr. Page?" Bobby said.

"Yes?"

"Could you just tell us why we're here?" As always, the kid went for the gold.

They hit the basement level, and Lucas pushed through the doors. Then he held out his open palm, and Whitaker placed a portable hard drive in it. Lucas held the device up. "I'm back with the FBI on a consulting basis. We've got four people who have been killed by a sniper. The bureau's people haven't been able to link them in any capacity, but they are not random. What I need from you is to find out what the commonality is."

"We're working for the FBI?" Bobby asked. "Will we be able to put that on a résumé?"

Lucas looked over at Whitaker. She gave him a blank shrug, so Lucas answered it on his own authority. "I'll make sure that you all get letters of reference from the senior agent in charge of the case."

Lucas handed the hard drive to Bobby. "What you have there is the entire history of all four victims. The last victim, Atchison, is more than likely a victim of opportunity, but don't take anything for granted—just be aware of the possibility. Everything from personnel files from their respective agencies to their credit card statements to their email passwords—absolutely everything the agency has assembled on them from the unknowable to Big Data—is in there."

Lucas keyed them into the lab, locking the door behind them. This was the hub of the university's brainpower, a corridor-filled underground wing that very few people got to see. The subterranean tech chamber was home to the university's servers, the temperature- and humidity-controlled space home to massive doses of computational might. It also looked really cool.

The lab tech, a woman named Cecile Rasmussen, whom everyone

simply called Raz, came over. She was dressed in a pair of jeans and a sweater that was either ironic or the ugliest thing Lucas had ever seen: a thick green shag with Rudolph emblazoned on the front in bright-colored yarn, his nose an actual red light bulb that blinked. "Raz, this is the group I called you about."

Rasmussen opened her arms to the space, indicating that it was all theirs. "Take the big lecture monitors; Dr. Page said you'd need a lot of eyeball real estate. I set you up with enough juice to model most of the known universe. If you need me, just yell," she said and walked off, disappearing into the maze of air-cooled corridors that snaked off to points unknown.

Lucas walked over to the corner that Rasmussen had roped off for them. "No one else is coming in here, so you'll have the space to yourself. But I have a few caveats."

Nadeel already had his laptop out and was slaving to the big screens. "Such as?"

"Such as you are being given very personal information on every aspect of these victims' lives. If any of this is leaked—I mean *any* of it—I will consider it an ethical violation of your duties as my assistants, and you will be expelled. Beyond that, the FBI will charge you with a felony and pursue you in a criminal court. I don't think any of you here would do that, but I have to put it on the table."

Then, with warnings over, he went to work. "Don't waste your time with what's there. Look for what isn't there. Look for the holes in the patterns."

Bobby smiled and held up his hand. "Is that it? Or do you have more pontificating to do?"

Lucas looked at the kid for a hard second. "Three of these victims are connected somehow. Maybe all four. The bureau can't find it, but it's there. Besides their choice of careers, something else links these people. I want you to find it."

Bobby plugged the hard drive into his laptop, and the five massive monitors lit up. "Do you mind if we get to work now?" he said and dropped into the zone.

As they walked away, Whitaker said, "I guess all you eggheads are like that."

"Like what?"

"Pricks."

Lucas ignored her and checked his watch. "We have to get back to Oscar's."

57

The West Village

The suited acolytes were done milling about the machine shop floor, no longer deeply immersed in their slow-motion process of black-lighting, dusting, and photographing the total environment. Most of their equipment was packed back up, and the static-free suits were bagged and put away.

Oscar's office was exactly as it had been the day before. Except for the dead man scabbed to the chair, a tumbler of bloody scotch sitting amid red flecks on the coffee table in front of him. Oscar's teeth were inside, the blood and booze separated into different densities, a smiling tequila sunrise.

The fire was long since dead, but the flue was open, and the wind generated a sad moan that seemed the perfect soundtrack.

Whitaker stood in front of Oscar's chair. Lucas didn't know much about her, and he knew absolutely nothing about Oscar except what he had witnessed the day before, but it was obvious that she was upset by his death. Her lip didn't tremble and no tears formed in her eyes, but her movements were nowhere near as smooth as usual.

Crime-scene investigation had never been part of his job description, but he had absorbed enough of it through a natural curiosity coupled with crime-scene osmosis. The process had been refined into a science by the bureau, beginning with the larger gestalt and refining focus down to the minutiae, eventually arriving at a very specific category. And standing there, staring down at the Kafkaesque earthly vessel Oscar's murderer had left behind, whole passages out of the FBI's *Violent Crime Investigation Manual* came back to him. There was no way to miss what this was: a sadistic murder.

The bureau's crime-scene people were there, and Whitaker summoned their lead over. His name was Denver Williams, and he was filling out his second decade with the bureau. Which meant he had the tired, bored look that anyone who spends enough time around the dead eventually develops.

"Special Agent Whitaker," Williams said in way of a hello. He simply nodded at Lucas, probably because he didn't remember his name from the scene the other night at Hartke's murder. "We've had two separate visits here, at different times. Two individuals were present for the murder, and they tracked blood out when they left; we found it on the staircase going down, leaving traces right up to the back door. Men's boots, large size. We'll type them at the lab. There are no signs that any of the locks were either compromised or picked, so we have to assume that Mr. Shiner let his murderers in or that they had a key. But it's the third set that's odd."

Whitaker didn't say anything; she just listened. Lucas stood behind her, watching her body language.

Williams continued, "Sometime after the murderers left, a third person entered the building. Again, through the back door. The blood spatter left a strong and defined pattern on the carpet, and the third visitor picked up trace evidence, but it was already dry. Which meant that they were here at least three hours after the murder. Since Mr. Shiner was already dead, we have to assume that this person had a key."

"How was he killed?" Whitaker asked.

Williams nodded down at the corpse dried to the chair. "We won't know the exact COD until the ME takes him apart, but a good guess would be that gunshot to his head punched his clock. Everything that happened before was window dressing. He died around six last night. It looks like the slug didn't exit the body, so the ME'll be able to give you more specifics."

Oscar's head was tilted to one side, and his brain was spilled all over his shoulder and down into his lap. His mouth was open, the hinge on one side of his jaw gone and burned from the muzzle blast. And the rest of the wounds said that Oscar had been visited by the angel of pain before the bullet had extinguished his life.

Lucas turned away as Whitaker and Williams talked more shop, his attention drawn to the collection of ammunition on the mantel. Shells of every conceivable size, shape, and caliber were still neatly organized. But something had changed since the last time they were here. "Whitaker," he said, interrupting the CSI man's monologue.

She looked up from Oscar's body and came over.

Lucas nodded at the display of bullets. "This is not the same as yesterday."

"What do you mean?"

"A round is missing." Lucas aimed his green anodized finger at a point in the fence of ammunition where a shell was missing. "Two rows back—a .300 Winnie Mag."

Whitaker was staring at the empty slot in the display when her phone rang. Without taking her eyes from the mantel, she pulled it from her pocket and answered with a curt, "Whitaker."

She listened for a few seconds, punctuating the dead air with, "Of course," and "Okay." After nodding a half dozen times, she hung up and turned to Lucas. "Analysis of the ammunition we found in Atchison's basement came back. The machining and bonding process is identical, and the tooling marks match. But the ferrous kernels they contain are not meteoric; they're stainless steel."

"And?" He could tell there was more by her expression.

"Kehoe wants us at the office ASAP; a French terrorist cell just released a statement claiming the shooter."

58

26 Federal Plaza

Zeke Tran hung up the phone and clicked the cursor over the check box on the screen, connecting to the next number on the list. He was one of three agents cold-calling law enforcement agencies that didn't have a statistical presence in reporting crimes to the bureau's national crime database—the N-DEx.

Not that Tran believed that this was how they'd find their guy; news had already come down that it was some French asshole who had turned to the dark side. This was a monumental waste of his resources, and he would much rather be out there questioning people, taking notes, and developing theories. None of which his first-year status as a probationary agent even remotely qualified him to do.

Tran hit the automatic dial tab, and the computer connected him with the next agency on the list—a sheriff's department in Carlwood, Wyoming. As the line connected, he scanned the bureau's information sheet on the office, noting the size of their force and the demographics: population 5,003 souls as of last census; one sheriff; three deputies; one part-time dispatcher; average snowfall of 109 inches.

Tran could tell that the call transferred to a cell phone. It was answered with, "Sheriff's office. How can I help you?"

Tran went into his pitch, honed over a day of cold-calling. "This is Agent Zeke Tran of the FBI. I'm calling from our field office in New York City. Who am I speaking to?"

"This is Deputy Arch Stanton."

"Deputy Stanton, I need to speak to your CO. How can I reach him?"

There was a pause before Stanton said, "How do I know that this really is the FBI?"

This had happened at every single one of the departments Tran spoke to. Welcome to the age of paranoia—*necessary* paranoia. "If you check your call display and then run that number through Google—you have data in your car?"

"Yes, we do."

"Just run the number, and it will come up as one of ours. If you prefer, you can call the New York office and ask them to transfer through to my extension. I'd understand. But it's urgent and has to be done in the next few minutes. We're in the midst of an investigation."

"I heard. Nigger shooting folks."

"We don't have a suspect, Deputy Stanton, and I'd appreciate it if you'd not use racial epithets."

There was a pause followed by, "Racial wha—? Oh, you mean *nigger*? Sorry. It ain't a racist thing. It's not like we're talking about Cam Newton or anything. I just—"

Tran cut him off. "Deputy Stanton, I don't have a lot of time. How do I reach your sheriff?"

Tran could hear Stanton typing on his console computer, the telltale *clack-clack-clack* of technology badly in need of an upgrade. But not all counties had the tax base for new equipment. Tran had spoken to a department earlier in the day where the sheriff's phone line was his home number.

"You check out, Mr. Tran." And with that, Stanton gave him the sheriff's cell number. "Sheriff Doyle is on duty right now. If you have any trouble reaching him, just give me a call ba—"

"Thank you, Deputy Stanton," Tran said, hung up, and dialed the sheriff's number.

The man snapped on in one ring, his voice echoing with computer-generated wobble. "Doyle here."

Tran went into his pitch again, wondering how many more times he'd utter the same sentence in the next few days. "Sheriff Doyle, this is Agent Zeke Tran from the FBI. I'm calling from our field office in New York City."

"What can I do for you, Agent Tran?"

Tran's delivery was committed to memory. "We're looking for a crime that for whatever reason hasn't made it into the N-DEx. It would be a murder or attempted murder involving a large-caliber rifle, most probably a .300 Winchester Magnum. This crime would have happened within the last three years. It's probable a law enforcement officer was the target; it's probable that this crime took place in the winter months, most likely at dusk or dawn; it's probable that the crime took place in extreme cold, maybe during inclement weather; it's probable that the shooter used an elevated position. We're looking for a long-distance shot, something that tables out beyond eight hundred yards. The shooter would have fired from a spot that wasn't easy to find, and they would have left very little behind in the way of evidence. And it's probable that the shooter used a unique type of ammunition—possibly armor-piercing."

"Jesus," Doyle said.

"What?"

There was silence for a few moments before the sheriff came back on with, "You got a crystal ball?"

59

Reuters

Late Saturday afternoon, the Islamic State's news agency, Amaq, claimed that an arm of their organization positioned in France is responsible for orchestrating the murder of four law enforcement officers in New York City. The press release lacked the usual fundamentalist flair of earlier press releases, which was an earmark of the organization's communiqués until the death of their propaganda chief, Wa'il Adil Hasan Salman al-Fayad, also known as Dr. Wa'il, who was killed in a U.S.-led coalition airstrike on September 7, 2016.

"The attack on law enforcement peoples [sic] in New York City was carried out by an Islamic State fighter. More deaths are to follow. God is great," the release in Amaq stated.

(Reporting by Milad Almasi, writing by Kenneth Dent, editing by Mary Ignatius)

Lucas sat in one of the ubiquitous conference rooms at the bureau offices with Kehoe, Graves, and Whitaker. He was watching Graves's lips move, but he had stopped listening. Graves was going over an official press release from a faction of a fractured terrorist organization that had set up shop in one of the crumbling neighborhoods of the Middle East. They were loosely affiliated with ISIS and even more loosely affiliated with reality. And as far as Lucas could tell, the claims the group were making were complete and absolute horseshit.

Graves was ticking off points and weighing in on merits. By the time he finished the communiqué, Lucas was ready to throw a chair through the window.

His irritation must have been evident, because Graves chimed in with, "You have something to add?"

Lucas took a breath and counted to three. "If this were their baby, they'd have claimed responsibility right after Hartke. Or warned of it coming."

"What makes you say that?" Graves sounded like he was humoring a small child.

"Basic added PR value. This is a bang-for-the-buck organization. They know that going up against the FBI is a losing philosophy; it's only a matter of time until they are caught, so getting in on the game at the earliest possible point garners the most publicity. But they didn't claim it early because the first shooting could have been a single random act of run-of-the-mill, good old American firearm violence. They didn't know a second killing was coming, or they would have said as much. All they know is that someone is killing people in a manner that fits well with their brand. Which was why they scrambled to get that letter together; it fits their narrative. It doesn't matter if it turns out to be true; most Americans go nuts when you mention ISIS, even if they're not a threat in any statistical way."

Graves rolled his eyes at that. "Not a threat? You want to talk about that?"

"Not really, but I will." It wasn't hard to see through the statistics. "Since 9/11, fewer than two hundred Americans have been killed on U.S. soil by what could credibly be called Islamic extremists. Fewer. Than. Two. Hundred," Lucas said very slowly. "Your basic

Muslim extremist is not any real threat—and I'm not saying that can't change in an instant—but as things stand, they pose less of a statistical problem than being eaten by your own house cat. The real threat is your Christian neighbor. Those yahoos kill, what?—twelve to fifteen thousand Americans a year. The Iron Man of the mass-shooting championship is your average American asshole." He turned to Whitaker and asked, "How many mass shootings this week alone?"

Whitaker's eyes cycled up as she said, "Six in the last five days."

Lucas turned back to Graves. "We can chalk half of those up to the Silly Season. But this country has more mass shooters that are American-made than lottery winners. How's that?"

"You sound like a liberal," Graves said slowly.

"I am not a fucking liberal," Lucas snapped. "Or a conservative. Or a Marxist, socialist, or anarchist. I'm just a human being. But I understand numbers." Lucas leaned forward, pointing his good eye directly at Graves. "I have no problem with gun ownership; I just hate that those same people refuse to understand that by having a gun in their possession, they trip the stats up into epidemic territory. The problem with the Second Amendment is that it tricks people into the unsaid belief that when it comes time to complain, they have the right to do so with said guns. Check out the stats on virtually every mass shooting in the fucking history of this country and you won't find a radical Muslim behind it; you'll find a good old boy or mental case—raised on the belief that guns are a God-given right under the umbrella of the Constitution, granted by Jesus. The guise is to fight tyranny so when things don't go their way, they automatically—and unconsciously—associate any perceived slight as both tyranny *and* a chance to express their rights. Otherwise, what's the point of owning ten thousand rounds of ammunition? Don't like your boss? Tyranny! Can't get laid because you're an unappealing individual? Tyranny! Koreans now own the 7-Eleven where you used to buy your Big Gulp? Tyranny! And the asshole takes up his complaint with an assault rifle. A Muslim does this and your Second Amendment supporter calls him a terrorist; when you tell them a *real American*—their words, *not* mine—did it, it's a false flag. Apparently, believing that a secret world order carries out atrocious crimes in order to garner public sympathy in an effort to take their guns away is more believable than the truth, which is that having so many guns out there is a cultural mistake. I've said it before—there's a crisis of stupidity in America. All you have to do is look at the numbers around the world. So yeah, I stand by my point. Up to this juncture in time, your average American has absofuckinglutely nothing to fear from Muslim terrorists from a statistical standpoint. At least not now."

Graves shook his head. "That's not what they feel, and it's still a free country."

"Who are you now, Newt Gingrich? This isn't about feelings; this is about facts. Numbers don't lie. And although everyone is allowed to have a position, not all positions are created equal. There are experts in any given field; one person's ignorance is not just as valuable as another's *knowledge,* and the fact is your average American has to worry about his neighbor more than terrorists by *orders of magnitude.*"

"You're kind of an asshole," Graves said, staring Lucas down.

"Graves, life is a nuanced sport, and you need to wear your critical-thinking pants." He smiled over at him. "So do me a favor, and pick a number between one and fuck you."

Kehoe held up his hand. "Gentlemen, this is getting us nowhere."

Lucas nodded. "I just hate stupid."

Graves glared at him.

Kehoe took back the reins of the meeting. "I appreciate your concern, Dr. Page. But we have our marching papers via a joint recommendation between the DHS, the DOJ, and the NSA." He gave Lucas that look again, the one that said he was missing part of the equation. "And Interpol pushed the Frenchman across our desk. I'm not going to say that it's out of my hands, but we go *where we are told to.*" Kehoe took a sip of tea before continuing. "We're focusing on Froissant. We need to release a statement to the media—including photos—so we can find this guy. I want to run him down, and I want to do it before someone else gets killed."

Graves nodded at the letter. "Media is already drafting a release with Froissant's bio."

"Have legal take a look at it to make sure there's nothing in there that will come back later to bite us in the ass." Kehoe turned to Lucas. "You see anything wrong with releasing this?"

Lucas had absolutely no idea why Kehoe was asking him, only that he had a reason. The obvious answer was so his objections would be a matter of record. "Only that you will be looking for the wrong man."

"You don't think there's a possibility it's the Frenchman?"

How many times did he have to say this? "I *guarantee* it's not the Frenchman."

"Then why is Washington so sure?" Graves asked.

Lucas shrugged. "Because the only people who end up there are the only ones who shouldn't? I don't fucking know. But if you want to follow the ravings of idiots, be my guest."

There was a knock at the door, and one of the probationary agents clogging up the corridors of the building came in. Lucas recognized him from Kehoe's state of the nation speech yesterday morning. "Mr. Kehoe, sorry to interrupt. I'm Probationary Agent Zeke Tran."

Kehoe nodded a *get to the point*.

"I just got off the horn with a small sheriff's department out West." Tran nodded at Lucas. "They had a murder thirty-six months back that fits our shooter's MO."

Lucas pushed up and back, rising out of his chair. "How closely?"

Tran held up his notes. "He used a mountain instead of a rooftop, but other than that, it's the same. Middle of a snowstorm at sunrise. Hit the driver of a moving car."

"Who'd he kill?"

"A deputy."

"Where was this?" Kehoe asked.

"Carlwood, Wyoming, sir."

Lucas saw something flash over Kehoe's features, like a spark riding dry air, and then it was gone and Kehoe turned to Lucas and Whitaker. "Do the follow-up."

They stood, and Graves's phone rang. He picked it up and listened for a few seconds before snapping his fingers at them, stopping them. They turned, and he asked the caller to hold on. "Ballistics matched the slugs Atchison put into your friend Dingo. It was the same weapon that killed Oscar Shiner *and* Billy Margolis."

60

John F. Kennedy International Airport, New York

The runway slid under the belly of the Gulfstream G550 as the dual Rolls-Royce turbofans propelled them down the snow-swept tarmac. There was an instant when the cabin began to shudder, and Lucas thought his teeth would rattle loose. But human engineering beat out gravity and they were airborne, the laws of physics pushing him into the luxurious leather seat. The earth began to unfold beneath and behind them before it was lost as they headed up into the storm.

The updates to the bureau's infrastructure over the past decade included their fleet of jets, and the new wings were impressive. Besides the Connolly Leather and bubinga paneling, the cabin was outfitted with top-drawer communications equipment, computers, and a minibar that would make a nutritionist proud. But Lucas was just happy he didn't have to fly commercial. He hated clearing security, a process he saw as basically pointless (and invasive—his prosthetics always lit up the scanners and he hated dealing with the TSA simpletons). There were myriad ways to sneak weapons or explosives through. But he understood why they were there: to make the huddled masses feel less threatened. More of that feelings-over-facts that Graves had brought up back at the bureau, another manifestation of the dumbing down of America. It was one of the reasons that Lucas wanted to grade student papers with a cigarette lighter instead of a red pen.

Graves and the body politic of the FBI were still convinced that the Frenchman was responsible even though all the evidence said otherwise. But not Kehoe; he was a lot of things, but he was by no means stupid. And he was most definitely not an intellectually lazy man. He had always been able to focus on the big picture, and Lucas wondered if he had been sent out West so he'd be out of the way, or if he was helping Kehoe in some unknown manner.

But there was definitely a reason—Kehoe didn't do *anything* without a reason.

He had signed off on their trip to Wyoming to examine a three-year-old crime scene—not the actions of a skeptic. The fuel alone would be worthy of an accounting report, massive investigation notwithstanding. Which brought Lucas around to the *why* part of it all: Why had he sent them across the country?

"Page?" Whitaker interrupted the questions ticker-taping through his mind.

He turned away from the window.

"We've got a little under four hours to Jackson; if you want to stretch out, the seats in the back fold down." She nodded at her purse. "I've got Seconal if you need a little extra help."

"Do I look that bad?" She was facing the damaged side of his body, and after two days of shitty sleep and too much coffee in the tank, he no doubt looked like Frankenstein's monster in need of fresh paint and a good waxing. The bolts in his neck were probably rusty, too.

"Yes, you do."

Lucas turned back to the window. Back to the storm they were rising through. And back to the questions he couldn't shake.

The biggest question of all being: *What was Kehoe not telling him?*

61

The panel assembled on Fox News was deeply immersed in the scientific analysis of the Ferguson effect, which was no doubt the only logical explanation for the recent killings of four law enforcement officers in New York City. The panel was headed up by a cliché in a suit who looked like he was hawking hair care products, toothpaste, or both. He kept smiling into the camera as the other guests rolled out their theories. The Ferguson effect was bound to be responsible for more killings unless immediate legal steps were taken to shut down Black Lives Matter for what it was—a terrorist organization. These were criminals. These were African American thu—

And then Smiley McSmileyface's expression changed as his producer piped in through his earpiece and the chyron swinging across the bottom of the screen shifted ideologies.

"Sorry to cut this short," Chuckles said to the panel of experts—one former lawyer for the DOJ who had been fired for taking bribes; a former model turned spokesperson for a grocery chain; and a retired police officer who was now a celebrated author on the coming race wars in America. "But we have breaking news that the Islamic State has just claimed responsibility for the shootings."

.

At that, Chuckles turned to the camera and did his best to look like he knew what he was talking about. He managed a reasonable imitation of a news anchor as he read from the prompter. "According to the new ISIS propaganda chief, the four law enforcement officers recently shot in the city of New York were killed by one of their fighters. They have not released any additional information, only that more killings are to come and that God will grant them victory." At that, he turned back to the panel.

The disgraced lawyer was the first to speak. "As I said, this is clearly the fault of sloppy foreign policy under the last Democratic president, and it's clear they wanted to deflect the blame to the African American lobby in order to conceal their Muslim sympathies so that hardworking, plain-speaking Americans can't . . ."

CNN had become the New York City Shooting Channel. No other news existed, not even in America. They ignored the mass shootings unfolding across the country just as they did every week. They ignored the storm blanketing the northeastern states and the closed schools. They ignored the pileups on the beltways, the religious freedom cases being fought in the Supreme Court, they ignored the stock market plunge and the airline strike. They ignored the protests in Germany and the power outages in Venezuela.

They ignored.

And ignored.

And ignored.

But they did it with graphs. And charts. And videos and interviews and cool graphics and way too many commercials.

They did it in suits.

And dresses.

They did it outside and indoors.

They invited experts and laymen to voice their opinions.

They did survey after survey. Then they announced the results.

The only thing they did not do was report any facts.

62

The Upper West Side

The mosque on West Eighty-sixth and Amsterdam had been under sporadic government surveillance for the past fourteen years. It was on the watch list for every agency that had a finger in the anti-terrorism pie, from the DHS to the NSA to the FBI. The focus of their attention was usually on the center for Islamic studies that operated out of the offices, but the mosque proper, and its imam—Kifah Elseyed—had been a fixture in governmental memos since the Arab Spring of 2011.

The past three days had certainly been some of the busiest in the way of good old-fashioned governmental peekaboo. Email had been scanned; cell phone records collated and analyzed; visitors photographed and run through databases; banking monitored. All in search of a French national turned jihadi named Philippe Froissant. And now, with news of Middle Eastern terrorists claiming responsibility for the four dead law enforcement officers, the men in the apartment across the street were filming on a twenty-four-hour schedule, going so far as to use night-sensitive gear after sundown.

Surveillance on this particular mosque was not the result of random anti-Muslim sentiment. Imam Kifah Elseyed had been promoting elements of radical Islam for years, and in the heightened tensions of the past few days, the analysts with the FBI had upgraded his threat classification. The imam, American by birth, was a fixture in the homegrown radical Islam movement; he had recently been charged with inciting hate and was out on bail, awaiting trial.

The pair of agents from the Department of Homeland Security took turns at the binoculars. They had very little in the way of concrete orders other than to look for Froissant. If they saw him—even if they *thought* they saw him—they were to call in a tactical squad. Until that happened, they were to observe and report. And to make sure the camera was always running.

Even in the midst of a storm that had slowed the metabolism of the entire city, the imam's white Toyota Sequoia arrived precisely on time. The side doors to the mosque opened and two assistants—a euphemism for *bodyguards*—stepped out, looking up and down the street. They motioned for Elseyed to come forward, and he emerged from the mosaic-decorated doors in a fur coat that covered his robe. He was a small man, with a round physique and a distinctive walk the agents were by now familiar with.

The steps had been shoveled and sanded, but the freezing temperatures kept them icy, and he made his way cautiously, occasionally reaching out to steady himself on the arm of one of his assistants. He paused at the bottom step while they opened the door for him.

The imam took a step, and it was as if he had walked into a guillotine and his head popped off his neck, sending a black arc of arterial spray into the air. His body stood there for a second, and there was a brief instant of silence before he went to his knees and the sound of the shot whistled in.

He fell over and the steps around him quickly went red.

63

State Route 39, outside Carlwood, Wyoming

Lucas cradled the travel mug of coffee in his gloved hand. It was his fourth of the morning and it was doing its job, binding with his blood on a molecular level and providing him with the mental fuel to face another day of trying to find meaning in the meaningless.

The sun was coming up over the mountain behind him, painting the road in early-morning pastels. It was freezing here, much colder than back in New York; he had never experienced temperatures like this, and he wondered if something was wrong with his central nervous system. It was a wet, humid cold that needled down into his bones like a dental drill. Each time he pulled in a lungful of mountain air, his nostrils froze together. It sucked.

"Right here?" he asked.

"Right here," the sheriff said from somewhere behind him.

Whitaker stood ahead of them on the road, her shadow stretching out in front of her as she surveyed the terrain. She was in her FBI parka and vapor-barrier boots and looked as comfortable as the sheriff, no doubt the Midwest roots serving her well.

Lucas finished off the coffee and placed the mug down on the hood of the sheriff's sport ute, a monstrous vehicle that had a kangaroo bar welded to the front, an extra tire fastened to the back, and three separate long weapons inside. All four quarter panels and both bumpers were decorated with CSPOA stickers, the proud head of a bald eagle staring defiantly into the future the main graphic. If you were worried about the zombie apocalypse, it would be hard to find a better ride this side of a King Tiger.

Sheriff Brice "Bronco" Doyle was a tall man a few years into his fifties, with a solid set of shoulders and a head that could have been hammered out of a paint bucket. He had thick white hair offset by a beard that, with the right tending, could rival Billy Gibbons's. He had a cross pin on his lapel beside the American flag, and he carried a pair of pistols in a tooled old-time holster that had the mirror images of Jesus worked into the pockets. Doyle gave the impression that he was the kind of man you'd want at your side when you ran out of ammunition and the cannibals made it over the fence. But there was nothing humorous about his disposition, and he didn't smile much. But what weirded Lucas out was that for a small-town sheriff on the edge of civilization, he had yet to swear.

Doyle walked ahead and knelt down a few paces past Whitaker. He touched his gloved fingertip to the icy road. "Near as I could figure it, Jameson was right here when he got hit." He lifted his arm and pointed to forty yards beyond where his knee touched the earth. "He came around that corner, straight into the sun."

Not much in the way of lead time, Lucas recognized, and he slapped another mental Post-it up on the board in his head.

Before coming out here, Doyle walked them through the file. It was back in the sport ute, but the sixty or so photographs were in Lucas's pocket. He pulled them out, and they stuck together in the cold as he thumbed through the pile. When he found the one he was looking for, he held it up: it had been taken from this same vantage point. As now, it was the midst of winter, and the road was plowed but heavily crisscrossed with tire marks. One set emerged from the countless impressions and shot off frame, toward the guardrail. The photos were dated January 9 and would be three years old in a little over two weeks.

Lucas turned to the mountain, a rutted chunk of ancient geological animosity that reached up into the sky, the top hidden in low-slung clouds. He pulled out the Leupold and sighted in on the tree line a little over five hundred feet up.

Doyle stood up and went into narrator mode. "Deputy Jameson was delivering a prisoner from our county jail to Jackson. Local man. Not a career criminal, just a career dumbass.

"It was somewhere between seven and seven thirty when Jameson rounded that corner. His prisoner was cuffed to the bar in the backseat, passenger's side. Jameson got to about where I'm standing when the round punched through his windshield. Hit him square in the fillings. The Explorer swerved right, sped along until it hit the corner, jumped the guardrail, and tumbled down that slope into the river."

Lucas looked down at the river, seventy-five feet below the road. It was a good-sized flow that displaced a lot of water per second, and even now, in this inhuman deep-space temperature, it was too rough to freeze over. It rumbled by, gasping great gulps of steam into the air that weighted the nearby trees down in a white shroud. Weird cauliflower lumps of ice grew on the branches down by the water, opaque milky tumors built up over time.

Doyle went on, "It took us four days to get the car out of the river and up the hill. Jameson's body had been washed out, but his prisoner was still cuffed in the back." Doyle smiled sadly and shook his head. "Drowned." The word hung in the air on a lungful of condensation. "Coroner said the tumble down the bank broke his wrist in two places. He broke it another four times trying to get out of the cuffs after they went into the drink.

"We found Jameson half a mile downriver, snagged up in some branches. Big hole punched right through his head."

"Did you find the slug?"

Doyle was silent for a few ticks of the clock before he shook his head. "From what we were able to piece together, the round went through the front windshield, then through Deputy Jameson's head. After that, it went through one of the back windows—we never could figure out which one. The roll down the bank and four days in rushing water did a lot of damage—all of the windows were gone. I had divers in there, and all we found were a few handfuls of glass."

Lucas thumbed through the photos until he found the ones he was looking for—images of the deputy's SUV, taken in a garage back in town. The lighting was shitty, but there was no mistaking that the windows had all been smashed out. A fragment of the windshield remained, peeled away and curled up like the lid from an anchovy can.

"You still have this vehicle, Sheriff Doyle?" Lucas asked, knowing what the answer would be.

"We scrapped it." Doyle shook his head. "And we never did figure out where the shot came from."

Lucas turned back to the mountain and nodded. "Five hundred feet up the side of that hill, approximately where the trees end. To the right, beside that pile of geological shit." He cranked his aluminum hand up, and the sun from behind lit up his fingers.

Doyle kept his focus on Lucas. "What did you say you did at the FBI, Dr. Page?"

"I didn't." Lucas pocketed the scope.

Lucas turned back to the corner where Jameson's 4×4 had come from. He connected the dots in his head, doing what he did. The wind and cold and humidity disappeared, and he was back in time. Back in Doyle's car. Back in January, three years ago.

He looked up at the mountain, focusing on the tree line. It was about twelve hundred yards out. Except for the car coming straight on, it was nearly identical to the shot that had killed Hartke—at least from a geometrical perspective.

He turned back to the corner that Jameson had come out of just before a man with a rifle had ended his time on earth. Behind it was the guardrail, thirty yards of field, and the river beyond. A lot of terrain to cover if he got the men with the metal detectors out here.

He looked over at Whitaker, and she was examining him, not doing a very good job of hiding her curiosity. He nodded and shrugged. "It's possible," was all he said. But they needed a way to tie this killing directly to the ones in New York; otherwise, all they had was a handful of conjecture held together by hope—not much in the way of a solution.

Whitaker shifted out of observation mode and turned to Doyle, who was also looking at Lucas.

"Suspects?" she asked.

Doyle shook his head. "Nothing. We're a rural area, so there's enough bad ideas to go around. Mostly domestic violence and booze-fueled stupidity. Drugs and break-ins. ATV accidents and suicide. One dumb chain of events after another." He stopped at that and nodded at Whitaker. "Most criminals don't mean to be criminals; they just don't have the brains to stay out of trouble. I'm sure it's the same in the big city."

It was Whitaker's turn to smile sadly and nod. "You have no idea."

"Yeah. Well," he said as if those two words held all kinds of meaning.

"How long was Jameson on the force?"

"About eighteen months, give or take."

"He ever live out East? New York? He ever visit?"

"Jameson? He was proud that he had never left the county, never mind the state. New York?" He smiled at that. "I can't picture Billy Jameson in New York City. If you knew him, neither could you."

"He the kind of guy to make enemies?"

Doyle snorted out a laugh. "He was a good kid. Some guys, you know, you slap a badge on them and it goes to their head. Kills their humility. Not him. He liked people, and people liked him. Didn't hand out too many speeding tickets to the locals, which earned him a lot of friends. I used to bust his butt at the end of every month; I told him we depended on the revenue. He'd just smile and say these people were his neighbors and that his father said you never crap where you eat. Lived with his ma. Never got angry. He really didn't deserve what happened to him."

Lucas was still staring up at the mountain. "Yet someone killed him anyway."

Doyle shrugged. "And you got a Muslimist shooting cops down on the streets of New York." He straightened up and rested a gloved hand on his holster, his fingers curling down and touching Jesus's crown of thorns. "Life ain't fair."

Lucas turned to Doyle, and his line of sight dropped to the man's holster, to the dual images of the Lord. "On that," Lucas said. "We can agree."

64

When they got back to town and asked about food, Doyle suggested a joint down the block. The distance between the station—a former insurance brokerage in a strip mall—and the restaurant clocked out at 305 steps for Lucas. But the wind funneling down the street made it feel like they were crossing Elephant Island in Shackleton's footsteps, and by the time they stepped into Mackey's Restaurant and Grill, he was ready to light his clothing on fire just to get a little warmth into his bloodstream.

Mackey's was a typical rural family hotspot, complete with tablecloths that looked like western shirts minus buttons overseen by a platoon of taxidermied mule deer hanging in the rafters.

They ordered coffee before sitting. Since arriving in the tiny hamlet the night before, Lucas developed the theory that becoming an alcoholic out here could be a useful survival mechanism; ethanol in your blood kept it from freezing. After their lips started working again, they ordered food and both lapsed into their own personal silence.

Lucas's expression must have been telegraphing his concentration, because Whitaker asked, "What's going through your head?"

Lucas wanted to shrug, but he was afraid that his ears would snap off and fall into his collar. "What have we found here, other than a reason to appreciate warm clothes?"

"A small-town deputy who was killed for no apparent reason with no leads and very little to tie his killing to the ones back in New York."

"Yet here we are, trying to find a link." He wrapped his good hand around the mug, willing more warmth into his hand. The weather here really was a completely different animal from back in New York.

"You think there is one?"

Lucas turned the question over in his head a few times before answering. "The general mechanics of the murder look very similar in everything from weather conditions to yardage to elevation to type of target. But that's all we have—similarities. Without a way to concretely tie our shooter to Jameson's murder, we're just wishing." He took a sip of coffee and noticed that it was already getting cold. "But it *feels* like our guy. Not that that means anything."

"What about the missing slug?"

"I was thinking about that; an off-the-shelf .300 could easily go through a windshield at twelve hundred yards, go through a human head, then exit a back window. Jameson could have been killed with a regular deer-hunting round. Problem is, one of our armor-piercing rounds would do the same thing at that distance and elevation—through the windshield, through Jameson's head, and out the back window."

"So we need to find that slug," Whitaker offered.

"Ideally, yes. But that will take time. There's a good square mile to search, and most of it is either under ten feet of snow, or is occupied by a river; the chances of never finding it are better than I'd like to think. Which means we need another way to connect Deputy Jameson's killing to the murders in New York—if there is one. That connection lies in linking Jameson to Hartke, Kavanagh, and Lupino."

"And we still haven't figured out how they are related to one another."

"Which brings us back to why the fuck are we here?" he said into his mug. Crawling around on that frozen road earlier made him feel like an actor in a Scandinavian film noir—all that had been missing was a Volvo and a little more silence. "At least Doyle doesn't have his head up his own ass."

"Did you see the CSPOA stickers on his SUV?"

"The eagle stickers?"

"You don't know what they are, do you?"

Lucas shrugged. "Fraternal order of sheriffs or some such deal."

She shook her head. "Constitutional Sheriffs and Peace Officers Association."

"Okay."

"The CSPOA is of the opinion that since local law enforcement, and sheriffs in specific, are the highest authority in a county, their power supersedes that of the federal government, including the FBI, ATF, and DHS. They feel that they are the only ones who can decide what's constitutional and what's not in their own backyards—they value the concept of interpretation. They pick and choose the laws they want to uphold."

Lucas interrupted with, "Idiots convinced of their own superiority always make me nervous."

"Me, too. Especially when racism is baked into the formula. From a certain perspective, they are vigilante anti-government people masquerading as patriots under the guise of authority. It can be a bad combination."

"Like your Jade Helm people?"

Whitaker smiled. "Exactly."

The waitress, a woman in her sixties with pineapple earrings and pink Nikes, brought their order over. They were both silent as she slid the plates onto the table. She gave Whitaker a dirty look, then walked away without asking if they wanted anything else.

Whitaker picked up her fork. "Doyle is not happy that we're here, asking questions."

Lucas looked out the window at the snow whistling down the street. "Neither am I," he said, going to work on his food.

Lucas was one mouthful into his mushroom omelet and Whitaker had barely dented a BLT with extra cheese, mayo, and mustard when his phone buzzed. He checked the screen and was surprised to see Bobby Nadeel's number come up—almost as surprised that his phone worked out here.

"Dr. Page." Lucas never dropped character with students.

"Dr. Page, this is Bob Nadeel."

Lucas could tell Nadeel thought he had good news.

"I think we've found something that might help you. It's not very big, but it's a definite link between your victims."

Lucas put his fork down, wiped his mouth with his napkin, and tried not to yell when he said, "What?" He checked his watch, which was still on East Coast time. He had handed the data off to Nadeel and the other kids—what?—less than twenty-two hours ago.

"We know how the victims are related. I'd like to take the credit, but Caroline was the one who nailed it. She's better at abstract thinking, and it was her algorithm that picked it up."

Whitaker saw the change in Lucas's expression, and she put her sandwich down, took a swig of coffee, and wiped her mouth. She leaned forward to listen.

Nadeel continued, "We entered everything on that hard drive you gave us into spreadsheets, and I mean *everything;* I don't think we left out a single byte of data. The obvious avenues were employment, schooling, and social circles. There's a theory regarding social structures in beehives that denotes that hive members don't interact with others of a higher—"

"It's called eusociality, Bobby. Can you get to the point?"

"Sure. Of course. We went through the obvious avenues to connect the victims, but to be honest, we didn't put as much backbone into it at the front end as we could have. It's not that we were being lazy, it's just that like you said, the FBI's digital people have already gone at this with their big bad supercomputers. So we did as you directed and concentrated on the holes in the data, focusing on what *wasn't* there.

"We factored in the kinds of phone calls that people usually make—you know, spouses and kids and work and mechanics and siblings and credit card companies. Then we looked for calls that each victim should have made but didn't. Nothing stuck out. Same thing with credit cards; we looked for things that should have been there but weren't. It took us all night, but Caroline's algorithm—which was real old-school, by the way: Euclidian—came through."

"Bobby?" Nadeel was playing this up for political reasons, but Lucas was cold and tired, and his omelet was starting to wrinkle.

"Sure. You can forget Atchison. He has nothing to do with the rest of the gene pool. But the other three victims have a hole in their service records during January, eighteen years back. The dates aren't all identical, but there is an overlap of six days where all three were not present anywhere—January 7 to 13. Hartke was off from January 5 to 15; Kavanagh from January 7 to 13; Lupino was gone from January 5 to 16."

Lucas emptied his coffee without taking the phone from his ear.

"So we dug in on those dates. Not one of the victims used their cell phones during those six days. Same thing for credit cards, which was anomalous; there isn't a six-day period on any of their credit card histories that is inactive. The longest we could find was a two-day break on Kavanagh's statement over Christmas break in 2009." Nadeel paused. "We did a countrywide search for those six days, focusing on events that would involve law enforcement. We came up with a massive list of criminal events—you wouldn't believe the shit that goes on in this country when you look at the stats. It's amazing that the whole country hasn't been shot by their neighbors."

"Bobby?"

"Yeah. Sorry. Only eleven percent of crimes during those dates spanned more than a single day; four percent spanned more than two days; two incidents spanned more than three days; and a single one spanned five, beginning on the first day of our six-day period. It's an eighteen-year-old case—an arrest by federal marshals that went wrong. A family got pinned down in their cabin, and the good guys jumped the gun. Everyone died. The government didn't release the names of the personnel or officers involved, so there was no way to tie your victims to this event. But those six days were bugging me.

"So I did a little research and found out that since 9/11, the federal government has the right to redact personnel from reports destined for review—even the FOIA can't free the files for a period of ninety-nine years after a case is closed. So I went off-road; I searched WikiLeaks and found three-hundred-and-seven internal FBI and DOJ memos referencing the event, all dumped a little over three years ago. We searched for your victims but found nothing until we reduced their names to initials and, well, there they were. All three were involved in an incident that became known as Bible Hill. And you'll never guess where it is."

Lucas thought back to Sheriff Doyle standing out on the road, looking up at the mountain. About where Deputy Jameson had gone in the river, drowning a small-time criminal in the back. "Carlwood, Wyoming."

Nadeel was silent for a moment. "How did you know?"

Lucas looked up into the rafters, at the crowd of glass eyeballs staring down. "Lucky guess."

65

Lucas watched them flex their respective muscles, establishing alpha. Doyle was leaning against the rifle rack in his office, both hands resting on the tooled Jesus twins on his holster. The long guns behind him were greased and dusted, the bluing worn down on the high spots. He eyed Whitaker for a few quiet seconds before saying, "Whyina hell would you want to go up there?" The declaration was the closest thing to swearing the sheriff had demonstrated so far. He shifted his weight, and his hands crept back over the pockets of his holster so they were resting on the rubber grips of the dual Glocks.

Whitaker stepped forward. "Because we would."

Lucas could see that she had switched gears into combat mode. So could the sheriff. "Don't be so sure," he said, and it was hard to miss that it sounded like a thinly veiled threat.

Whitaker walked over to the rifle rack until she was almost nose to nose with the man. "I appreciate your position, and as much as I'd like to tell you that you're allowed to have opinions, you're not. Our brothers-in-arms are out there being murdered by someone, and I need to know who. You either become part of the solution right fucking now, or you're part of the problem." She smiled at him, and it wasn't a friendly expression. "And you do not want to get me angry."

Doyle was silent for a moment, and it was obvious he was thinking through his options. "We need a plow to get up there this time of year. We stopped clearing the road on the county dime to cut down on pilgrims going up."

"Pilgrims?" Lucas asked. "What kind of pilgrims?"

The sheriff tried to pick an eye to focus on, finally settling on Lucas's good one. "The kind who don't like tyranny."

Whitaker kept the voltage in her voice dialed up. "So get us a plow. I'll pay for it."

Doyle was trying to put the pieces together. "What does Jameson's killing have to do with Bible Hill?"

Whitaker answered as if there were nothing to think about. "They are independent incidents." Which was the safest way to handle things.

Doyle nodded at that. "I know that. I just want to be sure that *you* know that. Jameson was still in high school when Bible Hill happened."

"And you?"

He paused, and the mass of his larynx pumped once with a swallow. "I had no choice. You people stormed in here with two dozen agents and a ton of bad ideas. I told you not to go up there. I told you it wouldn't end well. I tried to help."

Whitaker flexed rank again when she said, "I need to see your files."

Doyle smiled at that. "Lady, I don't have any files. You people took everything."

Whitaker didn't look convinced. "Can you remember who was in charge?"

"Sure." Doyle nodded. "Some asshole name of Doug Hartke."

66

Bible Hill, Wyoming

It wasn't hard to see why they had named this place with such reverence. The ground below his feet dropped off, and the old-growth coniferous forest was dappled with patches of green poking through the snow. It was the kind of view that could make you believe in God if you didn't understand the general mechanics of the universe. Or weren't interested.

Lucas and Whitaker had gone through the appropriate motions, digging through the FBI archives to replicate Nadeel's findings. Whitaker found a basic case summary, totaling less than six thousand words, and the picture it painted was ridiculously incomplete. They needed something solid to take to Kehoe. The link was here. Somewhere. They had passed the threshold for coincidence.

Lucas turned away from the HD image of the world stretching into forever. Back to the mountainside. Back to the burned-out cabin and litter-strewn clearing. Back to where a family had been killed.

Whitaker and Doyle were standing up at the foundation near the stone chimney reaching into the sky like a charred bone. They were speaking softly, Doyle pointing here and there as he went through the chain of events that led to a disaster so terrible that it had been struck from FBI memory. On the way up here, Doyle had laid out his version of events. It was not pretty, not particularly erudite, and very disturbing.

Doyle had been very matter of fact about it all, but Lucas didn't have a great deal of faith in the man's loyalty to their cause, and he took everything at less than face value. After all, the FBI was the very government that his bumper sticker confirmed he didn't respect. But his delivery jelled with what they knew, and the predictability of the story didn't make it any less heartbreaking.

Carl and Elisabeth Quaid had had enough of life in the city. Their growing mistrust of the way civilization was heading was fueled by the ministry they attended, the Covenant of the New Order, a fundamentalist End Times congregation with Christian Identity roots. Certain that the apocalypse was imminent, Quaid and his wife bought three hundred acres in the mountains using a distant relative's inheritance. They built a cabin. A smokehouse. A larder. All overlooking God's country.

For a lot of years, everything had been good. Their children spent their time doing what kids did. Tommy, Forney, Ursula, Ruby, and Esther never really knew any other life, and they were devoted to their parents and their teachings. Quaid made a living operating heavy machinery for a local roadwork crew and buying and selling guns in his spare time. Elisabeth homeschooled the children. They had a vegetable garden, and Carl hunted to fill the storeroom. Carl split logs in the fall to heat the house through the winter. They had two dogs, German shepherds—Boomer and Keylor. They cut their own Christmas tree, and Elisabeth canned vegetables. They enjoyed the sunrises. Life was hard work, but they were good at it.

Then one Monday, Carl Quaid sold a trunkful of semiautomatic AR-15s to someone he barely knew in the parking lot of a Waffle House in Jackson. Quaid had a dealer's license, and the transaction was completely legal, but things got complicated when the customer became upset that the weapons weren't fully automatic. Quaid told him to file down the hammer hook—or remove the disconnector—but after the back-and-forth became heated, Quaid took one of the assault rifles apart right there on the hood of the car, modifying it with his Gerber pocket tool. When he put the rifle back together, a dozen ATF agents jumped out, read him his Miranda rights, and led him away in handcuffs while his three-year-old twin daughters watched from the backseat. Turned out the customer was an ATF informant.

It was a bullshit charge that any decent lawyer could have sold as entrapment. But Quaid stood by his actions; he had done nothing wrong. After he posted bail, he refused to show up for the trial date. And when Sheriff Doyle was asked to deliver the arrest warrant for failure to appear, he had driven up there and tried to talk it out with Quaid. He told him that the powers that be were pissed and that he should take it to court. Worst-case scenario, he explained, Quaid could plea it down. Quaid said he believed in his constitutional rights under the Second Amendment, and he thanked Doyle for his efforts before telling him that the only way he was coming down off the mountain was feetfirst.

Doyle said he was stupid enough to relay Quaid's comments to the Wyoming branch of the ATF. It was a decision that would haunt him until the day he closed his eyes. Lucas didn't say anything to that, but he understood those kinds of regrets.

Three months and five days after Carl Quaid failed to appear in court, the ATF and FBI showed up on the mountain.

The Quaid cabin overlooked the single road that climbed to their gate, and they saw the convoy coming. They were prepared. But it is impossible to stand up to the government of the United States in any meaningful way, and things were bad from the beginning.

By the time the ATF, FBI, local SD, and U.S. Marshals arrived at the cabin, the gate was locked and the drive was blocked by a series of chained logs.

But the dogs were out, and the government made their point by killing both. They left Boomer and Keylor on the road, and in the subzero weather, the convoy of government vehicles spread them out in a long red smear on the ice and snow. Doyle cited this as merely one instance out of many that amounted to unnecessary mental cruelty, paramount unprofessionalism, and supreme negligence. Lucas couldn't disagree with the man. Doyle pleaded with the feds to leave and let him bring Quaid in when things calmed down. He was ordered off the mountain.

Things went from bad to worse when an FBI sniper positioned on an outcropping of rock five hundred yards from the cabin took a guess shot at a figure he later testified he believed to be Carl Quaid.

Doyle claimed that there was footage locked away in some unknown FBI vault that showed the nine-year-old boy's head disintegrating. The thought brought back images of Atchison's skull taking the full wallop of the sniper's round.

Doyle said the boy would lie out in the yard for the next four days, like the dogs.

Things continued the spectacular downward spiral as mistakes compounded, sending the entire operation into the shitter of the irrevocably fucked. Two FBI agents and one ATF officer died from what ballistics would later determine to be "friendly fire." One of the senior agents from the FBI would fall off a cliff, rendering him brain-dead; Doyle wondered out loud if he was still on life support all these years later.

But the big cinematic finale occurred on the fifth day.

It was an errant shot that should not have been let go. But one of the government men who had been out in the cold for too long didn't realize that frostbite was setting in and one of his fingers twitched.

The bullet ricocheted off the doorknob.

Right into a propane cylinder.

Technically, there was a *clink*.

Followed by a partial scream by Elisabeth Quaid.

And a *bang*.

But no one really heard anything but the mushroom cloud motherfucking *whump* that rose into the sky like an angry fist reaching for God.

The cabin burned through the night, the first half hour punctuated by endless rounds of stored ammunition going off, the heavy punch of twelve-gauge shells offset by the high-pitched crack of .223 rounds complemented by what the forensics investigators would later discover was over a hundred thousand rounds of .45 and 9 mil in the basement. *Bing. Bang. Pop. Crack. Zing.* And the occasional *boom*. All recorded on government footage that would remain sealed for ninety-nine years, a time capsule that future generations could look back on and weep.

They found most of Elisabeth; her charred corpse was wound around her baby, their bones intertwined in burned human macramé. They weren't as lucky with Carl Quaid; all they managed to cull from the embers were his feet bones, a few ribs, and his skull. The big Kodak moment were the children. They were discovered in crispy little pieces of bone that would take a month to identify, their itty-bitty pieces spread out over half the hillside.

All the government agencies involved would be drawn into an investigation that wasn't as monitored as it might have been due to the lack of plaintiffs. There was a closed trial. And a secret settlement. Doyle was flown to Washington, D.C., where he sat in a hallway for three days, sipping vending machine coffee and listening to court clerks come out and tell him that they'd soon call him as a witness. But they never did, and he was sent home without ever answering a single question.

Not that any of it would have made a difference. The Quaids were dead, and the money went to Elisabeth's sister, another hard-line fundamentalist who would disappear from public life. Promises of reform and future transparency were made. But after the legal dust settled and the documents were sealed, the event was lost to communal memory.

Which brought Lucas back to Doyle fingering Hartke. Either Doyle was lying, or Hartke had put the past into a box and buried it in the earth. Hartke could be shoehorned into a lot of stereotypical topography, and the strong, silent type would top the marquee, so it would be easy to explain why he had never mentioned Bible Hill. Besides, no one talked about their old cases, it was an unwritten rule in the bureau. But there was too much coincidence here, and Lucas felt that he was being set up in one of Kehoe's games.

The question was: *How?*

Lucas walked up the hillside, through the deep footsteps he made on the way down. It was colder up here than down in town, which was some kind of black magic. Not only did his nostrils close up, but the cold was so aggressive that when he blinked his lashes froze together, only to come apart like crazy-glued zippers. He couldn't understand how anyone could take this weather. Not with any sort of regularity.

Back at the cabin, Doyle and Whitaker looked as if they were finally starting to feel the temperature, and Lucas momentarily gave in to schadenfreude. He lifted his aluminum hand and jabbed a thumb at Doyle's SUV parked at the mouth of the drive behind the city plow they had rented for the morning.

"You good?" Doyle asked.

Lucas turned to the snow-covered charred remains of what had once been a family home. "No, but I'm ready to go." And he headed back to Doyle's 4 × 4.

67

Milliner, Wyoming

The sign at the town limit of Milliner denoted a population of 4,032 souls. It was a handsome hamlet that sported all the usual amenities, most of them buried under snow that looked like it had been here since megafauna still roamed the area. Lucas was once again amazed that human beings could brave these elements for a good chunk of the year without getting scurvy, starving, or committing suicide.

They drove through town, past the single car dealership with a mobile home for an office, two bars, a combination hair salon / post office, and a Chinese restaurant that looked like it had closed some time before the first moon landing. There was a white spired Presbyterian church, a gas station / convenience store combo, gun store, and a pawnshop. Along with a grocery store, one gas station, and a bank.

The immediate knee-jerk reaction was to compare Milliner to ten thousand other towns spread through the country, represented everywhere from stock photos to movies. But the truth was Lucas found every one he had ever visited to be different on so many levels. They had been built by different people, grown by different people, and occupied by different people. There was a homogeny because they were American, but there was nothing generic about them. Not when you really took off the blinders. And the farther apart they were, the more their differences showed. It was simple math. And there was something true, something attractive, about each and every one of them—even the run-down ones.

They decided that a cold call would garner the best results. There was a lot bothering Lucas, and he didn't want to add local law enforcement with misaligned sympathies to the list. Sheriff Doyle's CSPOA stickers were still bugging Whitaker. That Doyle had helped them was some kind of testament to luck; Lucas just couldn't figure out if it was out of brotherly fidelity to the law enforcement officers back in New York who had been killed, the death of his own deputy on that icy road three years ago, or a real desire to help Lucas and Whitaker because they faced the pointy end of a spear on the same side of the fence—a little of the old *the enemy of my enemy is my friend* thinking. It certainly wasn't out of a love for the FBI. If nothing else, Doyle had been clear about his feelings on the bureau in general and Hartke in specific. It was hard to miss that he felt betrayed, which was something they had in common.

And after reading the skimpy files they could find, Lucas understood why; it was a classic example of governmental overreaction combined with not enough thinking. And the closed hearings and archival amnesia highlighted that everyone concerned wanted this to be gone. And it was. To everyone.

Everyone except the man with the rifle.

The patronizing voice of the GPS politely—but firmly—directed them ten miles past town before telling them to turn left. Whitaker paused on the shoulder in front of a drive heading into the forest that looked like the mouth to Mordor. She checked her sidearm.

"Nervous?" Lucas asked, realizing that he was externalizing.

"It's not like these people like the FBI."

"Yeah, I was thinking about that."

"Check your sidearm."

"I don't carry one."

"Funny," she said flatly.

"I'm not kidding."

Whitaker eyed him for a few quiet seconds. When she saw that he was serious, she reached around to the small of her back and pulled out a tiny chrome semiautomatic. "The sights are filed off and it's difficult to hit anything beyond thirty yards, but it's loaded with hollow points that will put down a rhinoceros." She held it out. "It holds six shots."

Lucas stared at the little pistol in her palm. Her skin offset the bright polish of the weapon. He shook his head and said, "I've never met a rhinoceros I couldn't reason with."

"You'd rather have it and not need it than need it and not have it." Her eyes narrowed. "Trust me."

"Statistically, guns don't save people."

"There are lots of stories to the contrary."

"I'm not shooting anyone. Guns are for weak people. Or frightened people. Take your pick."

"Personally, I feel guns are for protecting me from other people with guns."

"That's the beauty of this country—you're allowed to believe whatever you want, even if the numbers say otherwise."

"And they stick you with me." She slipped the pistol back home. "I must have pissed Kehoe off." She pulled into the forest.

The snout of the rented SUV wound through a thick canopy of old-growth coniferous forest, and the road was a dark ribbon punctured by little bolts of sunlight piercing the thick roof of branches.

After a hundred yards of heavy shade intermittently pierced by dancing winter sky, the trees opened up and the road furrowed between a pair of old stone pillars that grew into an arch of intertwined deer antlers. They crept beneath the decaying architectural sculpture, and its shadow crawled over the hood like animated snakes. The tires crunched on the snow. When they were through, it was as if they had gone back in history, and for the second time that day, Lucas understood why some people felt the need to think that a god had created the earth for humans.

The road wound into the distance over a gently rolling field that dead-ended in a tree-lined ridge looking down on a house, barn, and three outbuildings. The sun cut down through a cleft in the stone wall behind the ranch, illuminating the field in a blanket of colors like a Monet oil painting. Anywhere else in the world, this chunk of real estate would have cost a bucketload of money. Here, where there were no factories, burgeoning IT start-ups, palm trees, or infrastructure, the place cost less than a decent German automobile.

Whitaker drove slowly through the field so they would see them coming. They weren't sure how things would unroll; Myrna Mercer—Quaid's sister-in-law—would react how she would react. Judging by everything Whitaker had highlighted on her social media accounts, she would not be the welcoming type. At least not to a pair of federal badges.

Myrna had a propensity for friending and following gun ranges, gun manufacturers, and pro–Second Amendment activists on several social media sites. She was a proud member of the NRA and a charter member of the Covenant of the New Order. She was a hunter, collected little crystal bells, and was part of a quilting club called the Sisters of America. She was the shy one.

Myrna's husband, Grant, was a prototype for anti-government sentiment. He had been with the 173rd Airborne in Vietnam and was one of the 130 critically wounded on Hill 875 in the summer of 1967; he took a round in the back that confined him to a wheelchair. He came home to run a mechanic's shop in Milliner for the next half century. His social media accounts painted a pretty specific portrait of a man who had a lot of anger and a general distrust of the powers that be.

The rest of the file was filled with basic givens, general internet Big Data—they had both graduated from high school, but Grant had tried his hand at college when he got back, earning a degree in accounting. They owned two vehicles—a Jeep Grand Cherokee and a Ford F-150—both more than a decade old. Grant still reported a little income from his on-site mechanic business, and their one daughter, Doreen, had moved out three years back. They had no credit cards, and it looked like they had never traveled out of state— at least not in the past decade. They never made long-distance phone calls, but they did receive two a month from D.C., from their daughter.

All of this had been discovered without a warrant, and Lucas wondered how that was even possible.

They were two hundred yards from the house when he spotted them on the road ahead. Six large dogs that blocked their path. There were four shepherd mixes and two that had strong pit bull genes— don't-fuck-with kind of dogs. Whitaker slowed down, and the dogs parted to let them through. Once they passed, the barking started, and they closed up the rear. Not that they'd be able to stop the SUV if Whitaker ripped it into reverse and pounded down on the gas, but it was a nice little bit of psychological warfare.

They pulled up in front of the house. The other outbuildings shot off the rotunda like spokes. The doors to the big wooden barn were open, and several trucks and cars stood inside. Like the guns in Oscar's shop back in New York, they were in various stages of repair, restoration, or plain old decay. There were three other buildings, one that looked like a woodshed and another that had to be a smoke-house, followed by a small Quonset hut that had a single human-sized door in the front.

A woman with a rifle stepped out onto the porch. Her social media accounts put her at sixty, but she had that lean, energetic look a lot of city people lose by the time they are fifty. She kept the rifle pointed at the ground, but her index finger was out, over the trigger guard.

Lucas took her in. *Welcome to America, Land of the Free, Home of the Afraid.*

The dogs circled the SUV in a cacophony of barks.

Whitaker waved at the woman and said to Lucas, "That's a Sig SG 551. Don't get in front of that thing."

Lucas looked at the weapon. "No shit."

The old lady whistled a three-note alert, and the dogs abandoned the SUV to go to her side.

Whitaker dropped the shift into park, opened the door, and said, "Keep your hands where she can see them."

"I thought we were looking for rhinoceroses, not old ladies with machine guns." He followed her out into the cold.

"You lost?" the woman asked.

Whitaker followed her own advice and kept her hands out in the open. "We're with the FBI, ma'am—I'm Special Agent Whitaker, this is Dr. Page. I was hoping to speak with Mrs. Myrna Mercer."

The woman shifted on her hip, and the rifle muzzle made a small circle. "How am I supposed to know that you really are the FBI?" she asked. "Not that it makes any difference. I don't want to speak to you nohow." Good old star-spangled paranoia at its best.

"May I show you identification?" Whitaker asked.

Lucas took up position a little to Whitaker's left, in a spot where Myrna Mercer could keep an eye on him without taking her attention from Whitaker. He also realized that it would make it a lot easier for the old woman to shoot both of them.

Myrna nodded. "It'd be a start."

Whitaker pulled her ID and held it up before taking a few steps toward Myrna.

Myrna didn't even bother to check it. "What do you want?"

Lucas kept his head pointed at the old lady but ran his eye over the windows. The muzzle of a shotgun poked through the curtain beside the door. Probably the old man—it was perfect wheelchair height.

"I'd like to talk to you about what happened to your brother-in-law."

Myrna shifted her weight, and once again the muzzle of the rifle traced a little circle at the ground. She stared at Whitaker for a few cold seconds. "No, you don't."

"I'm sorry?"

Myrna raised the rifle and aimed it straight at Whitaker's head. "You want to ask me about them dead agents in New York City."

68

The house smelled of burned hardwood and dogs and stew on the stove. There were enough deer heads to replace the ones in the family diner back in Carlwood if they had a fire, and a stuffed wolf stood guard by the door, his plastic tongue snapped off and gone. The mantel was decorated with a few family photographs, and the wall above was adorned with a selection of bolt-action hunting rifles that hung on an antler rack. The bottom space was empty, no doubt home to the angry-looking rifle Myrna had greeted them with—and still held now. The house was comfortable and a little messy in the way that happens when time gets to a certain point in a couple's life.

It definitely didn't appear that they had spent much of the settlement money. These were not people who wanted names on the paintings on their walls or prancing horses on their vehicles. They just wanted to be left alone to live out their time without any more assholes shooting their loved ones.

Whitaker sat on the sofa, facing Myrna in her La-Z-Boy by the kitchen with the big Sig resting across the arms. Lucas stood at the fireplace, enjoying the warmth of the hearth. Grant was in a wheelchair by the door, and the dogs lay at his side, looking like there was nothing they wanted more than an attack command.

Myrna was a no-nonsense woman with the clipped diction and purposeful body language of someone who didn't like to waste time. At least not with FBI people. She was five feet in her big shearling slippers and wore jeans and a plaid shirt with pockets on both breasts. Her hair was long, once red and thick like Erin's, now run through with gray and pulled into a bun. Grant was a decade older and sat lopsided in his chair, emotionless and unmoving other than the occasional grunt. His gut covered his belt buckle and spilled over a pair of too-skinny legs covered in old jeans and ending in cowboy boots that hadn't seen polish in a long time. There was a shotgun—a twelve-gauge pump—on the back of his chair, and a sidearm—this one a chrome .45—in a tooled holster hanging off the right arm of his chair. Nope, these folks were not spending the settlement on finery.

The Mercers were kind enough to offer coffee, and at first Lucas wondered if it was poisoned. Then he realized that they weren't monsters, they were just old people who didn't trust a government that had let its servants murder their loved ones for no real reason.

"So you know about the shootings?" Whitaker asked.

Myrna nodded solemnly. "The message boards is lit up with it. Fox and Breitbart, too." She took a sip of her own coffee, but her right hand never left the handle and trigger of the big ugly Sig. Her focus never shifted off Whitaker.

"Someone is hunting federal agents. Five people are now dead."

Myrna shook her head. "Four people are dead."

"It's five."

The old lady shook her head. "That imam ain't worth more'n a cockroach."

She pronounced the word *eye-mam*.

Whitaker went silent.

Lucas pivoted a little to bring heat from the fire to distant parts of his body, and it brought his line of sight to the photos on the mantel. There was a single photo of Grant when he was younger—

just a kid, really—all ribs and biceps under a palm tree. He had a cigarette in his mouth and an M16 in his hands, taken during his time with the 173rd Airborne in Vietnam. There was another, more recent—in his chair at a rifle range, wearing a sweatshirt with his airborne insignia on it, a younger man with a flat top, a lopsided grin, and the same sweatshirt beside him, a hand on Grant's shoulder, the banner behind declaring it old-timer's day for the 173rd. Lucas felt wistful as he compared the two pictures, separated by what—fifty years?—and realized that life rolled over everyone.

Grant spoke up. "Why are you here?" There was no finesse in the question, just a brutish search for information.

"We have reason to believe that whoever is killing these people is somehow connected to your sister and brother-in-law's deaths."

"You mean their *murders*." Grant rolled forward through the throng of dogs that automatically lifted a forest of tails.

"Yes, that's what I mean." Whitaker looked up at him and nodded. "Connected to your brother-in-law's murder."

That seemed to be the right answer, and Grant nodded definitively before switching gears. "You accusing us?" It was difficult to blame him for being hostile, and Lucas realized that they were only inside because Myrna had invited them in—Grant seemed more like a sic-the-dogs kind of guy.

Whitaker held up her hand. "Of course not."

Whitaker was doing well, and Lucas decided that the mute act was the way to go; for some reason, Whitaker and Myrna were connecting. Maybe it was because they both liked guns. Maybe it was that invisible woman thing that he saw Erin and the girls do. But whatever it was, he would only screw it up if he opened his mouth. So he played the mute, nodding or shaking his head at the appropriate junctures in the conversation.

"The shooter has intimate knowledge of what happened on Bible Hill. I don't know where he got this knowledge, and I was wondering if you had any information that might point us in the right direction. Have you spoken to anyone about what happened?"

Myrna looked at her for a few cold seconds. "Spoken to anyone? No, Agent Whitaker, I haven't *spoken to anyone*. I'm not allowed to. That was part of the deal. You people gave me a bag of money, and I'm not allowed to discuss how you shot down my family. How's that for *land of the free*?" She stared Whitaker down for a few seconds more before turning to Lucas. "I lost my blood up there, and you're asking me for help?"

One of the photos on the mantel was of Myrna in her younger days—a good ten or fifteen years back—she was kneeling on the ground, the butt of her hunting rifle resting on a mule deer, its bloody tongue lolling out. Her daughter stood beside her—Doreen was maybe seven or eight, about Laurie's age—hand on her mom's shoulder. Lucas suddenly wished he were back at home with his kids, decorating the tree or playing with the Luigi board. Anything had to be better than being in this house of sadness.

Lucas couldn't help but wonder if Grant Mercer's country had done as much for him as he deserved when he came home minus the use of his legs. A lot of men either fell between the cracks or were ignored altogether. He wondered when the people who were so keen on buying bullets and bombers for the country would see fit to give the boys who used that stuff medical coverage befitting their sacrifices. But they'd need empathy for that, something that the people in Congress seemed to be missing on every conceivable level—unless it was tax breaks for billion-dollar companies; that one they had down.

Whitaker kept at Myrna. "Whoever is killing these people knows about what happened at your brother-in-law's cabin."

"What makes you say that?" the old woman asked.

"I'm afraid I can't share that with you. But I can tell you that he knows things only available to people with intimate knowledge of what happened. I know you don't want anyone else to get hurt over what happened on Bible Hill. There's been enough suffering already."

Myrna locked Whitaker with that hunter's stare she displayed in the photographs. "You people ain't too smart."

"What do you mean?"

Lucas couldn't tell if it was an act or if she really didn't know what Myrna was going to say next.

Myrna leaned forward, and her face went cold again. "If it's so secret, did you ever stop to think that maybe it's someone in the FBI?"

69

Carlwood, Wyoming

The hotel room smelled of tobacco smoke and Lysol and scented lubricant and laser ink from the little HP they bought at the general store in downtown Carlwood. Every surface in the room was piled with papers, birthed from the dead printer cartridges piled on the snot-green shag beside the dented garbage can. There was a grease-stained bag filled with burger wrappers and crunched plastic water bottles on top of the television. Welcome to room 9 of the Buck Stops Here Motor Lodge, population: 2.

Lucas's eye felt like it was too large for his socket, and he put the pages down, clamped it shut, and listened to the circuits in his head hum in protest.

"You okay?" Whitaker asked from somewhere else.

They had been at this for hours now, and it felt like another day. "Just tired of the nothing." He opened his eyes.

The latest victim report on the imam from New York was in front of him. More surgical precision with a .300 Winnie Mag. It was like this guy was ivory hunting, only taking the trophies that would make headlines. But now he had crossed the line from proactive to reactive in denying he had a master. With that one death, he had finally sent a decipherable message: *Don't make an ass out of you and umptions.*

The shooter was letting everyone know that he wasn't out there for someone else—he was doing this for his own reasons. And killing the imam had been a poignant fuck-you and a warning to any other terrorist agencies thinking about hanging their shingle around his neck.

And now they had Doyle's sour sentiments about Hartke, compounded by Myrna Mercer's pronouncements that the only people left who knew about Bible Hill were those in the FBI. Which, Lucas hated to admit, made sense from a certain perspective.

But what did that give him and Whitaker in the way of options?

And they still hadn't tied Jameson's murder in with those of Hartke, Kavanagh, and Lupino back in New York. At least not beyond anything circumstantial. Jameson most definitely had nothing to do with Bible Hill. So how was his death connected to their shooter?

They couldn't call Kehoe until they had something solid. And Lucas was having trouble swallowing all this without a way to link it all together. All he had was a sea of dotted lines.

Lucas stood up and cracked another bottle of water from the plastic-wrapped case purchased at the gas station. "You?" Their coats were spread over the radiator under the window but they both wore their boots; neither wanted to catch cooties from the carpet.

"I was just reading the report on the mosque killing in New York. The lands and grooves from the slug they found embedded in the steps match our guy. Same round. Same weight. Same weird core. Same same *same.*" She closed the laptop and tossed it onto the bed, which squeaked for what had to be the ten millionth time in its sad life. "And we're up to three copycat shooters now. A man hit three pedestrians in Brooklyn, but they'll all be fine; there was a shooting down in the Bowery—UPS driver took a round in the hip, but they caught the guy trying to get on a bus with a rifle case two blocks up; a third down on Canal Street—someone took a shot at a tourist but missed. No .300s in the lot."

He put the bottle of water away, then crumpled the empty and tossed it into the garbage can. "You find any mention of Hartke in this pile of dogshit?" He hated wasting time on something that might be a witch hunt dreamed up by a sheriff who was still angry at losing a deputy. Not to mention having a cinematic mistake by the FBI and ATF forever scarring his record in a tiny little outpost on the edge of civilization.

"Nothing in the files by the FBI proper. He never got a promotion; he stayed a field agent for twenty-eight years even though he had an exemplary record."

"Not according to Doyle."

"Not according to Doyle," she repeated. "No."

Lucas thought back to all the time he had spent with the man and realized that Hartke had never spoken about his past. He was a here and now kind of man with nothing in the way of regrets, his three biggest data points being two bad marriages and an old Dodge that sucked up money like a vengeful casino. He had never hinted at bad career juju like Bible Hill. Not even close.

Whitaker picked up a long-cold burger. "So we have Doyle mimicking WikiLeaks. But there's no way to tie Deputy Jameson's death directly to Bible Hill or Hartke, Kavanagh, and Lupino. So it's a big bag of coincidences and not much more."

Lucas leaned forward and stretched, reaching for the floor. His prosthetic locked, and he had to twist his back and flex his shoulder to unkink the elbow joint when he got back up. It made an audible *clink*. "If our shooter is somehow motivated by Bible Hill, why would he kill Jameson? It doesn't fit the narrative. He wasn't even working for the local SD when the Quaid incident went down. I can't believe that our shooter would kill a deputy and an innocent bystander simply for target practice. He would—" And Lucas stopped as the gears in his head meshed, and it came to him. "The other victim in Jameson's cruiser, the one who drowned in the back—what was his name?"

Like an appliance, all her lights went on, and she picked through a pile of papers until she came up with Doyle's docket on the Jameson killing. She opened it. "Here . . . it . . . is. Second victim was one Donald Francis Doowack."

Lucas smiled, and he could tell that half of his face was too tired to obey by the way Whitaker looked at him. "What if Doowack was the target?"

Whitaker's eyes narrowed for a few seconds as she connected the dots. Then she reached for the phone.

It took her a few minutes to get through to one of the archivists back in New York, an agent named Carla Zubrowka.

Whitaker knew her and got right to the point. "Carla, I have you on speakerphone with Dr. Page, who's helping us—"

"Sure. We met yesterday. What can I do for you?"

"I need you to run down an offender history. His name is Donald Francis Doowack. That's *D-O-O-W-A-C-K*. Deceased January 9, three years back. Possible resident of Carlwood, Wyoming. No last known address. No known aliases. That's everything I can give you. Do we have anything on him in the system? And check the ATF's database."

They could hear Zubrowka's fingers doing the Big Data Dance on the other end of the country. "Here we are. Doowack, Donald F. White male. Sixty-one years of age at the time of his death. Petty criminal with a background of firearms violations—mostly parole problems. Did three stints in state penitentiaries, all under two years. The rest of his collars look more like warnings. That's pretty much it. I'll email you the package . . . now . . . let's migrate over to the ATF's system. Here we go.

"Let's . . . see . . . same arrests. Same charges. Doowack was also listed as an ATF informant for a short stint twenty years back."

It felt like someone snapped their fingers inside Lucas's head. "Is there a record of his involvement in an ATF sting operation for illegal firearms modification?"

"Give . . . me . . . a . . . seco—yep, right here. It's a nineteen-year-old file. He purchased twelve AR-15s from a subject the ATF was interested in—name redacted. But I can tell you it was part of a broader investigation into a Christian Identity group in Wyoming called the Covenant of the New Order."

"Did this sting operation take place in the parking lot of a Waffle House?"

"Let's . . . see." There was a pause that ended with, "How did you know?"

This time, Whitaker got to say it. "Lucky guess."

70

Whitaker dropped the phone back into her pocket after hanging up. "The high-value target wasn't Doyle's deputy."

"Apparently not, no."

"So Jameson was just a bonus? A twofer?"

"Yep."

"And Doyle didn't know that Doowack was the ATF informant who roped in Quaid?"

"Again, no."

"And now we have a straight line from Doowack to the Quaids on Bible Hill, and the way he was murdered ties him to Hartke, Kavanagh, and Lupino in New York."

A nod this time.

"Doyle said that Hartke was the man in charge?"

"Yep."

"And he was killed first?"

Another nod.

"This is a revenge narrative."

"Looks like," he said.

"Jesus." Whitaker sat down on the bed, which groaned again. "If

Doyle's telling the truth, and Hartke was in charge of the team that screwed up on Bible Hill, there are more people on our shooter's list. Kehoe has to unseal the file so we can put the remaining agents in protective custody." She looked over at Lucas. "You see any holes in this?"

Lucas shook his head.

"And you think that this is all about revenge?"

"Occam's razor."

Whitaker smiled at him. "You're not as dumb as Graves says."

Lucas allowed himself a smile and took another slug of water. It tasted of cheeseburger and hotel room.

71

42,000 feet above sea level, over Iowa

Lucas took a root beer from the minifridge and dropped back into the plush leather. Whitaker was zonked out in her seat across the cabin, head back, mouth open, doing a pretty good job of not snoring. They were well above the storm smothering the entire Northeast with more frigid temperatures and snow. Up here, the sky stretched into forever, and the stars blinked like musical notes. The darkness was dropping off behind them, the first hues of morning creeping into the sky ahead. He could still see the Orion OB1 Association off to his left if he turned his head. His focus automatically zoomed out, until he was looking at the constellation proper, its four brightest stars—Betelgeuse, Bellatrix, Rigel, and Saiph—enclosing the famous belt of the hunter. Supergiant Red, Blue, Gamma, and Kappa Orionis, among the most distant visible to the naked human eye. Lucas had been staring at that particular constellation since he was a child, and it never ceased to amaze him in its beauty, complexity, and deceptive permanence.

There was a little bump of turbulence that shook the ice cubes in his glass, and he was back on the plane with Whitaker, his root beer, and a mind full of doubts. He checked his Submariner; the

Gulfstream G550 would be touching down in New York in two hours, somewhere just after 9:00 a.m. He had been running on adrenaline again, and he was beat.

When they had called Kehoe from Wyoming, he listened patiently as they ran through everything they had discovered. And when they were done, his voice kept the same stoic cadence it always had when he delivered the anomalous response of, "Fuck."

Kehoe was dismissive of Myrna Mercer's claim that someone in the bureau might be involved. But even over the phone, Lucas could hear the circuits humming behind the façade of calm. Kehoe had always been of the self-contained variety, and sharing was not part of his general approach to management, but he wouldn't be able to write anything off until they had the shooter in front of a judge. And that someone inside might be the problem wasn't completely unthinkable.

He had Lucas and Whitaker go over everything one more time and asked the right questions. Then he told them to get back to New York.

Lucas knew that the first thing Kehoe did after they hung up was to call the director of the bureau to get the DOJ to unseal the files on Bible Hill. And as quickly as bureaucratically possible, teams would be dispatched to round up all the agents involved. While they were being shipped off to parts unknown, no doubt to live out the investigation in shitty motels under some variant of the name *Smith*, each and every one of them would be vetted to make certain they hadn't been filling their off hours by hunting their former associates. It wasn't an unreasonable assumption since everyone on the other side of the Bible Hill mess was now dead.

Lucas couldn't see the statistical probability that there would be any more agents who had been involved in the Wyoming fiasco in New York; that three had ended up in the city was some kind of dumb luck.

Before heading back East, Lucas and Whitaker had a quick meeting with the boys from the local field office in one of the lounges at the Jackson Hole Airport. All concerned traded what they knew, what they suspected, and what they were looking for—the Wyoming team having the least to contribute at this point. The local special agent in charge was a man by the name of Rod Ziegler, who struck Lucas as another no-nonsense type very similar to Whitaker. Before they had all gone their respective ways, Lucas and Ziegler had talked a little, exchanged cards, and promised to help each other out.

The Wyoming office would do what the bureau was designed to—take apart the Bible Hill history one DNA strand at a time. And they would keep going until they found something useful.

At this point, it was simply a matter of wearing down the leads.

But that still left a lot of the heavy lifting to the New York office. At least for the immediate future. It was possible that now that they'd taken the shooter's food supply away, he'd leave the area. But Lucas doubted it—this guy had put too much legwork into this to give up now. And he was very good at shifting his focus.

72

The Bronx

Special Agent Grover Graves watched the three blacked-out Econolines disappear into the snow before they were at the end of the block where he knew they would turn left for their journey downtown. When the convoy was gone, he nodded a thank-you to the NYPD officers who had escorted him here, giving them a two-finger salute and a smile. They got in their cruisers and drove off.

It was early morning now and it was bright out, but the sun was hidden behind a thousand miles of snow. Graves couldn't remember the last time he had seen a bright blue sky, and in some remote part of his brain he wondered if he would ever see one again. If nothing else, this winter had taught him that there was no such thing as reliable when it came to the weather. Unless you were looking for more snow and cold.

That was the last of them—a woman by the name of Wendy Carson—and she was their fourth pickup of the morning. Which meant they were done. The others were already in safekeeping, locked down under the watchful eye of the bureau. All over the country, local field offices were going through the same procedure, collecting alumni from some ancient bureaucratic SNAFU out West.

Carson had been a hostage negotiator back in the day. But she had been retired for fifteen years and couldn't have looked more surprised when Graves, ten federal agents, and six cops had shown up, demanding that she throw some pj's and a toothbrush into a bag (and to stay away from the windows while doing it). She was now safe, and Graves could take a break.

After a middle-of-the-night call from Kehoe (didn't that fucking guy ever sleep?), Graves had spent the early-morning hours coordinating the pickups. He thought that Page and Whitaker were wrong, but Kehoe believed them, and that was all that counted. Maybe now Page would go back to gimping around his classroom where he belonged.

If Page had one flaw, it was that he overthought things. Kehoe had put it in simple terms. Page saw the world as complicated because he was unable to see it as simple—it was just the way he had been built. Other people looked at flowers in the park and all they saw were pretty colors. Lucas saw nutrients in the dirt they grew in and the sunshine that fed them and the bumblebees that pollinated them. And then he'd focus on one element, like the bees, and obsess that from every conceivable mathematical standpoint they shouldn't be able to fly. He would factor in components like lift and drag and gravity and windage and wingbeats per second, and he'd work out the math. All while everyone else was looking at the flowers.

And that's how he had found Bible Hill—while everyone else had been looking at what was there, Page had been looking at what *wasn't*. Or at least that was how Kehoe had explained it.

Graves wasn't convinced that the shootings were connected to Bible Hill. Or anything else Page and Whitaker had dug up. That their three victims had worked together was no big surprise—the law enforcement gene pool was limited, and at a certain level, everyone had worked with everyone else. It was like one of those conspiracy corkboards, with the colored yarn connecting all the pushpins. Everyone knew, and had worked with, everyone else.

Graves was pooped and needed a little downtime. He'd head

home for a shower and a solid six before going back down to Federal Plaza to hump it through the next part of forever.

He pulled out his Ray-Bans and they were cold on the bridge of his nose. He saw a bodega on the corner, which translated to coffee.

Graves was used to long hours and late nights, but with the cold thrown into the mix, it took a lot out of him. The same thing happened in the piss-warm humid days of July. As he got older, the weather was more of an obstacle than he liked. He didn't want to think of himself as aging, but trips to the doctor were getting closer together, and his hardware seemed to be breaking down in increments. Shit was starting to add up. A bad knee here, a lower back pain there. A cold last year that had taken three months to shake. Blood pressure that was a little higher than the doctor liked. Bouts of insomnia. And he was chowing down on Tylenol like they were fucking Tic Tacs, which he hadn't started doing until last year. No, getting old wasn't for pussies, they were right about that. But coffee helped, even if it was just a little warmth for the belly.

The bodega was like a thousand others in the city, a space no larger than a small garage that held about fifty million things—all packed so tightly that you'd think it was some sort of a contest. Every neighborhood had one, and besides the indispensables like Tampax and condoms, they could always be counted on for cold beer in the summer and *café con leche* in the winter.

The guy behind the counter was a skinny little Latin dude wearing a big furry hoodie, who looked like he wanted to be somewhere else. His indifference was shared by the cat asleep on the register. But the guy smiled at Graves, even if it was a little forced. "Yeah?"

"I'll have a coffee and a Powerball." Graves liked the little joints and tried to spend a few bucks every time he went into one. Like everything else, they would eventually give way to progress.

The man filled a paper cup, and Graves told him to leave the lid off. He cycled up a lottery ticket and Graves paid, scratched the sleeping cat behind the ear, pocketed the ticket, and left the little store.

Back outside, the cold hit him, but the coffee was warming his hand and he stopped to take a sip.

The cup touched his lips and he pulled in a sip, careful not to burn his lips.

But he never finished swallowing.

Or heard the shot that killed him.

73

Columbia University Medical Center

While the bureau went into endocannibalism mode, devouring its own data in massive gulps, Lucas visited Dingo in the hospital. He was still in a coma but incrementally better. The few tempered statements the doctors slipped into their updates still hinted at the possibility of bad things to come, and Lucas understood that the situation was worse than they were letting on. They were fun that way. But they hadn't mentioned a priest, a rabbi, or a lawyer, so Lucas was doing his best to be hopeful, which was some kind of a minor miracle.

The bureau hive was humming, their anger now focused on Graves's murder. They had opened a dialogue with the media in an effort to bring back a little useful information. They had finally released the names of the victims, and the public relations department had outlined things that the citizenry could do to help.

Graves was in the morgue having his body violated by a stainless surgical blade and oscillating saw. The bullet had gone right through him. He was alive. And then he wasn't. And that was that. Roll credits.

He had died on one of the busiest corners in the Bronx, the instant of his death captured by a CCTV in the bodega where he had just purchased a coffee. Lucas refused to watch the footage—he wouldn't learn anything from it—but he had been told that the round had punched through the coffee cup then gone right through his front teeth. Graves stood there on the sidewalk for a good second before his body got the message that it was dead and he fell over as the vestigial impulses sent to his muscles blipped out. It was a mental image that Lucas was having a hard time shaking. He had never liked the man and was now destined to remember him forever—as opposed to simply forgetting about him when he walked off this job. Horror—the gift that keeps on giving.

Which meant that Lucas had been right; now that they had taken the last few people off the shooter's shopping list, he had lashed out. Which was both good and bad. Up until now, he had shown a control and precision that had been all but impossible to crack. He had no doubt spent months on surveillance; everything from Hartke to Lupino to Kavanagh dictated it. But Atchison, the imam, and Graves were all put together in a limited time frame with little to no planning. He hadn't made a mistake yet, but he would. It was only a matter of time.

The thing that brought Lucas a modicum of peace was knowing that Erin and the kids were safe. Their shooter knew who he was, and his family was the easiest way to track him. With them gone, and Lucas in a hotel, he'd be off the guy's radar.

And everyone else on the job had been given directives to change their routines. Every agent on the case was staying with family, friends, or in a hotel.

But that still left a lot of law enforcement targets out there. It was impossible to turn your head in Manhattan without seeing a uniformed police officer. And when all you have is a hammer, everything tends to look like a nail. Or a target.

There were countersnipers positioned around the city, which was causing its own particular set of problems with reports of men with rifles on rooftops coming in around the clock. City hall and Federal

Plaza were the most heavily guarded, with a dozen eyes covering all the nearby terrain.

All because one man with a rifle was unhappy about something.

Only it wasn't merely *something*.

It was Bible Hill.

The slug that went through Graves had shattered the window of the bodega behind him, gone through the cash register, then detonated a coffee maker. All while barely missing a cat. It was the same meteoric round. Another elevated position. Another evidence-free crime scene. Another example of fancy footwork, supreme skill with a rifle, and the ability to adapt to a changing situational landscape.

Same. Same. Same. Same. Over and over and over. *Groundhog Day* on perpetual loop.

Lucas left Whitaker back at the office in the suit she had been wearing for the past three days. She was going through the Bible Hill files that Kehoe had received from the DOJ under a special warrant.

There was no one left alive to bring attention to the case—and since Myrna Mercer had accepted a wheelbarrow of blood money in exchange for her silence—it was supposed to stay buried. Gone from public consciousness as if it had never really happened at all.

Except that their shooter had a very definite set of feelings on the subject.

Lucas was at the window, looking out on the city, while Dingo fought his invisible war, aided by the respirator and a litany of IV bags. His citizenship card had been delivered to the nursing station, and his passport was back at Lucas's house. Along with Alisha's final adoption papers. Kehoe was making an effort. Maybe a real stab at an apology after all this time. Maybe they were both letting it all go.

The rest of the personnel who had been involved in Bible Hill were all in protective custody now. There were four in New York City, and after the shooter was done here, Lucas had no doubt that he would have headed off to other pastures—the most likely being Houston, where three of the people involved in Bible Hill had ended up. That so many were in New York was some kind of a statistical anomaly.

Lucas couldn't stop the questions in his head.

Or stop thinking about Bible Hill.

It all started there.

With Carl Quaid. And somehow, almost two decades later, it had morphed into a hunting trip in the concrete jungle.

Outside, the snow still swirled down in clumps, burying the city in a new ice age. Most of Manhattan was crippled in one way or another, and basic infrastructure and core businesses were at the point where they could no longer operate effectively. The cabs and their Uber asshole counterparts were the only cars out—most drivers too afraid of the snow to risk the safari into the arctic wonderland; the waste management trucks weren't running because the garbagemen couldn't get through the banks to the curb to pick up the trash; delivery trucks couldn't ford the narrow streets or the back alleys; grocery stores, markets, and restaurants were sold out of basics; and even the subway schedule was a mess; many of the outdoor trains were freezing up—particularly the electronic brake systems—and the chain reaction was affecting the entire transit system. In the simple jargon of a twenty-first-century urban planner, everything was fucked.

But not to the man with the rifle. Half a week and he had won himself a place in history. This guy was the post office motto come to life—they'd be talking about him for years. He'd make it into the textbooks at Quantico. Leonardo DiCaprio would play him in the movie. He'd live forever.

But who was he?

And what was his connection to Bible Hill?

And the Quaids?

Myrna and her husband now had the unforgiving focus of the Federal Bureau of Investigation pointed at them. The Jackson, Wyoming, branch of the bureau, coupled with the men Kehoe had sent out, were digging up everything they could on the couple, all under the shadow of a warrant that Kehoe had long-armed to a federal judge, all backed up by what Lucas and Whitaker had learned from Doyle.

It was all so fucking convoluted that Lucas wondered if there was a straight line anywhere in the equation.

The roof across the street was six stories down and identical to five thousand others in the city, an empty flat space that supported a water tank and a bunch of HVAC units. Maybe an electrical panel and a forest of satellite dishes. And it was the perfect perch for a man with a rifle.

Just like that tree-lined ridge back in Wyoming.

Wyoming.

The Quaids.

The Mercers.

A man with a rifle.

It was there somewhere, hidden in the—

And then he got it.

It was right there.

Like everything else on this one, it wasn't in what was there.

It was in what *wasn't*.

Lucas gave Dingo's hand a squeeze and left the ICU.

74

26 Federal Plaza

There is no other governmental agency as difficult to rile up as the Federal Bureau of Investigation, but the killing of two of their agents had managed to accomplish precisely that. Electricity sparks in the dead air between angry people, and the rooms of the bureau offices were filled with determined human voltage.

Lucas cornered Kehoe in his office. They talked it through, and when Lucas finished, Kehoe simply nodded and said, "Do it."

Again, the solution was to be found in the holes in the equation, not the parts they could see. Which required a whole new approach, one recalibrated to look in the places that weren't technically places.

Lucas spent an hour on the phone with Rod Ziegler, his new contact at the Jackson, Wyoming, branch of the bureau. Ziegler was the lead man interviewing the Mercers, which meant he had access to all facets of the investigation out there. What Lucas wanted wasn't the usual information that they could find by simply logging in to the appropriate databases. No, Lucas needed a little legwork, persuasiveness, and the ability to think in abstract terms, all of which Ziegler had demonstrated at their meeting in the Jackson Hole Airport. When Lucas was done explaining what he wanted, Ziegler went off to locate the appropriate haystack in which to find their needle.

That was four hours ago, and the interim had been spent running down the familiar dead ends that make up the bulk of most cases. Lucas and Whitaker were going through Oscar's purchase records for the past year when Lucas's cell lit up with Ziegler's number.

"Dr. Page here."

"Dr. Page, Rod Ziegler. I pulled all the bank records I could for the Mercers, and you were right, they're cash kind of people. And you were right that even people who don't like the government have to take a check on occasion, especially when they come *from* the government. We already had the appropriate warrants for the bank records, so that saved a lot of time. Like you recommended, I went to their actual branch in Milliner and pulled up everything in their file.

"That chunk of settlement money is gone; I couldn't find it anywhere. Federal law dictates that banks have to keep detailed records, including copies of all checks, for a period of seven years. But with server space being cheap, a lot of banks keep records longer than that; the Milliner branch had the Mercers' records going back ten years, and the money has been gone all that time, so they cashed out more than ten years ago."

"And Grant Mercer?"

"His mechanic business operated on a purely cash basis—not a single check deposited in all the ten years I could dig up. Paid all his business expenses with cash. Same goes for taxes and payroll. Never took a check. Never wrote a check."

"Except for his veterans benefits," Lucas said.

"That's right. I stopped at the five-year mark like you specified and checked the back of every single check he cashed. You were right about that, too; Grant had someone else cash a few of his veterans benefits checks for him."

Lucas figured that Myrna would be the one to cash his checks, but with the two of them getting older, and the winters out there being what they were, there was every reason to believe that the Mercers didn't go into town much in the winter.

Ziegler continued, "I found the first countersignature fifty months back, in November. Over the next sixteen months, a man by the name of Kirby Clibbon cashed five checks for Grant Mercer."

Lucas could tell by the way Ziegler's tone was changing that he was getting to the good part.

Ziegler didn't disappoint him. "Clibbon was with the 173rd Airborne."

Lucas thought back to the photos of Grant when he was younger, just a kid, all ribs and hope and smiles posing under a palm tree with an M16 in his hands, somewhere in Vietnam half a century ago. "That's Grant's old unit," Lucas remembered out loud.

Ziegler continued. "I spoke to all the tellers, and none of them really knew Grant all that well, but I pulled personnel records and found a woman who used to work there who has since retired. She remembered Kirby Clibbon. She said she used to see him around town with the Mercers' daughter, Doreen. They dated for a spell."

And with that, the final pieces of the puzzle snapped into place, and Lucas snapped his fingers at Whitaker, who looked up from the file box taken from Oscar's shop.

"What can you tell me about this Clibbon guy?"

Across the country, Ziegler flipped through his notes. "Clibbon, Kirby Jonathan. Born March 9, 1987. Lieutenant, 173rd Airborne. Two tours in Afghanistan. Honorably discharged four years and five months ago."

"That's Kirby Clibbon? *K-I-R-B-Y . . . C-L-I-B-B-O-N*?"

"That's it."

"Okay, give me a second."

Lucas waited while Whitaker punched Clibbon's name into one of the laptops. When she was done, she turned it so that Lucas could see the image. It was the same kid from the photo on the Mercers' mantel—the picture of Grant at the old-timer's event, a smiling country boy with a flattop beside him. "How long did he date Do-reen Mercer?"

"Not long. We found his old address through a local utilities com-pany and talked to the landlord. He said Clibbon just canceled his month-to-month one day. Moved away to find work."

"When was that?"

"Thirty-six months ago; January 9."

Lucas felt his rib cage drop by a full size. "That's the day Deputy Jameson and Donald Doowack were killed."

"Yes, sir, it is."

Lucas wanted to reach through the phone and give the guy a kiss. "What did you find?"

"I couldn't come up with an address. No utilities. No tax re-turns. No library cards or email addresses. At least not in his own name. We were able to find an address for the Mercers' daughter in D.C., so I looked for Clibbon there and came up with zip."

Lucas heard a *but* coming.

"But what you said was bothering me—that we'd find what we were looking for in the spaces between the knowns; everyone has someone who knows where they are. It took two phone calls, a little foul language, and a nudge from a judge friend, but I found Clib-bon. He's on the mailing list for his old unit. It appears to be a busi-ness address, but at least you have a starting point."

"Where is he?"

"About thirty blocks from where you are right now."

Lucas turned to Whitaker and tried not to let the adrenaline seep through his skin. He was about to say thank you and hang up when something hit him. "What did Clibbon do in Afghanistan?"

Of course the only answer Ziegler could give was, "He was a sniper."

75

The entire information-gathering apparatus of the Federal Bureau of Investigation fastened its sights on Kirby Clibbon, former Airborne sniper, current person of interest, and prime suspect in the murder of six law enforcement officers, one imam, and one former ATF informant.

Contrary to how action movies portrayed omniscient government surveillance, Clibbon wasn't instantaneously located by a drone and taken down by a tag team of Humvees filled with armor-clad storm troopers using shiny aluminum spearguns and high-def body cams. The ultimate collar would be done by six plainclothesmen while he was out buying a new skin for his iPhone. Or a SWAT team would be sent into his apartment while he slept.

But before the wheels of justice moved in to take him down, they needed to be confident that he was their guy. That was not to say they would simply leave him out in the open without some kind of surveillance. Three pairs of agents were watching his apartment (he wasn't home). Three more pairs were positioned around the garage where he worked as a general mechanic (he wasn't there). And everyone in the city was looking for him.

Lucas was asleep on the sofa in Graves's old office when Whitaker blew in. "Wake up, Page."

Lucas opened his eyes and took a deep breath that he powered with a cat stretch. He blinked, made sure his prosthetic eye was aligned properly (when he slept with it in, it tended to dry out and rotate up to the left so it looked like his head had been wired by Tim Burton), and sat up, reaching for his Persols.

Whitaker held out an FBI mug of coffee. Lucas took a sip and realized that his hand was cold.

She dropped a pile of papers on the desk. "You were right. Clibbon is our guy."

Lucas ran his tongue over his teeth and took in another mouthful of coffee. He smiled and thanked her. "Were we able to place him at any of the sites?"

"We found surveillance footage of Clibbon at number 3 Park Avenue. He didn't go in, but he walked by twice on the day of the shooting. His boss checked the worksheets and said Clibbon was supposed to be out test-driving customers' cars at those times."

With the influx of caffeine, the little spinning hourglass in his operating system stopped. "Any of the others?"

Whitaker pulled a color photo from the stack of papers. "We've got this."

It was an image lifted from security footage from the Roosevelt Island tram. Lucas checked the time stamp; it had been taken twenty-eight days ago, at 6:23 a.m. Commuters huddled together, doing their best to keep civil while packed into a confined space with strangers, three hundred feet above a polluted river. One of them was Kirby Clibbon. He was sandwiched in between a small, thin man in glasses on one side and a heavyset black woman on the other. A tall man in a Russian fur hat stood behind him, earflaps buttoned up, buds plugged into his head—he was reading *The New York Times*. And a small woman with freckles and a parka with a fur-lined hood read a Robert Ludlum paperback a foot to his left. Clibbon was watching Carol Kavanagh, the ATF agent who would be shot on that exact tram, standing in that exact spot, three weeks later.

Lucas handed the photo back. "One place? Maybe. Two? As statistically probable as me winning the Gregory Hines tap dancing award."

Whitaker fingered through the papers and came up with another photo. "What about three?" she asked. "This is from one of the cameras at LaGuardia." She handed it over.

The image was of a sedan—Lucas couldn't tell the make—on a road beside the water. The license place was enhanced, but there was no way to see who was driving, the interior was hidden in shadow.

"I can't see a face," said Lucas.

"We ran the plate, and the car is the same one that Clibbon was supposed to be test-driving when he was spotted outside number 3 Park Avenue in that first photo. Belongs to a floor manager at ABC Decorating. The guy has no connection to Clibbon other than he sends his car there for servicing. There's a key cutter at the garage where Clibbon works, and it's no big stretch to imagine him making a copy and 'borrowing' the guy's car at night while it's parked in front of his house. This photo doesn't place Clibbon in the vehicle, but it's pretty damning in its own right."

Lucas handed it back. They were there, in the final stretch, making up for all that lost time.

Even so, Lucas couldn't help feeling like they were eight people too late.

Kehoe came in. "Clibbon was spotted two blocks from his work. I gave the green light; SWAT's taking him down."

76

Midtown West

Moses and Coco General Mechanics and Tire Wholesale was sandwiched between a parking garage and a sporting goods warehouse on West Forty-seventh between Tenth and Eleventh. There were six graffiti-covered bay doors and a single pedestrian entrance with *Office* painted overhead, highlighted by a large, red, asymmetrical arrow that jabbed down to the riot-gated portal. All six roller doors were down, but only one of the round exhaust vents puffed carbon monoxide into the atmosphere.

Kirby Clibbon cut down the block, looking like any one of a thousand other people in the city at that particular moment—just a guy in his winter coat carrying a guitar case. The snow squeaked under the treads of his boots, and in the failing light of late afternoon, his shadow played along the snowbanks.

He was halfway down the block—in front of the shuttered doors of Jax's Sports—when he was boxed in by a pair of unmarked vans that plowed up onto the sidewalk, scattering garbage cans and snow mounds.

His reaction time was good, and he dropped the guitar case just as the doors blew open and black tactical insects burst forth in synchronized aggression.

The SWAT men swarmed over him like soldier ants taking down a spider.

And it was finally over.

77

Precisely thirty seconds after Kirby Clibbon was arrested on suspicion of eight murders, the FBI opened the door to his apartment under the direction and protection of the appropriate warrants. They went through his home with the famous patience of their kind, dissecting the space one square inch at a time. They emptied the bookshelf, which contained mostly tactical manuals, although there were several classics, notably a first edition of *A Rifleman Went to War*, the iconic sniper's tome. They packed up his laptop and external hard drives, his three cell phones, and his address book. They took his journals and carted his filing cabinet away.

Kirby Clibbon had a fascination with guns, and the offshoot of this was an apartment loaded with ammunition. The bureau people found nearly thirty thousand rounds, about evenly divided between the Winchester and Remington brands.

But the big payoff came in the closet.

They found the rifle behind the hangers of work shirts. It was locked into a custom rack with two hardened steel padlocks. It was a .300 Winchester Magnum. The bureau people would photograph it in situ before carefully removing and bagging it with latex-gloved hands so as not to disturb any trace evidence. But the real focus would be ballistics.

It happened when they went to move the hangers.

To call it a booby trap would be a misnomer. It was a simple and relatively crude invention using no more than four feet of piano wire, a twenty-pound sledgehammer head connected to a trigger on the clothes bar, and a little ingenuity.

The tech who moved the clothes for the photographer heard the *zing* and had time to jump back, but the device had not been designed to harm people.

The damage was not extensive. But it was enough to put a slight bend in the barrel.

The rifle would never fire a round again.

78

CNN, Breaking News

"We have new details regarding the suspect arrested by the FBI mere moments ago in Midtown Manhattan. Sources in the FBI confirm that the man apprehended is believed to be the sniper who murdered eight people, including six law enforcement officers—personnel from the ATF, FBI, NYPD, and a Wyoming Sheriff's Department—a New York imam, and a Wyoming resident. The suspect's name has not been released, but our sources tell us that he is a man in his late twenties with an extensive military record, reportedly an Afghanistan veteran.

"While we wait for the press conference at Federal Plaza to begin, we have—for the first time in our studio—gun rights advocate and president of the NRA, Dwayne Laroche. Mr. Laroche, thank you for being here."

"My pleasure, Wolf."

"Mr. Laroche, over the past few days, you have refused to condemn the actions of the sniper stalking our city. Now that we have a little more information on him, are you willing to maybe walk that endorsement back a bit?"

"First of all, Wolf, I never endorsed the alleged suspect. What I *did was suggest that until we know all the facts, we should suspend rush judgments to ban all firearms in urban centers. Now, before I continue, I reserve the right to modify or change my comments in the future. But let's look at the facts as we now know them.*

"With the recent phenomenon of police overstepping their assigned authority, the citizens of this fine country are increasingly worried about their safety. From a Second Amendment standpoint—and, Wolf, I am sure you and your viewers know that one of the foundation walls of the Second Amendment is for the right of citizens to defend themselves against the tyranny of the government—it is conceivable that this individual was defending himself against tyrannical governmental employees and—"

"Don't you think that is a bit of a stretch?"

"I'm not finished. When the investigation is over, and if we find out that this individual is, in fact, the victim of governmental overreach or even criminal actions on behalf of the government, then it could be argued that he was defending and expressing his God-granted Second Amendment right.

"And if you look at the imam he allegedly killed, the man preached a doctrine diametrically opposed to the rights and freedoms guaranteed by the Constitution. It could be argued that he was an enemy of America and that this young man did America a great favor. And while we are on the subject of the Second Amendment . . ."

79

26 Federal Plaza

His hands were cuffed to the leather belt encircling his waist, which was, in turn, fastened to the manacles on his ankles with another four feet of hardened chrome chain. The contraption only allowed him to move in a tight-stepped shuffle, but now that he was attached to a table, he didn't think that exercise was one of their objectives. It was the beginning of the waiting game.

Kirby Clibbon knew there was a roomful of excited people at the other end of the camera in the corner, slapping one another on the back for a job well done.

They had the temperature turned down and the humidity cranked up, and Kirby recognized the clumsy attempt at psychological warfare. If they really wanted to get his attention, they'd need to pump him full of LSD, fold him into a fifty-gallon drum with a bag of camel spiders, turn up the Michael Bolton, and leave him in the ground for a week. Barring that kind of determination, this was going to be a one-sided conversation.

The door opened, and a tall black chick in a suit came in. Not one of those deep blue motherfuckers who were always hanging out down in eyes-and-teeth-park—no, this gal was good old American, that common mixture produced by the union of too horny and too stupid that filled every inner city in the country. She looked pissed, but they *all* looked pissed. It was one of those character traits they couldn't hide with all the education in the world.

The second person was a white guy who definitely walked the walk. He wore a suit that his FBI salary definitely couldn't pay for and he had the polished movements of an expensive finishing school—Kirby had seen a few guys like him back in the forces, all visiting senators or governors or other useless hand-shaking positions—men who couldn't change a tire if their fucking lives depended on it. He looked all calm and collected. Kirby knew calm. He knew collected. And this guy had them both down. Of the two, it was the white dude in the suit that he'd have to watch—his type specialized in fucking the workingman; it was just how they were put together.

This was the FBI, so Kirby didn't expect good cop / bad cop. He expected polite conversation followed by threats of deep dark holes for the rest of his life—boilerplate government cliché kind of speak. He had been ready for this for a while now. That it had taken them this long was some kind of a miracle. The rest was up to him.

The black chick sat down facing him, and the nice suit took up his place in the corner. None of this mattered because Kirby had nowhere else to be right now.

"Mr. Clibbon, I'm Special Agent Whitaker. That's Special Agent in Charge of Manhattan, Brett Kehoe."

Kirby just stared down at his forearms, adorned with left and right Mr. Horsepower tattoos; three years of dealing with Haji sand niggers in Afghanistan, followed by his time yessiring those fucking Hasidic Jews down at the garage, had taught him a lot about how to ignore people.

The Nubian went into her sales pitch. "You know why you're here. We know why you're here. The AR-15 in your guitar case will be how we kick things off. For starters, you are going to be indicted on Criminal Possession of a Firearm, under Penal Law section 265.01-b.

It's unregistered, so that's a straight five if we make a point of it. And we *will* make a point of it.

"The firearms charge gives us everything we need to keep you locked up for a few days as we go through your life, one tiny bit at a time. We're eventually going to convict you of the murder of six law enforcement officers and two civilians, including the two murders you committed in Wyoming three years back. We have you at the scene of three of the murders before they happened, which shows clear intent and premeditation. If you don't want to spend the rest of your days at the bottom of a deep dark hole in our federal penal system, you might want to consider helping us out here." Whitaker opened her hands in a way that showed they were at the point in the monologue where she expected some kind of response.

Kirby could not believe the lack of imagination they were showing. These two couldn't scare a cat. He kept his focus on the Woody Woodpecker images, cigars clamped in the corners of their mouths.

"Do you have something you'd like to say?" Whitaker pushed.

Kirby lifted his focus and locked her in a heavy-lidded thousand-yard stare. Just who the fuck did these people think they were dealing with?

After thirty seconds of silence, he turned and spoke to the camera. "I want a lawyer. A *white* lawyer." And with that, he closed his eyes and went into himself.

80

The Long Island Railroad

After the elegant interior of the bureau's Gulfstream G550, the Long Island Railroad car possessed all the panache of a garden shed. Yes, the walls and ceiling were paneled in nicely vacuum-formed plastic; yes, the seats were upholstered in a man-made blue-and-green pseudo-leatherette; yes, they had tried to do away with hard corners à la Steve Jobs. But the general effect could only be described as *modern extinct* with a hint of *ugly* thrown in.

From Penn Station to Montauk was three hours and three minutes, with a five-minute stop at Babylon, fifty-eight minutes in. Lucas liked the train almost as much as the kids did. There was something about the passengers and the rhythm that gave the whole exercise a sense of adventure, like you were really going someplace. Maybe it was because of the destination. They'd get to the beach, and when they walked into the house, it had *that smell,* that beach smell.

Tonight it was business mannequins thumbing their phone screens offset by college kids in Canada Goose parkas. Lucas hated cell phones. But not because they were isolating people from one another—he remembered way back when the Walkman first hit public consciousness. No, what he hated was the identity crisis they had imparted on young people.

But he was in a good mood, and he remembered to forget about the world for a moment, on the countryside sliding by, and for some reason thought back to that night all those years ago when Mr. Teach had called him home from school.

He took the train down from Boston, arriving late at night.

Mr. Teach answered the door. He was in one of his impeccably tailored suits, but his hair and beard would still do a bushman proud—they had gone gray over the past few years. Lucas gave him a hug, and Mr. Teach had tears in his eyes.

It was a warm spring evening, and all the windows, including the doors to the balcony, were open. The silk curtains hung limp in the night air, and the apartment smelled like furniture polish, perfume, and home.

As he walked through the space, he saw that the painting of Mrs. Page's mother was not there, and he assumed that it was on loan to a museum or gallery.

Mrs. Page was awake when he went to her room. "I've been waiting for you, Lucas." In all their time together, she had never called him anything else.

He went to the bed and kissed her, then sat down at her side. "A heart attack?"

She shrugged and took his hand. "My dinner guests were so boring, I just couldn't take it. I would have much preferred a stroke that made me speak in gibberish, but this was the best I could do under the circumstances." She smiled at the joke and gave his hand a squeeze. "I so miss our talks. It's lonely here without you."

"I can come back. There are a lot of good universities in the city."

"No, you can't. You have a responsibility."

"To whom?"

"To yourself. And to me. Life is going to give you some difficult choices, and when it does, you make them."

Mr. Teach came in with a root beer for him and a lemonade for her.

She took a sip and made a face that got him smiling. "Like our first time together, remember?"

"Have I ever said thank you?"

She waved it away. "Every single day. With your enthusiasm and kindness and discipline. You have been the single greatest joy of my life—my *very long* life—and my only regret is that we won't have more time together."

He tried to take a sip of his root beer but it suddenly tasted very flat. "Don't say that."

She held out the lemonade, and he put it on the nightstand. Then she took his hand again. "It's all right. You're still young, but life will teach you—my death will teach you—that this is all very temporary. The trick is knowing that it's short—finding value in that commodity *time* you seem so fascinated by." She paused and caught her breath. "But I didn't have Mr. Teach call you home to give you life lessons. I hope I've done that enough already. I called you home because I need you to know about a few things.

"All of this," she said, waving her hand, signifying the room, the apartment, her life. "Is going away. The fortune my grandfather made has run its course. My accountant tells me that the last market collapse made a larger dent in the portfolio than I can recover from. There are debts and obligations. There is a small trust that will pay for your education—and not much more. But I want to do one more thing for you, Lucas. I want you to have a little insurance for the day when you need it, so I put something into a trust for you years ago. Something the creditors won't be able to touch—the painting of my mother."

Lucas remembered the first time he had seen it all those years ago, when Mr. Teach had walked him through the apartment and he thought he was in a palace. And for years after, that painting had looked down on him while he did his homework at the big desk in the living room. Every line, hue, detail, and crack in the pigment was as much a part of himself as any physical object could be. The portrait was of Francesca Johnson, Mrs. Page's mother, done by John Singer Sargent during her twenty-second year.

"Don't look so puzzled." She smiled up at him. "Mr. Teach has already had it crated up; it is at my barrister's office so the debt collectors can't get their hooks into it through some loophole. It is very valuable now but will only increase. Put it somewhere and leave it there. One day, you may have a wife and a family, and it will pay for a house. Or the education of your children. Hold on to it as long as you can. I was hoping to leave you more, but I haven't made the best decisions with my money." She smiled weakly. "That's another thing—don't trust stockbrokers or bankers. They're worse than the religious boobs. They don't have the imagination to invent anything other than confidence games. It is a recipe for disaster. They can't help themselves, it's what they were bred for, but that's no excuse."

"I don't need the painting. I don't—"

"Lucas," she said, a little sternly. "Of course you don't *need* the painting. But you will be able to focus on your education and career a lot easier if you don't have to worry about subway fare."

And that was his turn to smile. Every New Year's Day, they took the subway downtown to the site of her grandfather's long-razed first factory. Lucas always got a kick out of watching her count out the change at the token booth, Mr. Teach standing back, her own private guardian angel. "Okay," he said.

"I am glad you like learning, my boy. When I was young, about a thousand years ago, people wanted an education so that they could better their financial position. Now, with the rise of the merchant class, the buying and selling of things no longer makes education a necessity. People amass wealth without realizing that they need to amass knowledge to better use that wealth—the Peggy Guggenheims of this world are dying. Those stupid people I see on television are the future, and they will fight you every step of the way. They will try to make you like them."

"Don't worry about that."

"Good." She waved her hand again, this time signaling that commerce was over. "Now tell me about school."

They spent the rest of the night talking about his studies and friends and how he was enjoying Boston and the girl he was dating and his upcoming studies in England and myriad topics of no immediate import. They drank lemonade and root beer, and the doctor came in to administer blood thinners, and for a few hours they were like they had been that first day, all those years ago.

He got to tell her that he loved her one last time. And just as the sun was bleeding into the morning sky, Mrs. Page died.

The train hit some turbulence, and he was jostled back to the blue-and-green vinyl and the smell of too many passengers and not enough fresh air.

He looked up and blinked one time, feeling his eyelid get caught on his bad eye. He took his pocket square and used his original fingers to reach up behind the dark lens, rotating the prosthetic.

He refolded his pocket square before turning to the polished character reflected back at him in the window.

He had kept the painting crated up for years. Through his first marriage. Through the stint in the hospital. Through tough financial times and upticks in the art market. Until that day that he and Erin realized they needed someplace to raise their family. And when he sold it, Mrs. Page once again took care of him. But even she would have been shocked at how much her mother's portrait would eventually be worth. After the brownstone, there had been a significant chunk of cash left over, enough to last him the rest of his life. He gave a good slice to Mr. Teach, who was by that time almost eighty and living in Florida, spending his days golfing and two-for-one-ing it at happy hour on Casey Key. Lucas was grateful to be able to return some of the kindness Mr. Teach had shown him over the years.

After the house and Mr. Teach, Lucas followed her advice, keeping it out of the markets, away from the parasites who ran Wall Street. She had been right about them as well.

And as he sat there, staring at his reflection in the window, her words came back to him. *They can't help themselves. It's what they were bred for.*

They.

Can't.

Help.

Themselves.

The voice of the announcer added a score to the image staring back at him. "Babylon, Long Island, next stop."

What.

They.

Were.

Bred.

For.

And it all slipped into place.

All of it.

Myrna Mercer.

Margolis and his disappearing magic bullets.

Detective Atchison's house in Jersey.

Hartke and the sealed hearings.

Oscar.

Bible Hill and Sheriff Doyle with the tooled Jesus holsters.

Hartke and Kavanagh and the imam.

And Kirby Clibbon and the destroyed rifle hanging in his closet.

Lucas stood up as the train pulled into the station. His prosthetic was running fine, but his good leg had fallen asleep, and he had a difficult time resetting his internal gyroscope. He stood in the aisle, holding the seats so he wouldn't fall over as the decreasing speed pulled his center of gravity forward.

A woman behind him said, "Mind if I get by?"

Lucas turned toward her with the right side of his face. He couldn't see her straight on, but he caught a reflected view of her in the window with his good eye. He knew she was looking up into his disconnected prosthetic, visible at this distance, even behind the tinted lenses. "Please give me a second," he said politely, but firmly.

She scurried to the rear exit, mumbling under her breath, the word *cocksucker* somewhere in the mix.

Lucas waited for the pain to bleed out of his leg. By the time the train rolled to a stop in the town of Babylon, the pins and needles had dulled to a numb electrical current.

He hobbled down the steps and stopped under the awning. He didn't want to call in the Indians unless he was certain, so he stood there as the snow came down, staring off into the distance, looking for holes in the storyline.

He couldn't find a single one.

The train started to pull away, and Lucas watched the faces of the people in the lit windows as it got up to speed. He didn't realize that his phone was in his hand until the final doubt had left the station with the train.

He dialed Whitaker's number, and when she answered she sounded different—maybe even relaxed. "Dr. Page! Hey, man."

"I'm in Babylon, and I need you to send someone for me." He looked up at the snow coming down; a helicopter wouldn't get through this.

"Why?" She didn't bother to hide the concern in the question.

Lucas watched the train continuing on to Montauk, where his family would be waiting. "I made a mistake," he said as the last car was swallowed by the snow. "Kirby Clibbon isn't our shooter."

81

The Time Warner Center, New York City

Dashon Jenkins had been polishing the floors of the shops at the Time Warner Center on Columbus Circle since the day it opened, and in all that time, he had seen hundreds of thousands, possibly even *millions*, of people walk by. Very few of them ever noticed the floors, but that was fine by him. He didn't do this for them; he did it for himself. He took pride in his work—otherwise, what was the point? It was one of the few things his father had taught him before taking off to Baltimore. This dedication served him well outside of work, too. He got his GED five years ago and was halfway through earning a college degree. He owned a triplex on Staten Island that was almost paid off, which was more than most of the people out there. Nope, he didn't give a shit that those motherfuckers never noticed him.

The building attracted tourists by the busload, from well-dressed Italians to the inflated folks from Florida; there were Chinese tourists who followed the guides with the signs; and the chubby schoolkids in yoga pants who couldn't take a single photo without their own fat faces in it. In all that time, he had become an expert in reading people. From the slick lawyer assholes who charged through, to the famous news folks from upstairs at CNN, he could tell who would nod a hello and who would walk by like he wasn't there. And from the instant he saw him, Dashon knew the guy with the red face and all the bodyguards who plowed through earlier wouldn't so much as look at him.

But it wasn't until he saw that same red face on the television screens around the building that he understood why. The dude was on CNN, going on about how everyone in the United States should carry a bazooka.

While he ran the polisher, Dashon read a few of the comments that ran across the bottom of the screen. The guy was really getting into it with one of the hosts. He believed that law-abiding citizens should own any gun they wanted. Apparently, he had statistics that showed the country would be a lot safer if every man, woman, and child carried a gun. Without knowing anything about him—the subtitles said his name was Dwayne Laroche—Dashon could tell he wasn't being 100 percent truthful. Dashon knew that what he really meant was that all the *white* people should own guns. Those white assholes who loved their guns usually had a pretty standard set of feelings for the black man. Not that Dashon was a racist—it was just that in his experience, any honky who believed in guns tended to also believe that black people shouldn't be allowed to have them. Not the ones who said they believed in law and order. And especially not the cops. Googling *Philando Castile* would show you how the Man felt about brothers carrying guns—even legal ones.

He could tell by looking at the man's face that he wasn't really an activist or true believer. Nope, this guy was just another salesman trying to make a buck. They had called it *branding* in the marketing course he took last semester. The guy wasn't selling a product, he was selling an idea, and Dashon knew that could be a dangerous thing. All you had to do was look at those rednecks down South who screamed about believing in the Lord just before throwing a noose over a branch. Or those Muslim brothers who weren't happy unless they took a whole city block with them on their trip to the sky. As far as Dashon was concerned, the selling of ideas should be illegal.

As he read the subtitles on the big screen beside the Hugo Boss store, he had to give Mr. Laroche credit for sticking to his guns . . . ha ha. He wasn't going to be swayed by the news anchor. And certainly not by anything as ridiculous as logic. No, the transcript showed the thinking of a man welded to his ideas.

. . . and if we were all armed, we'd be much safer. I carry at least one firearm on my person at all times, and I guarantee that I will not be a victim of firearm violence because, as the facts clearly demonstrate, the only thing that stops a bad man with a gun is a good man with a gun. Furthermore, my training and belief in the use of firearms for personal protection ensure a safe environment for those around me. I become, in a way, a guardian angel to those who need . . .

When Dashon swung back, Mr. Laroche was off the screen and the blonde with the big eyes and small brain had moved on to another guest.

He put a lot of square feet under his polisher, gradually forgetting about Mr. Grand Dragon until he came ripping through the lobby again, this time angrier than before, which was some kind of a motherfucking miracle.

Laroche stormed by, walking straight through Dashon's path, his bodyguards clearing the way as if he were the quarterback for the Giants. Not a single one of them acknowledged him, not even when he had to skid to a halt and dropped the coffee he was carrying.

Honkaloid assholes.

But he had been through this enough times to know that getting angry wouldn't help no one, so he simply cleaned up his coffee with some paper towels and went back to work.

He was swinging the big Koblenz polisher around a garbage can by the entrance when one of the front doors shattered and something zipped by his head, whistling into the ATM in a bloom of sparks.

Dashon jumped and looked up. *What the fu—?*

Outside, the Grand Dragon stumbled back.

The sound of the shot rolled in. The screams began. And the Klansmen started running around like it was Black Friday and white cotton sheets were 90 percent off. People stomped on one another in their race for the doors, and a crowd spilled onto his polished floor, scrambling for cover.

Laroche's men muscled in, half carrying and half dragging him. They held the body with one hand each, free hands waving pistols around. Dashon tried to step out of the way, but they headed straight for him, leaving a dark red smear on his freshly cleaned floor.

He put his hands up.

They dumped their man on the floor, and Dashon saw that his head was pretty much not there anymore. There were two ears and a flap of hair. But nothing in between. No face. No forehead. No chin. And no more fucking ideas to sell. The dude was canceled.

Dashon fell back on the only thing left to say when faced by a bunch of white men with guns. "I didn't do it!"

"Call an ambulance!" ordered one.

"Get us a first aid kit!" yelled another.

Dashon dropped his hands. Did that guy just ask for an ambulance? An ambulance wasn't going to save that motherfucker. No one could unscramble that cracker's head without a magic Rewind button.

Dashon held up a roll of duct tape. "How about this?" he asked.

82

Columbus Circle

Lucas stood in the middle of Columbus Circle waiting for Whitaker to finish up inside. The shot that killed one Dwayne Laroche—former president of the NRA and current gun crime statistic—had not come from the roof of one of the nearby buildings. It had come from under a parked car—a pickup truck, to be specific. From a little more than four hundred yards away.

The first rule of evolutionary mechanics was adaptability, something their shooter had in abundance.

There were still two ambulances parked in front of the building, but Laroche had been wheeled down to the morgue. After the forensics guys finished their trickery, the coroner's Tupperware canopic jars—plastic bins containing brains, hair, and some skin—were carted away. But it was all a formality. No one doubted what had killed Mr. Laroche: his own principles.

The bureau boys found the spot where the shot came from long before Lucas rolled up in the back of the Babylon sheriff's cruiser. The two-hour trip in from Long Island had been a sullen experience since the officer—one Deputy McKinnley—resented being delegated the status of Uber driver.

The pickup the shooter hid under was registered to a man named Leo Grabinsky, who owned a tourist shop on Broadway that sold everything from bobbleheads of Joey Ramone to New York Yankees merchandise. The bureau impounded his truck to go over the undercarriage in search of trace evidence, but Lucas knew they wouldn't find anything.

The pickup had been parked down Broadway, on the east side. A perfect vantage point to see the entrance to the Time Warner Center. They had pulled the CCTV video, and Lucas watched it a handful of times.

Two of Laroche's bodyguards had exited the towers via the southernmost door; a third held it open. Laroche stepped out, followed by three more bodyguards. He then took a step toward the back door of the limousine, and that was the last intentional movement his body ever performed.

For a man who espoused the use of firearms for personal protection, the more than eighteen handguns found on his party didn't lend much credence to his argument. Someone wanted him dead, and now he was. And there had been plenty of good guys with guns on the scene.

Lucas watched Whitaker cross Broadway, weaving between the emergency vehicles. As she approached, she held up her phone. "I love Patton Oswalt. Listen to this tweet. *Irony: Being shot by a nut with a rifle minutes after going on TV to defend the right of nuts to own rifles.*"

Columbus Circle was closed to traffic, and the NYPD had the place on lockdown. And there seemed to be hundreds of emergency response vehicles on-site—everything from police cruisers to the bureau's submarine-sized command vehicle.

Lucas kept staring at the building across Broadway. People make mistakes; it is hardwired into our evolutionary past as a way to learn. And people with guns make mistakes *with guns*. There wasn't really much of an argument in arming all the citizens, but the people who sold death worked very hard to make Americans believe the line, regardless of what the numbers showed. After all, it wasn't about anyone's safety; it was about making money. They weren't buying protection—they were being sold fear.

Inside the television-like glow of the lobby, they were drilling the slug out of the ATM, raining sparks down on the marble tiles.

Whitaker turned to look back at the scene in the lobby. The unmistakable figure of Kehoe was there, stage left, watching over his people. With Graves dead, Kehoe would act as interim head honcho until he appointed another SAC—which he would do by morning.

"Why would a gun nut kill the president of the NRA?" she asked.

Lucas didn't have to think about that one. "She's not a gun nut. She was making the same point as when she nailed that cleric—denying allegiance. And I think she knows that it was the bullshit that these idiots sell that killed her family."

"So what do we do?"

"We go talk to Kirby Clibbon and see if he'll help us out."

"You think he'll say anything?"

Again, Lucas didn't have to think about the answer. "Nope."

"Then why bother?"

"So when this is all over, I can tell myself I did everything I could."

83

26 Federal Plaza

Lucas had met men like Kirby over the years, and he always wondered how they kept it all under lock and key. It never won them a lot of friends, but they very rarely got pushed into corners not of their own choosing.

Kirby was doing a good job of hiding what was going on behind his eyes. "I'm not talking to *anyone* without my lawyer," he repeated. "This conversation is *over.*"

Lucas leaned forward, meshing his flesh fingers with his green anodized ones. "I need your help."

"No shit."

"You want her to die? Because that's how this ends—with her in a box." Lucas hoped the kid would do the smart thing. "She's going to make a mistake."

Kirby locked on Lucas's good eye for a few seconds. And maybe it was because he saw the logic in Lucas's pleas, or maybe because he no longer cared, but he stepped out of character and said, "I once hunted her in the mountains to see how good she was. Four days in March. Forty below with no sun or moon for ninety-six straight hours. She didn't eat or sleep or drink." He didn't look like he was trying to make a point. Or win an argument. He looked awed. "Four. Fucking. Days. Man, I know SEALs couldn't hack that kind of abuse. Your crippy ass certainly ain't going to find her." He smiled. There was nothing humorous in it. "She's been at this her whole life—she was born to do this. A little hate goes a long way."

Lucas thought back to the night she had taken Atchison out on his front steps—it was all he could come up with in the way of camaraderie. "She saved me."

Kirby smiled sadly at Lucas, as if he just realized he were dealing with a small child. "You're the cripple teacher with all the mongrel kids? Sure, she saved you—for last. So you can watch everyone you love die, just like she had to." Kirby put his head down on the table. "Now, get me my fucking lawyer or get the fuck out of here. I'm through talking to dead men."

84

Grant Mercer answered the phone in one ring. "Yes?"

"Mr. Mercer, this is Dr. Page of the FBI. I was there with Agent Whitaker—"

"I'm not senile."

"Of course. Look, I need to know where she is."

"She?" the old man halfway across the country repeated. "I don't know what you are talking about."

Lucas closed his eyes and pushed the frustration away. "I need your help, Mr. Mercer."

"You need *my* help? The FBI is here, Dr. Page. They ripped my house apart and took my dogs."

"We're just trying to prevent anyone else from getting killed."

Grant laughed. It was a slow, rattling sound that could have been generated by a mechanical pump. Then he said, "Good luck with that," and hung up.

85

Lucas paced the floor of the office at 26 Federal Plaza, cycling through the events of the past few days. The conference table was littered with thousands of pieces of paper, ranging from police reports to old copies of credit card bills to crime-scene photographs.

Between the digital information in Lucas's head and the massive amount of paper data, there was a significant pile of zeros and ones to wade through.

He had been at this for hours as Whitaker was doing her own mental connect-the-dots. Lucas circled the table counterclockwise. Turning left was easier on his bad leg, and he was tired and distracted and didn't feel like falling through a window. Every now and then, one of them would have a light bulb moment and they'd go into the pile of paper. So far, all their big ideas had turned out to be snake eyes.

What they *had* managed to do was piss off Kirby Clibbon and Grant Mercer.

She was supposed to be in D.C., but they couldn't find an address for her anywhere there. The D.C. bureau was running around, following leads, but their reports were coming in loaded with big fat nothings.

She called her folks twice a month from D.C., and they had tried to track down the cell number, but it was a prepaid deal, and the phone wasn't showing up on the networks; it had only been used to call that single number. They had traced the purchase of the phone to an AT&T store three years back, but it had been bought with cash, which, after this much time, was a complete dead end.

Which meant that she went to D.C. twice a month to make the calls. The bureau had pulled the logs, and every single call she made home had been traced to within six blocks of Union Station up until October, after which the calls came in from various locations along the Beltway. They tried to pull all the surveillance footage for the New York and D.C. terminals, but they only went back sixty days, which meant they no longer had CCTV video of the dates she had been there.

Like everything else she had done, there were no mistakes in the formula, and Lucas wondered if Kirby was right, and she'd just keep on doing this until she died of old age.

Where was she?

The obvious answer was New York; they had a roomful of bodies to prove that one very important point.

"You hungry?" Whitaker asked.

Lucas didn't raise his eye from the table. Or answer her.

"You see, us humans need food. Didn't your alien leaders teach you that before they sent you here?"

Lucas looked at the photos. They didn't have much. And what was there was out of date. They had precisely three pictures of her— one old snapshot from when she was six and the two photos from the mantel at the Mercers', collected and transmitted by the Wyoming branch of the bureau two hours earlier. They couldn't find a single piece of government identification connected to her name— and she had not been issued either a passport or a driver's license.

No school photos. No social media accounts. So what they really had was nothing more than a very general, and very stale, impression.

One of the bureau artists who specialized in missing children had updated her face, adding enough years to give them a general idea of how she *might* look now. The media were doing what they did, and the image was already burned into the national consciousness. But even if it were dead-on, which the artist had assured them it wasn't, all she had to do was change her hair or put on glasses and she would look like a million women across the country.

She was out there, hiding in plain sight.

"Huh?" Whitaker prodded.

Lucas looked up at her. "What?"

"Food?"

"What about it?"

"Do you want some? There are ten diners within a block of here. I can get us anything you want, although I'm partial to tuna melts. Want to see a menu?"

"No. Thanks. I'm—menus?" And the alarm in his head went off.

"Yeah, menus: they're lists of food items and corresponding prices. You get them at restau—" She stopped when she saw that Lucas wasn't paying attention again.

He pulled through the mountain of papers until he found the one that he was looking for: the stack of photos from Atchison's house in Jersey. He flipped through the deck with his green finger, creasing the photos as he went, until he found the one of the contents of the desk in the basement. He taped it up on the whiteboard, over the felt-tipped scribbles he had spent the night generating.

Then he went to the old crime-scene photographs from Margolis's apartment, going to the one of the fridge. He taped it up beside the other one.

Then he did the same with the photographs from Oscar's place, this time focusing on the pile of papers on his desk by the telephone. He taped it up beside the other two and took a step back.

Whitaker came forward and looked up. "Jesus Christ," she said.

Lucas grabbed his coat and began to thread his prosthetic through the insulated sleeve. Even though the photographs had been taken at different crime scenes, there was a matching item in each—a menu from the Amphora Diner.

86

Whitaker gave Nick Papadopoulos, the owner of the Amphora Diner, a quick rundown of who they were looking for, including a general description and what few facts they had. It took about thirty seconds before he said, "You're looking for Connie."

87

The SWAT team held position in the hallway, four on one side, five on the other.

This was a standard sweep with a green light to kill anything that didn't raise its hands without being asked.

The entire apartment building had been evacuated in an effort to prevent an errant round shifting someone from the civilian category into the innocent bystander column.

The point man pulled back the metal battering ram. He got a thumbs-up and slammed it home, taking the door off the hinges in one massive punch that rattled the floor and splintered wood.

The SWAT men rushed in, going through the place in less than twelve seconds, their calls of *Clear! Clear! Clear!* offset by the sound of doors crashing into plaster.

The CO came back out into the hallway and called down to Whitaker. "It's empty."

Lucas followed her up the steps, and they cut through the gauntlet of black-clad tactical soldiers. Before the CO could say anything, she said, "Don't worry, we won't touch anything." These kinds of people tended to be big on booby traps.

They did a quick walk-through, taking in the general dynamics. The apartment was neat and boring, with very little in the way of personal touches. They split up.

Lucas looked around the bedroom, and it wasn't hard to see that Ruby Quaid, known to her boss and coworkers as Connie Ridzik and raised as Doreen Mercer, didn't believe in a lot of unnecessary clutter. The only furniture was a single bed. Other than that one luxury, the room was completely bare. The open closet held two wire coat hangers, one supporting a waitress uniform from the diner, the other empty. The living room had a folding nylon camp chair and a beat-up card table. There were no books or magazines or any other personal items, as if no one lived there at all.

"Page," Whitaker called from the kitchen, the crystal ring of panic in her voice.

He stepped through the open archway. Whitaker was looking at the fridge, and he moved around beside her to see what had her so spooked.

A photograph was taped to the fridge. A boy was in the foreground, his tongue lolling out while he made a goofy face as snow came down. Four other children were in the frame, all in the background, enjoying the winter in what Lucas recognized as Central Park. Erin stood in the background, Lemmy at her side.

88

Off Fire Island

The chopper ripped up the coast a mile off the south shore of Long Island. It appeared that they were zipping over the waves in a speedboat. But the illusion dissipated when you realized that the Bell 206 JetRanger was pulling more than 120 knots straight into a snowstorm.

The ocean threw slush up at the windshield, and visibility faded a little over thirty yards out, but Lucas didn't notice any of these incidentals—he was trying to get Erin on the phone. Since loading into Whitaker's Navigator at the Quaid girl's apartment, he had been pressing Redial in a Skinner box loop, trying to contact his wife.

Maybe Erin and the kids were curled up in front of the tube, watching one of their standard Christmas movies, and house rules were being followed, everyone's phone off and stored in the big fruit bowl on the kitchen island.

In all their time together as a family, this was the first time Lucas wished they had a landline at the beach house.

After what had to be the three hundredth redial, Lucas took a breath and focused on Whitaker across from him, her back to the pilot. She was speaking to the Southampton Sheriff's Department.

She was on a different communications link, and Lucas couldn't hear anything through his headset, but judging by her lip movement and facial expressions, she was forgoing niceties in exchange for expediency.

Whitaker signed off and gave him a look that was all questions.

He shook his head and keyed the mic on his headset. "Nothing. You?" His own voice was tinny and distant, as if it were being broadcast from inside a shipping container.

Her voice wasn't much better. "Southampton SD has a cruiser on the way, and they are going to shut down Route 27 between South Lake Drive and Oceanside. If she's not already there, she's not getting there."

Lucas went through the geography in his head—that was the narrowest point on the entire isthmus and probably the easiest bottleneck on the route. But with everything Ruby Quaid had done so far, circumventing a roadblock hardly seemed like an insurmountable task for her.

"Luke, she might not be anywhere near there."

He knew Whitaker wasn't wrong—going to Montauk would be a dumb tactical decision and out of character with everything else Ruby had done; until now, her targets could all be shoehorned into her revenge narrative (except for the imam and Laroche, who both fit the role of warnings).

He checked his Rolex and pressed Redial for the 301st time.

89

Montauk

Ruby Quaid lay in the snow, her world reduced to the tunnel of the scope. She had her eye fastened on the door, a white rectangle against gray cedar shingles—1,350 yards out, according to the range finder. The weather out here was worse than in the city, but the wind was at her back, pushing in from the north, and would work in her favor.

The ugly snout of the hunting rifle was aimed at Lucas's house across the field and through the drive where the trees opened up. She wore white snow pants and a white parka, and even from ten feet away, she was invisible. She was comfortable and deadly and barely grown up.

She didn't feel the wind or the snow or the cold. She had become immune to the worst nature could throw at her long ago on the hunting trips up in the mountains. She could lie out here all night. She had proved that on the roof of number 3 Park Avenue; she knew standard protocol would be to review the security footage of the stairwell cameras going back at least six hours. If they were determined, they would go back twelve. When they found nothing, they might go back twenty-four hours. But more than that? No one expected a shooter to stay on a roof for thirty hours before a kill. It made no sense.

But that's exactly what she had done.

Thirty.

Hours.

She could outwait all of them. Again and again and again.

And she could outthink them.

She wondered if they had figured out how she got down from that first roof. It was no great feat if you had a little imagination; all she had needed was an accurate SWAT uniform, which she purchased through some of Kirby's friends. After killing Hartke, she skirted the perimeter of the roof on the outside wall, then shimmied down between the HVAC units. She crawled up inside one, hiding in the open space of the coil for two hours until the SWAT people showed up. Predictably, the initial team walked right by her. (And why shouldn't they have? She had climbed down from the windswept wall, and left no prints in the snow.) When the roof became crowded, she had simply climbed out of her blind and walked down the stairs in the stream of law enforcement people.

The dying sky glowed in the storm, and it was hard to tell where the earth ended and the heavens began.

There hadn't been enough time to scout out their schedule, but families tended to operate on a regular timetable, especially when they had kids. And nothing made an evening walk more of a certainty than a dog.

So she lay there, waiting for Lucas's family to take their dog out for his evening poop so she could shoot them down.

Ruby had no malice toward them. At least not the kind she had had toward Hartke or Kavanagh or Lupino; that had been a festering sickness that was still with her, even though she had taken their heads off. She would carry it with her until the moment she died, an event that was probably not that far off. She'd kill the family. Then maybe get one or two more on her list.

But in the end, they would do what they did and run her down.

They would win. But she wouldn't let them take her alive. No, she was going to be with her family. And she would be buried on Bible Hill with her mom and dad and brothers and sisters. In the arms of Jesus overlooking God's own country.

Her parents had settled up there after God told her father it was a safe place. Her mother, who was really her aunt, raised her on the story. Her father had been out hunting on the mountain and stayed up there one night after getting pinned down by a storm. He had taken a big buck and didn't want to leave it behind any more than he wanted to risk losing it on the way down, so he camped out for the night. He was a born woodsman, like his father and grandfather had been, and spending a night in a snowstorm was as easy for him as it now was for the daughter he never got to know in any mean-ingful way.

He had been sitting at the fire, eating some beans and venison, when it whistled out of the sky. It hit a tree on the slope, a big pine leaning out over the valley. The trunk detonated in a shower of sparks and splinters that sounded like the earth opening up and the tree top-pled over the edge, crashing into the forest below.

God couldn't have been more clear if he had pressed his finger into the earth; this was the spot he wanted Daddy to raise his family. Away from the cities and the government and the people who wanted to take what you had simply because they were too lazy to work for it themselves.

But they had come nonetheless, orchestrated by Doug Hartke—a man whose name she wouldn't learn until a few years ago, thanks to a document dump on one of the websites Myrna scoured. Myrna had told her the truth since she was a child, the way the people from the FBI and ATF had murdered her family and burned her house to the dirt. They used to take trips up there sometimes. And in the fall and winter, when no one else was on the mountain, they would hunt up there. It was where she learned to use a rifle and dress a deer and live in the snow, all with the angels of her family looking down.

By the time she was fourteen, she was going up there by herself for a week at a time, in the worst weather God could conjure up. She knew he was training her; there was no other way to see it. Not if you opened your heart to Jesus and your eyes to the signs.

He was training her for something, and that something was no secret. He wanted her to get revenge.

An eye for an eye.

A death for a death.

A rifle round for a rifle round.

A family for a family.

Amen.

Then, one night four years back, she found the meteor. It was a few hundred feet below the charred chimney of her home, wedged into a crevice. She was tracking a muley up through the forest, and when she sighted him in, she had knelt down to take the shot and her knee touched something that was much colder than the snow and ice covering the world. She knew what it was, because like everything else about her family, Myrna had told her about it.

God was once again speaking through the rock he had dropped from the heavens.

She showed it to the uncle she now called Father, and he figured out that it was mostly metal. And it didn't take much discussion for them to figure out that metal from the heavens had only one divine use: to smite evil. And there was nothing more evil than the men who had killed her family. And that was when she was born for the third time.

She had done so much to get here, endured a lot of indignities that she hoped wouldn't upset her dead parents too much. The men she had used—Margolis and Atchison and Oscar and even Nick at the diner—had been necessary evils. She had done terrible things with them. Even Kirby had been a means to an end, and she hoped he could someday forgive her.

Night was coming in fast, but the snow would amplify whatever light there was and help her sight them in. Of course, her muzzle blast would be visible, but so what?

Once she began shooting, the bigger ones would move fastest, but the little ones would be harder to sight in. She'd hit the mother first, then pick off the older ones, moving down to the little girl. She'd save the dog for last, which was more than they had done for her brothers and sisters.

And when it was all over, Dr. Page would know that he had sided with the wrong people.

It wasn't difficult to see that life had already taken a lot from him. His Wikipedia page described a man who had come as close to meeting God as you could get. The world had taken a lot from him.

She was going to take everything else.

And then he would know how she felt.

90

Montauk

They were in the basement television room, watching Ralphie Parker wax poetic about a Red Ryder air rifle, when the doorbell rang. Lemmy lifted off the floor with a high-pitched fart that made the children laugh, and Erin proclaimed it the perfect time for a pee break.

Kathy, their neighbor from down the street (and the only person in the neighborhood who hadn't headed to warmer climes for Christmas) said she needed another glass of sauvignon blanc. Maude, always the resident pragmatist, said the fart was the dog's way of letting them know he needed to go out. They all got up.

"Any drinks?" Erin asked as the visitor *bing-bong*ed again.

After taking the order of two juice boxes and one milk, Erin headed upstairs after Kathy, Maude, and the dog, whom she could now hear woofing at the front door.

Once upstairs, the ringing graduated to knocking—an incessant rap that egged Lemmy on.

Maude was getting her coat off the back of one of the kitchen chairs, where she'd put it to dry after their last walk. "Must be those

Jehovah's Witnesses people again. Maybe they have some questions about the lecture on evolution Dr. Luke gave them the last time."

"Cut it, kiddo," Erin said as she walked by the kitchen island. All the phones in the fruit bowl were lit up with missed calls, blinking in various shades of digital frustration.

Outside, the Christmas lights were working overtime, sending bolts of blinking red and white into the kitchen.

Kathy took Erin's coat from one of the other chairs. "Mind if I come with you, Maude? I could use a little fresh air."

"If you want, but it's snowing pretty hard."

Erin ignored Kathy and Maude and pulled her phone from the pile, giving it a cursory glance: seventy-one missed calls.

What the hell?

Then the visitor knocked again, sending Lemmy into another bout of barking. "I'm coming!" she yelled and slipped around Maude, heading for the blinking lights at the front door.

91

Somewhere south of Long Island

Lucas waited for voice mail to kick in again as he listened to Erin's phone ring. He was about to disconnect when she answered. "Luke? Jesus, what's going on?" He could hear all kinds of commotion in the background, not the least of which was Lemmy barking.

"Erin, listen to me—"

"Hold on, someone's at—"

In the background, Maude piped in with, "Those aren't Christmas lights; it's the police. I'll get it."

"No, I'll get it," Erin said.

"*Erin?*"

She no longer had her ear to her phone, and he helplessly called her name again.

"Erin!" he repeated, the fear coming out this time.

On the other end of the line—at what felt like the other end of the universe—Erin gave Lemmy a sit command.

"Erin!" Lucas yelled.

The sound of the locks being unbolted.

"Erin!" Lucas screamed so hard that the copilot turned around in his seat, startled by the noise rising above the engine.

There was a pause.

The sound of voices—male voices. *"Sorry to bother you, ma'am. We were told to—"*

There was an ugly *smack*—the unmistakable sound of a slug whacking into bone and tissue.

Erin's scream.

A second round connecting with meat.

Erin's scream hitched up a dozen octaves.

Then the sound of the first shot rolled in.

Another ugly *smack*.

Followed by two more rifle reports.

And the phone went dead.

92

Montauk

Ruby watched the SUV from the Southampton Sheriff's Department fishtail up the road, lights thumping. It could have been heading to any points east, but the lights implied a purpose; Ruby had scouted the entire eastern tip of the island, and none of the homes between here and the lighthouse were occupied.

She took a breath and automaticity kicked in, training and routine overcoming thought and effort.

She kept the crosshairs locked on the vehicle and peeled back the finger on the shooter's glove. The cold air licked her sweaty index, and the pad froze to the metal as she touched the grooved surface of the trigger.

The Chevy slowed for the turn into Dr. Page's drive, but it was moving fast and almost slid past the opening. The driver outsmarted the corner, hitting the gas hard over the last two hundred yards to the house.

It pulled up in front and parked near the garage. Two figures emerged—local deputies clad in the usual rural cop attire of big boots and winter parkas. As they moved toward the front door, their dark clothes flashed blue and red in the cruiser's lights.

She slowed her breathing.

Slowed down the wind and the snow and time itself.

And concentrated on her pulse, picking out the still place between heartbeats when her body was completely at rest.

The two men from the sheriff's department moved to the front door with the overbearing display of import she had seen a thousand times in law enforcement people—a physical manifestation of the foolish belief that they were the ones in control.

The taller deputy reached out and rang the bell with a slow, deliberate motion.

The second man hung back, near the steps. He was looking around, and for a second, it appeared as if he stared straight at her.

The taller deputy rang the bell again.

And once again waited.

Inside, shadows flicked across the windows as the family roused from whatever they had been doing off camera. A light went on. Again, figures moved behind the glass, throwing shadows.

The front door opened.

And without even thinking about the process, Ruby squeezed the trigger.

The first shot hit the deputy closest to the door right at the base of the skull. Before he began to fall over, she chambered another round. Zeroed in on the other officer.

And fired.

She acquired Page's wife and bolted another round.

Ruby zeroed in on the head atop the red parka. Held her breath. Waited for her heart to fall between beats. And gently squeezed the trigger.

She brought the scope down from the recoil just as the copper-jacketed iron-cored slug drilled into the figure more than ten football fields away.

The woman's head was there. And then it wasn't. And all that remained was the blowback from her brains dripping down the shingles.

Ruby bolted another round and panned over the ground floor, searching the windows for one of the children.

She'd settle for the dog.

93

South of Long Island

Lucas was still staring at the telephone when it lit up with Erin's number. "Erin?"

"Luke. Oh Jesus, fuck. They're *dead*."

Lucas tried to process what she said. "What?"

"I . . . I . . . we're in the basement. In the furnace room. Kathy's dead. Two policemen are dead. What do I do?"

Whitaker held up her hand—three minutes out.

"I'm almost there."

"What do I do?" she repeated.

Lucas thought about Ruby Quaid, about how she had been raised like a poisonous reptile in a closed terrarium where all she had learned was hatred and fear. This all hinged on what she would do next.

The Quaid cabin had been obliterated in a fireball brought on by a sniper's bullet. Is that what Ruby would try? There were plenty of ways to start a fire.

Would she go into the house? Would she execute his family up close?

He wasted valuable seconds trying to think like her.

Until now, she had done all her killing at a distance.

And then it hit him. "Erin, I want you to stay on the phone with Agent Whitaker here." He nodded across the cabin and Whitaker keyed in.

"I'm here, Erin," she said into her mic.

"Luke?" Erin asked.

"I have to do something. Give me a few seconds."

Whitaker picked up with, "Have you got an escape route?"

Lucas clicked off and went to the recording of the last call he had with Erin, stored on the onboard computer. The unit was basically a glorified digital recorder and operated with a poor man's version of the same software astronomers used to analyze radio waves collected from deep space; Pro Tools for cosmic musicians. Which meant it had all the right features.

He played back the recording of Erin and him on the phone a few moments earlier, fast-forwarding to the point where the sheriff's deputy said, *Sorry to bother you, ma'am.*

Marked off the time.

And listened.

He ran through it again. And again. And again. Each time isolating some other piece of the equation, until he had it down.

Six separate sounds—three rounds hitting home and three shots ringing out.

He marked off the sonic events, isolating the hang time between each round hitting home and the sound of its report.

Physics was physics, and he calculated for muzzle velocity, bullet mass, powder load, and loss of momentum. He split the seconds into parts too small for the human ear. Then he did some quick calculations.

If the rounds were the same as the ones taken from Atchison's basement (except for the material used in the ferrous core), Ruby Quaid was roughly 1,325–1,410 yards from the front door—depending on wind.

Lucas thought about the beach house. About the wooded drive. The 250 yards from the road to the house. The almost perfectly north-south orientation of the building. About the field across the highway where he took Lemmy to poop in the summer.

He keyed his mic, cutting into Whitaker and Erin's conversation. "Erin?"

Her voice rose through the sound of the rotors and the *clink-clink-clink* of the machinery in his head spinning the numbers like a Curta adding machine. "Luke? Oh God, what do we do?"

"The shooter is across the highway in the field. Near one of those shacks filled with all the old fishing shit that run off Cliff Drive. Stay in the basement—we'll be there soon. I have an idea."

"How long is *soon*?" Her voice was shaking, but she was trying to keep it together for the kids.

"Two minutes. Stay where you are. I'll find you."

"Don't go anywhere," she pleaded.

"I'm right here," he said, then muted the external mic and asked Whitaker how far out the SWAT team was.

"They took off thirteen minutes after we did, and they're in a bigger helicopter, so we're looking at eighteen, maybe twenty minutes."

"Twenty-two," the pilot chimed in over their headsets.

"Swell," Lucas said, then went back to Erin. "Do you hear anything?"

"No."

"Okay. Good." He was trying to figure out what Ruby would do. "Tell me exactly what happened. I need to figure out what she's going to do next."

"She? She who?"

"The shooter is a girl. Please, Erin, tell me what happened."

"The police rang the bell while we were watching a movie. Maude was going to take Lemmy for a walk, and Kathy was going to join her—she put on my coat. She saw I was on the phone, so she opened the front door. I was beside the big clock by the stairs and he . . . um, I mean *she* shot the policemen, then Kathy."

"Kathy was in your coat?"

"Yes."

And with that, his software cycled up the final line of code, and he knew what Ruby Quaid would do next.

94

Montauk

The pilot came in low, lights off, using the beach and the house as cover from the shooter. The wind was blowing due south, pushing the sound of their rotors out to sea, which suggested that she wouldn't hear them. But the Nomex blade tips were moving faster than the stabilizers, and they'd generate a subsonic shock wave; if Ruby was in the right spot, the *thump-thump-thump* would travel below the frequency of the wind as if it weren't there.

They landed on the beach in a spray of water and snow that blocked out the world for a few seconds. Lucas told the pilot to stay right where he was and ran for the house with Whitaker, who had her service pistol out.

The house was dark, and Lucas simply punched through the window on the back door with his prosthetic while Whitaker covered his back.

He moved low through the kitchen, which put all kinds of stress on the good knee that was doing all the work. The front of the house was lit up with what looked like their Christmas lights if you didn't know that a police cruiser was parked out front, cherries spinning.

Lucas tried the basement door—*locked.* He knocked softly. "It's me."

When Erin opened it, the kids cheered, and both she and Lucas hissed for them to be quiet.

He gave her an intense hug that he didn't want to end. "Come on!" he said, motioning the kids upstairs with his prosthetic. "We have to go."

"What about the policemen? Kathy?" Erin asked.

Whitaker held up her hand. "I got it." And she disappeared into the dark.

The kids filed up, and Lucas made sure they kept low as they headed to the back door in the dark. Even Lemmy moved with slow, deliberate motion, the benefit of pack observation serving him well. Wind and snow whistled in through the broken door, and it was impossible to miss the sound of the helicopter down on the beach.

All the kids looked petrified except Alisha, who thought this was some sort of a game.

They crouched below the back door and slipped on boots and coats—Maude had to use a pair of Lucas's sneakers because her boots were at the front door from her last trip to take Lemmy out.

Just as they were heading out, Whitaker came back, looked at Lucas, and shook her head. "All three textbook," she said, leaving out details that might scare the kids. Or Erin.

Lucas led his family through the path he had forged up from the beach. He went last, putting the dog between him and Whitaker, so that Ruby would have to go through him and Lemmy first. He knew it would only buy his children a few more seconds, but it was the best he could do.

They somehow made the trek without the whistle of Ruby's rounds coming in, and by the time they were down on the frozen sand, Lucas had a pretty good idea where she was going and what she planned to do.

The helicopter was only designed to carry four passengers, but Lucas ushered all five children in on top of Erin, pushing Lemmy's big ass against the far door. Then he gestured for Whitaker to get in.

She shook her head. "If I get in, there's no place for you."

"I don't have time to argue. I know where she's headed, and I have to beat her there."

Whitaker stood her ground and shook her head. "Until this is done, I'm made out of glue."

"That's sentimental but unnecessary. Get on the fucking helicopter."

Whitaker didn't budge.

Lucas added, "Please."

She shook her head.

Lucas let his plan play through in his head one single time, then nodded. "Okay. We both get in. But after that, you listen to me no matter what."

She seemed to think that over for half a second, looking for holes. "You screw me on this and I'm going to shoot you in the foot," she said as they squeezed into the cabin.

Lucas pulled the door shut, and the pilot turned his head and yelled into the back, "We're overloaded, and it's going to be a bit bumpy! Hold on!"

They ratcheted up into the sky and swung out into the storm over the Atlantic.

95

Montauk Point

Ruby focused on the spire of the lighthouse ahead, her snowshoes *shish-shish-shish*ing as she ran. The eyeholes on her balaclava were frosted with frozen perspiration, but she was warm in the carefully picked clothing; given the right gear, she could live outside for weeks. But this wasn't cold. Not in any real sense of the word. When it came to freezing, there wasn't a place in the world that could compete with the hills of Wyoming.

Her rifle was across her back, and each time she took a step, she felt it pull a little to the left. But she was making good time and wondered how much of a break she'd get before the police showed up—first the locals, then the FBI. At least she had plenty of ammunition.

They would be looking for her by now. Even a little local sheriff's department would know that she had been the one to kill Dr. Page's wife and those two deputies. There would be a few standard procedures like a roadblock and house-to-house searches. But these were easterners, and they wouldn't be smart enough to bring dogs out after her. Not that they'd be great in the snow, but they'd force her to move faster. No, using dogs required smarts, which was definitely missing in these people. They were good at killing un-armed families, but when it came to someone who knew what they were doing, their success rate dropped predictably. No matter what tactics they used to hunt her down, they'd eventually find themselves here, on this hill, facing the lighthouse.

Facing her.

She crossed the parking lot, steering clear of the one lone car in the corner, left here a few days ago judging by the thick wedge of snow capping the roof. The plow hadn't come by in several hours, and she was leaving a clear trail—but what the snow didn't fill in, the wind would take away.

They wouldn't know she was here until she started shooting. And by then, it would be too late.

As long as she didn't wait for them to surround her, she had a chance. If she controlled the high ground, she controlled them. The trick would be in keeping them from setting up snipers; if she could do that, they didn't have a chance. At least for a while.

She climbed the small knoll that bordered the parking lot, crossed Old Montauk Highway, and headed up Lighthouse Road toward the Christmas-light-decorated spire on the hill. She looked for tracks, but the drive was scoured bare—no one had been up here for hours.

The lighthouse and main building looked like a postcard, and at any other time she would have stopped to admire the scene; if there was one thing Myrna had taught her, it was to enjoy what little time you had because it could all be taken away in an instant.

She jogged up Lighthouse Road. Her core temperature was up, and she could feel a puff of hot air forced out of her collar with each step, her body now a sweat-generating piston.

She wasn't even winded by the time she crested the hill and made the front steps of the access building. She expected the door to be locked but the parks people left it open—they probably didn't expect any burglars out here, which saved her a few seconds. (There wasn't a commercially available lock that she couldn't pick.) Once inside, she blocked the door with the Coke machine, wondering why it wasn't plugged in. The defense wouldn't stop a battering ram, or even a single determined man, but it would offer her protection from gunfire if she had to come down here.

With the barricade in place, she moved through the building to the base of the tower. There were 137 steps to the top, which stood 110 feet above grade, giving a perfect 360-degree view that would make her nearly invincible. At least until they brought the siege equipment like they had at Waco. But how many would be dead by then?

The answer was, of course, *plenty.*

She shed her backpack and rifle, laying the big Remington down on the pack; she never stood her rifle against, or leaned it on, anything—Myrna had taught her that was the best way to knock it over and pooch the sights. And without a scope, the rifle was almost useless.

And there were still bad people to kill.

She went to the back exit and pushed the other vending machine in front of the door. The parks department had shuttered up the windows, so that was something she wouldn't have to do; this was as protected as she would get. If they wanted to storm the hill, she had no problem with that. She'd paint the fields around the lighthouse with their blood.

It wasn't much warmer inside, but there was less wind, which helped. She wasn't moving now, and in a few minutes her core temperature would drop and her sweat would cool on her skin and she'd start to shiver. But she'd fight through it. She always did.

The lighthouse was automated, and the parks people only checked on it twice a day—the last time two hours ago. (She had seen the parks SUV pass by Page's beach house.) So she'd be alone until the police made it this way.

Ruby shouldered the pack and picked up her rifle for the 137-step trek to the top of the world.

She was halfway through her second complete loop up the stairs when a voice somewhere in the dark ahead said, "Hello, Ruby."

96

Montauk

After the helicopter banked out over the Atlantic, Lucas held the headset up but didn't put it on. "Head east, along the coast," he directed the pilot. "A little more than a mile up on the tip of the island is a lighthouse. Drop me on the beach below it—hook around the tip and dump me on the north side." Across the cabin, the kids were all huddled around Erin, who was watching Lucas with an expression he had never seen on her before. Lemmy was kneaded in between the kids, head on Maude's lap, eyes closed as he slept.

The pilot's voice came in over the headset. "We've got a strong wind on the north side. How about I drop you off at the front door?"

"It has to be the north side. Set down on the beach, let me off, then get the fuck out of Dodge." A helicopter left an identifiable disturbance in snow, and Lucas didn't want her to know he was here. She would look for something like that, even at night. And Lucas and the kids had walked around up there in the summer—the north side was an easier trek up the hill.

"You're the boss," the pilot said, banking the bird and swinging up along the coast.

It wouldn't be a long trip, and Lucas had a lot to say. He looked at Erin and mouthed the words *I love you.* She nodded an *I know* and turned to the kids.

"You stay with them," he said to Whitaker, who had her headset on now. "Take them somewhere safe. And I need you to get a message to the SWAT team and the local SD, which means you can't come with me.

"Ruby knows there's no escape route, especially now, and she walked in here anyway. Which means she has a plan. And she's only built for one thing." His words warbled to the thrum of the rotors. "She will assume we think she's left the area. Or is trying to. And the local SD will do a neighborhood sweep. We're on a peninsula, and the only logical way would be to sweep from west to east—or to start at both ends and move in. A mile west of here to a mile east of here. Which ends up at the lighthouse, another elevated position. And we don't want her in an elevated position. All she'd have to do is wait for a few cars to show up and she'd have her aria to go out on."

Whitaker shook her head. "Why would she throw her life away? She doesn't strike me as the suicidal type."

Lucas shrugged. "I don't think she cares. Not anymore. But if she gets off this island, she will cause a lot more damage. Make sure they block off all escape routes—the entire breadth of the island; a roadblock won't stop Ruby Quaid."

Whitaker pulled out her little rhinoceros pistol. "Are you taking this with you?"

Lucas looked down at the semiautomatic. Then at his children. Then at Erin, who was watching the conversation without being able to hear what was being said. Then back at Whitaker. "I'm good."

Whitaker rolled her eyes. "One day, your principles are going to get you killed." She slipped the pistol back into the holster as the pilot swung the chopper around the tip of the island.

The lighthouse blasted a beam of bright white through the squall, and the interior of the aircraft blossomed supernova, which had all the kids shield their eyes. Then they were past, and the pilot brought the bird down on the ice-covered beach.

Lucas leaned forward and gave Erin a kiss. Then he smiled at the kids, hollered *I love you guys,* and stepped out into the storm.

Whitaker asked, "What are you going to do?"

"Don't worry." Lucas looked up the hill at the lighthouse. "I have a plan," he lied.

97

Montauk Lighthouse

He stood in the dark on the welded iron stairway that served as the spinal column for the tower. It thrummed and vibrated with the shifting building, transferring the energy from the storm outside, down through the bedrock, and up through the soles of his feet. It felt as if the structure were stretching.

There was every reason to believe that she would come this way. Of course, she might do something else completely. Ruby Quaid had proved to be smart. And she performed exceptionally well under pressure.

But being here felt right.

He stripped the cord from the Coke machine downstairs, soaked up his footprints with a mop from the utility room, and went looking for a way to end this thing.

When they had revamped and renovated the lighthouse a few summers back, they had switched to an LED fixture that, for all practical applications, ran on little more current than your average toaster oven. But the old mains were still wired into the box; the big junction was bolted into an alcove halfway up the staircase. The key was tucked into a hole in the stone above.

After rigging his defensive gamble, he stepped onto the small rubber welcome mat.

He wondered if she'd even show up. Whatever she did next, it would be smart; it would be out of character for her to start making mistakes now. But even if you factored in her youth and stamina and determination, the past week had to have been rough. Fatigue was always the big one; everything else was secondary.

But some people always had more rocket sauce in the tank. What had Kirby said? *A little hate goes a long way.*

And Ruby had most definitely gone a long way. Nation-states had trouble fielding people who could do what she had. And she was really little more than a child, a young woman with a rifle.

His teeth had been chattering for a while when one of the doors in the building opened. The stone structure took in a massive gulp of arctic air, then pressurized, and the door slammed somewhere down in the dark.

He fought the shivers building up as he listened, straining to hear the sounds of human clatter above the storm breathing through the cracks in the building. There were footsteps. Something was dropped. A zipper being undone. Grunts. Something heavy—probably the Coke machine—being dragged across the stone floor.

Then the footsteps faded for a few moments—a silence that was marred by another heavy machine being dragged across the floor, no doubt the back entrance. Then the footsteps came back.

And someone began to climb the steps.

98

Southampton Sheriff's Department

The FBI chopper touched down in the parking lot, a makeshift landing pad denoted by two dozen magnesium flares thrown down in the snow. As soon as the skids stopped bouncing, the door opened and Whitaker climbed out. She helped the kids and Lemmy out first, followed by Erin. They all ran for the open doors of the station house, hunching to keep below the slowing rotors.

When the aircraft was empty, Whitaker walked over to the big man in sheriff's gear standing at the edge of the burning almost-circle and asked, "You Hauser?"

He nodded, and she came back with, "Thanks for all the help on the phone."

A troop of deputies stood behind him, cradling shotguns and looking like they expected an invasion at any moment.

The big man replied, "After your call, I spoke with your SWAT team, and right now they're still—" He checked his watch. "Six to eight mikes out."

Whitaker took that in. "I don't think we have time to wait. We need to quarantine the tip of the island, but we might have a problem up at the lighthouse."

"Problem?" Hauser asked as they headed to the station house.

"We might have a sniper up there."

Hauser stopped. "I just sent three cars up there."

99

Montauk Lighthouse

As they stared at each other, something sparked between them that at any other time would have been an understanding. About why they were here; about why she had done what she had; about why she was still trying to do it. And about who they both were.

But he couldn't figure out why she had gone after his family. It was petty, which was something he wouldn't have pegged her as. And looking down at her, at the freckled face rimmed by the fur collar, he saw all the broken children who had come through his life, and he got it; he represented all the things she either hated or had not been allowed to have.

She had never really been allowed to be a child. Not when her parents had pulled her out of society to teach her their fanatical interpretation of God's word. And not after her family was dead and she was being raised by a bitter woman who wanted revenge for what had happened to her sister and brother-in-law's family. Ruby Quaid's life had been taken away at Bible Hill, and she never got it back.

Lucas's focus went from her eyes to the muzzle of the rifle pointed straight up, back to her eyes.

Her focus shifted from his one good eye, down to the thick electrical cable with the exposed copper end he was holding on to, then back to his eye.

He needed to stay in control of the situation. "This can end."

"This is all there is."

Lucas nodded down at the cable in his hand. "You don't have a lot of options."

The muzzle of the rifle moved in small circles as she spoke. "I've watched lots of people die. It's easy." In that instant, she really was just a little girl. With freckles and a rifle. "Dying don't take nothing. Living? That's something else."

"Why do you think I'm here, freezing my ass off, looking for you? Because you need someone on your side."

"You ain't my friend."

"You're right—I'm not. I don't keep weak people as friends."

"You think I'm weak?"

"I *know* you're weak. You could have taken what happened to you and turned it around, but you went out and did the same thing that was done to you—you destroyed a lot of good people just because you *could*. You're just like everyone else out there; you have no imagination."

"That's not true."

"How is it not true?"

She was silent for a few furious seconds as the building vibrated in the storm. "They killed my family."

"Your father had plenty of chances to make good decisions, and he pissed them all away. You want to blame someone, blame him. It's not a very complicated equation."

"There are people who believe in what I did."

"Sure there are. Stupid people. Uninformed people. Bad people. No one else has to die," he said. "Not even you."

She smiled at that. It was a lost, lonely smile. "The bad guy always has to die."

Lucas shook his head. "The universe doesn't believe in good and bad, right or wrong. It's a violent place, and you are just a fractal representation of the chaos."

She seemed to think about that for a second before nodding. "Yes," she said. "I am." And she began to lower the muzzle.

Lucas threw his prosthetic hand out. Trying to stop her. Trying to get her to listen. Trying to save her life.

But she was no longer interested.

He released the cable.

The muzzle was down now. Almost at his chest.

The wire unfurled.

Lucas had time to flinch before the air went electric as current sparked from the copper braid to the metal steps in a single flash of blue that grounded Ruby Quaid with 480 molten volts of pure Con Edison. She bellowed like Karloff as she got hit with enough current to jump-start a small star. There was a staccato *pop-pop-pop* as her muscles contracted, breaking bones and shattering joints, and she squeezed the trigger while she danced in place. The muzzle flashed, sending a round into the wall as every atom in the immediate universe surged through her skeleton.

Her lips sharked back, and there was another great twitch, and her jaw slammed shut, taking off her tongue and bottom lip.

Her head kinked to one side and her eyes crossed and her hair caught fire.

There was another Jacob's ladder weird blue flash outside as the main transformer for the property blew in one massive bang, and the whole shithouse shorted out.

All the light bulbs in the 130-foot shaft exploded in one final eruption of electricity and blown glass.

And then it was over.

She stood there, on fire. Crackling in the dark.

But without the current to pull her strings, gravity took over, and Ruby flopped back into the stone wall. She let out a grunt as her lungs collapsed, sending out a final breath of black dust that slipped away in the air current.

Lucas stepped off the small rubber mat that had separated him from a trip to the promised land. All he saw were the melted soles of Ruby's smoking boots, and the air smelled of burned hair and melted nylon, and the familiarity of it all was too much, and he bent over and threw up.

100

Lucas sat on the front steps to the lighthouse. The electrical building down by the maintenance shed was on fire, the blown transformer too much of a boost to contain. The flames licked into the sky, sending a feather of greasy smoke up into the snow coming down. He had called Whitaker and she was on the way with the cavalry.

The first of the Southampton Sheriff's Department vehicles blew through the trees in the distance, a fleet of lights flashing behind. The SWAT team had been sent back to New York; whatever there was to clean up could be handled through the joint efforts of the local SD and the FBI.

And here they were.

Lucas hoisted himself up. There was a slight tingling in his skeleton, and he was aware that his being alive was more than a minor miracle. His prosthetic limbs offered the opposite of protection from current; if nothing else, his metal arm and leg converted him into the kind of potential human electrical disaster that AC/DC wrote songs about. The possibility of bad things happening was greater than he had wanted to admit.

The big Chevy Suburban barreled through the corner on Old Montauk Highway, fishtailing up Lighthouse Road, and Lucas recognized the wheelmanship as Whitaker's. The half dozen vehicles behind her took the corner at a more restrained pace, and he smiled in spite of the taste of puke in his throat and the smell of fried human being in his nostrils.

The Suburban stopped in front of the steps, and a forest of faces peered at him from the interior. Erin was in the passenger's seat, and the kids were in the back, waving and grinning like the world's tiniest cheerleading squad. Lemmy had his butt pressed up against the window.

Whitaker and Erin stepped out at the same time.

"You okay?" they asked in stereo.

He shrugged because it was the simplest answer. Then he jabbed a thumb over his shoulder. "She's about forty steps up."

"Is she okay?"

He shook his head. "Not really."

Whitaker came around the front end and headed up the steps to the lighthouse.

Behind her, doors on the six official vehicles opened, spilling law enforcement officers out onto the snow.

Erin came over, and he pulled her into a hug. Her nose crinkled up, and she said, "You smell like a melted Frisbee."

"Hello to you, too."

"Is it really over?"

"Yes."

And with that, she sank her face into his chest and began to cry.

After a few moments, he asked her, "You ready to go home?"

"Home here?"

"No. Home to the city."

Erin turned to the kids in the car. "Who wants to bring Uncle Dingo Christmas presents in the hospital?"

The kids hollered a unanimous *I do!,* and Lucas smiled for what felt like the first time in his life.

"So let's go," he said. "But you drive."

"They won't mind you stealing their SUV?"

"You're kidding, right?" And with that, he climbed in and snapped on his seat belt.

Erin started the 4×4 and swung around in a tight arc, and they headed down the hill to Old Montauk Highway. Lucas watched the spire of the lighthouse in the rearview mirror, fire from the blown transformer licking up into the sky. By the time they were on the highway, the dark building had been swallowed by the storm, the only visible point being the shed that was still on fire.

In a few minutes, he was asleep.

101

Columbia University Medical Center

From the hall, Lucas watched Dingo entertain the kids from his hospital bed. He was wearing a candy necklace they brought him and trying to get Hector to put a bedpan on his head, an idea the other children thought was wonderful. There were presents on the windowsill, half-hidden by torn wrapping paper and recycled Christmas bows. If there was one thing Dingo was good at, it was entertaining kids, even when he could barely keep his eyes open.

He wasn't able to sit up yet. There were two tubes that vented liquid from his body, one from his lung and the other from his bladder, but he was now out of the ICU and already making bad jokes.

When Lucas held out his new passport with the gold eagle embossed on the cover, Dingo said that he was no longer sure he wanted it. Then he smiled and took it from Lucas's hand, only to point out that they could have used a better photo. Like hate, a little humor went a long way.

The bureau was combing through the rubble that Ruby Quaid had left in her wake and, along with the dead, there were a lot of questions to answer. Kehoe had gone into damage control mode—Ruby Quaid most definitely did not fit the narrative handed down by the politicians, and now, with hindsight being the mother of invention, the double-speak, finger-pointing, ass-covering, and plain old lying had already started.

In the end, Kehoe's motives for pulling him aboard hadn't been all that complicated. He had most definitely needed Lucas—the results proved that. And if it had turned out to be a foreigner following the bent decree laid out by some invisible man in the sky, Lucas could have been relegated back into mothball mode with no one the wiser and only a few pieces of silver missing from the coffers. He had paid lip service to the Frenchman narrative while simultaneously setting Lucas loose to do that thing he did. More of that strategic thinking he was known for. Which wasn't really any big surprise—people don't change, not really.

Of course, when Lucas lined it all up, the job had been more than just Kehoe making the right choices; it had also been an olive branch of sorts—a partial apology for how he had reacted all those years ago. For words spoken and deeds done. Which said a lot about his character.

All to stop a girl with a rifle.

When it was all tallied up, there were fourteen dead bodies in her wake if he included collateral damage like Atchison's partner. And of course there was Ruby herself. And they'd probably find more. It was a remarkable accomplishment when you thought about it.

That night on the train, Lucas had figured a lot of it out. Not the whole story, but he'd turn out to be correct on the broad strokes.

They were exhuming the remains of the dead Quaid children, and Lucas was certain they'd learn that one of the girls—one of those little corpses from Bible Hill—would turn out to be Myrna Mercer's biological daughter, Doreen. Myrna and Grant had no doubt loved their nephews and nieces, but with Grant in a wheelchair and the cabin to manage, taking in five children would have been difficult. So their daughter spent time with her cousins up on Bible Hill, and they spent time with Carl and Elisabeth Quaid's children one at a time. What was it that Myrna had said?

I lost my blood up there.

At the time it made sense. Now, it made more.

She had lost her own daughter. And raised Ruby as her own child, as Doreen.

And Myrna's mission of revenge had been born, delivered to the girl she was raising as her own with the force of Scripture behind it, teaching Ruby that it was not only her responsibility to go after the people who had killed her family but also her sacred duty.

They had cashed out the settlement—the blood money, as she rightly called it—years ago, a little at a time so as not to raise any suspicions. They stored it until Ruby needed financing. Myrna had been at the trial back in D.C. and it wasn't hard to imagine her staring down all the agents responsible for murdering her family, quietly etching their names in blood somewhere on the hate-filled walls of her mind. Myrna's plan was borne. Years later, the man responsible for Quaid's arrest—Donnie Doowack—surfaced, and *planning* became *action*. Ruby went out into the world with a backpack of money, a hunting rifle, and head full of bad ideas.

After getting to New York—or was it before?—setting up another identity would have been simple. She changed her name and started up a new life—one that included two trips a month to D.C. to call Myrna, which was really just a smart way of establishing an alibi. And in New York, the waitress job was just something for her to do in case anyone came asking about how she lived. But she spent her weekends and evenings with Kirby. And his militia friends. Learning about urban warfare and how the police operated and where to source everything from fake identification to specialized ammunition to SWAT uniforms.

Which of course brought her to Oscar's doorstep.

Oscar had no doubt modified the ammunition for her, but it looked like he had stolen the original Nosler rounds from a job he had done for one racist cop and erstwhile arms dealer, Detective Michael Atchison—who, it turned out, had stolen it from a man named Margolis after killing him for a reason they would probably never know.

But Oscar fucked up. He stole fifty rounds from the wrong people so he could give it to a girl who had somehow become a friend—Ruby Quaid, who was by now living under the name of Connie Ridzik. Ruby Quaid was nothing else if not adaptable, and getting men to like her was one of her strongest traits. That duffel bag and blue sweater up in the office above the shop that afternoon had been hers.

He had missed it because it had been in plain sight. Like the modified round that had been on the mantel the first time they were there.

Hiding in plain sight.

Oscar had modified the rounds for her, using a rock that had fallen from the sky as a source for the iron in her skimmed rounds. They'd probably never know why Ruby had chosen meteoric iron, only that it held some significance.

That morning Lucas and Whitaker visited him must have been a wake-up. Maybe he got scared. Or maybe he didn't care anymore. After all, the cancer feeding on him with an exponential appetite no doubt delivered a little extra dose of don't-give-a-fuck-ism that tended to be a side effect of the disease.

And when they had explained the round to Atchison, it hadn't been a stretch for him to figure out which gunsmith they had spoken with. So he and Roberts paid old Oscar a visit. The crime-scene people said two people had killed him, and ballistics matched the slugs to the same pistol that had killed Margolis earlier and would try to kill Dingo later. So Atchison and Roberts went to work on Oscar to find out where the ammunition he had stolen from them had gone.

Maybe he had held up, maybe he had spilled what he knew. But he died anyway.

The CSI minions were certain that after Atchison and Roberts left Oscar's dead body in the chair by the fire, a third person had visited. Someone with a key.

Someone who had taken the .300 round from the display on the mantel—no doubt one of Ruby's magical rounds.

Ruby.

She had gone in to clean up all signs of herself.

But she had forgotten the menu. The same one that Atchison had in his basement. And Margolis had in his house.

Had she been with all of them at some point? Was she the mystery girlfriend that Atchison had heard about from Margolis's neighbors? Had the waitress uniform in Atchison's closet been hers as well? Which meant that maybe she had used Atchison's pistol to kill Margolis. Maybe she had taken the Nosler rounds from his place. Maybe Atchison had killed Oscar for some other reason.

There were a dozen ways to string the narrative, but they all came back to a child who had never really had a chance at a decent life.

It was dizzying to think about, and Lucas realized that he was much happier unraveling the mysteries of the cosmos because they were simpler than the dramas that continually played out in the theater of the human soul.

The one aspect Whitaker didn't understand was why Ruby hadn't started her killing with Doyle. But Lucas saw that it reflected the way she had handled the terrorist cell claiming ownership as well as the murder of Laroche; she wasn't welded to ideas; she was welded to people. And Doyle had tried to help her father, which had no doubt saved him; he was her people, one of the tribe. That he had failed didn't matter; that he had tried to help did.

And through it all had been Whitaker. Lucas had asked for her after that first night, but when he looked back on events with the clarity of resolution, he now knew that Kehoe had set him up. Another one of his moves.

She was a great agent. And a decent human being. He was thinking that he had never asked for her first name when his cell phone buzzed in his pocket.

It was a text from Whitaker.

It displayed a single word: *Alice.*

Lucas smiled and turned back to the scene in the hospital room. Hector and Damien were explaining the made-up Luigi board game to Dingo, who had already chewed through half of his candy necklace. Alisha was sitting on Laurie's lap in one of the ugly vinyl chairs, just enjoying being kids for a moment. Maude was helping Erin trim the stems of the flowers on the window ledge, and he realized that they had all grown up a little in the past couple of days. He, too, maybe.

Outside, the snow had started back up.

Lucas walked to the window and pulled the curtains.

Acknowledgments

The Big Hug goes to my agent and friend, Jill Marr, for always being an honest and constructive voice at the edge of reason (and for using her magic wand at all the critical times)—once again, you have changed my life. Kelley Ragland at Minotaur also gets a seat in the lifeboat—her support came at a time when I needed someone else to see the magic—thank you for setting this big monster in motion (and for grinning while doing it). Keith Kahla, my editor at Minotaur, who is now officially a brother in arms—his editorial chops, sense of humor, and begrudging kindness not only won me over, but forced me to rise to the occasion; without him, this truly would be a lesser book. Hector DeJean for seeing the world through a similar prism and Paul Hochman for having read all the same books as I did growing up—my marketing and PR gurus. Alice Pfeifer, who is too young to remember The Jam, but should have a song named after her nonetheless. And of course none of this would be possible if Andrew Martin hadn't put all of these people together to do that voodoo that they do—give the man a drink; he's earned it.

Everyone at the Sandra Dijkstra Literary Agency, who manage to keep my life organized and the paperwork flowing flawlessly (which is no small feat when your client does not own a cell phone and spends most of his time at a cabin in the mountains, preferring to be left alone): Andrea Cavallaro for getting my work published in more than twenty countries (all while fighting Vikings on her days off); Thao Le, for making sure I cash the checks; Elise Capron for holding the lines; and Sandra Dijkstra, who makes sure everyone has a sharp sword. I cannot see fighting any of these battles without you.

My friend and former editor, Kevin Smith, for talking me into putting down the pointy objects on more than one occasion; Johnny Russo, for not getting mad all the times they kicked us out of the Friars Club; Eyre Price for always helping me see the end of the story when I thought I had walked right by it.

I also need to thank all of the foreign publishers who stood behind my work from the beginning—I now have readers around the globe, which was something I never saw coming; the earth is indeed flat.

As always, I have to thank the Writer who made me want to do this above everything else—Rod Whitaker. He gave me a high bar to aim for. And made it look easy.

I would also like to thank Shane Black, John Carpenter, Walter Hill, and Christopher McQuarrie for teaching me more about storytelling than I could ever remember—their fingerprints are all over this thing.

Gene Simmons for all the times he told me to go big. And for the encouragement. The Godzilla conversation still stands out. Thank you.

Murray Head, for telling me to embrace the hard times and put it into my work. And for always giving me a place to stay.

An unsung hero in the novelist's life is the beta reader, and Diane Laheurte is the gold standard—you are the best.

John Roberts, without whose influence Lucas would never have found his way into a classroom.

And all the people behind the curtain who had a hand in this happening—you know who you are.